WOMEN OF COURAGE...
WOMEN OF PASSION...

DEVLIN'S PROMISE continues the stirring saga of the American frontier and the unconquerable men and women who dared to journey across the plains in search of a land they could call their own. This is the story of Devlin Branigan and Angelica Corrall, a man and a woman desperately fleeing pasts that threatened to destroy them both—only to discover a glorious future in each other's arms.

PASSION'S PROMISE

Angelica stood before the fireplace, the light turning her nightgown into little more than a gossamer mist, a mist that highlighted the shapeliness of her form. She was clearly naked beneath the flimsy material. Her silhouette was outlined in gold by the firelight at her back. Cascading hair fell in waves over her shoulders and down her back, the dark red tresses glowing with warmth.

Never had Devlin known a woman so lovely. Never had he wanted a woman as much as he wanted her. The desire began as a slow heat, devouring him by inches until he was consumed by it.

"Angelica," he whispered thickly.

Put something on, his mind protested as he struggled to remember all the reasons he couldn't allow this to happen. *Put something on before I do something we'll both regret later.*

"Angelica, you don't know what you're doing."

Her breath was warm against his skin. "Yes, Devlin, I Do."

Other *Women West* Books by Robin Lee Hatcher:

PROMISE ME SPRING
PROMISED SUNRISE

Also by Robin Lee Hatcher:
DREAMTIDE
THE WAGER
GEMFIRE
PIRATE'S LADY
PASSION'S GAMBLE
HEART STORM
THORN OF LOVE
HEART'S LANDING
STORMY SURRENDER

DEVLIN'S PROMISE

ROBIN LEE HATCHER

LEISURE BOOKS  NEW YORK CITY

A LEISURE BOOK®

July 1992

Published by

Dorchester Publishing Co., Inc.
276 Fifth Avenue
New York, NY 10001

The name "Leisure Books" and the stylized "L" with design are trademarks of Dorchester Publishing Co., Inc.

Printed in the United States of America.

With special thanks to:

Holly Turner of ICD for encouraging me to set *Devlin's Promise* in her "neck of the woods."

Laura Cameron-Behee of the Snohomish Historical Society for the time she spent tracking down information about Snohomish County since 1885.

Catherin Pickerill of the Central District Health in Boise, ID, for her assistance in answering my somewhat weird questions about typhoid fever.

To a special friend,
Darlene Layman,
with thanks for hauling me around
Snohomish County, WA
(not to mention the two years we spent
together in "La La Land").

Prologue

Colorado, March 1885

If the Kid had to die, Devlin Branigan would just as soon be the one to bring about his demise. The problem was how to do it. It wasn't like he could challenge him to a shootout at high noon on Main Street.

Devlin groaned as he rolled onto his back, pain shooting out from the bullet wound in his right shoulder.

Damn! It was bad enough when young punks wanted to make their reputations in fair fights. It was even worse when they started ambushing a fellow from behind.

If Jake Thompson hadn't found Devlin in that gully three days ago and brought him back to his place, Devlin would have bled to death before nightfall. He was lucky to be alive.

And something told him his luck had about

run out. Instinct warned him that whoever had shot him wasn't going to give up so easily. He'd be back once he found out Devlin wasn't dead, and Devlin knew he'd better be ready to shoot it out or be long gone from here before he was discovered.

He opened his eyes and stared at the ceiling of Jake's shack, his thoughts dark and gloomy.

Look at him. Thirty-five years old with nothing to show for it except a broken-down horse, a Colt Peacemaker .45, a saddle, a change of clothes—and the dubious honor of being known as the man who shot and killed the outlaw Chiver McClaine. Hell, it wasn't even Devlin Branigan who had the reputation as a gunslinger. It was a man folks called the Devil Kid. A legend.

And, as far as Devlin was concerned, a myth.

Yeah, look at him. He was the guy who was going to run the Yankees and carpetbaggers out of his Georgia home back in '67. He was the hotheaded youth who'd bragged to his brother—as Tucker and the rest of the family were leaving for Idaho Territory—that the next time they saw each other he'd be holding the deed to Twin Willows Plantation. Oh, he was one tough kid back then.

And here he was, eighteen years later, a hole in his shoulder and eight bits in his pants pocket. Wouldn't his mother be proud if she could see him now?

Eighteen years. He hadn't seen his mother or any of the rest of the Branigans in all that time. He hadn't wanted them to see what he'd become. But suddenly, as he lay there feeling sorry for himself, shut up in this miserable little cabin in the middle of nowhere, needles of pain tormenting him, he wished he could see them. He wished there were some way he could change the last eighteen years and become something other than what he was—a gunslinger without faith in himself or any hope for the future.

But he couldn't change the past, so what was he supposed to do? Ride into Boise and say, "Here I am. I couldn't get Twin Willows back, but I've managed to traipse all over the West and get shot at by the best of 'em. I'm now known as the Devil Kid. Rumor says there's no man faster. Aren't you all proud of me?"

But if the Kid were dead, if the Devil Kid didn't exist anymore, that would change everything. He wouldn't have to go through the rest of his life looking over his shoulder, wondering when the next gun-happy youth would show up. He'd even be able to see his family again.

So now all he needed was a way to kill the Kid without getting himself killed in the bargain.

Chapter One

Devlin ignored the first knock. Jake wasn't home, and there wasn't anyone else who knew that he was here—unless his whereabouts had been discovered by his ambusher.

He reached for his gun, hanging in its holster on the end of the bed, and stared at the door, waiting. He wasn't as good a shot left-handed, but he could do some damage. Hopefully, enough to save his hide.

His head thundered with the sound of a thousand drums, punishing him for his night-long affair with the whiskey bottle. After ten days of being holed up in this shack with only his pain, his own dismal thoughts, and Jake's company, getting drunk had seemed a good catharsis for what ailed him. Now he thought differently.

Another knock, hesitant, tentative.

Devlin frowned. He could be wrong, of course, but he seriously doubted that the fellow who'd ambushed him would come meekly knocking at the door. If his ambusher had known Devlin was inside, he would have barged in, guns blazing, without announcing his presence first.

The sound came again, with more emphasis this time.

Damn! Whoever it was wasn't going to leave him in peace until he chased them off.

Still holding his Colt .45, he pushed himself up from the chair with the heel of his left hand and crossed the room. Holding his right arm close against his body to alleviate the spasms of pain in his shoulder, he moved silently toward the lone window and eased aside the ragged cloth that served for a curtain. A black buggy, pulled by a gangly sorrel gelding, stood directly outside the window. He edged closer to the glass, but he still couldn't see who was at the door.

Again the knock.

The throbbing in his head and the fiery tentacles of pain in his shoulder increased. He slipped his revolver into the waistband of his trousers and reached for the latch.

"All right. All right. Hold your horses." He jerked open the door. "Jake isn't . . ." His voice died in his throat.

He noticed her eyes first. Dark green, like a lush carpet of lawn after the spring rains. They sloped up at the corners and were fringed with dark sable lashes.

He noticed her hair next. Burgundy, like a

fine claret. It was swept high on her head, thick curls framing her face, its deep color glowing in the afternoon sunlight.

Her skin was smooth and pale, with just the right hint of color over high cheekbones. Her mouth was sensuous, full and inviting. And, Lord help him, her dress did nothing to hide the generous curves that proclaimed her all woman, despite its high neckline and long sleeves.

"Are you the Kid?" Her voice had a husky, breathless quality. She watched him with a direct gaze. "The Devil Kid?"

His eyes narrowed, and his whole body went on alert. "Who wants to know?" He glanced beyond her, quickly scanning the stretch of land that surrounded Jake's tiny house on the prairie.

"Angelica Corrall. I'm a friend of Jake's." She tilted her head slightly to one side. "I'd like to speak with you."

"What about?"

"I... I have a proposition for you, Mr.... Kid. Please. May I come in?"

A proposition? Curiousity got the better of him. He stepped back and opened the door wide. "Why not?" He waved her in with his hand.

She moved past him with a delightful rustle of skirts. He caught a whiff of her cologne. A warm scent. Sensuous, like her mouth.

His gaze swept the length of her again. If she weren't dressed like a lady, he would think she was interested in the Kid to build a reputation of a different kind. It had happened before. There was some prestige in being the Devil Kid's woman. He'd found it true wherever he went.

A grin curved his mouth, his headache forgotten. At least in that arena he deserved his notoriety. He knew how to please a woman.

And this lady looked like she'd be able to set a man's soul on fire.

He mentally reined in the first stirrings of desire. He wasn't exactly in the right physical condition to follow through with them, even if the lady were willing. And he had more than enough problems at the moment without the added complication of a female.

Angelica turned, her unwavering gaze once more meeting his. "Well . . . I suppose the best way to go about this is to just speak my piece and be done with it."

That voice. It sent shivers of awareness up his spine.

"Usually is," he replied. "Have a seat."

She obeyed, sitting on the edge of a precarious-looking chair, not daring to recline against its back. Devlin leaned against the dry sink. He rested his revolver against his thigh and gave her a look that said, "Continue."

"Well . . ." She drew a deep breath. "Mr. Kid. . . . Jake told me what you said last night."

Devlin was instantly suspicious. Jake wasn't much of a talker, and for that matter, neither was he. Devlin couldn't remember the previous night except that he'd started drinking early and kept at it into the wee hours of morning. For all he knew, he could have done more than his share of talking, or he might not have said anything at all. He'd been feeling mighty sorry for himself—he remembered that much.

"Just what was it I'm supposed to have said?" he asked, his expression and voice neutral.

"That you'd like to go see your family in Idaho. That you wished the Devil Kid didn't exist and you could be somebody else." Her eyebrows drew together. "Jake assured me you aren't wanted by the law. Is that the truth? You're not an outlaw?"

"That's true. I'm not a wanted man." He didn't know why he bothered to answer. He should just invite her to leave. He didn't see any purpose in answering her questions.

She sighed again. "All right then. Here's my plan. The Devil Kid has a reputation with a gun and with the ladies. Am I right?"

Devlin shrugged, neither confirming nor denying her statement.

"So nobody would think to look for him with a wife and child, would they?"

"A wife and . . ."

"If you were to travel by train with me and my son to Washington Territory, no one would think you were the Devil Kid. You could shave off that beard of yours and put on a suit and no one would ever suspect you're a gunslinger.

You'd be a family man, going to homestead in Morgan Falls."

"Morgan Falls?"

She pulled a wrinkled piece of newspaper from her reticule and thrust it toward him. He gazed at her for a lengthy moment before taking it from her hand.

Homesteaders! it proclaimed in bold print. *Morgan Falls is bursting with wonderful resources. Only 45 miles north of Seattle and seven miles from the Snohomish River, Morgan Falls is destined to be one of the most desirable and healthy localities in Washington! Lumber, mining and agricultural opportunities abound. For further information address Bert Farland, Morgan Falls, Washington Territory.*

Devlin fingered his beard, then pulled his hand away. What was he doing? Was he actually considering this crazy plan of hers?

Hell, there was no question about it. He *had* had too much to drink last night.

"Mrs. Corrall, I think you've got the wrong—"

"It's *Miss* Corrall." Her chin lifted. "Jake told me you'd like to see your family in Idaho but didn't want them to know about . . . well, how you've been living since you saw them last. We could stop in Idaho for a visit on the way to Washington. I promise you they would never think I was a . . ." Her cheeks flushed with color and her gaze dropped to the floor. Her voice was even huskier when she continued.

"They would never think I was anything but a lady."

"Listen, Miss Corrall. What makes you think I want to go to Washington?" He was practically shouting at her. "Besides, I don't have the money to buy a new suit, let alone take me and two more to Washington on the train. And even if I did, what would you be getting out of this deal?"

She rose from her chair. "I will pay the cost of the train passage." Her gaze flicked over him. "And for a new suit of clothes for you. As for what I would get out of this deal . . ." Again her chin lifted. There was a defiant glitter in her green eyes. "I would get a name for my son. He won't have to grow up being ashamed of his mother."

"Wait a minute!" He pushed off from the dry sink. "I'm not about to marry you or anyone el—"

"I don't want you to marry me, Mr. Kid. I just want your promise that you will *pose* as my husband for the next eighteen months. After we've built a house and harvested the first crop, you'll be free to leave. When you're gone, I'll tell people you died while on a trip back East. I'd be a widow, and my child wouldn't ever be called a bastard again." She drew another deep breath and met his gaze with an unflinching one of her own. "That's what I would get out of this deal."

* * *

He stared at her with eyes as black as midnight. Was he considering what she'd said or did he simply think her mad?

He wasn't what she'd expected. She'd heard he was devilishly handsome and always popular with the ladies. She'd thought there would be an aura of danger about him. She'd expected to see a gun belt slung across his hip, the holster strapped to his thigh and a bloodthirsty look in his eyes. But she didn't see anything she'd expected in the man standing before her. Instead of handsome or dangerous, he looked tired and haggard, dark circles under his eyes and beard unkempt. He moved stiffly, like he was still in pain, although she'd been led to believe he was nearly mended.

He certainly wasn't her idea of a gunslinger, especially not the Devil Kid.

But if he wanted to put his past behind him as badly as Jake said he did—or even half as badly as she wanted to escape hers—he just might take her up on the offer. One way or the other, she had to leave the little hole-in-the-wall town that had been her prison for too long now. She had to get Robby away before he was old enough to understand people's cruel looks and remarks.

And she had to get away before Lamar returned.

Ever since she'd seen that advertisement for Morgan Falls, she'd been thinking about starting over again, somewhere far away from here, somewhere away from the snide looks and ugly whispers. A little farm, a place to grow her own food, a place where she could be independent. She knew she couldn't do it all by herself, and her savings weren't enough to hire a man to build a house, till the land, and plant the first crop. But once that was done, she was certain she could manage on her own. Once that was done, she wouldn't ever need a man in her life again.

Only, she'd run out of time. She couldn't just dream about it any longer. She had to get away and get away now. Surely a man like the Devil Kid could help her. He was quick with a gun. Fearless, Jake said. Lamar wouldn't dare . . .

Suddenly she was aware of the way his eyes were perusing her. She knew that look. It spelled trouble.

"There's one more thing you should know." She looked him straight in the eye, her head held high and proud. "There are no . . . *marital* duties included in this arrangement. If you ever need a woman to . . . well . . . you will certainly be free to pursue those interests elsewhere, as long as you're discreet."

He didn't so much as blink an eye. "Fair enough." He leaned once more against the dry sink. "How old's your boy?"

"Two."

"Where's his father?"

She didn't hesitate. She didn't blink an eyelash. "He has no father."

A wry smile lifted one corner of his mouth. "Every boy has a father somewhere."

"Not my Robby," she answered firmly. "Robby's mine and mine alone. He's a good boy. He'd cause you no trouble. And neither would I. I promise you that, Mr. Kid."

He shook his head slowly as he walked over to the open door. He stood there a moment, then stepped outside. She could only see his back, but she imagined his intense gaze scanning the lonesome prairie that made up Jake's front yard.

Naturally, he was going to turn her down. She'd known he would. It had been crazy of her to even come out here. After all, what was she offering him in return? Very little for a year and a half of hard work. She'd hoped, after listening to Jake talk about the Devil Kid and how he wanted to change his life, that this might be a solution for them both, that he might be as desperate as she.

But, of course, that wasn't the case.

She shouldn't be surprised. Nothing much had worked out for her the past few years.

Perhaps it was just as well that he wouldn't accept. She didn't know anything about this man, except the little that Jake had told her this morning—and Jake wasn't always the most reliable source, no matter how good his intentions. With her past, it was probably better not to get mixed up with a man like the Devil Kid. She would just have to find some other way to get out of Wood Bluff.

"Have you been to Denver before?" he asked without turning to look at her.

She hesitated, feeling a cold dread squeeze her heart. "Only once. A few years ago."

It wasn't *really* a lie.

Devlin turned around and looked at the lady standing in the middle of Jake Thompson's ramshackle cabin. He must have drowned his brain in whiskey last night or else he wouldn't be thinking her plan made sense.

But it *did* make sense. She was right about it being the perfect cover. No one would look for the Devil Kid with a wife and child. He knew he wouldn't be able to handle a gun for a while, not for weeks yet and not with anything bordering on speed and accuracy. He wouldn't be safe here at Jake's much longer, either. This plan of hers would give him time to lie low and heal up.

He let his gaze slide from her face to her gown. It was simple but fashionable and well made. She apparently had the money to get them out of here. Of course, he didn't have any intention of staying with her for a full year and a half. He might want to give up his life as a hired gun, but he didn't hanker to be a farmer instead. When he was ready to move on, he'd find somebody else to help her with her place. He wouldn't just walk out on her. He still had a few scruples left.

Devlin wasn't fooling himself. He didn't think he could change his life so easily. He couldn't escape the past eighteen years simply by changing his clothes and shaving off his beard. But it would give him some time ... and he could go to Idaho to see his family without them ever knowing the truth about him.

Then ... well, then he'd just have to see what happened.

"All right, Miss Corrall, you've got a deal."

She gasped. Her hand fluttered to her throat in a gesture of disbelief.

"You send me the money for that new suit with Jake. I'll meet you in Denver at the end of the week."

"But I ... Denver ... I'm not sure ..."

"Would you care to rethink your offer?"

"No," she answered quickly. "I'll be there. Where do we meet and what day?"

"Do you know the Windsor Hotel?" he asked as he reentered the house, coming to stand before her. "I'll meet you at noon on Friday in the lobby of the Windsor."

"No!" she cried as the color faded from her cheeks. "Not the Windsor."

Devlin recognized fear on a person's face when he saw it. He'd seen it often enough in his life. Shoot, he'd *felt* it often enough. There was more to the lady's story than what she'd told him. She was running from something. She needed help, and she was looking for it from him.

She'd made a poor choice. He wasn't the type to take on damsels in distress.

Knowing she was hiding something from him, that she was afraid and running, should have been a good enough reason to change his mind. He had troubles of his own. He didn't need to add hers. But he didn't change his mind.

"We won't be staying there, if it's the cost you're worrying about," Devlin explained calmly. "We'll simply reunite in the lobby."

"No. Please. I'll meet you at the stage office." She drew in a breath as she straightened her shoulders and lifted her chin, the calm facade slipping back into place. "It makes much more sense. The wife and son being met as they arrive by stage. No one would suspect we're anything but what we appear to be."

She was watching him with those wide, green, still-frightened eyes of hers, and he had a sudden urge to comfort her. He squelched it.

"I suppose you're right." Devlin took hold of her hand. "The Branigan family, seeing each other for the first time in months. Should be a touching scene."

"The Branigan family?"

Her hand was small and warm within his. He could smell her earthy-scented cologne once again. She was beautiful. Beautiful and sensuous, although he didn't think she was aware of it. He could imagine worse places to hide out than with a woman like Angelica Corrall.

Looking into her eyes, he felt a renewed prickle of desire. Maybe helping a damsel in distress wouldn't be such a terrible undertaking.

He raised her hand to his lips. When he straightened, he revealed the grin that had always made the Devil Kid so irresistible to women. "Angelica, may I introduce your husband? The name is Branigan. Devlin Branigan."

Chapter Two

Devlin sat in the hay loft, one leg hanging out the open window. He could hear Old Joe singing softly somewhere in the barn below him. Moonlight spilled over the red earth of the barnyard. Up at the house, his mother and father were having a party. The sounds of laughter and music and genteel conversation floated to him on a warm March breeze.

As far as Devlin was concerned, there wasn't any place better in the whole world than Twin Willows Plantation. Of course, he was young and hadn't traveled much, but he was certain he was right.

He supposed, when he was old enough, that he would have to go off to college, just like his brothers, Grady and Tucker, had done and his father before them. He'd just as soon not leave, but going away to school would be preferable to disappointing his parents. His father was the best lawyer in all of Georgia, possibly all of the

South. His mother was without a doubt the finest lady anywhere.

Sometimes he wished he could stay a boy forever, that things would never change.

He frowned, thinking back on this afternoon as the guests arrived. He'd listened to the conversations as everyone stood about the drawing room. The talk had been political, as it always was of late. The possibility of war was on everyone's minds.

"The Yankees think they can tell us what to do," Bertrand Pickard had said. "You mark my words. They think they can march down here and take our darkies and our lands away from us and we'll do as they want. They're going to find out how wrong they are."

Devlin tossed the piece of hay he'd been chewing on out the window.

Damn Yankees! Just let them try to take Twin Willows away from his family. He'd fight every last one of them if he had to, but they'd never take the Branigan home. His father said he was a better shot than either of his brothers had been at his age. He'd brought down his first deer last year.

If he had to, he'd lick the Yankees singlehandedly, but he wasn't going to let anybody take Twin Willows.

Chapter Three

Angelica turned slowly, her gaze moving over the familiar room. She had never imagined that it might be difficult to leave this house. She'd always hated living in Wood Bluff. For two and a half years this wretched little town had been her prison. Now she was getting out, and she found that she was afraid to leave.

Marilla Jackson entered the sitting room, carrying Robby in her arms. As soon as the little boy saw Angelica, he leaned toward her, arms outstretched. "Mama."

"The boy knows somethin's not right," Marilla said as she passed the child into his mother's arms. "Are you certain you should be doin' this? It's not too late to change your mind."

"I've got to do it. If I don't, Lamar will come and take Robby away." Angelica stroked the silky hair atop the toddler's head, then lifted her gaze toward the other woman. "You know he always takes what he wants."

Marilla nodded, her expression grim.

Marilla Jackson was Angelica's only friend in town. The woman owned one of the local saloons, which made her as much of an outcast in the eyes of the good people of Wood Bluff as Angelica.

When Lamar Orwell had first brought her here, he'd left her with Marilla. At first, she hadn't trusted the attractive blonde. Why should she have? It had been clear to her that Marilla was another of Lamar's mistresses. A former mistress, as it turned out, but that hadn't eased the pain of his betrayal any.

By the time Robby was born, however, the two women had become fast friends.

Marilla shook her head. "But where will you go? Are you goin' back to the theater? Who's gonna take care of the boy if you do?"

"I haven't decided what I'll do yet or where I'll go. I'm just going away." She offered a tiny smile. "And even if I did know, I wouldn't tell you. If you don't know where I've gone, you can't tell anyone."

They both knew whom she meant. Lamar wasn't going to be happy about her running off this way. He'd told Angelica he wanted Robby, and Lamar wasn't one to give up easily when he decided he wanted something.

Angelica frowned. "Marilla, you don't think he'll try to hurt you, do you? I . . . I wouldn't want that to happen on my account."

"Don't worry about me, sugar. I haven't run a saloon all these years without learnin' a thing

31

or two about protectin' myself. Besides—" she paused a moment, her expression grim "—I know Lamar as well as you do. Prob'ly better. I can handle him."

Angelica nodded, then set her wriggling son on the floor and watched him run across the sparsely furnished room. She wondered again at her sense of loss. This hadn't ever truly felt like a home, although she'd tried to make it one after Robby was born. It wasn't much of a place, but it was the best she'd been able to afford after leaving her room above Marilla's saloon. Over the past two years, Angelica had added her own little touches to the small clapboard house. She'd embroidered the curtains at the windows, and she'd made the rug beside the fireplace.

Still, it wasn't a home. This house, like this town, was merely the place she'd lived in since Lamar discarded her.

"I was such a fool," she whispered.

Marilla came up behind her and wrapped her arms around Angelica's shoulders, then pressed her cheek against the young mother's dark hair. "Women have always made fools of themselves over men. It's the way things are. Always have been. Always will be."

"Not for me," Angelica replied in a firmer voice, shrugging off her friend's embrace. "Not ever again."

"Sugar, I hope you don't mean that. There's plenty of good men out there if you'll just look. Don't let Lamar sour you on the lot."

Angelica shook her head. She meant what she'd said. She wasn't ever again going to trust a man with her heart. She'd trusted Lamar, and look where it got her. Folks here in Wood Bluff thought her no better than a whore because of Lamar, because of Robby.

And maybe she wasn't. She'd given herself to Lamar without even a promise of marriage. But she'd been young and in love and had been so sure that he loved her, too. After all, he was a wealthy and respected gentleman, and she was his lady. She'd believed he meant to marry her.

Of course, his wife would have found that objectionable.

It still stung to remember the night she'd learned that Lamar was married. It had been the same night she'd told him she was expecting his baby. She'd thought he would tell her they would be married at once. She'd thought he would be happy about the child.

She'd thought wrong.

Angelica shook off the dark memories. She wasn't the same helpless, pregnant girl who had arrived in Wood Bluff with no money and nowhere to go. She'd carefully hoarded and saved during the past two years, dreaming of the day she could shake the dust of this town from her feet. She was going to go away where Lamar could never find her or her son. She was going to make a life for herself and Robby where people didn't look down their noses and sneer and talk about her behind her back.

"Well," Marilla said softly, "if you're set on leavin', you'd best get over to the hotel 'fore you miss the stage for Pueblo."

Angelica turned around to meet her friend's gaze. Suddenly she embraced Marilla. "I would have died of loneliness if it weren't for you. I wish there was something I could do to repay your kindness."

"Seems Lamar did me a favor, bringin' you here. It was mighty nice to have a friend. I'm gonna miss you and Robby more'n you'll ever know."

"And we'll miss you," she whispered in response.

Marilla ducked her head, trying to muffle her sniffling. "You get the boy and be on your way. And someday, when you figure you're safe, you write and tell me where you are and what's happened to you. I'll be right here in Wood Bluff, waitin' to hear from you." Marilla turned and walked out of the small house without a backward glance.

Devlin stepped out of the bathhouse and paused on the boardwalk. Beneath the wide brim of his Stetson, his gaze swept the length of the busy Denver street, watchful for any signs of danger. It felt strange to stand there without his gun belt strapped around his hips, but he'd decided it wouldn't fit his new image of farmer and family man. He'd settled for hiding his Colt inside the sling that supported his right arm.

With his left hand he fingered his freshly shaved jaw. It would take some getting used to. He'd first grown his beard at the age of eighteen, when he'd thought it would make him look older, tougher, more of a man. He'd thought to fool the Yankees into thinking he was someone to be dealt with, someone more like his brother Tucker. It hadn't worked, of course, but by the time he'd realized it, he'd become accustomed to the beard and had kept it. It had been a bit of a shock, seeing his whole face again after seventeen years.

Thinking of it reminded him why he'd been to the barber in the first place, and a quick glance at his pocket watch told him the stage was due in soon. He turned to his left and walked down the boardwalk toward the stage office.

You're crazy for going through with this, Branigan, he thought as he crossed the dusty street, then turned right.

He'd tried to find out more about Angelica Corrall from Jake, but the old man had been as stubborn as one of his mules. The most Jake had been willing to say was that Angelica was a real lady, even if she wasn't married to the father of her boy, and Devlin darned well better treat her like one or he'd have Jake Thompson to answer to. Then the old man had told Devlin he'd consider it a mighty big favor if he'd help the gal out by getting her safely to Washington and starting that farm she was so set on having.

Devlin's instincts told him there was plenty more to know about Angelica. Like why she was in such a hurry to leave Wood Bluff. He knew she was a lady in trouble, and he knew she and Jake both thought Devlin was the man to help her.

Well, the two of them were wrong. He couldn't even help himself.

Still, there he was, dressed in the new suit her money had bought for him. He'd sold his horse and saddle, tucked his Colt into his sling, and packed his few belongings—including his gun belt and second revolver—in a small carpetbag. It looked like he meant to keep his promise to Angelica, at least the part about getting to Washington.

Guess that proves you're crazy, he silently told himself.

He slowed his long strides as he approached the stage office, once again on the lookout for danger. It was second nature for him to locate every bystander—man, woman, and child—before making his own presence known. He felt the need even more now that he wasn't wearing his gun.

There was a woman seated on a bench outside the stage office, a traveling bag near her feet. Through the open doorway of the building, he could see a man behind the ticket counter, a green visor shading his eyes. Across the street, two trail-dusty cowboys lounged on a bench outside a hotel. A few doors down, a woman entered the mercantile, a small child in her arms. Several horsemen passed by in the street. A buckboard followed, driven by a grizzled-faced fellow, the back of the wagon filled with supplies.

It felt safe enough, normal. He'd put his faith in such feelings before. He did so again now.

The woman outside the stage office looked up as he approached, then turned her gaze back toward the street when Devlin stepped into the building.

"Afternoon," the clerk greeted him, glancing up from the ledger he'd been toiling over.

"Stage up from Pueblo be in soon?"

"Should be, mister. You takin' it out of here?"

"No, I'm here to meet...ah...my wife. She's been visiting relatives for a few weeks."

The clerk checked the clock against the wall. "Well, you shouldn't have much of a wait. Stage's been runnin' on time most of the week."

"Thanks." Devlin turned around just as the pounding hoofbeats and the "whoa" of the driver announced the stage's arrival.

"See? What'd I tell you? On time again." The clerk hurried from behind his counter and out the doorway.

Devlin followed, stopping in the shade of the awning as the stage rolled to a halt before the office.

Clouds of dust rose from beneath the wheels, then blew on down the street as if still following a phantom coach that had yet to stop.

Sweaty horses snorted, shook their heads, and stomped their feet. Leather creaked and chains rattled.

"Howdy, Matt," the clerk said to the driver, squinting into the afternoon sun from beneath his visor. "Many passengers?"

"Just a woman and her boy." Matt hopped down from the driver's seat and reached for the door.

For a split second, Devlin considered walking away before Angelica descended from the stage, but only for a split second. He needed a place to hide. How much trouble could one woman and a little boy be? A few months from now, he'd be off on his own again.

He stepped forward and waited for his "family" to disembark.

Angelica drew a deep breath and tightened her arms around her sleeping child. Her fears and anxieties had increased tenfold over the last half hour and had doubled yet again as the stage rolled into Denver.

It had been nearly three years since she'd left this city in Lamar's buggy, escorted out of town in the dark of night. She'd been scared and ashamed and afraid. At first, she'd held out hope that Lamar would realize his love for her, that he would send for her again, that he would leave his wife and marry her and claim his child. But the hopes had dimmed with time.

Then, little by little, with Marilla's help,

she'd begun to understand the truth about Lamar. He wasn't at all the man she'd thought him to be. But she hadn't known the full truth of his cruelty until a month ago, when he'd come to take her son.

She never should have stayed in Wood Bluff. She should have gone away even before Robby was born. But what would she have done? How would she have survived? Shame and depression had left her lethargic. Now it could be too late. If Lamar found her . . .

The door of the stage opened, and the driver's dusty face appeared.

She banished thoughts of Lamar. She had more important concerns. For instance, what if the Devil Kid wasn't there? What if he'd taken her money and gone off on his own? And if he was there, waiting for her, what then? Was she doing the right thing? Could she trust him with her and Robby's safety? Would she be able to manage on her own once they were in Washington? Would her money last long enough? Was Morgan Falls the right place for them? Would they be happy there? What if . . .

"We're here, ma'am," the driver said, holding out his hand to help her to the ground.

"Thank you," she murmured. She shifted Robby in her arms.

"Let me take the boy fer ya, ma'am. He looks a mite heavy."

"He is," she confessed, realizing that her right arm had gone to sleep while holding him.

The driver reached in and took Robby from

her, then stepped back to give her room to exit. Drawing another deep breath, Angelica lifted the hem of her skirt slightly and stepped down from the stagecoach.

A wave of fear swelled, threatening to engulf her as her anxieties replayed in her head. *She was in Denver. She was in Lamar's city. What if someone should recognize her? What if...*

"Mrs. Branigan, you are a sight for sore eyes."

The deep voice came softly from behind her. The unfamiliar name wouldn't have caused her to turn if the man hadn't seemed to be standing so close when he spoke.

She swung around, then tipped her head back as her eyes followed the length of the man standing before her.

"I've missed you," he said before pulling her close with one arm and lowering his mouth to hers.

She was too surprised to move, to think, even to breathe. His lips teased hers with a gentle pressure. They were warm and tasted clean. His skin felt smooth against hers, and he smelled of bay rum.

When he released her, she stepped backward, her eyes wide, her mouth tingling, her breathing rapid. She was struck dumb not only by his kiss but by his appearance. This couldn't possibly be the Devil Kid! Not the man she'd visited in Jake's shack.

The scraggly beard was gone, revealing a face far more handsome than any she could have imagined. He had a long nose, slightly flared at the nostrils, and prominent cheekbones. His thick eyebrows were the same raven-black as the hair on his head. His complexion had lost the sallow shades of illness, replaced by the golden-kissed tones of the sun.

But it was his eyes that caught and held her attention. They weren't bloodshot and sunken beneath dark circles of weariness and pain. They were commanding and sharp and . . . and they left her feeling uneasy.

Then he smiled, and she felt as if she'd been spinning like a top for several minutes.

He stepped around her. "And there's my son. Robby, my boy, I've missed you."

Angelica turned in time to see Devlin take Robby from the driver's arms. The boy was awake now, and he was returning Devlin's grin as if they were the greatest of friends. They looked surprisingly natural and right together. The odd, twirling sensation returned to her stomach.

"You found your parents well, I trust?" Devlin asked as he reached down and picked up the portmanteau the driver had set on the boardwalk.

"My parents?" she echoed stupidly, feeling disoriented, as if she'd arrived at the theater in the middle of a play.

He chuckled, stepping forward to kiss her cheek. "Let's go home, Mrs. Branigan," he said in a stage whisper. "You can tell me all about your visit after you're rested."

She nodded, almost believing they had a home together. As he turned and started walking, she fell in at his side. They were several blocks away from the stage office before her senses returned.

She glanced sideways at him. "What was that all about, Mr. Branigan?"

"You wanted folks to believe we're a family, didn't you?" He met her gaze. "So now they do."

"You didn't have to kiss me." There was that awful spinning sensation again.

He chuckled, and she saw a twinkle in his black eyes. "Seemed a good idea to me. Those two fellas won't likely forget the family they reunited today. Husband glad to see his wife. Father glad to see his son." He looked away; his expression sobered. "Anyone looking wouldn't know who we really are."

Angelica stopped suddenly, fear icing through her. There *was* someone who might see and know who they really were. Someone right there in Denver.

"Give me Robby," she demanded, needing to feel her son safely in her arms.

Devlin looked at her. "I don't mind carrying him."

"*Give* him to me."

The fear was back in her green eyes. Devlin stepped forward and handed the boy to her. He wanted to ask what caused the anxiety he saw so clearly on her beautiful face. Then he told himself he'd be better off not knowing.

He'd get her to Washington, give himself time to heal up, and then be on his way without a lot of complications.

He took hold of her elbow. "Come on. I've got us a room for the night at the hotel. We catch the train for Cheyenne early in the morning."

Chapter Four

*It was the company's last night in New York City
when the Countess of Brunbrook came backstage
to meet the players, although Angelica didn't
know who she was until later.*

*All the actors and actresses, stagehands and
musicians, even the theater company's manager,
talked in hushed tones while they waited to be
introduced to the tall woman wearing a sparkling
tiara. Angelica's mother, easily the prettiest
woman in the room, a woman who was rarely
flustered, seemed in awe of the countess.*

*Angelica was in awe herself. She had never
seen anyone so regal before. She longed to ask
her mother who the woman was and why everyone was acting so strangely, but she'd been
warned before about children getting in the way
backstage, and so she sat and watched in absolute silence.*

*As she turned to leave the room, the countess's
cool, assessing gaze fell upon Angelica, who was*

seated on a crate in a dim corner. The woman stared at the girl for what seemed an eternity before gliding toward her.

"What an uncommonly beautiful child," the countess said as she stopped before the crate. "Have you ever seen such extraordinary eyes before, Richard? Or such hair?"

The man beside the countess shook his head. "No, my lady, I have not."

"Whose child is this?"

Angelica's mother stepped forward, her face flushed. "Mine, Lady Sloane. This is my daughter Angelica." She bent her knees, placing her head close to Angelica's. "This is Lady Sloane. She's a countess from England."

Lady Sloane took hold of Angelica's chin and tipped her head back. "Are you going to be an actress like your mother when you grow up, my child?"

Angelica stared, wide-eyed, at the countess. "No," she answered breathlessly, "I want to be a lady like you."

She heard the chuckles from the people behind Lady Sloane, but the countess didn't laugh. "I'm afraid you Americans don't have countesses, my dear child. It is an English institution to which one is born. One does not simply decide to become a lady." The countess smiled tolerantly, then turned and left.

It was something Angelica would always remember.

Chapter Five

Devlin held the door open, and Angelica walked past him into the hotel room.

There wasn't much to it. A bed was pushed up against the far wall. Next to it, two spindle-backed chairs sat on either side of a washstand which held a cracked pitcher and matching bowl. Across the small, narrow room stood a sorry-looking chiffonier. The lone window was covered with a faded curtain, daylight filtering through the worn fabric.

"We'll only be here one night," Devlin said behind her, as if apologizing.

Robby wriggled in her arms, and she gladly set him on the floor as weariness rushed over her.

"Here." Devlin took her elbow and guided her to a chair. "Sit down. We'll go for supper after you've had a while to rest."

"Thank you, Mr. Branigan," she said softly as she settled onto the hard wooden seat.

She glanced toward the bed. She really didn't care about eating. What she would like was a nap. She hadn't slept last night after arriving in Pueblo, and the long stagecoach ride to Denver today had left her exhausted. Perhaps she should ask Devlin to go to his own room while . . .

Her gaze snapped away from the bed and across the room to where he was standing. As she watched, he set his hat on the chiffonier, then removed his suit jacket. Beneath the coat he wore a white shirt, and his arm was in a sling. At his feet were two bags—the portmanteau she'd brought with her from Wood Bluff and a smaller one. His.

He didn't have his own room. He would be staying with her. Not just tonight but until they reached Washington and could build their own house. The charade would have to continue whenever other people were around.

She'd known that this would be the arrangement when she'd proposed the idea to him. Why did it feel so awkward now? She was twenty-six and the mother of a two-year-old son. It wasn't as if she'd never shared a room with a man before, she reminded herself, feeling the old, recurring shame wash over her.

He glanced her way. For a moment, his expression seemed to mirror her doubts. Then he smiled. It was a slow, warm, devastating smile, and she felt its magnetic pull. He was a dangerous man, this Devil Kid. Much more dangerous than she'd thought when she first met him—and it had nothing to do with his reputation with a gun.

Alarmed by her reaction to his smile, shaken by the lingering effects of his kiss, Angelica rose quickly from the chair. She wouldn't allow him to use his charms on her. She'd learned her lessons about men. What Lamar hadn't taught her by experience, she'd learned from Marilla.

She held her head high and thrust her chin forward defiantly. "I think we'd best be certain we understand each other, Mr. Branigan. We may be pretending to be man and wife, but I won't be mauled by you in the middle of the street or anywhere else. I'm sure I made myself clear when I said to you that there are no intimate favors included in our bargain. I've heard about you, and I've no intention of becoming another of the Devil Kid's conquests. The last thing I need is to have my life complicated by a gunfighter."

She saw the anger flash in his black eyes, but she refused to quake before it.

Devlin took a step forward. "As long as we're speaking our minds, Miss Corrall, let's make sure *you* understand *me*. I don't need a woman bad enough to traipse across the country with her and her boy just so I can get her into my bed. Believe it or not, I'm not after your *intimate favors*." Sarcasm laced his words as two more long strides brought him face-to-face with her. His voice lowered. "You came to me with this plan, remember, Miss Corrall? Now,

I don't know who or what you're runnin' from, but if I think a kiss is going to help folks believe we are who we say we are, then you darned well better believe I'm going to kiss you."

He towered over her, his handsome face darkened by outrage, his eyes narrowed, his mouth in a grim line. For one terrible moment, she thought he might kiss her again.

For one terrible moment, she realized she wished he would.

Devlin spun away quickly before he did something he knew he would regret later. He grabbed his hat and slammed it onto his head, then picked up his suit coat and strode out of the room and down the stairs.

He should have known better than to agree to help her. He should have refused and sent her on her way. He could still do it. He could get his bag and light out of Denver. He could buy back his saddle and horse and get rid of these fancy duds and set out on his own, just like he'd done for more years than he cared to count.

He cursed as he pushed his way through the doors of the closest saloon. He glanced around the near-empty room before walking up to the bar.

"Whiskey," he told the barkeeper.

What made Angelica Corrall think he was so hard up for a woman he'd try to trick her into his bed? Hell, he'd never tricked a woman before. They'd all come willingly enough.

The moment the barkeeper set the whiskey glass before him, Devlin picked it up and tossed the fiery liquid into his mouth.

He imagined Angelica then, just as he'd seen her minutes before, her insolent chin jutting forward and her eyes filled with stubbornness. He remembered the anger and fear and uncertainty he'd seen written on her face, and he felt the same urge to help her that had gotten him into this mess in the first place.

He couldn't deny the surge of desire he'd felt when he'd kissed her beside the stagecoach, either. He could feel it stirring again as he remembered the feel of her mouth against his, the sweet taste of her lips, the warm fragrance of her cologne. It had been a long, long time since Devlin had seen a woman as beautiful and sensuous as Angelica Corrall. Her kelly green eyes weren't darkened with kohl nor were her lips painted with rouge. She didn't need enhancements such as those. Her beauty was natural, honest.

"Give me another," he told the barkeeper as he slid his empty glass across the bar.

Damn! What was he doing here, pretending to help this woman and her boy? She was right. He *was* a gunslinger, just as she'd said, not some chivalrous knight of old.

Devlin had believed in chivalry once. He'd admired it in his older brother Tucker, and in his father. He hadn't been too young to recognize that quality in them and to want to be the same when he was a man.

But that was before the Yankees had come to Georgia, before his family had been torn apart, separated from one another like chaff in the wind.

That was before Devlin had lost his belief in the triumph of good over evil, right over wrong.

That was before he'd lost sight of things like honor, faith, and hope.

Devlin drank his second glass of whiskey more slowly, enjoying the feeling as it burned its way down his throat.

He supposed the real reason he was here with this woman was because he wanted to see his family, not because he cared about helping Angelica. He'd been thinking about his mother and Tucker a lot since he'd been shot. He didn't know why. Perhaps it was a sense of his own mortality. Actually, he didn't care what the reasons were. He just knew he wanted to see them both again. And he wanted to see his sisters, Shannon and Fiona, and his little brother, Neal. They were all grown by this time. Probably had families of their own. He wouldn't know them and they wouldn't know him.

Now *there* was what he wanted most of all. He wanted to see his family without any of them knowing what he'd become in the years they'd been apart. With Angelica and the boy at his side—and Angelica's money for the train fare—he could see them without having to read disappointment in their eyes.

His shoulder began to throb, as if to remind him of one more reason he'd agreed to take Angelica to Washington. He couldn't very well deny it. He needed this disguise as much as she did. He needed to lie low until he could draw his gun again. Then he would gladly bid her farewell.

Devlin turned his back to the bar and leaned against it as he stared out at the street through the swinging doors of the saloon.

Well, Miss Corrall, he thought, *seems like you're stuck with me for a while, whether you like it or not.*

"Hungry, Mama."

Angelica turned from the window as her son tugged on her skirt. "I know." She reached out and smoothed the dark curls away from his face. "We won't wait for Mr. Branigan any longer."

"Misser Bran'gan?"

Oh, dear. She hadn't thought about Robby's part in this charade. He couldn't be expected to say "Mr. Branigan" when they were alone and "Pa" when they were with others. He was only two, after all.

Angelica knelt on the floor beside the boy. "Mr. Branigan is your pa, sweetheart. That's what you're to call him. Pa."

Robby's face screwed up, as if he were trying to understand what she was saying.

But how could he understand? Robby had no idea what a "pa" was. He'd seen the man who'd sired him only once. She'd learned the hard way that the accident of conception didn't make a man a father. Certainly it hadn't made one of Lamar.

A familiar cold sensation gripped her stomach at the thought of Lamar with Robby. It left her feeling empty, frightened, helpless.

"Hungry, Mama," her son repeated.

"All right, Robby." She smiled at him. "Let's go find a place to eat."

She picked up her bonnet from the bed where she'd laid it earlier and placed it on her head, tying the ribbon beneath her chin. She was just pulling on her matching gloves when the door opened behind her. She spun around as Devlin stepped into the room, then closed the door again.

"Mr. Branigan," she whispered, realizing that she'd been afraid he wouldn't return, realizing that she'd been afraid she had made him so angry he would abandon her in Denver.

He stared at her, not moving, not speaking, just studying her with those magnetic ebony eyes.

Robby pulled on her skirt again. "Eat, Mama."

"Sorry I'm so late," Devlin said curtly. "Let's go down for supper."

She nodded.

"Come here, boy," he said to Robby.

She was surprised at how quickly her son obeyed. Robby didn't usually take to strangers, especially men. They'd lived a quiet, reclusive life in Wood Bluff, and except for Marilla, they'd had few visitors in their tiny house. Angelica's artistry with a needle and thread had made her popular with the local ladies as a dressmaker, but few of them had ever acknowledged her on the street and no one had ever thought to become her friend or pay a visit to her home.

As for the men of Wood Bluff . . .

Bitterness burned in her chest as she recalled the hurts and insults she'd sustained from the moment she'd told Lamar she was expecting his child. She felt hot tears forming behind her eyes as she watched Devlin pick up Robby with his good arm and hold the boy against his side.

"Mr. Branigan . . ." she began, stepping toward him, intending to retrieve her son.

"Bran'gan," Robby echoed, grinning as he looked at the man holding him.

Devlin glanced toward Angelica. She felt herself growing warm beneath his gaze, confusion replacing the resentment of moments before.

Softly, she said, "I think he'd better call you Pa."

"Bran'gan," Robby said again, louder this time.

Devlin nodded. "I reckon you're right. How do we get him to do that?"

"I suppose I should call you Pa whenever he's listening."

He nodded. "The rest of the time, you can

call me Devlin." He turned and opened the door, then looked back at her expectantly. "You don't have to worry about me bothering you, Miss Corrall. You offered me a way out when I needed one, and I appreciate it. Even a two-bit gunslinger like me knows how to behave like a gentleman if the circumstances call for it. I mean to treat you like the lady you are. I'm probably most of the things you think I am. Maybe I'm worse than you think. But I'm as good as my word. We'll see my family and let 'em think I'm a nice, respectable family man. Then I'll get you to Washington, get you settled in on that farm you think you want, and after that, I'll be on my way. You've got my promise on it."

"Thank you, Mr. Branigan." She swallowed her tears, surprised to find that she believed him. Surprised even more that she sympathized with him. She wasn't sure why he would need her sympathy, yet she felt his discouragement as if it were her own. "I'm sorry, too. I overreacted earlier, and I apologize for the things I said. It's just that I'm not used to . . . I haven't . . ."

He shook his head. "You don't have to explain anything to me. Now, let's go feed the boy. He's hungry."

Chapter Six

Devlin sat astride the lanky sorrel and watched as his mother dropped the keys to Twin Willows into Harlan Simmons' waiting hand.

He knew that this moment would be burned in his memory forever. The white trim of the red brick manse turned golden by the warm spring sunshine. The fields lying fallow. The black buggy pulled by a broken-down nag, and the larger carriage piled high with all the Branigans' remaining worldy goods.

His mother moved stiffly but with great dignity as she turned her back on her home and walked toward the waiting vehicles that would carry the Branigans away, not just from Twin Willows but from Georgia itself.

Oh yes, he would remember this moment.

How could Tucker allow this to happen? How could he give up and quit fighting and let the likes of that dirty carpetbagger have their plantation? If Devlin had a gun, so help him, he'd shoot the man where he stood.

The buggy started down the drive, carrying his sister Shannon and his great-aunt Eugenia toward Atlanta. His brother's gaze turned on Devlin. For a moment they just stared at each other, then Tucker strode toward him.

Devlin's anger surged. He hated his brother for turning tail and running. He hated his father for giving up, for taking his own life rather than fight the Yankees anymore. Perhaps he even hated his mother a little for her calm dignity in the face of such disaster.

Well, he wasn't going to be like them. He wasn't going to quit. He was going to keep fighting the Yankees until he took back what was his.

He'd beat them. So help him, he would beat them.

Chapter Seven

Despite himself, Devlin found he was curious to know more about this woman. He wished he hadn't stopped her from saying whatever she'd started to say back in the hotel room. He wished she would explain everything to him— who she was and what she was afraid of and why she was running away to Washington.

He watched as Angelica patiently helped Robby with his supper, cutting his meat into tiny bites, mashing his potatoes with her fork. There was a special light in her green eyes that was always there when she looked at her son.

He has no father.

Every boy has a father somewhere.

Not my Robby.

As their exchange echoed in his memory, he couldn't help wondering about it. Just who was the boy's father? How had Angelica ended up a mother without a husband? She was no woman of easy virtue. He would bet on it. So what was the truth? It was just one more missing piece to the puzzle of Angelica Corrall.

She looked up at that moment, and their gazes met across the table.

It wasn't going to be easy, he thought, pretending to be her husband and remaining a gentleman at the same time. Even now, he had to resist the urge to kiss her, to taste again the sweetness of her mouth, to feel her soft breasts pressed against his chest.

"I suppose," she said, "you should tell me about your family since I'm going to be meeting them in a few days."

"Yeah," he answered abruptly, jerked from his private musings. "I suppose I should."

He thought back to the last time he'd seen the family together. Seventeen and self-righteous, he'd sat on his horse and watched them drive away from Twin Willows, headed for Missouri and the start of the Oregon Trail. His sister Shannon had remained behind, too, for a short while. The last time he'd seen her was at Great-aunt Eugenia's funeral. Then Shannon had followed the rest of the family west.

Hell, he didn't even know if they were all still alive. He only knew about Tucker because he'd become a well-known judge in Idaho Territory. Devlin hadn't been surprised the first time he'd seen his brother's name in the newspaper. He wouldn't have expected less from him. Tucker had said he was going west to make a difference, to make sure nothing like the War Between the States ever happened again. He'd said he was going to take part in the shaping of the country's future.

At least Tucker had done what he'd set out to do, unlike his younger brother. Devlin hadn't succeeded at anything, unless staying out of jail and keeping one step ahead of the law could be counted as something.

Angelica reached across the table and laid her hand over his for just a moment, then withdrew it as he looked up to meet her gaze. "Tell me. If we've been married long enough to have a son Robby's age, you surely would have talked about them in the past."

"Our family's plantation was called Twin Willows. It was the home of the Branigans for three generations."

"It survived the war?"

"It survived . . . but we had to leave."

He remembered the empty paddocks, the barren fields, the house stripped bare of many priceless possessions. He remembered Harlan Simmons as he accepted the keys from his mother.

"My mother's name is Maureen," he continued. "Prettiest woman in four counties, my father always said. Green eyes and auburn hair. A little like you, I guess. My father's name was Farrell. He died after the war." He couldn't bring himself to tell her how. Even after all these years, Farrell Branigan's suicide remained a painful scar on his memory. At first, he'd hated his father for giving up that way.

He understood it a little better, now that he was older and had experienced defeats of his own, but it had been difficult to forgive.

"I had five brothers and sisters," he continued. "My brother Grady was killed in the war. My oldest brother, Tucker, is a judge up in Idaho Territory. He moved the family there in sixty-seven. Tucker was always the smart one in the family. Then there's my sister Shannon." He grinned to himself. "She's three years older than me. She was always hot-tempered and bullheaded. A lot like me when I was younger. I wonder if she's still the same."

"Don't her letters give you any clues?"

Devlin shook his head. "I haven't seen or heard from any of them since they left Georgia. And they don't know where I am."

"But . . . that's so long ago!" Angelica's eyes rounded, and she looked at him with something akin to pity.

"Yeah. Eighteen years." He turned his head and stared across the restaurant. "They probably think I'm dead. I ought to leave it that way." He'd just as soon let the matter drop, and his tone of voice said so.

But Angelica wasn't about to let that happen. "You said there were six children," she prodded gently. "Tell me about the others."

Reluctantly, he was drawn back to the memories.

"Tell me," she whispered.

"I've got one younger brother and one younger sister. Neal and Fiona. They were just little kids when they left Georgia. It's hard to think of them as being grown with families of their own, but I suppose they do."

"Why didn't you go with them?"

He brought his head back around, causing their gazes to collide. "Because I was young and idealistic, and I thought that right always prevailed in the end. I thought I could do what the whole Confederate Army couldn't. I thought I could save the South from the swarm of locusts that came after the shooting stopped. I've found out since then that locusts are everywhere and right doesn't always win."

An uncomfortable silence stretched between them.

Devlin rose abruptly from his chair. "I'd better get you back to the room. It's getting late and we've got an early train to catch."

She nodded. "We could all use some sleep."

As he looked down at her, something told him he wasn't going to sleep much tonight.

Angelica stared up at the ceiling, but she couldn't see anything in the ink-black darkness of the room. Beside her on the bed, Robby flopped over onto his stomach. She stretched out a hand and touched his back, assuring herself that all was well. Then she turned her head toward the center of the room.

She couldn't see Devlin, but she could hear him breathing.

"There's not room for all three of us in that bed," he'd told her. "You and the boy can share it. I'll sleep on the floor tonight."

She'd been relieved when he said it, but she couldn't expect him to keep sleeping on floors. She would have to allow him to sleep in her bed one of these nights, she thought as a nervous fluttering began in her stomach. Nervous, but not fearful.

She pondered again how easily she had come to believe this man. She'd believed him when he said he would behave the gentleman. She believed that he wouldn't force himself on her, even if they did share the same room and the same bed.

She had no more reason to trust Devlin than any other man, and yet she did. Maybe it was because he didn't look at her the way the men of Wood Bluff always had—with scorn and lust. Not that she hadn't seen the flashes of interest, perhaps even desire, in Devlin's eyes, but it was tempered by a sort of respect, as if he truly believed she was a lady.

Perhaps he didn't know that one had to be born a lady. She couldn't become one simply by wanting it. Ladies were born, not made. Angelica had proved the countess right by her own actions.

Her thoughts returned to the man sleeping on the floor. It had surprised her tonight, when he was talking about his family, to see the gentleness in his eyes, to hear it in his voice. It was one more thing about him that didn't fit the title "gunslinger."

Angelica turned onto her other side and

pulled the blankets up over her shoulders.

What was the matter with her? Devlin Branigan was a man. That meant he was trouble from the word go. She was with him only because he could help her build that new life she wanted in Washington Territory. She didn't care if he was a gentleman who loved his family or if he was a cold-blooded gunman, as long as he helped her and Robby reach safety. She didn't care as long as he helped her escape Lamar.

She drew Robby's warm body close to her own and rested her chin against the soft curls on his head.

You think you can keep the boy from me? You're wrong, Angelica. I'll see to that. Haven't you learned yet that I keep what's mine?

"He mustn't find us," she whispered as she lightly rubbed her fingers over the little boy's arm. "He mustn't ever find us, Robby."

No, it didn't matter who or what Devlin Branigan was, as long as he helped them get away from Colorado and Lamar. She would do anything, use anyone, if it meant finding a safe place for her son. She would lie, cheat, and steal if she had to. She would sleep with the devil himself if it would help her elude Lamar's powerful grasp.

She heard Devlin sigh, and pictured him in her mind as he'd looked when she'd gotten off the stage—so tall and strong and handsome. She remembered the feel of his mouth upon hers and was filled with an unwelcome wanting.

The Devil Kid . . .

Sleep with the devil himself . . .

She shivered uncontrollably even as her skin grew warm. She closed her eyes, trying to clear her mind of such thoughts, and prayed for the release that slumber would bring.

Chapter Eight

Angelica was hungry. It was hard to remember a time she hadn't been hungry—or cold or tired. Certainly not in the years since she'd arrived at the Hardigan Orphanage. It wasn't that Mrs. Hardigan didn't try to provide for the orphans under her care. There were just so many of them and too few resources to go around.

The door to Mrs. Hardigan's office opened. "Come in, Angelica," the tall woman said in her commanding voice, the one she always used when speaking to her children.

Angelica rose from the chair outside the door and followed Mrs. Hardigan into her office. She wondered what sort of trouble she'd gotten herself into this time.

It seemed to Angelica that she'd been in hot water most of the time since she was brought here after the fire. She either cried too easily or laughed too loudly. She was forever telling stories about traveling with a company of actors to the *younger children, and most of these stories were found to be of questionable taste in the matron's opinion. Mrs. Hardigan didn't approve of Angelica's "theatrics" or "flair for the dramatic." She was forever trying to mold the girl into a biddable young woman who, at the very least, might find a position as a schoolteacher or a governess for a respectable family.*

Angelica stopped just inside the doorway.

"This is the child I was telling you about," Mrs. Hardigan stated to the couple standing near her desk. "Angelica, this is Mr. and Mrs. Brown."

"How do you do?" she asked politely.

Mrs. Brown's gaze moved from Angelica's face to the bodice of her dress.

Angelica was already embarrassed by the early development of her breasts and was aware of how tightly her dress fit her. She was even more embarrassed when she was scrupulously studied by people like the Browns, as if she were a freak or something.

Mrs. Brown moved her eyes to her husband and found him staring at the same place. "I'm sorry, Mrs. Hardigan. This girl won't do."

"But why not, Mrs. Brown?"

"She is too old. We want a younger child. Besides, look at her. There's no telling what things this girl has done or might do. We cannot take just anyone into our home. Her parentage . . . Well, we have a social standing in the community which we must consider." Mrs. Brown gripped her husband's arm and urged him toward the door. "Good day."

67

The door slammed behind them.

Angelica didn't need Mrs. Hardigan to say anything. She knew that no one was going to adopt her and take her out of this place. And when a man like Mr. Brown leered at her breasts, she was more afraid that they would than that they wouldn't. She would rather stay here and be hungry than live with someone like that.

"Perhaps I shouldn't tell people that your parents were actors. If they thought you came from a family of quality—"

Angelica's chin shot up a notch. "My father had plenty of quality, and my mother was a fine lady," she stated emphatically. "And someday, I'm going to be a lady, too."

She spun on her heel and marched from the office before the tears could begin to spill over.

Chapter Nine

The passenger car was crowded for the trip from Denver to Cheyenne. Devlin escorted Angelica down the center aisle and into a vacant seat next to the window. He set Robby on the seat across from her, then sat down beside the boy. Angelica glanced at Devlin briefly before moving her gaze out the window.

Neither one of them had spoken more than a dozen words all morning. Devlin had been dressed when she awoke, then had left the room while she performed her morning ablutions. They'd eaten breakfast in the hotel restaurant, rarely even looking at each other, let alone speaking. Angelica should have been grateful for the solitude, but she wasn't. She felt on edge and irritable.

She hadn't slept well during the night. She was anxious to be gone from Denver. There were several reasons for her frayed nerves, and she was convinced that none of them had anything to do with the man seated across from her.

She heard Robby's laughter and looked at him. He was grinning at someone across the aisle, and Angelica followed his gaze.

"What a handsome lad," the middle-aged woman said. "As handsome as his father, isn't he?"

Fear constricted Angelica's throat and paralyzed her limbs. Who was this woman? Did she know Lamar? Had she been following them?

Slowly, good sense cleared her thoughts. The woman meant Devlin, not Lamar. She hadn't said they looked alike, only that they both were handsome.

"Yes," she replied at last. "Yes, he is."

She glanced toward Devlin and Robby as she spoke, comparing them to each other. Robby's hair was dark brown, not black like Devlin's. He had umber eyes rather than ebony, and his complexion was fair like hers. Robby didn't look the least bit like Devlin Branigan, but she realized her good fortune if others thought there was a resemblance. It meant her plan for escaping Lamar's clutches was working.

Robby stood up on the seat, then sidled up beside Devlin. "Bran'gan," he proclaimed loudly. "Bran'gan."

Devlin's eyes met hers before he drew the boy onto his lap. "That's right, son. Bran-i-gan. Robby Branigan."

He said it so naturally, she almost believed

him herself. He was very quick, covering for Robby's innocent blunder with the skill of a born actor. She couldn't help but wonder what other glib lies he could tell with equal ease.

Devlin looked at the woman across the aisle. "He's a bright boy. Not much of a talker, but he knows his name. Don't you, son? Can you tell her your name is Robby?"

"Bran'gan," he replied, then laughed.

"I'm on my way to see my first grandchild," the woman responded proudly. "My daughter and her husband live in Cheyenne. How about you folks? Where are you headed?" Her gaze moved back and forth between Angelica and Devlin.

Devlin replied for them both. "We're headed west to homestead. We've always wanted a place of our own. We've just been to Colorado to visit my wife's parents before we move on. Could be a long time before we can make it back this way."

"How nice for your parents to get to see you and your son," the woman said to Angelica. "I wish my daughter could come visit me more often, but it's difficult with the baby and all. She—"

The car made a sudden surge forward as the train pulled away from the depot. The woman's hat fell forward over her eyes, abruptly ending the conversation.

Robby broke free of Devlin's arms and scrambled across the seat to the window. His eyes were wide with excitement. "Mama!

71

Mama!" he exclaimed, his small hands splayed against the glass.

"I know. Isn't it wonderful, Robby? So much better than the stagecoach. Pretty soon we'll be moving very fast, and the ground will just fly away. We'll be in Washington before you know it."

Devlin leaned forward and spoke in a low voice. "And when were you last on a train, Mrs. Branigan?"

She looked at him without answering.

"Don't you think I need to know a little about my wife before we see my family? There'll be plenty of questions from all of them. We'll be in Boise in just a couple of days. I told you my story. Now it's your turn."

He was right, and she knew it. She needed to keep up her end of this bargain, as well. She needed to help him convince his loved ones that he was a happy family man. But it had been a long time since she'd told anyone about herself, a long time since anyone had cared enough to ask.

Of course, Devlin wasn't asking because he cared about her. He simply needed to know so that they wouldn't be caught in an embarrassing situation later. He was merely being practical, and she needed to be practical, too.

Angelica clenched her hands in her lap and lowered her gaze. She spoke in a whisper, causing him to lean forward until their heads nearly touched. "My parents were actors. They traveled all over the country, performing in farces and Shakespearean plays, singing and dancing. They were wonderful people. They died in a theater fire in San Francisco when I was ten."

He had large hands with tapered fingers. Clean but not soft. Strong-looking hands, the kind that could wrestle a cow to the ground for branding or build a fence to keep the stock in. And yet gentle hands, the kind that could hold a small boy without hurting him. Fine black hair lay flat against the back of his wrists. She could see it peeking from beneath his white cuff as he rested his left forearm on his knee.

"Go on," he encouraged softly.

She met his gaze, then looked away again. "I didn't have any other family, so I was placed in an orphanage in San Francisco. I hated it there. Mrs. Hardigan didn't approve of my family's background. I don't think she liked anything about me. She couldn't find a family to adopt me, although I think she tried. I was simply too old. I was very lonely at the orphanage. Besides, I was used to traveling all the time. I felt like a prisoner. I left there on my seventeenth birthday and joined a theater company. I wanted to be as great an actress as my mother had been."

Angelica had been good, too, and for a long time she'd been happy. From the night she played her first lead in a play, she was an enormous success. Her beauty and talent had drawn men to her like bees to honey, all of them set on seducing the sultry actress with the voluptuous figure, the abundant burgundy hair, and the flashing green eyes. But Angelica had resisted them all.

She'd tired quickly of the vagabond life of the theater. She'd found it hadn't been the traveling she'd missed during the years in the orphanage. Being with her parents had made going from town to town seem exciting and wonderful, but it hadn't been the same without them. What she'd really wanted, she'd learned, was marriage and a home and children. She'd wanted to be part of a family again. She'd wanted to love and be loved in return.

She'd also meant to remain a virgin for the man she would one day marry.

"And did you?" Devlin prompted gently.

She glanced up, startled, wondering if he could read her mind. "Did I what?" She felt her cheeks growing warm.

"Become as great an actress as your mother."

"I was told so," she said after a lengthy pause. She wondered if he'd noticed her embarrassment and guessed why.

He seemed to notice everything with those eyes, she thought. A gunslinger's eyes—especially ones as black as his—should be cold and heartless. His weren't. His seemed ... tender and understanding.

She looked away, fastening her gaze on the passing landscape beyond the window. "I was twenty-three when I left the company after the close of the show in Denver. A few months later, I moved to Wood Bluff. That's where Robby was born."

There was a lot she wasn't telling him. Like who Robby's father was. Was he another actor? Is that why she'd left the theater? Had he broken her heart? And why did she leave Denver for a small town like Wood Bluff? Why didn't she just pretend to be a widow? Why let everyone know she wasn't married?

Devlin wanted to ask those questions and more, but she looked so sad, he couldn't bring himself to cause her any more distress.

Impulsively, he reached forward and folded Angelica's hands within his. "Now let me tell you about us." His eyes twinkled with good-natured encouragement, hoping to drive the melancholy look from her pretty face. "You and I met in Denver. I'd been pushing cattle for a few years and was on my way to ... hmmm ... let's say Montana." He scratched his head. "Must have been back about ... oh ... eighty-one, I'd say. I stopped in Denver and decided to take in a play. When I saw you up there on the stage, I decided to stay in Denver awhile longer. I went back to your dressing room that same night and managed to be introduced to you."

An answering grin pulled at the corners of her mouth. "I, of course, wanted nothing to do with a saddle tramp. Cowboys were not my cup of tea."

"But my charm won you over," he added, turning on his full-fledged smile. "I promised you I'd settle down and quit runnin' cattle if you'd do me the honor of marrying me."

"And I gave up the theater to become your wife."

He caught a whiff of her cologne, found himself staring at the fullness of her lower lip and remembering how sweet she had tasted when he'd kissed her.

"Where have we lived, Mr. Branigan, since our marriage?" Angelica asked.

Lord, he loved the husky quality of her voice. It warmed him to the bottom of his boots.

"Devlin?"

"Hmmm? Oh ..." He straightened as he released her hands. "Small town in Colorado called ... ah ... Harpersville. I was the deputy there. That's where our son was born."

He saw her gaze move to Robby who was still staring out the window, excitement written on his face. When she looked at Devlin again, her smile had disappeared.

"You speak your lines very well, Mr. Branigan. You missed your true calling. You should have been an actor instead of a gunfighter."

Angelica reached forward and pulled Robby into her lap, as if to protect him from contamination. Then she turned with Robby to gaze out the window, pointing at the passing landscape and whispering to him softly.

The wall she'd thrown up between herself and Devlin was invisible but seemingly impregnable, causing Devlin to wonder if he'd only imagined the lighthearted banter they'd shared moments before.

Blasted female. If she didn't cotton to spending time with a gunslinger—or having her son exposed to one—she shouldn't have sought him out in the first place.

The dull ache in his shoulder intensified. He frowned and pulled his hat low over his forehead, then dropped his chin toward his chest and sought comfort in sleep.

Clackity-clackity-clackity...

The rhythmic sound of the iron wheels against the rails soon lulled Robby to sleep. Angelica laid the boy on the seat beside her, then glanced surreptitiously at the man across from her. He, too, appeared to be asleep. She lifted her head and viewed him more openly.

She could try to deny it all she wished, but the truth was, she found Devlin Branigan far more attractive than was wise. Whenever he smiled at her, her breath caught in her throat. Whenever he lowered his voice and leaned toward her, her pulse jumped. Whenever he perused her with ebony eyes, she felt warm and desirable.

She felt it all now, just looking at him and remembering.

Clackity-clackity-clackity...

She pressed her gloved hands against her cheeks, trying to cool the flush she knew must be evident.

What was happening to her? Had she learned nothing in the past three years? Did she want to make the same mistakes all over again, this time with a gunman?

Clackity-clackity-clackity...

She turned her head toward the window as she lowered her hands to her lap and clenched them together.

She was being ridiculous. She wanted nothing more from this man than his help to get her to Washington. She simply needed a good night's sleep. She'd been tense ever since Lamar's visit to Wood Bluff. She'd slept little and spent countless hours worrying that she wouldn't find a way out of that town before he returned.

Penelope wants to adopt a child. I came to take the boy back to Denver with me.

Did he know yet? Did Lamar know that she'd left Wood Bluff? Was he looking for her even now?

Clackity-clackity-clackity...

Be sensible, Angelica. I can give the boy things you never can. He'll go to the finest schools and know the very best people. What can you hope to give him?

Angelica leaned her forehead against the train window. She knew what she could give Robby that Lamar Orwell couldn't. Love. He'd never loved anyone but himself. He didn't even love his wife. He stayed with Penelope only because her father was rich and powerful, even more rich and powerful than Lamar. And Lamar wanted Robby because keeping his wife happy also kept his father-in-law happy.

You think you can keep the boy from me? You're wrong, Angelica. Haven't you learned yet that I take what I want and I keep what's mine? I'll be back for him.

Clackity-clackity-clackity . . .

He'd meant it, of course. He'd meant to come back and take Robby from her, forcefully if necessary. It wasn't because Lamar harbored any fatherly instincts for Robby. Lamar had never even seen his son until the day he'd come to Wood Bluff to tell her he meant to take Robby back to Denver.

Angelica turned her gaze upon her sleeping child. Lamar hadn't even planned to acknowledge that Robby was his son, she thought angrily. He'd merely intended to tell his barren wife that he'd brought home a child they could adopt.

How could she have ever thought herself in love with such a man? Angelica wondered now, recoiling from the memory. As young as she'd been, she still should have recognized the lies and the ease with which he told them. She should have seen how ruthless he was when dealing with others. She should have guessed that he was already married, that he never intended to marry her, that she was only a pawn for his pleasures.

Oh, how could she have been such a blind and utter fool?

Well, never again. She would be the mistress

of her own fate. Never again would she let emotions rule her head. Never again would she let desire beguile her into a man's bed.

Clackity-clackity-clackity . . .

As if in response to that last thought, she turned her eyes upon Devlin, only to discover him watching her in that disconcerting manner of his.

Clackity-clackity-clackity . . .

Was it the train making all that noise or the crazy rhythm of her heart?

Clackity-clackity-clackity . . .

She couldn't be sure.

Chapter Ten

*"You know what I like most 'bout you?" Her
voice was languorous and tinged with pleasure.*

*Devlin pulled the girl close against his naked
body, causing her unbound honey-colored hair
to spill over his chest. "What's that?" He nuzzled
her neck with his lips.*

*"You don't treat me like white trash. You treat
me like I mattered. Like I got feelin's."*

*"Of course, you have feelings. You're no dif-
ferent from anyone else."*

*"That's not what most of the men who come
here think. Long as I make them feel good, it
don't matter 'bout me. You're not like that. You
care. You're a real gentleman, Devlin Branigan,
and you make me feel almost like a lady."*

*He could hear the thickness in her voice, rec-
ognized the threat of tears. It surprised him. In
all the time he'd been coming to see Polly, she'd
never done anything but smile and laugh.
"You're not going to start crying, are you?"*

She sniffed. *"Polly Saunders? She don't cry. Hasn't shed a tear since she first come to Ma Spencer's."*

He couldn't help but admire the girl's bravado. He understood what it took to show the world a stoic face when everything was falling apart. Maybe that was why he always asked for Polly. Because they understood each other.

"That's good. No tears tonight." He ran his fingers slowly up her back. *"I want to remember you smiling."*

"Will you remember me?" She braced herself on one elbow and looked down into his face. *"Will you really?"*

Devlin pushed her tousled hair back, hooking it behind her ears. She was pretty, with dainty features and wide blue eyes. She couldn't be more than nineteen, if that. She'd grown up on a farm in the hills of Georgia, a happy life from the things she'd told him. But her father and brother had been killed at Shiloh, her mother had died before the war was over, and Polly had had no place to go.

"No man could ever forget you, Polly. You're too pretty to forget."

She gave him a pitiful smile. "I wish you didn't have to go. It don't seem fair. You wanted back your place so bad an' all."

Polly was just one of Ma Spencer's girls, working to support herself the only way she knew how. She'd never had much, probably never would. But whenever Devlin needed a warm place to hide from the disappointments and frustrations, he could always find sanctuary here in Polly's arms. In a way, he would always cherish her for that.

She snuggled back down into his embrace, laying her head on his shoulder. "Tell me again where it is you're goin'."

"Just west. I thought I'd head for Texas first. There's lots of land there. Maybe there's room for me."

"You ever comin' back?"

"I don't think so, Polly." Bitterness and sadness filled his chest. "I don't think I'll ever come home again."

Chapter Eleven

The Oregon Short Line Railroad stopped in Nampa in the middle of the night. Devlin touched Angelica's shoulder, gently awakening her.

"Time to get off," he whispered.

She gazed at him sleepily. "Do we have to change trains again?" Weariness laced each syllable.

"No. This is the end of the line."

Angelica straightened slightly and turned her eyes toward the window. "We're in Boise City?"

"No," he said again. "The train doesn't go into Boise. We'll take the stage in the morning."

"Oh." She yawned.

"Come on." Devlin lifted Robby from her lap and braced him against his right shoulder, ignoring the throbbing the boy's weight caused to flare. He pulled his arm from the sling and placed his hand against Robby's back. Then he reached out with his left hand to take Angelica's elbow and help her to her feet. "Let's find us a place to bed down for the night."

She didn't argue with him. She was probably too tired to even realize what he was telling her. After nearly forty-eight hours of travel, including changing trains and long periods spent waiting in depots, Angelica was exhausted.

"You'll have to carry one of the bags, Angelica."

"Hmmm?"

"Our luggage. I can't carry it all and Robby, too."

She tipped her head back and looked up at him. Her face was shrouded in shadows, yet he knew exactly how she must look. Eyes slightly puffy. Cheeks pale. Wisps of dark hair pulled loose from her prim chignon and curling around her face.

Entirely too beautiful for her own good—or his either.

"Is Robby asleep?" she mumbled.

"Just like you." He smiled. "Grab my bag. It's lighter. I'll get yours."

Angelica did as she was told, then led the way off the train. She paused on the platform, obviously disoriented and uncertain where to go.

"This way," Devlin said as he stepped up beside her, then headed into the depot. Moments later, having asked for directions to the nearest hotel, Devlin guided his sleepy companion toward their lodgings for the night.

It wasn't easy, signing the register and paying for the room, with Robby in his arms and Angelica leaning against his other side. The clerk was not overjoyed at being awakened in the middle of the night. He glowered at the little family before him as he slapped the key down on the counter.

"When's the morning stage into Boise?" Devlin asked the man before he could turn away.

"First one's at ten."

"Thanks." His arm tightened around Angelica's back. "Upstairs," he whispered in her ear. "Then you can go back to sleep."

As soon as she started walking, he picked up her portmanteau from the floor where he'd set it earlier, then followed behind her.

The train must have stopped again. They weren't moving. She wondered what time it was. She wondered if they would have to change trains again or if this was just another whistle stop.

It was several more minutes before Angelica was conscious enough to realize she was lying on her side, stretched out comfortably on a soft mattress, not curled up on a hard train seat. Her head was resting on a plump pillow, and she was unmistakably covered with a sheet and blanket. She opened her eyes and blinked several times to clear them.

Sunlight streamed through a part in the curtains, spreading a soft light over the room. Her gaze immediately found Robby, who was lying on the floor next to the bed. A blanket was twisted around him, his legs and arms poking out of it. His mouth was open, his eyes tightly closed.

She tried to remember how and when they'd arrived at this hotel, but her mind was blank. She couldn't recall a thing.

But why should she care how she'd come to be there? It was too wonderful to be in a real bed instead of jostled about by the movements of the train. Absolute heaven, in fact.

With a contented sigh, she rolled onto her back—and bumped against another body.

She held her breath, not daring to move, knowing without looking whom she would see there when she did find the courage to look, and wondering why her heart was beating so funny at the thought of it. Slowly, as she forced herself to begin breathing again, she turned her head on the pillow to look at the man beside her.

Devlin's black hair had the same tousled look that Robby's did when he woke up each morning. As she watched him, he mumbled something in his sleep. The blanket lay across him at mid-chest, and she had a clear view of his union suit. The sleeves were pushed up his arms, and several buttons were open at the chest, revealing black, curly chest hair against sun-bronzed skin.

She slid away from him, instantly aware of the heat of his body so close to her own. She closed her eyes for a moment, trying to calm the sudden racing of her heart. She drew a deep breath, let it out slowly, then repeated the process two more times. When she opened her eyes again, she found him watching her.

"Morning," he said drowsily. He rubbed the dark bristle on his chin with his hand. "Guess it's time we were up."

"Where are we?" Angelica whispered.

"About twenty miles or so outside of Boise. We catch the stage at ten."

He was handsome even with the shadow of a beard on his face. It was tempting to reach out and brush the hair back from his forehead. It was tempting to feel the stubble on his chin, then run her fingers down the column of his throat, rest her hand upon his broad chest and feel the muscles there. It was tempting . . .

Angelica reined in her unsettling thoughts. She wasn't about to let weariness play havoc with her mind.

She grasped the blanket as she sat up, prepared to rise, then fell back on the mattress and yanked the bedclothes up under her chin. She was wearing nothing but her thin chemise and cotton drawers.

Devlin chuckled. "Would you like me to turn my back?"

She didn't remember arriving here. She didn't remember disrobing and getting into bed. She didn't remember Devlin climbing in beside her.

Her heart started another series of wild palpitations.

What else didn't she remember?

"Well, I can't wait around all morning." Devlin tossed off the blankets and rose from the bed.

His short-legged union suit was much too snug for decency. It left little to her imagination. Yet Angelica couldn't seem to take her eyes off his back, watching as he pulled on his trousers over long legs and tight buttocks. He paused and stretched, then slipped on his shirt before turning to face her.

The moment their gazes met, Devlin's face broke into a grin, as if he knew she'd been watching him as he dressed.

"You'd better get up," he said. "I don't know about you, but I could use a decent breakfast."

She continued to lie there, the blanket clutched beneath her chin.

His grin broadened. "It's not like I haven't seen a lady's undergarments before." He smoothed his hair back from his face with his hands.

Angelica knew it then. She knew it beyond a shadow of a doubt. *He* had undressed her and put her to bed.

"I'll go check on a place to eat." He was still smiling as he shoved his hat over his hair. "I'll be back for you and Robby." He opened the door and left the room.

She didn't move for a long time. She simply stared at the closed door and let her embarrassment ebb and flow. Or was it embarrassment she felt?

She closed her eyes and imagined his hands moving over her body, slowly loosening each button of her gown, then sliding the dress off her shoulders. She could almost feel his fingers gripping her ankle as he tugged to remove her shoe. Her skin tingled, and her stomach grew taut.

She groaned, angered at herself. What was wrong with her? She'd never had such thoughts about any man before. Not even Lamar when she'd thought herself in love with him.

Did she really desire this man, this... this gunslinger? Was she so eager to get another child to raise alone? She'd never even enjoyed the act of lovemaking. Her own experience had proved that it was an act meant for the enjoyment of men. For a woman, it was merely a means of keeping a man content and a necessary step in procreation.

"Hellfire and brimstone!" she swore softly, sitting up and casting aside the blankets. "You're not so daft that you'd ever give the man liberties. Mr. Branigan will find that out."

By the time Devlin returned, Angelica was washed and dressed, the tangles brushed from her hair and the burgundy tresses captured in a knot at the nape. Robby was awake, and the portmanteau was packed and waiting by the door.

She was prepared for Devlin emotionally as well. She was determined not to let his good looks or his charms affect her again. It was not the end of the world if he'd seen her in her undergarments, and she was not the least bit disturbed by seeing him in his. Devlin Branigan was merely a means to an end. Nothing more. Certainly nothing to her.

"I'm ready, Mr. Branigan," she said, lifting Robby into her arms. "Shall we go?"

Devlin had mixed feelings as the stage rumbled toward the upper end of the Boise Valley. It had been eighteen years since he'd seen or heard from anyone in his family. They were all strangers to him now, as was he to them. What would they have to say to one another? Would he even be welcome? What if they had learned that he was the Devil Kid and despised him for it?

No, he decided. They couldn't know he was the Devil Kid. No one, not even Devlin himself, had spoken his real name in more than a decade. Not until he'd uttered it to Angelica the day they'd met out at Jake's place.

No, his family wouldn't know what he was called, but they might guess what he had become in the years since they'd seen him last. Did he really think a new suit, now covered with dust and wrinkled from travel, could make him respectable?

Devlin gazed out the window of the stage, noting the many small farms and ranches that lay along the river. To the north and east of the serene valley, rolling foothills, brown and barren, rose toward the pine-covered peaks of the Boise mountains.

Very different country from Georgia, he thought. There would be no Twin Willows here.

Twin Willows... The name was evocative, stirring up a myriad of memories: acres and acres of cotton basking in the hot Georgia sun, songs from the servant quarters drifting toward the house on an evening breeze, his father reading law books in the library, his mother sitting on the veranda as she sipped her morning coffee, honeysuckle and magnolia perfuming the air. He pictured the two-story, red brick manse that had been home to the Branigans for three generations. Devlin had been born there, in the master bedroom, as had his father before him. Devlin's grandfather had helped build the house with his own two hands. They'd all thought Branigans would live there for many more generations to come.

Devlin wondered if the house was still standing or if the yellow-bellied carpetbagger who'd stolen Twin Willows from the Branigans had managed to destroy it by this time. When Devlin had given up his quest to regain title to the land, deciding to leave Georgia for good, he'd gone to see the place one last time. The lands had still lain fallow, and the house had seemed to look back at him with despair. It was a bitter memory, one he'd been unable to forget.

"Devlin?"

He turned toward the soft, husky sound of Angelica's voice.

"It will be all right." She offered a gentle smile. "We were married four years ago come August first. After the wedding, we moved to Harpersville where you were the deputy."

He'd wondered if she would remember a single word of his fabrication about their life together, but she'd remembered all of it.

"Our son was born February fourth of 1883," she told him. "I think you should try to remember that."

Devlin glanced at Robby, seated beside her. He was a good boy. A man would be proud to have such a son.

"February fourth," he repeated. "I'll remember."

The stage slowed as it reached the outskirts of town. Devlin glanced once more out the window, then dropped his suit coat off his right shoulder and removed the sling. He grimaced as he slid his arm into the sleeve of his coat.

"What are you doing?" Angelica asked, eyes wide and disapproving.

"I can't very well tell them I was shot."

"Why not? You were a deputy. Deputies get shot at all the time. You could have been wounded in the line of duty." She frowned. "I've seen the way you wince with pain. Your arm should stay in that sling until it's completely healed."

He shook his head. "I don't want them to know I was shot. I don't want them asking any questions." He leveled a determined gaze on her. "And that settles it."

She nodded in reluctant agreement. "As you wish." The look she gave him seemed to mock his authoritarian tone.

A moment later, the stagecoach rocked to a halt.

"Here we are, folks," the driver called to them, then hopped down from his high perch and opened the door. "Welcome to Boise City, capital of the territory."

"Thanks." Devlin stepped to the ground. He turned and helped Angelica out, then lifted Robby into his arms. "Can you tell me a good place to stay?" he asked the driver.

"Best place is the Overland." The grizzled man pointed down the street. "East and Main Streets. Can't miss it."

"Thanks," Devlin said again.

"You an' the missus be stayin' long?"

"Not long. Just visiting family." Devlin gave Robby to Angelica, then picked up their luggage.

"Family, huh? I know most folks around these parts. I come here back in seventy-five. Nice place to live. What'd you say your name was? Maybe I know your—"

"The Overland, you said?"

"What? Yeah, that's right. The Overland Hotel. Right up the street thataway. Like I said, maybe I know ..."

Devlin began walking before the man could pry more information from him. He didn't feel much like talking about why he was here. In fact, he wasn't too sure but what he should get back on the stage and ride out again. It would probably be better for everyone if he did.

Angelica's hand closed around his arm, squeezing gently. He looked at her, but she remained silent.

It didn't matter. For some crazy reason, he felt better just knowing she was with him.

Chapter Twelve

Angelica opened the door to her dressing room, then stopped and stared at the sight before her. The small space was filled to overflowing with flowers. There was hardly room for her to step inside.

"They pale beside your beauty, Miss Corrall."

She turned around. "Mr. Orwell, really. You mustn't..."

He'd been sending her flowers since the first night they'd met, but he'd never done anything like this before.

"Oh, but I must. And I will, until you agree to have supper with me again. You cannot imagine how lonely I have been without your company. You, my dear lady, are the sun and the moon. You are the music and the stars. You are the very heartbeat of my existence."

Angelica couldn't help smiling at her persistent suitor. "And you, sir, are ridiculous." She glanced toward the other actors, watching in the hallway, and felt herself blush. "Come in, Mr.

Orwell, and quit making a scene. You're embarrassing me."

"What care I for making a scene if you spurn
my attentions, Miss Corrall? Take pity upon this
poor soul. Say you'll dine with me tonight. Tell
me you won't turn me away."

She grabbed his wrist and pulled him into the
crowded dressing room before he could say anything more.

The sweet fragrance of hothouse flowers filled
the room. Lamar was watching her with barely
disguised desire. She felt both excited and frightened at the same time. She'd been sought after
before, of course, but never by anyone as handsome or rich as Lamar Orwell. The times she'd
allowed him to take her out to supper after the
evening performances they'd gone to the finest
restaurants. He'd showered her with compli-
ments. He'd given her expensive gifts. And he'd
always treated her with the utmost respect, like
a lady. He'd never even tried to kiss her, although
she knew he wanted to.

She wondered if she might be falling in love
with him. She'd never been in love before. Was
this what it was like? Feeling so uncertain and
frightened and bewildered? She was definitely flattered by his constant attention. Could he be falling in love with her, too?

Lamar took hold of her hand and raised it to
his lips. Looking at her over the back of her hand,
he said, "You know I won't let you leave Denver
when the play closes. I cannot bear the thought
of not seeing you again. You must give up the

theater. You must stay in Denver with me. I'll see that you have everything your heart desires."

"You want me to stay?" she whispered.

"I insist upon it, Miss Corrall. One thing you will learn about me, my dear, is that I always get what I want. Always."

She envisioned a home and children, happiness and laughter. Lamar was offering that to her. He was offering her a life of security and love and all the things she'd ever wanted. As his wife, she would be respected. No one would turn their nose up at her because she was an actress. No man would assume that they could take liberties with her because of her profession.

"Dine with me at the Windsor," he said softly, his light blue eyes staring intently into hers. "It will be an evening you won't forget. You cannot say no, Miss Corrall. I won't allow it."

"Then I'll say yes, Mr. Orwell. What else can I say?"

Chapter Thirteen

Tucker Branigan leaned back in his leather upholstered chair and closed his eyes. Lord, he wasn't sure what to do in the Chin Wong case. His gut told him the gardener had simply been in the wrong place at the wrong time, despite all the evidence that said the man was a thief and murderer. Tucker was convinced that Chin Wong really didn't know anything about the death of the grocer he'd supposedly robbed and then stabbed.

There had to be some way to find the truth. Tucker wasn't willing to sentence an innocent man to prison or death, not while there was any hope of discovering who the real culprit was.

He sighed. It was days like this that made him question the wisdom of changing sides of the bench—or at the very least, wish he were arguing with someone over the benefits of statehood or votes for women or philosophical differences on any number of subjects. Anything but deciding the fate of a man he thought guiltless.

A light rapping sounded on his door.

"Excuse me, Judge Branigan," his clerk said as he poked his head through the open doorway.

"What is it, Sedgewick?"

"There's a gentleman here who insists on seeing you. He won't give his name, sir. Says he knew you in Georgia."

In Georgia? That was a lifetime ago.

He frowned, suspicious yet curious. "Any reason you think you shouldn't let him in?" Tucker asked, mindful that he'd earned the enmity of a man or two over the last eighteen years of practicing law in the territory, first as an attorney and more recently as a judge.

"I think you should see him, sir," Sedgewick replied, a strange expression on his face.

"Well, show him in then."

The young man nodded and backed away from the door, closing it as he did so.

Tucker straightened in his chair and pulled it closer to his desk. He leaned his forearms on the polished wood surface, assuming his most judgelike demeanor as he waited.

It wasn't long before the door opened again and a tall man stepped into the chamber.

For a split second, Tucker thought it was his younger brother Neal. The raven-colored hair was the same as Neal's, only longer around the collar. The black eyes were the same, too, only this man's had a world-weary look about them, as if he'd seen too much during his lifetime, the sort of things he'd just as soon forget if he could. The fellow was both taller and older than Neal, and his walk was different, as well.

My eyes are playing tricks on me, Tucker thought as he rose from his chair. No one could look this much like his brother.

His brother . . .

"Good God . . ." he whispered. "We thought you were dead."

Devlin didn't move, didn't smile, didn't speak. He simply stared at his older brother.

Tucker's beard was gone, his face as clean-shaven as Devlin's. There was a touch of gray in his sandy brown hair. Eighteen years had added more character to his face, and he'd put on a little weight. Tucker also seemed to have grown shorter, although Devlin knew that was a trick of time and memory. It was Devlin who'd added several inches to his height since the two men had last seen each other.

Tucker looked good. Damn good.

"No, I'm not dead," Devlin replied softly.

Tucker was around the desk and across the office in the blink of an eye. He threw his arms around Devlin and embraced him tightly, pounding him on the back in enthusiastic welcome.

Devlin swallowed the groan that rose in his throat as needles of pain pierced his shoulder.

Tucker stepped back, his hands still clasping Devlin's upper arms. "I can't believe it. We'd given up hope. We tried to track you down in Georgia years ago."

Devlin was certain his brother wanted to know why he hadn't sent word where he was, why he hadn't come to Idaho before now. He was glad Tucker didn't ask. He wasn't ready to answer those questions just yet.

"Mother . . . is she . . ."

"She's well. And happy. She and her husband live out on a ranch across the river from my place. Neal runs Green Willows for them now."

"She's *married*?"

"Almost eighteen years. Same as me."

Devlin shook his head, disbelieving. He'd known that things would be different, but not this different. He'd been afraid that Maureen Branigan might be dead. Anything could happen in eighteen years, and she was nearing sixty by this time. But he'd never considered she might be married again. Almost eighteen years? That meant she'd married a man Devlin had never seen not long after the family left Georgia. How could she have done that? His father was barely cold in his grave when they'd left Twin Willows. How could she have married someone else so soon?

As quickly as the indignation rose in his chest, it dissipated. Who was he to judge what his mother had done? He could only hope the years had been happy ones for her.

Tucker patted Devlin's shoulder again, then guided him to a pair of overstuffed leather chairs near the fireplace. "Sit down, Dev. I imagine we've both got plenty to catch up on."

For over an hour, Devlin plied Tucker with questions, skillfully avoiding saying anything about himself. He learned that Tucker's wife's name was Maggie, that they'd met on the journey west, and that they had six children, the oldest almost sixteen, the youngest not yet a year old. He learned that his sister Shannon had never joined the family in Idaho but was living outside Cheyenne, Wyoming, with her husband and three children. He learned that Neal and Fiona were both married, and that Fiona had a daughter.

He also heard stories of the Branigans' experiences on the Oregon Trail and the first years they were in Idaho, building their homes and their ranches, Tucker establishing his law practice.

Finally, Tucker rose from his chair, saying, "We'd better get you out to Green Willows. If Mother learns I've kept you from her, there'll be the devil to pay. You can tell us all about you and what you've been doing once everyone gets there."

"There's one thing I'd better tell you now," Devlin replied as he got to his feet. "My wife and son are waiting at the Overland Hotel."

"Your wife and ... Why didn't you say something? Why didn't you bring them here with you?"

Devlin's voice was low when he answered, "I wasn't certain I'd be welcome."

"Why wouldn't you be?" Tucker asked, looking surprised.

"I've been gone a long time, Tuck. Our parting wasn't a pleasant one. Remember? Besides, I didn't have a very good excuse for not writing and letting Mother know I was all right. I didn't even know for sure if she was alive. I only knew about you 'cause I read your name in the paper. Judge Tucker Branigan. Made me proud to know you'd done what you set out to do. Real proud."

"Why didn't you come sooner, Dev?"

"Pride, I guess. I never could get Twin Willows back, of course. You were right about that all along. I don't know what I thought I was going to do, anyway. I was just beating myself against a brick wall, just like you told me not to do. Guess I wanted to prove something before you saw me again."

"And did you?"

Devlin shrugged—and tried not to think what he'd really done with his life. "One thing I did right was marrying Angelica. Why don't you come meet her?"

Tucker grinned. "I'm ready. Let's go."

Angelica paced back and forth across the hotel room, pausing each time by the window to gaze down at the street below.

Devlin had been gone an awfully long time. Had something gone wrong? She didn't know what she expected to go awry, but she was afraid it would if it could. After all, Devlin had said he hadn't seen his family in eighteen years. He couldn't possibly know what to expect or what his reception would be.

Or worse, what if someone in town had recognized him as the Devil Kid? What if someone tried to call him out? He didn't even have his gun with him. What if . . .

She stopped suddenly in the middle of the room, closed her eyes, and drew a deep breath. She was letting her imagination run wild. She had to pull herself together. Devlin wasn't a child who needed her fussing and pampering. In fact, she was the one who needed his help and protection. It was silly of her to be acting this way. There wasn't a single logical reason for her behavior.

"Mama, this?"

Angelica glanced down at the wooden toy in Robby's upheld hand. "It's a horse."

"Mama, this?"

"It's a *horse*, Robby," she repeated, her tone abrupt as she turned her eyes from her child to the window. *Where is he? What could be keeping him so long?*

She heard Devlin's voice in the hall and knew immediate relief. He was all right. No harm had befallen him. She let out a deep sigh.

The door opened before she could move from her spot in the center of the room. Devlin entered first. On his heels came another man. He was not quite as tall as Devlin, and his hair and eyes were brown rather than black. And yet there was an unmistakable resemblance.

She knew without being told that she was looking at Tucker Branigan.

"Sorry I—" Devlin began.

Two lengthy strides carried the other man to her. "I'm Tucker. And you must be Angelica. Welcome to Boise City . . . and to the Branigan clan."

She didn't have time to reply before he gave her a warm hug.

Tucker took a half-step back from her. "It's easy to see how you caught my brother's eye. I don't reckon I've seen anyone prettier than you since I met my Maggie." He glanced toward Devlin. "She's even got the coloring of the O'Tooles, doesn't she?"

Devlin was silent for a long moment, then answered, "Yes, I guess she does."

Tucker's gaze returned to Angelica. "Our mother was an O'Toole before she married Father. All the O'Tooles had auburn hair and green eyes. The hair isn't quite the same color as yours, but close. Very close." He grinned. "Mother's going to take a cotton to you. The whole family will." He looked down at the little boy standing near her side. "And you must be Dev's boy. Hello, Robby. I'm your Uncle Tuck."

A lump formed in Angelica's throat. Uncle Tuck. Robby hadn't ever had an uncle before. He'd never had any family but her. It was ridiculous, but she felt just a bit like having a good cry.

"How old are you?" Tucker asked as he lifted Robby into his arms.

Robby tried to hold up just two fingers, but his thumb kept poking up, too.

"He was two in February," Devlin said as he joined the others in the middle of the room.

"Two, huh? Well, you're a fine-looking boy, Robby Branigan." Tucker looked at Angelica. "I'd forgotten how grown up they are at two. Our youngest boy is six, but we've still got Gwen, the baby. She's only seven months, and already she's shooting up like a weed." He turned toward Devlin. "Get your things together. It won't take us long to ride out to the ranch. My buggy's just down the street."

"We don't want to put you out," Angelica protested.

"Put us out? Maggie and Mother would skin me alive if I left you to stay at the hotel. You can live with us until you find a place of your own."

Angelica glanced quickly at Devlin, eyes wide.

He met her gaze, then said, "We won't be staying on here, Tucker. We're on our way to Washington Territory."

"Washington?"

Angelica moved away from the men, picking up the items she'd unpacked earlier and returning them to her portmanteau. "It's my fault," she explained. "I've always wanted to live in Washington, ever since someone . . . a friend . . . told me about it. Devlin promised me that when Robby was old enough we'd have our own place there." As she turned around, her gaze met with Devlin's.

"One thing I never do," he said softly, still looking at her, "is fail to keep a promise to Angelica."

It was unsettling, the way her stomach fluttered in response to his words.

"It's not hard for me to understand that," Tucker interrupted. "I'm the same way with Maggie. And if I don't get the three of you out to meet her right away, I'll be sleeping in the barn with my faithful hound dog."

Devlin grinned at Angelica. "I know what you mean. I've made do with the floor a time or two myself."

Angelica felt herself flush, remembering how she'd felt that morning lying in bed next to him. She suspected he wouldn't volunteer to make do with the floor again. She wasn't even sure she wanted him to.

Chapter Fourteen

Buckshot put down his glass and turned his back to the bar. "Reckon we'd better be gettin' back to the herd."

Devlin nodded. "How's your jaw?"

"Long as I can chew old Cookie's supper, I reckon it's fine." Buckshot rubbed the spot on his chin where the hot-headed youth had punched him. "Young fool. Tryin' t'call me out like that. He won't live to see twenty if he don't watch what he says to his elders."

Devlin knew that what his friend said was the truth. If Buckshot were the sort of man to lose his temper, that kid would have been dead before he'd known what hit him. Devlin didn't think there was another man alive who was faster with a six-gun than Buckshot Jones. 'Course, folks wouldn't know it by looking at him. The grizzly old man was about the scruffiest-looking saddle bum this side of the Mississippi. Maybe on both sides. Buckshot didn't look like he had enough energy to hold a gun, let alone draw and fire it before a man could blink.

Devlin shoved away from the bar and headed toward the swinging doors of the saloon, Buckshot right behind him. He squinted up at the hot summer sun as he paused on the boardwalk.

The old cowpoke slapped him on the back, then untied his big paint and swung into the saddle. "Let's go, Kid. The cows are waitin' for us. MacCory will be wonderin' what kept us in town so long."

"Comin'."

They rode through Dodge at a lazy pace suitable to the temperature of the day. Things were quiet. Devlin figured it was just plain too hot for most folks to be working any harder than they had to.

Most folks, but not all. Like cowboys, for instance. Cowboys just kept working, no matter what the weather. He'd been in the saddle when he'd have sworn he could fry an egg on his hat brim. He'd been in the saddle when the snow was blowing in his face so hard he'd thought his eyes would freeze shut. And he'd been out in every kind of weather in between those two extremes.

Devlin grinned to himself. Surprisingly enough—at least to himself—he liked the life of a trail hand. He supposed that was mostly because of Buckshot. The weathered cowpoke had taken an interest in him when Devlin had first ridden into Robert MacCory's camp and asked for work.

Angry. Bitter. Ready to pick a fight with anybody and everybody. That was the best way to describe Devlin back then. Others had avoided the fiery-tempered young man with a chip on his shoulder, but not Buckshot.

Because of Buckshot, Devlin had even been giving some thought to going on to Idaho after this drive. His friend thought he should. Buckshot kept telling him there wasn't any shame in admitting you'd failed, not if you'd done your best. Maybe his friend was right. Maybe it was time for Devlin to see his family. Maybe he'd even ask Buckshot Jones to go with him.

From the corner of his eye, he saw a flash of sun against metal.

"Nobody laughs at me, old man!"

The angry shout was followed by a gunshot.

Even as Devlin drew his gun, he saw Buckshot tumbling off his horse. He fired at their ambusher, saw the fellow fall face first into the dusty road, then spun his horse around and hopped from the saddle.

Buckshot was dead.

Chapter Fifteen

It was a little like being back in the theater again, only everything was improvised. She had no lines to memorize, at least not at first. She had to be ready for anything. She had to keep track of her own tales, making sure she told the same story each and every time.

And today was only one performance in a show that would run for many months.

Angelica glanced across the parlor. Her gaze met briefly with Devlin's. He smiled at her, and she felt a slight breathlessness before she looked away.

He was a superb actor, she thought, trying to calm the crazy beat of her heart. Every time he'd looked at her today—lovingly, like a husband—even she'd found it convincing. He made it too easy to get caught up in the pretense and forget that she was only playing a part.

Of course, it was vital that they play their

parts well. Angelica knew that, if she could convince these people that this was reality, she could convince anyone. If Devlin's own family believed they were husband, wife, and son, she could quit worrying about others suspecting the truth. She would be free of the past for good.

Not that she didn't feel a bit guilty for her masquerade, seated here in the warmth of Tucker Branigan's parlor. After all, Devlin's mother and sister-in-law had greeted her with open arms and more warmth than she had ever known. Angelica hadn't expected it to be like this. She'd had reason to believe that Devlin had been estranged from his family. After all, he'd stayed away from them for nearly two decades. She'd expected them to, at the very least, be skeptical of her.

But they'd welcomed her as if she'd always been a part of the family.

"Why don't I show you around the place?" Maggie Branigan's gaze strayed to the opposite side of the room.

Tucker and Devlin were seated on either side of their mother. Maureen Foster was holding Devlin's hand and looking into his eyes as if she couldn't look at him long enough or hard enough.

Watching them, Angelica felt hot tears burn her throat. It had been so very long since anyone had looked at her with so much love.

"I don't imagine they'll miss us," Maggie continued. "And the rest of the family won't be here until supper time. Tara will keep a close eye on Robby and Gwen. Won't you, Tara Maureen?" She glanced down at her twelve-year-old daughter sitting on the floor with the two children.

Tara nodded as she set another block on the pyramid she was building. "I'll take care of them."

Angelica drew a deep breath as she rose from the sofa. *Enter, stage left*, she thought, preparing herself for what had to be a gentle but direct interrogation. Her initial meeting with Tucker had been fairly simple. A woman would be more difficult to fool.

"Let's start outside. It's such a beautiful day, and spring is my favorite season." Maggie led the way through the doorway.

His mother's auburn hair was streaked with gray, her face creased with age. While Devlin had considered that she could be dead after so many years, he'd never imagined her changed in any way. He'd always remembered her as she'd been when he was a child. The prettiest woman in four counties, his father had said, and Devlin had agreed with him. No one had ever held a candle to Maureen Branigan.

Maureen touched his cheek for the second time in the past five minutes. Tears still glittered in the corners of her eyes. "I never thought I'd see you again," she repeated. "I thought I'd lost you, just as I lost Grady and your father."

114

It seemed childish—no matter how much he might want to—to tell her how often he'd longed to come, how many nights he'd thought of her, imagining her sitting on the veranda at Twin Willows, and how often he'd pined to see her again. Nor could he tell her why he'd stayed away. Maureen Branigan would never understand why a son of hers would take up the life of a gunman, living by a different law than the one his brother practiced. It would be an affront to all that the Branigans had stood for.

"I missed you, too," he said, hoping the simple words would convey the feelings he couldn't actually say.

Why? her eyes asked. *Why didn't you come sooner?*

But he knew she wouldn't voice the question. At least, not yet. For now it was enough for them just to be together.

"Tell us about Angelica," Maureen prompted. "She's so very lovely."

"She was an actress when I met her. That was in Denver back in eighty-one." The lie fell glibly from his tongue. "I never saw anyone more beautiful than Angelica." That, at least, wasn't a lie. He glanced toward the doorway, wondering where Angelica and Maggie had gone. Talking about her, he found he wanted to look at her, just to see if she was as beautiful as he recalled.

"Does she still perform?" Tucker asked.

"No." Devlin shook his head as he returned

his gaze to his brother. "She gave up acting to marry me. I promised her, if she did, that I'd take her to Washington when we had the money to start our own place."

"Where in Washington?" his brother queried.

"A settlement called Morgan Falls. Judging by the advertisement we saw, my guess is it's a small town with big notions." He shrugged. "But there are homesteads available, and Angelica's got her heart set on us having a ranch of our own. When we leave here, we'll take the train through to Portland, then go by steamer around to Seattle. From there, I'm not sure if we go overland or up river by boat."

"How soon?" his mother asked softly, her expression once again sad. "How soon must you leave?"

"By the end of the week. There's a lot of work waiting for us before winter comes. We've got ground to clear and a house to build and supplies to put up."

Maureen nodded. "I remember what it's like, starting over with nothing. If you stayed here, you wouldn't..." She stopped herself abruptly, then squeezed his hand as she gamely smiled at him. "Washington isn't so very far away. With trains and steamers, we can get there in no time. We'll come for a visit."

"Sure you will, and we'll do the same." Devlin didn't allow himself to think of the day when he would leave Angelica and Robby and strike out on his own once again.

This was just the sort of place Angelica had always dreamed of having. When she was living at the orphanage, she had often closed her eyes and envisioned a home just like this—a big, sprawling house filled with children and plenty of love and laughter. She'd forgotten it for a while after she'd decided to become a great actress like her mother, but the dream had returned to her before she'd met Lamar. Perhaps that was why she'd been so eager to believe he wanted the same things she did. Perhaps that was why...

Beside her, Maggie stopped walking. "See the cabin over there?" She pointed toward the river where a small log building was nearly obscured by trees and underbrush. "That was our first home. It's where Tucker brought me as his bride. Kevin was born there just before we moved into the big house."

Angelica heard a special warmth in Maggie's voice. She glanced at the woman and found her wearing a secret smile.

"I guess that first year we were on this place was the hardest, but it never seemed so bad, not as long as we had each other. You'll find that's true when you get to Washington."

Angelica nodded but didn't attempt to reply, certain her words would get caught in the sudden thickness in her throat.

"Maureen would love to keep Devlin here," Maggie continued softly. "You can't blame her for hoping. Eighteen years is a long time for a mother not to see her son."

"I know." Angelica turned her gaze once more on the log cabin. *If we were really married, we could stay here*, she thought, causing her heart to stumble.

But they *weren't* really married, she reminded herself firmly. They were only pretending. Next year, Devlin would ride away, leaving Angelica and Robby all alone.

That was how she wanted it, too. She wanted to be alone with Robby. She'd made this bargain with Devlin only so Lamar couldn't find her, only so she could get safely to Washington and build her own place. Then she wouldn't need Devlin any longer. She wouldn't need him or his family or anyone else either. She would be just fine on her own. She would be just fine.

Maggie put her arm around Angelica's shoulders and squeezed lightly. "Don't worry. Maureen understands. You and Devlin have dreams of your own. She's not the sort to try to keep her children tied to her apron strings. She only cares that he's happy. And the way Devlin looks at you, it's easy to see you make him happy."

Angelica could only nod and hope that Maggie couldn't read the guilt in her eyes. Maggie's blithe acceptance that all Angelica had said was the truth only made Angelica feel worse.

"Come on. We'd better get back to the house. The rest of the clan will be arriving soon." Maggie laughed. "By the way, don't let us frighten you. We're a large, rather boisterous lot and a bit overwhelming at times, but we're mostly harmless. And everyone's going to love you and Robby. I just know they will. I do already."

Angelica shoved her guilt into a dark corner of her mind and allowed herself to relax, lured by the warmth and friendliness she'd felt ever since Tucker had walked into her hotel room. Would it be so terrible to enjoy the affections of this family for just a few days, even though it was based on a counterfeit marriage? She wouldn't be harming anyone. She was actually doing them a favor, making them all believe that Devlin was something other than what he was. Why shouldn't she take pleasure in their acceptance?

She offered a hesitant smile. "I think I'm going to like all of you, too," she said to Maggie. "And I can't think of one reason to be afraid."

Marilla's shoulder slammed against the chair. Reflexively, she raised her arm to protect her face from another blow as she stumbled backward, trying to maintain her balance.

"Tell me where she is," Lamar demanded as he stepped toward her.

She lowered her arm slightly. "I've told you, I don't know."

He was too quick for her. Before she could move out of reach, the back of his hand struck her cheek, knocking her head against the wall. The room swam before her as tears of pain welled up in her eyes. Her ears rang. Even her teeth hurt.

"I brought her to Wood Bluff so you could keep an eye on her," he shouted. "Where were you when she left? Why didn't you stop her from going?"

Marilla straightened, trying to ignore the pounding in her head as she met his gaze. She forced the quiver from her voice. Come hell or high water, she'd show him she wasn't afraid. She'd show him he couldn't push her around like this. "You don't own me, Lamar. I'm not your woman any more and haven't been for years. I don't owe you a damn thing, and neither does Angelica."

Lamar's face darkened. "Why, you two-bit floozy. Where do you think you'd be if it weren't for me?"

"I sure as hell wouldn't be stuck in this hole folks call a town. Who knows? I might even be happy if you hadn't dumped me here." She started to move around him.

He grabbed her arm and jerked her back into place. "You hear me, Marilla Jackson, and you hear me good." His voice was low, smooth, and deadly. "I mean to find that kid and take him back to Denver. If you get in my way, you'll regret it. You know I can do it, too."

She'd told Angelica that she could take care

120

of herself when it came to Lamar. She'd believed it at the time. But gazing into his cold eyes, she suddenly wasn't so sure. Once, many years ago, she'd found him immensely attractive. Tall, blue-eyed, and blond, he was one of the most charismatic men she'd ever seen. Now, he only filled her with dread. Lamar Orwell would stop at nothing to get what he wanted. From a dirt-poor nobody, he'd become one of the wealthiest, most influential men in Colorado. She hated to think what he'd done to get there. She'd be better off not knowing.

His grip tightened on her arm. "Now, you tell me what she said before she left. You tell me where she was going."

"Leave her be, Lamar," she pleaded. "You don't care about that boy. You don't even know his name, do you? You must have a half-dozen offspring runnin' around the streets of Denver with mothers who don't care where they are. Take one of them. Leave Angelica and her son alone. She loves Robby. He's all she's got. Leave 'em be."

"I'm not about to be saddled with another man's bastard. If Penelope's got to have a brat to raise, it damn well is going to have my blood. That boy's mine, and I mean to have him. Now, tell me where she's taken him."

Marilla whimpered as his fingers bit into the flesh of her arm—bit so hard she thought the bone might snap in two. "I don't know, Lamar. I swear I don't know. She didn't tell me anything. Maybe she didn't want me to know."

"Tell me what you *do* know."

When she didn't answer, he gave her arm a hard twist.

Marilla dragged in a breath. "She caught the stage three days ago. Or maybe it was four. I don't know. I didn't keep track. She didn't take much with her. I...I thought maybe she was goin' to see you, to ask you to leave her and Robby be. Maybe she's there lookin' for you now. I don't know anything else. I swear I don't."

He shoved her away from him, then strode to the door where he picked up his hat from a nearby table. Placing it on his head, he turned around to look at her again. "If I find out you kept something from me, Marilla, I'll be back. You hear me? I'll be back." A moment later, the door closed behind him.

Marilla's knees buckled beneath her. She grabbed for a chair and sank into it as the shaking that had started in her legs spread throughout her body. She covered her face with her hands, fighting the nausea that was twisting her stomach in knots even as she prayed she hadn't said too much.

"Hide, Angelica," she whispered. "Hide quick."

Chapter Sixteen

Angelica ran her fingers over the lawn-green fabric of her dressing gown. She'd chosen it because it was Lamar's favorite. She remembered the night he'd given it to her. He'd told her it was the same color as her eyes and that he wanted her to wear it often.

She glanced nervously at the clock on the mantel. He was late.

She turned and walked across the suite to one of the large windows overlooking the street. Dusk was settling over the city.

Where was Lamar?

Behind her, Lamar's favorite meal was growing cold on the table. A bottle of champagne was chilling on ice. She'd tried to think of everything that would make this night special.

She'd begun to fear that he was slipping away from her, that he was losing interest, that he no longer loved her. In the past few weeks, his visits had been rare. He'd stopped taking her out for supper or to the theater. They hadn't left her suite at the Windsor at all. He would drop in without warning, make love hastily, then dress and depart.

But things would be different now. When Lamar heard her news, he would declare his love and insist that they marry immediately.

She heard the key turning in the lock and spun to face the door.

Lamar's gaze took in the table and wine before finding her standing near the window. "What's this?"

Angelica stepped toward him. "I thought we might dine together."

"I don't have time tonight. What is it, Angelica? Your note said it was important that you speak with me." He removed his suit coat and tossed it onto a chair. "It had better be. I told you not to disturb me at my office."

"I'm sorry, Lamar. It's just . . . well, I haven't seen you for nearly two weeks and I—"

"Do you think I don't have anything to do but come running to you whenever you get lonely? Don't I come when I can?"

"Yes, I suppose you—"

He started to unbutton his shirt. "I'm not hungry for anything but you. Let's go to the bedroom."

She felt sick to her stomach. "Lamar, please. I must talk to you."

He let out an exasperated sigh, and his handsome face twisted with cold anger.

"Lamar, I . . ." She moved to stand before him.

"I love you. You know that I love you. I always thought that you ... well, that you loved me, too. Why else would you ..."

For some reason, she couldn't bear to look into his eyes any longer. They made her feel ... exposed and ... and dirty. She turned her back to him. *"Lamar, I'm going to have your baby. We can't wait any longer to—"*

He spun her around so quickly she nearly fell down.

"A baby? You're pregnant?"

"Yes. I—"

He struck her across the cheek with such force it knocked her backward. Her legs hit the sofa and she dropped onto it.

He moved toward her. *"You idiot. Don't you know anything? Why didn't you prevent this? Are you that stupid? Any whore in a saloon can tell you how to keep this from happening."* He moved his arm as if he would strike her again.

Angelica recoiled into the sofa.

"Penelope might forgive me for keeping a mistress, but a child ..." He blanched. *"If Alexander ever hears of this ..."*

"Who is Penelope?" Angelica asked softly. *"Who is Alexander?"*

The color returned to his face. His cruel eyes narrowed as he glared at her. His face was contorted with hatred. *"Penelope is my wife, you fool, and Alexander is her father."*

"Your wife?" The words were spoken in a horrified whisper.

"Did you think I'd leave her just because you

were going to have somebody's bastard and try to pawn it off on me?"

"Lamar, you know this is your—"

"How would I know? How do I know what you do with your time when I'm not here?"

She wanted to die. She was waiting to die. Please, God, let her die now.

He turned away and marched across the room toward the door, grabbing his coat from the chair as he moved past it. When he stopped and looked back at her, his expression was once more composed. "Get dressed. I'll send for someone to pack your things. You're leaving Denver tonight." He pointed his finger at her. "And if you ever try to contact me or my wife or tell anyone that this is my baby, you'll regret it, Angelica."

Chapter Seventeen

After five days, Angelica was no longer surprised when she opened her eyes in the morning to find Devlin sleeping next to her. There was already something quite natural about having him there.

Lying on her side, the pale light of dawn seeping through the curtains over the windows, Angelica looked at the man beside her. He was on his back, one arm curled over his face, shading his eyes. Black stubble covered his chin. A very strong, purposeful chin. So right with the long jawline, high cheekbones, and straight nose. Straight except for a slight bump near the bridge where, she supposed, he'd broken it in some barroom brawl. Tiny crow's-feet bordered his eyes and the corners of his mouth, and there was a small white scar just above his right eyebrow. It was a face with character, she decided. Much more than merely handsome as she'd originally thought.

She suddenly pictured the way he'd looked at her last night as they'd bid the family good night, recalling the ease with which he'd placed an arm around her shoulder and called her "wife."

But it was her own response to him that disturbed her. The endearment, no matter how artificial in reality, had sounded so right in her ears, just as lying beside him in bed, watching him sleep, felt natural to her now.

Far too natural.

She turned onto her other side and closed her eyes. Devlin Branigan was a man who could handle a lie as easily as he could handle a gun, she reminded herself. She'd had little choice but to trust him to get her to Washington, but she'd best not forget that it had to be a guarded trust. She had to remain wary for no other reason than that he was a man. She'd fallen once for a handsome face and a pretty speech. She wasn't going to forget herself again.

Yet, try as she might, she couldn't shake the memory of his arm around her shoulders, the affectionate twinkle in his black eyes when he looked at her, the soft sound of his voice when he spoke her name.

Unwelcome, unbidden, she remembered the time he'd kissed her beside the stage in Denver. The vision pushed all other thoughts from her head. She felt the warmth of his mouth, smelled the bay rum on his skin. She had the most frightening yearning to roll over and kiss him in return, if only to see if he actually would taste as good as she remembered.

"You awake?" His voice was deep, made gravelly by the last dregs of sleep.

Her eyes flashed open. Her heart raced uncontrollably. "Yes."

"Train leaves at"—he yawned—"noon."

Could he somehow read her thoughts? Did he know that she'd been thinking of his kisses? "I know."

The bed gave beneath his weight as he sat up. "We'd better get a move on."

"I know," she repeated, trying desperately to keep the breathlessness from her voice.

The bed shifted again as he rose. She could hear him moving about the room, listened as he poured water into the washbasin, then splashed it on his face, knew when he reached for his clothes and began to dress.

The door opened. "See you downstairs."

She thought she could feel his gaze on her back. "I'll be right there."

The door closed.

Angelica let out a deep breath and tried again to slow her pulse.

We're leaving today for Washington Territory, she thought as she sat up and lowered her feet to the cool wood floor. *We won't be around other people very often once we settle on our own homestead. We won't have to pretend that we're in love or feel things we don't feel. Then all this craziness will go away.*

Robby's laughter sounded in the hallway.

She turned her gaze toward the door, listening to Tara's faint whispers as the girl took Angelica's son downstairs for his breakfast.

Robby loved it here. He was coddled and pampered by all the women in the family and admired by all the men. He even had his own bed in the nursery, and Tara had made the boy her personal charge, leaving Angelica more free time than she'd had since Robby was born.

Well, her respite was over. Once they boarded the westbound train, she faced months of hard work. Years, actually. She might as well get started.

She dressed hastily, then loosened the thick braid in her hair and brushed it thoroughly before wrapping it into a chignon at the nape of her neck. Finally, feeling more like herself and much more in control, she headed out of the bedroom and down the stairs.

The Branigan family was gathered around the large table. Noisy, cheerful, they all seemed to be talking at once. Angelica paused in the doorway to the dining room and perused them.

Neal Branigan and his pretty wife, Patricia, were there again this morning. Dark, tall, and handsome, Neal was a younger version of Devlin, but without the rougher edges.

Devlin's youngest sister, Fiona Whittier, was there, too. She was holding her daughter, Myrna, and trying to get the toddler to eat, but all Myrna wanted to do was wriggle from her mother's arms and join Robby as he scurried around the table, giggling.

Devlin was deep in conversation with his brothers and their stepfather, David Foster. Angelica knew that Devlin had been ready to dislike the man his mother had married, but his resolve hadn't lasted long. It would have been hard for anyone not to like the former wagon master. She certainly hadn't been able to resist his easy smile and friendly manner.

Scattered around the table were Tucker's and Maggie's brood, all six of them, adding their voices to the general hubbub and commotion.

Angelica felt an arm circle her back and turned to meet Maureen's gaze.

"They're all here except Shannon. Nearly all my children together again. I didn't think I'd live to see this day."

Angelica felt the poignancy of the moment.

"I know Devlin's come to us because of you, my dear. He's been careful not to talk about what kept him away all these years, but I can see his life's been a hard one, just by looking into his eyes. He thinks I don't know, but a mother can tell. I don't believe that I'd have ever seen him again if not for you." Maureen's embrace tightened as she smiled gently at Angelica. "And I can see you've made him happy. For that, I thank you. I'm proud to call you daughter."

Angelica swallowed and nodded, unable to reply.

"Now..." Maureen's arm fell away. "We'd

better get you and your family fed and on your way. You've got a long journey ahead of you."

Angelica remained still as she watched Devlin's mother glide into the dining room. Maureen spoke softly to her children and grandchildren as she passed by them but didn't stop until she reached the far end of the table where Devlin was seated. He rose quickly from his chair and embraced her, resting his chin atop her head.

Angelica felt the sting of tears.

It shouldn't bother him so much, that look of sadness in Angelica's eyes, but it did. Perhaps it was because he was so immeasurably happy that he hated to see anyone not feeling the same way.

Of course, he didn't deserve to feel so happy, and he was well aware of it. He'd lied to his family about what he'd done, what he'd been. He was lying to them still about who he was, pretending to be a family man, pretending to love his wife and son. Funny thing was, it didn't feel like he was pretending most of the time.

Suddenly Angelica turned and disappeared down the hallway.

"I'll be right back," he said softly to his mother.

Maureen followed his gaze toward the place where Angelica had been. "Go on. We'll all still be here."

It took a bit of searching before he found

Angelica standing on the bank of the river.

"Something troubling you?" he asked as he stepped up beside her.

She didn't look at him. "No." Her voice was weak and without much conviction.

Devlin snapped off a dead branch from a willow, then leaned against the tree trunk. "Guess I haven't told you how much I appreciate what you've done. I never could have come here if it weren't for you. You know that, don't you?"

"It's not right, lying to your family this way." There was the sound of tears in her voice.

He straightened and stepped up beside her. Placing his hands on her upper arms, he turned her to face him. "You know Tucker now. You've talked to him. Would you want him to know his brother's the same sort he's spent his life trying to put behind bars? Would you want my mother to know that I've lived my life by the gun, and by the gun is probably how I'll die?"

"Your mother thinks they'll be seeing us again. She thinks they can come to Morgan Falls for a visit." She tilted her head back, lifting her gaze to meet his. "Your mother thinks I've made you happy."

"You have," he whispered.

It wasn't anything he'd planned to say. It just seemed the *right* thing to say. Just as kissing her seemed the right thing to do.

Devlin gathered her to him. With one hand

133

he cupped her chin, holding her gently as his mouth lowered to capture hers. His other hand pressed against the small of her back, drawing her close against the length of his body. The warm, heady scent of her cologne filled his nostrils.

For a moment he felt her surprise, her resistance. And then she leaned into him of her own volition. Her mouth softened. It parted easily as his tongue played across her lower lip. She tasted sweet, warm, inviting.

Or did he only imagine it?

Angelica pushed suddenly from his embrace. Her face was pale, her eyes enormous. "I told you not to do that," she whispered hoarsely.

"Angeli—"

"Don't ever do it again. I'm *not* your wife. We *are* just pretending. And I'm not responsible for your happiness. This is all just part of our bargain, to make people *think* we're a family. I've kept my part. Your family doesn't suspect that you're the Devil Kid, and neither does anybody else. Now you keep your part. You get us safely to Washington and help us get settled and bring in that first crop. And then you can go your own way. I don't care where you go or what you do after that, just as long as you go. I don't need a gunman complicating my life."

Anger rose in response to the disdain he heard in her voice. "Maybe it's time you told me what it is you're running from."

She sucked in a quick breath. "I'm not running from anything."

"Don't treat me like I'm stupid. You're not just after a name for your boy. You're hiding from somebody, and you're afraid. You thought you'd use me to protect you. Well, what if I don't want to be used any longer?"

"Do you mean to cancel our agreement, Mr. Branigan?" If possible, she was even more pale than before.

Blamed fool exasperating female! Why didn't she just tell him the truth?

He swiveled on his heel and started toward the house. "Get your things together," he called over his shoulder. "It's time we left for the train."

She couldn't move. She seemed rooted to the ground. She watched Devlin stride angrily away from her and had to fight the urge to call after him, to beckon him back to her.

He was right. She was afraid. But at the moment, her fear had nothing to do with running away from Lamar, and it had everything to do with Devlin Branigan's kisses.

She could still feel the tumultuous wanting that had flared in her belly in response to his mouth upon hers. It was a burning, searing need that left her aching for a more intimate touch. She'd wanted to feel Devlin's hands upon her bare flesh, and she'd wanted to put her own hands upon him. Even now, she quivered with the wanting.

She closed her eyes, dragging a deep breath

into her lungs. Then she let it out slowly, willing her traitorous desires to go with it.

She would *not* be lulled into a false sense of happiness and security by a mere five days in this house. Devlin Branigan was what he was, and she was what she was, and neither of them was what these people believed.

Angelica took another deep breath, and the shaking began to lessen.

The Devil Kid had always had plenty of women. She'd heard the rumors. She knew the truth. Naturally, he would think she would be willing to fall into his bed. It was obvious to anyone who knew she had an illegitimate son that she was a woman of loose morals.

Only, she wasn't. She was a woman who'd made a mistake with one man and had been forced to pay for it ever since. She wasn't about to fall for the Devil Kid's good looks and fatal charm like so many before her.

Another deep breath, and she felt her control return.

She didn't owe him anything more than they'd agreed upon. He wanted to put his past behind him, and that was what she was helping him to do. He wasn't looking to settle down for long in any one place. In another eighteen months, he would go his own way. She would never see him again. Then she would have the life she wanted.

Just her and Robby. Just the way she wanted it.

She glanced toward the sprawling gray

house and felt a sudden ache in her chest, then shoved the pain into some dark corner of her heart. It wasn't for her, a life like this, a home like this, filled with brothers and sisters, parents and grandchildren, aunts and uncles and cousins. That had been a foolish dream of a lonely orphan. Robby was all the family she would ever need. She didn't need anything or anyone else.

Above all, she didn't need Devlin Branigan.

Chapter Eighteen

It wasn't the things a man had done that passed through his mind as he lay dying, Devlin discovered. It was the things he hadn't done.

He opened his eyes and stared up the side of the gully. He'd tried several times to drag himself up the steep incline, but he'd been too weak. He'd lost too much blood while he was unconscious.

He wondered how long it had been since he'd felt the bullet rip through his shoulder, knocking him from his horse and sending him rolling down the hillside into the bottom of this ravine. Minutes? Hours, perhaps?

He considered trying one more time to inch his way up to the road, then rejected the idea. It was useless. He was growing weaker, not stronger. He would just pass out again, and next time he might not wake up. He'd just as soon spend his last few minutes on earth conscious.

He groaned and closed his eyes. He wished he could have seen his mother again. He wished he could have felt the warmth of her smile and seen the sparkle of approval in her eyes. He wished he could have shaken Tucker's hand and told him how proud he was of his older brother. He wished he could have seen Neal and Fiona now that they weren't children any longer. He wished he could have been part of the family again.

He wished he'd seen the Pacific Ocean. He would have liked to have gone to San Francisco. He'd always heard it was quite a city. He wished he'd had a chance to sit once again in a hayloft and feel a warm breeze whisper across his cheek and smell the magnolias and honeysuckle. He wished . . .

But a man didn't change things by wishing. He went through life, making choices, and then he lived with the consequences. Devlin was here, shot in the back, because of choices he'd made.

Simple, really. Real simple.

Still, if he had a chance to make a different choice, he wondered what he would have done. He wondered how his life might have turned out.

He wondered . . .

Chapter Nineteen

A spring snowstorm raged through the Blue
Mountains, the pristine whiteness seeming
harmless enough to the passengers inside the
train as it chugged up a steady incline.

Devlin turned his attention from the scene
outside the window to the woman across from
him. Neither of them had spoken to the other
since they'd boarded the train in Nampa. Not
that he was still angry with Angelica. He
wasn't. To be fair, she hadn't exactly invited
his advances. She'd made it clear from the
start what the rules of this agreement were and
that her favors weren't part of the package.

However, his promise didn't make him immune to her beauty. A man couldn't go to bed
every night beside a woman like Angelica without being all too aware of her. It wasn't just
sexual, either. Even in the daytime, he'd found
his gaze searching her out. He'd found himself
listening for her voice or her laughter. He'd

found himself waiting to catch a whiff of her cologne or to see her braiding her hair at night. After five days with his family, Angelica and Robby at his side much of the time, even he had begun to think of her as his wife, to believe the stories he told the others.

But now his equilibrium was returning. It was just this kind of fantasy, this sort of false sense of security that was likely to get him killed.

He frowned. It was still possible that someone would recognize him as the Devil Kid. He looked different, cleaned up and in a suit, his beard gone, but there wasn't anything he could do about his unusually tall height or the color of his hair and eyes. If someone was looking for him hard enough, they could still find him.

But he'd lived with that threat for most of his life. He didn't have to like it, but he could live with it. No, the niggling thoughts of danger weren't because of the Kid's reputation. These feelings had to do with Angelica Corrall and the homestead in Washington. It was time he found out why she was on the run, and why she'd chosen him to help her get away.

"Why Washington?" he asked softly.

She started at the sudden question, turning from the window to meet his gaze but not replying.

"Why did you choose Washington Territory?" he repeated. He knew he should have asked her long before now, probably before he'd agreed to come with her, but at the time it had only seemed important to him that he leave Colorado until he could heal up. "Have you been there before?"

"No."

"Then why Washington? There are plenty of other places to homestead."

He saw the flicker of fear in her eyes before she dropped her gaze to her folded hands. She shook her head and showed a weak smile, then shrugged. "I just want to go there. I hear it's pretty and green and that winters are mild."

She might try to hide her feelings from him, but the protective shell she'd thrown around herself was almost tangible. He wanted to knock it down. He wanted to break through the hurt and fear. He wanted her to trust him, to look at him as if he were something other than a gunslinger. It shouldn't have been so important to him, but it was.

He leaned forward and covered her hands in her lap with one of his own. "You're going to have to start trusting me sometime, Angelica. If you want me to protect you, I've got to know what from. I've been honest with you. You know who and what I am and why I agreed to this bargain of ours. Now you need to do the same with me. Tell me the truth, Angelica. Trust me."

She raised wide green eyes to meet his gaze. The look made his heart squeeze.

"Isn't it enough that I want to give my son a better life? He was always going to be the son of *that woman* in Wood Bluff. I don't want

142

that for Robby. He deserves better. It's not his fault that I ..." Her voice broke. Tears welled up in her eyes. "It's not his fault," she finished weakly.

"No. No, it isn't his fault." Devlin tightened his grip on her hands. "But that isn't why you're afraid."

She pulled her hands free from him and dashed the tears from her eyes. Her chin jutted forward as she lifted her head proudly. "I'm not afraid. I just want to go to Washington and have my own farm and raise my son in peace."

If she wasn't the most exasperating female he'd ever known, he didn't know who was.

Devlin glared at her, his patience slipping. It wasn't easy to keep his voice low and guarded, making sure that he wasn't overheard. "You might be a damned fine actress, Angelica, but you're a mighty poor liar. You're plenty scared. Jake didn't send you to me 'cause I looked like a husband or 'cause I needed a way out myself. I know the old goat better than that. He figured you'd need someone who could handle a gun. I admit I should have demanded to know why before now, but I didn't. So now I am." He leaned back against his seat and crossed his arms over his chest. "Tell me. Who's looking for you and why are you going to Washington?"

Angelica's gaze turned upon her sleeping son. She stroked his forehead with her fingertips. "Lamar went to Seattle once. He hated it. He said the rain made his bones ache. He won't look for us there."

"Who's Lamar?"

She didn't reply immediately. She just kept stroking Robby's face. Devlin could see her jaw working, as if she were trying to speak but couldn't. Finally she looked at him again. It wasn't just fear he saw in her eyes, he realized then. There was hatred there, too.

"Lamar Orwell. He's Robby's father, and he wants to take him away from me. But I won't ever let that happen. If you won't help me, I'll find someone who will."

"Orwell?"

Angelica nodded quickly, then turned her gaze back to her son.

Orwell . . . No wonder she was afraid. There weren't many people in Colorado who wouldn't be. Lamar Orwell was a man drunk on his own power. He couldn't be bothered with living within the law if there were quicker and easier methods of obtaining what he wanted. Devlin had seen Lamar a while back at the Cattlemen's Club, and it had been plain even then that the man was used to getting whatever he wanted. If he couldn't get it any other way, he simply took it.

Devlin thought a man like Lamar was more dangerous than any gunslinger he knew. He was dangerous because he hid everything he did beneath a veneer of respectability. He was like a snake in the grass, hard to see, striking without warning.

Yes, if Lamar Orwell was behind Angelica's

flight to Washington, she probably had good reason to be afraid.

"Maybe you'd better tell me a little more," he encouraged gently.

She didn't want to tell him more. She didn't even want to remember. She wanted so desperately to forget that any of it had ever happened . . .

December in Denver.

Angelica had been playing Desdemona in Shakespeare's *Othello*. Lamar had come backstage, asking to be introduced to her. The next day, he sent her flowers. Then he sent her gifts. Finally she allowed him to take her to supper.

Why hadn't someone warned her about him? Perhaps because no one ever interfered with Lamar Orwell. Or perhaps they'd tried to tell her and she hadn't listened. She had been too ready to believe whatever he told her. She had been twenty-two and eager for love and marriage and a family. He had been thirty-two and debonair, charming and wealthy, a real gentleman. He'd given her expensive jewelry and taken her to fabulous restaurants after the play each night and filled her dressing room with flowers and whispered words of adoration and devotion.

It had been in her suite at the Windsor Hotel where he first made love to her. She thought at the time that the quick coupling had followed a proposal of marriage, but later—much later—she realized it was what she'd wanted to hear, not what he'd actually said.

When the theater troupe moved on, Angelica had remained in Denver, certain that she and Lamar would soon be wed, desperate that she should find the happiness she thought awaited her with him. Even when he came to see her less often, even when he was harsh with her, she'd still told herself that he truly loved her and meant to marry her.

Month after month, she'd told herself the same thing—until that fateful night in June, the night she told him she was pregnant with his child . . .

The silence stretched on. As Devlin watched, her face grew pale and pinched. The look of stubborn pride was replaced by despair. She seemed scarcely more than a child herself at that moment, and he wanted to comfort her. But he didn't. He knew she wouldn't appreciate it.

Instead, he leaned forward and rested his forearms on his thighs. "Tell me, Angelica. I need to know what's going on."

"Lamar left me in Wood Bluff so his wife wouldn't hear that his mistress was pregnant." She glanced up at him. "I didn't know he was married until it was too late." There was a pleading tone in her voice, begging him to believe her.

Devlin nodded, careful to keep his expression neutral.

"I should have left Colorado after Robby was

born, but I was scared. I didn't know how I would take care of him. How was I to support us? I couldn't go back to the theater, not with a tiny baby, and I wasn't about to leave him behind. And since Lamar never came to Wood Bluff..." As her words faded away, she turned to look out the window.

It was growing dark. The snowy mountains had become little more than a gray blur. The passenger car was quiet, many of its occupants already nodding off to sleep.

"After the day Lamar took me to Wood Bluff, I didn't see him again until a few weeks ago. He didn't care what happened to me or the baby as long as his wife didn't find out about us." Angelica turned her gaze upon Devlin. The anger had returned and, with it, a steely glint in her green eyes. "His son meant nothing to him. Nothing! How could he not care about his own son?" The momentary show of courage vanished behind renewed fear. "He didn't care until his wife decided she wanted to adopt a child. Now he wants to take Robby away from me. He even offered to make me his mistress again if I cooperated. If I didn't, he'd take him anyway. I told him I'd see him in hell before I'd let him take Robby from me."

Devlin could imagine the scene. He could imagine how Lamar had responded to her defiance.

"He'll try to find me, but he won't be looking for a family headed for Washington. I took the stage to Pueblo a day early, then traveled as

147

Mrs. Branigan the next day to Denver. I assure you, I was very careful, Devlin. Lamar won't be able to find us now."

She could be right. She might have fooled Lamar. Shoot, the man might not even be looking for them. But Devlin didn't plan to take any chances. It was better to be prepared. From now on, he was going to take extra precautions.

The thought of Lamar threatening Angelica made Devlin's stomach knot up. He had the urge to find the man and tear him limb from limb with his bare hands.

Angelica wasn't the only one who would see Lamar in hell if he tried to take Robby away.

Chapter Twenty

Angelica was so intent on her sewing that she didn't acknowledge the first knock on her door. She assumed it was Marilla and that her friend would just walk on in when she didn't answer. When the knocking persisted, she laid the dress aside and rose from her chair.

She couldn't imagine who her visitor might be, unless it was Mrs. Clark. The woman was always complaining that Angelica took too long to finish an order, although it didn't keep her from buying all her gowns from Wood Bluff's finest seamstress. What the old biddy needed with so many dresses was beyond Angelica—there was certainly noplace to wear them in Wood Bluff—but she couldn't afford to turn down the work or offend the woman.

She opened the door, prepared to smile politely and offer a greeting. The smile never made it to her lips.

"Hello, Angelica." Lamar tipped his hat and

grinned. "Surprised to see me?"

She backed away from the door. "What do you want?"

"Now, is that a proper welcome for the man you love?" He followed her inside and closed the door. His gaze swept the room before returning to assess the woman before him. "I do believe you've grown even more beautiful, my dear. I never would have thought that possible."

"What do you want?" she asked again, repulsed by the way his eyes perused her.

Lamar removed his hat and tossed it on the table, then settled into a chair. "I wanted to see you again. It's been a long time. I was wondering if . . . if you'd kept the baby. Marilla tells me you did." He waved his hand at the chair across from him. "Sit down, Angelica. We need to talk."

What she wanted to do was dash into the bedroom, snatch Robby from his bed, and run out the back door.

Lamar seemed to read her mind. "You can't escape me, Angelica, so you might as well do as I say." He smiled again, lazily, as if he had all the time and patience in the world.

"We have nothing to talk about, Lamar. Certainly nothing to say about Robby," Despite her continuing denial, she warily sat down.

"Robby? So, it's a boy. Good. I prefer a son."

She'd been surprised before, then nervous and uncertain. But now she was growing genuinely frightened. "He's my son, not yours. Remember, that's why you brought me to Wood Bluff almost three years ago. You didn't want your wife to know about me. You even accused me of sleeping with other men."

"Three years?" He frowned. "My, my. Is it really so long? I'd lost all track of time. I assumed he'd still be a baby. May I see him?"

"No."

He quirked an eyebrow. "No?" His voice had lost its humor.

"Not until you tell me why you've come."

"Oh, very well. It seems my wife can't have a baby of her own. Now Penelope wants to adopt a child. I came to take the boy back to Denver with me."

She shot up from her chair. "Never!"

"Penelope won't know he's my son, of course. I'll tell her that the boy's father died tragically and that his mother can't take care of him any longer. Or perhaps she died, too. Anyway, that doesn't matter. We'll adopt the boy, and no one will ever know he's really mine."

Angelica walked over to the door and pulled it open. "Get out, Lamar. I will never let you take my son from me."

"Be sensible, Angelica. I can give the boy things you never can. He'll go to the finest schools and know the very best people. What can you hope to give him?"

In answer, she merely stared at him, allowing all her hatred to show in her eyes.

He rose slowly from his chair. "Perhaps you're right. Perhaps it wouldn't be fair to take him from you so quickly." He moved toward her with de-liberate steps, not stopping until only inches separated them. *"You might be able to convince me to take you back to Denver, too. That way you could see him occasionally. I could arrange it. I'd provide you with a comfortable place to live, and I'd come to you as often as I could get away from Penelope."*

She drew away from him, pressing her back against the door.

Desire flared in cold blue eyes. *"You could convince me right now. You could make sure you get to see your son again."*

"Get out," she croaked. *"Get out before I scream. I'd never let you touch me again, and I'll see you in hell before I'd let you take Robby."*

Lamar laughed. *"You think you can keep the boy from me? You're wrong, Angelica. Haven't you learned yet that I take what I want and I keep what's mine? I'll be back for him."* He raised his hand and stroked her cheek. *"And maybe you, too, my dear. Maybe you, too."*

Chapter Twenty-One

Devlin took complete charge from the moment Angelica told him about Lamar. And to her surprise, she was relieved to have him in control. It was a comfort to have someone else making the decisions, and rather nice to have someone strong to lean on.

"We'll get off the train at the next stop and go the rest of the way by horseback. I figure it'll take us about a week or ten days to get to Morgan Falls from here."

"Why can't we go on to Portland and Seattle as we planned?" she wondered aloud. "We'd get there so much faster by train and steamer, wouldn't we?"

"Because this way it will be harder for someone to trace us to our destination."

Angelica felt a sudden chill in response to the serious tone of his reply. She didn't question him further. She didn't need to. She knew he was thinking about Lamar. Devlin wasn't taking any chances, just in case Lamar was following them.

In the small town where they disembarked, they bought the necessary supplies to see them through their journey. Then Devlin managed to dicker the horse trader down to what Angelica thought was a reasonable price for two saddle horses and the essential harness.

A short while later, however, she eyed her steed with something less than enthusiasm. It wasn't the sorrel gelding's fault, although he certainly wasn't much of a horse—slightly swaybacked, ratty coat, deep-dished nose. But her problem wasn't with the horse as much as it was her own ability in the saddle. She'd never been able to claim that she was an accomplished horsewoman.

But, she assured herself, she was certain she could sit a saddle well enough to see them through the next week and a half, just until they reached Morgan Falls. Surely she could manage that.

Devlin led the way out of town. He held Robby in front of him, the boy's small hands resting on the saddle pommel. They rode for over two hours before Devlin stopped and allowed them to stretch their legs.

"Before we get to the next town, you need to do something about your hair," he told Angelica as he helped her down from the saddle.

"My hair?"

"Uh-huh."

"What's wrong with my hair?"

His smile wasn't so much amused as patient. "Nothing's *wrong* with it, Angelica, but the color's uncommon. It's not something a man would soon forget." His ebony eyes seemed to study her with unusual intensity. His smile faded slowly.

She felt his gaze upon her hair as if it were a physical touch. She shouldn't have been so pleased by his remark, especially when she knew he was only trying to protect her and Robby from discovery. Still, she couldn't deny her satisfaction that he found her hair unforgettable.

"Put on a bonnet or something." Devlin turned abruptly.

"I will," she whispered as she watched him walk away from her. For some unknown reason, she was the one now smiling.

They made camp while there was still plenty of daylight. While Angelica set about making supper, Devlin strapped his gun belt around his waist and walked off through the wooded area until he found a clearing.

His shoulder had been throbbing all day. He supposed it was because of the cool, damp weather. But he had to ignore the ache. He had work to do.

Lamar Orwell . . .

It was almost funny, he supposed. He'd tried to fool himself into believing that all he'd have to do was pretend to be a farmer with his own little family, and his life as a gunslinger could just be forgotten. He'd almost convinced himself that he could shave off his beard and all those gun-happy kids would forget about him, let him live out the rest of his life in peace.

It just might have worked, too, if the woman who'd devised the plan hadn't once belonged to Lamar.

Devlin chose a small branch on a log on the opposite side of the clearing. He waited the breadth of a second, then pulled his Colt from the holster and fired. The bullet hit the tree about six inches away from his mark, and the movement sent a bolt of fire streaking down the length of his arm.

He gritted his teeth, shoved the gun back into its holster, and selected another target.

Devlin wasn't a coward, but he knew what it was like to be afraid. He was feeling a bit of healthy fear right now. Although he'd seen Lamar only once, he knew his type well enough. If Lamar really wanted his son, he'd be sending men looking for him, and Devlin knew just the sort of men who would come, too. Men like himself. Hired guns. Hell, he could have been one of them, given different circumstances.

He drew and fired again. Closer this time. Just not close enough.

Angelica was afraid Lamar would steal her son. He wondered if she realized her own life was in danger. Lamar's men wouldn't hesitate to kill her. After all, the boy was supposed to be an orphan when they took him back to Denver. It would be much more convenient if it were true.

The next shot came within a half-inch of its mark. Still not good enough. He wouldn't get this many chances if they were found. He'd better be able to hit his target the first time he drew his revolver.

He reholstered the gun, then kneaded his shoulder with the fingers of his left hand, trying to work out the pain and stiffness.

He heard the snap of a breaking twig. In an instant, he'd whirled toward the sound, his Colt .45 already in his hand. He heard Angelica's startled intake of air just as his gaze connected with hers.

It was a long, tense moment before he spoke. Long enough for the galloping race of his heart to slow. "Don't ever sneak up on me like that, Angelica." His glance shifted to Robby, held snugly in his mother's arms. The boy was looking at Devlin as if he were a bad dream. Robby's eyes filled with tears, and he began to sniffle.

"It's all right, honey," Angelica whispered in the boy's ear. "Your pa was just practicing." She lifted her head to look at Devlin again, her eyes still frightened, still questioning.

Devlin slid the Colt into its holster. "Supper ready?"

She nodded.

He stepped forward. "Let's go eat. I'm hungry."

* * *

Robby had been afraid of him.

Devlin couldn't shake the memory of the little boy's expression. No matter how many times he tried to drive it from his thoughts, it lingered on, keeping him from sleep.

Robby had been afraid of him.

It was raining again. Just a light drizzle. He could hear it slapping the tent in a gentle rhythm. Usually he liked the sound. Not tonight. Not when the dampness had crept into his shoulder. Not when he was already having trouble sleeping.

Robby had been afraid of him.

The thought stung. It lay in his chest, festering, infecting everything else. He'd liked it that Robby had taken to him so quickly. He'd enjoyed being with the lad. He'd felt a level of satisfaction having folks think he was Robby's father. But even at two years of age, Robby had seen what Devlin really was, and now he was afraid.

"Is your arm hurting?" Angelica's whispered question surprised him. He'd thought she was asleep.

"No. It's all right. Go back to sleep."

The interior of the tent was as ink black as the inside of a cave. He couldn't see her as she rolled onto her side to face him, yet somehow he knew that was what she was doing when he heard the soft shifting of blankets.

"Dev...what made you become a gunslinger?"

He closed his eyes against the darkness all

around him, but he only found more darkness. It was in his soul, he supposed, and there was no escaping it there.

Her whisper was scarcely audible above the patter of the raindrops. "Please tell me."

He'd kept his own counsel for many years. He'd spent most of his adult life alone. It wasn't easy or even natural for him to talk about it. Yet, he was suddenly overcome with the desire to do just that.

"A man doesn't wake up one morning and decide to be a gunman. It just sort of happens to him. At least, that's the way it was for me."

He paused, remembering. How far? How far back did it really go? To the boy who'd lost his childhood to war? To the angry youth who watched his family riding away, leaving him and his pride to fight the Yankees in a vanquished Georgia? To the bitter young man who'd had to admit his own defeat?

Silently, he admitted to himself that he'd taken up the gun in his heart long before it had become a way of life.

"I was drivin' cattle with a man they called Buckshot Jones. Don't know why. I never saw him with a shotgun the whole time I knew him. He could do real fancy things with that six-shooter of his. He was the one who taught me how to quick draw. I practiced a lot, until I was nearly as fast as him."

He'd liked Buckshot. He'd been a tough old bird—gray hair, grizzled chin, skin like rawhide—but he'd had a good heart. It was Buck-shot who had given him the nickname Devil Kid. It was Buckshot who'd said, "Devlin's a regular devil with the ladies. Look at 'em, fallin' at his feet, an' him still just a kid." The name had been sort of a joke after that. It hadn't ever been meant to be more than that.

"We were leaving Dodge when we were ambushed by a kid with a grudge against Buckshot. Buckshot was dead before we even knew someone was layin' for us. I drew my gun and fired back. It was reflex more than anything, but I hit him. The kid died the next day."

Devlin swallowed the bad taste that rose in his mouth, the same sort of sick feeling he'd always felt when he'd shot someone. It wasn't right that Buckshot had died the way he did, and it wasn't right that that boy had had to die either.

"That's how reputations get started. A few months later, someone came looking for me. He'd heard the Devil Kid was fast, but he thought he was faster. He was determined to prove himself."

He was silent for a long while, blurred images from the past flitting through his head, the old loneliness in his chest squeezing his heart.

"Pretty soon, the only thing anyone wants to hire you for is to use your gun. So you use it, and then you move on. Always lookin' over your shoulder in case there's another fellow set on making a name for himself. And there always is."

Her hand came to him through the darkness. It lay gently on his shoulder. Her voice attempted to offer comfort and understanding. "You hated it, didn't you?"

He didn't answer. He'd said too much already. He'd wanted to leave the life behind, and look where it had gotten him. Perhaps he wasn't meant to live like Tucker and the others—with respectable jobs and homes and families. Perhaps there wasn't any hope for him. He was a gunman and that's what he'd always be, until the day somebody gunned him down in the street.

That would probably be the only way the Devil Kid would ever die.

Angelica left her hand on his shoulder until she finally heard the steady breathing that announced he'd fallen asleep. Then she drew her arm back and placed her hand over her heart.

She didn't particularly like the way she was feeling about Devlin Branigan. He was a tough, hardened hired gun. He'd never stayed put in any one place for long. He was notorious for his charm with the ladies. A man like Devlin probably didn't want or need her compassion.

And yet, her heart told her he *did* need it. He might be tall and handsome and strong and quick with a gun, but there was still a small measure of vulnerability hidden beneath that tough facade. She'd heard it in his voice tonight. She'd seen it while they were with his family.

And she understood what it was he felt, perhaps because she, too, had been trapped into a life she didn't want.

She rolled onto her other side and hugged Robby against her. It was dangerous to feel this way about Devlin. It could only lead to heartache. She would be better off to remember what he'd always been, to remember how she'd found him—broke and wounded. It would be better if she remembered that she didn't need or want anyone else in her life besides Robby.

It would be better. She just didn't know if it was possible.

Chapter Twenty-Two

Lamar felt the moisture forming between his shoulder blades. Next the sweat would bead on his forehead and along his upper lip, and his shirt would grow damp beneath his arms. It was always the same when he felt his father-in-law's disapproval.

Alexander Venizelos stood with his back to the room, filling a glass with brandy. "Penelope is unhappy, my son. Why do you not do something to make her happy?" He turned around, his beady eyes immediately finding Lamar. "I have always counted on you to make my daughter happy." He shook his head. "I never knew what my Penelope saw in you, but it was you she wanted more than any other. I always want what will make her happy. *You* must make her happy."

Lamar offered what he hoped was a confident smile. "I'm trying my best to do that, sir."

Alexander's bushy eyebrows arched in question. "The orphanages are not overflowing with children? You cannot find one child who needs a home and a mother who will love him?"

"You wouldn't want just any child as your grandson, would you, Alexander? The orphanages may be full, but I want Penelope to have a special child. One with the right breeding, the right looks and intelligence. Our son can't come from ignorant trash. When he's grown, he'll inherit all that I have."

"And all that *I* have," Alexander added as his forefinger traced the rim of his brandy glass. "But that will be a long time in coming."

Lamar glanced down at the thick Persian rug that covered the parlor floor. He tried to ignore the trickle of sweat that was making its way down his spine.

How he hated and despised the man! Always he had been forced to bow and scrape, just so he could get what was his due as the son-in-law of the powerful Alexander Venizelos. Wasn't it enough that he had married the man's horse-faced daughter? Was it *his* fault Penelope was barren?

"Perhaps you are right." Alexander crossed the parlor and sat on an off-white sofa directly across from Lamar. "If Penelope were awaiting her own child, it would take nine months before she held the baby in her arms. She can give you a little more time to provide for her." He frowned. "But do not take too long, my son, or I will wonder why."

Lamar felt the dampness beneath his arms

now, even as his stomach tightened. If Alexander should ever learn about Angelica—or any of the other women he'd bedded—Lamar's life wouldn't be worth two bits.

Alexander Venizelos was a hard, ruthless man whose only weakness was his daughter. He would think nothing of ordering a man's death—even his own son-in-law's—if it suited his purpose, but he was putty in the hands of Penelope. Whatever she wanted, he provided for her.

Seven years ago, Penelope had seen Lamar, an insignificant employee in one of her father's businesses, and decided she wanted him for her husband, and so Alexander had obtained him for her. Lamar had been willing enough. He'd decided that the wealth and power that came with being Alexander's son-in-law would make living with Penelope worthwhile.

And it had been, he supposed. Perhaps he wasn't respected, but he was feared. People knew better than to cross him. No one dared to speak against him. It was well known that he could be even more ruthless than Venizelos himself. Lamar had learned very quickly how to use money and power to get more money and power. Even his father-in-law wasn't aware of how much he'd learned. Yes, marrying Penelope had been worth it.

Besides, the old man wouldn't live forever. When he died, Denver would belong to Lamar Orwell. He could have all the women he wanted without worrying that Alexander would hear of it. Lamar could even send Penelope away if he wanted. Or perhaps he would just leave her alone in this house and let her wonder where he spent his nights.

But until then, he had to be careful.

"I won't," he replied, returning his attention to the conversation while hiding his agitation. "I'm as anxious to provide Penelope with a child as she is to have one. I only want it to be the right child. I want to give Penelope whatever she wants. After all, Alexander, she's my wife. Who more than I would want to make her happy?"

"Papa! I didn't know you were here."

The two men looked toward the doorway as Penelope entered the parlor. Smiling brightly, she walked to her father and leaned over to kiss first one cheek and then the other.

"We don't see you often enough, Papa."

Lamar observed them, father and daughter, and subdued a shudder. They were very similar, those two. Short, dark-haired, with long narrow faces and overlarge noses. But Penelope wasn't portly like her father. Instead, she was skinny and shapeless, like a scarecrow.

He suddenly envisioned Angelica, a woman beautiful beyond a man's wildest dreams. She was tall and generously curved. He'd thought he would be driven mad with desire before he'd managed to woo her into his bed. If she hadn't been so stupid, so careless, he might have been able to keep her as his mistress even after Alexander and Penelope had returned from Greece three years ago.

It surprised him now that he'd thought so little of Angelica. She'd rarely crossed his mind until Penelope's demands for a child had become strident.

The child was why he'd gone to see her. After all, why should he have to take someone else's reject when he could have his own offspring? But from the moment he'd seen Angelica again, the child had seemed secondary. He'd wanted her. She could have returned to Denver with him. She could have been his mistress, could have lived in style, could even have seen her son on occasion. Angelica should have seen the wisdom of such a decision. But she hadn't. She'd taken the boy and gone into hiding.

Damn her! Damn Angelica Corrall! How dare she defy him?

His jaw tightened as he felt anger heat his belly. He would find her and show her the error of her ways. So help him, he would teach her a lesson she wouldn't soon forget.

Penelope came to sit beside him, drawing his thoughts abruptly back to the present. She took his hand and revealed her toothy smile. "Tell Papa we don't see him often enough, Lamar."

He did his best to hide his raging thoughts, molding his expression into one of sincerity. "No, we don't, sir. You must join us for supper more often. Penelope misses you when you're not here."

Alexander nodded as he drew a thick cigar

from his pocket. "Then I shall do my best to come."

Rain fell steadily from a pewter sky, turning the lone street of Morgan Falls into a sea of mud. It oozed and sucked at their horses' hooves as Devlin, Angelica, and Robby entered the tiny settlement a week later.

Angelica felt a little like crying when she realized they'd arrived at their destination. She'd expected so much more. She'd expected Morgan Falls to be a *real* town, not just four unpainted buildings—the general store, the mill, and two houses.

A town? Morgan Falls wasn't a town at all. She thought of the advertisement that had brought them here. Where was the community bursting with wonderful resources? What foolhardy soul ever supposed that this hamlet was destined to be one of the most desirable and healthy localities in Washington?

Water dripping from the brim of his Stetson, Devlin drew his horse to a stop and dismounted in front of the general store. A sign in the window of the unpainted plank building announced that it also served as Morgan Falls' post office.

Angelica wondered how many people picked up their mail inside. She feared the answer would be very few.

Devlin looped the reins around the hitching post, then turned to help Angelica and Robby to the ground. He took the boy from her arms and held on to her elbow as he guided her toward the narrow boardwalk and awning that protected the entrance of the general store.

Angelica felt the cold mud seeping through the fabric of her shoes. The hem of her dress clung damply to her legs, chilling her even further. She shivered as she tried to pull her cloak more tightly around her shoulders.

"We'll ask if there's some place we can put up for the night," Devlin said as he opened the door for her. "Some place dry with a fire."

She glanced at him, realizing that he must feel every bit as cold and miserable as did she. He had been favoring his right arm even more than usual these past two or three days. She couldn't count the times she'd caught him rubbing his wound, his mouth set in a thin line. Still, his pain hadn't kept him from practicing his quick draw every night when they made camp. It served as a constant reminder that Devlin didn't think they were safe.

She shivered again as she moved past him into the store.

A man behind the counter—fiftyish, balding, with a pair of thick spectacles perched on the bridge of his nose—looked up as they entered. His face broke immediately into a grin of welcome. "Well, how do, strangers. Not a good day for folks to be travelin'. Come in, ma'am, and set yourself by the stove here."

Angelica did as she was told, sinking gratefully onto the spindle-backed chair next to a pot-bellied stove which was belching heat, a crackling fire within. She wanted desperately to remove her wet bonnet, but she remembered Devlin's admonition to keep her hair covered.

The man's gaze turned toward Devlin. "What can I get for you, young fella?"

"We're looking for a place to spend the night."

"The Widow Brighton, cross the way there, has an extra room she lets out every now an' agin. Course, we don't get many strangers through these parts, but Mary's more'n happy to have the company ever since her daughter up an' married my boy Joshua an' moved onto a place o' her own." He grinned, then asked, "Where you folks headed?"

Devlin removed his hat, sending a rivulet of water cascading from the brim onto the wooden floor. He raked his fingers through wet black hair. "We're looking to settle here in Morgan Falls."

"Well, I'll be." The man turned his head toward the back of the store. "Maud! Maud, come here."

A moment later, a short woman with gray hair bustled into the shop.

"Maud, come meet these folks. They say they've come to settle in Morgan Falls." His gaze returned to Devlin. "This here's my wife, Maud. My name's Bert Farland."

"Mrs. Farland," Devlin acknowledged with a tip of his head. "I'm Devlin Branigan. This is my wife, Angelica, and our son, Robby."

"Oh, my," Maud Farland responded, her gray eyes rounding and her expression appalled. "You poor dears. Look at you. You must be frozen to the bone. Bert, you get on over to Mary's and see that Rose's old room is made ready. Mrs. Branigan, you bring that boy of yours and we'll get you into something warm and dry. The men can see to gettin' your things over to Mary's. Come on now. I've got plenty o' hot tea and some good soup to warm your bellies."

Angelica glanced at Devlin.

He offered a weary grimace that she thought was meant to be a smile, then set Robby on the floor. "Go with your ma," he said softly as he straightened.

Angelica and Robby were whisked into the living quarters at the back of the general store and stripped of their soaked clothing. Angelica was commanded to put on one of Maud's nightgowns, which was far too short and only reached to mid-calf. Then she was wrapped in a scratchy but warm blanket.

"Land sakes, I'd love to have you folks stay here with us, but we just haven't the room. When we lived on our farm, we had us a big house. Course, we had to have us a big house, what with eight young'ns to raise. Our third boy, Joshua, lives out there now, him and his wife, Rose, and the baby. Oh my, Rose is going to be happy t'have another young mother in town. Oh my, yes."

Maud's steady stream of chatter droned on,

but Angelica was only vaguely aware of what she was saying. A weariness was stealing over her, exacerbated by the fire on the hearth and the warm tea which the kindly woman had prepared.

It wasn't long before she fell asleep, curled into a tight ball on the narrow sofa.

Devlin looked down at her. Burgundy hair, completely dry for the first time in days, spilled across the cushion of the worn sofa. Her long lashes kissed the pale skin of her cheeks. She looked peaceful, for a change. Peaceful and very, very beautiful.

He hated to wake her.

"Why don't you let the youngster stay here with me, Mr. Branigan?" Maud whispered behind him. "We've right taken to each other. He won't be no bother to me. I raised eight o' my own." She stepped closer, her voice lowering even more as she, too, gazed down at Angelica. "Prettiest thing I ever seen. You let her rest over at Mrs. Brighton's and come get Robby tomorrow."

Devlin thought it would be nice to sleep without fear of being awakened by the rambunctious two-year-old. He could use a good rest as much as Angelica.

"Go on, now. You carry your wife on over to Mrs. Brighton's. I don't reckon she'll even know how she got there, tired as the lamb is. And you tell her any time she needs someone to look after the boy, I'll be glad to oblige. Land sakes, there ain't enough young folk in these parts, and I miss havin' the little ones around. You come back and get him in the mornin'."

Devlin decided it would be pointless to argue with her. Besides, he was too weary to come up with any reason not to accept her offer.

Gently he slipped his arms beneath Angelica and lifted her against his chest. Her eyes briefly fluttered open, then closed again without focusing.

"Must we leave?" she mumbled.

"No," he answered softly. "We're going to stay."

She cuddled closer, her hands drifting up to clasp behind his neck. "I'm glad," she said with a deep sigh.

She was so incredibly beautiful, so soft and feminine, so stubborn and proud. And he was thoroughly enjoying holding her in his arms. The blanket had fallen open when he picked her up, and he had a delightful view of her full breasts beneath the white cotton nightgown.

An image popped into his head, an image of Angelica lying naked beneath him and how much he would enjoy running his tongue over the nipples of her breasts, hearing her moan with pleasure.

He felt a corresponding stirring of desire, and abruptly pushed the illicit image out of his thoughts. Angelica would not welcome it. Moreover, she wasn't his type of woman. The Devil Kid's women were fast and loose, women who wore plenty of makeup and very few clothes.

But what kind of woman would be right for a man known only as Devlin Branigan?

Troubled by the unwanted question, he nodded in Maud Farland's direction, then carried Angelica out the back door and down the muddy footpath to the boarding house.

Warm. So delightfully warm. And there were sheets on the bed. Real sheets.

Angelica knew she should probably be up, but nothing had felt this good since they left Boise. She just wanted to lie here, within the safety of Devlin's arms, until . . .

Her eyes flew open even as her breath caught in her throat.

She was, indeed, lying in his arms. Her head was resting on his shoulder. Her breasts were pressed against his side. She felt the heat rising steadily in her cheeks as she realized how intimately she lay against his hip, one leg lying atop his.

And with it came a longing, an aching for an even more intimate touch.

She closed her eyes, willing the unwanted desires to go away.

Devlin sighed and shifted, pressing her even more tightly against him. The rapid beating of her heart echoed in her head. She ran her tongue over her dry lips. She tried to swallow but found she couldn't. The ache in her loins increased.

She had no idea how long she lay there, not moving, scarcely breathing, before she knew he was awake and watching her. She knew it long before his free hand touched her arm, then slid slowly upwards. She knew it long before he rolled onto his side, crushing her to him and pressing his mouth against hers.

And her traitorous body responded. Like a drowning woman, she clung to him, opening her mouth at the insistence of his tongue. Never had she been so aware of her own desires as now. Never had she felt such a desperate longing.

It was wrong.

It was insane.

It was real.

His hand slid from her arm and covered her breast. Angelica moaned as her head dropped backward, exposing her throat to his lips. She felt frustrated by the thin fabric of her nightgown, wanted to feel flesh against flesh. Wanted it now before Robby woke up and . . .

Robby!

With extraordinary strength, she shoved Devlin away. She sat up, breathing frantically, her gaze flying around the small bedroom.

"Where's Robby?" she gasped.

"At Mrs. Farland's." He sat up beside her on the bed. His union suit was open down the front, revealing curly black chest hair against dark skin. His gaze—slumberous, sultry—watched her as he raked his hand through tousled hair. "He was asleep, and she offered to keep him so you could rest." He reached for her. His voice softened. "Angeli—"

"No!" She jumped out of bed, dragging the top blanket with her to hide behind. "You keep your hands to yourself, Devlin Branigan."

With terrible clarity, she knew she didn't fear Devlin. She feared her own reckless reaction to him. It seemed so easy for him to make her forget herself, to lose control. It was so easy for the fiery passions to be ignited, passions she'd never felt before, passions she didn't know how to handle. She couldn't afford to let that happen. She couldn't allow it. Not ever.

"Just stay away from me," she whispered, her voice quivering as she turned, her eyes searching for her clothing. "Just stay away."

Chapter Twenty-Three

With a satisfied sigh, Maud Farland sank onto a chair on the porch of the old homestead. She loved to come out here on Sunday afternoons. She enjoyed cooking beside her daughter-in-law, Rose, and looking after her granddaughter, Christine. She liked to sit on the porch and let her mind wander back through the years. It was one of the nice things about growing older, having so many memories.

Her gray eyes swept over the farmland that her husband and their boys had spent years clearing and cultivating, years when there hadn't been another living soul between here and Snohomish, except for the Indians. Just her and Bert and the children. Those had been good years. Real good years.

It hadn't been easy to leave this house, but Bert had been dead set on platting a town and bringing other folks to this neck of the woods. So he and Cord Brighton, Mary's husband, had done just that with four hundred and eighty acres of land. They'd built the general store and the Brighton house and the mill. They'd widened the road between Morgan Falls (named for Morgan Farland, the oldest of her boys) and Snohomish. And they'd started placing advertisements in papers around the country, proclaiming the greatness of Morgan Falls, Washington Territory.

She shook her head, feeling her husband's disappointment. Bert just couldn't understand why people hadn't flocked here by the droves. There was lots of land to be had for the taking. All a man needed was a strong back and plenty of sweat.

Just look at what Lars Johnson and his boy had accomplished. And how about the Newton family, and them with no sons? Maud grinned, thinking of the five Newton girls. She imagined it wouldn't be long before Rebecca and Thomas had five sons-in-law to help around the place, judging by how quickly their daughters were developing into young women.

It had been two years since the Newtons had moved onto their homestead, four since the Johnsons had come, and still no newcomers to the town itself. Maud had begun to fear that there never would be any others.

But Bert Farland wasn't the type to give up easily. He'd kept on sending out advertisements, encouraging people to move to Morgan

Falls. Even after Cord drowned in the Snohomish River a couple of years back, Bert had kept on believing that folks would come. The right folk. Good, honest people with families to raise. Not just men out to strip the land of its trees and its wealth, but families with roots to put down. Men and women and children who planned to stay on.

"See, Maudie," Bert had told her right after the Branigans had ridden into town. "I told you more'd come. You just wait. Morgan Falls is gonna grow, just like I said."

She thought of the Branigans now, and a small frown puckered her forehead. Nice young couple, but from what Mary Brighton said, things sure weren't right between them. Of course, maybe it was just because he was working so hard, up early and gone until late. It had been the same for two weeks, ever since they'd first arrived.

Maybe things weren't quite as bad as Mary had made them sound. Maud hoped not. She had a feeling about those two. When she'd seen them together that very first day, she'd thought of her and Bert when they were young and falling in love.

"Mother Farland."

Maud turned toward the door, her gaze settling on her daughter-in-law who was resting a tawny-haired toddler on her protruding abdomen.

"Christine's awake and wants her grandma."

"Here now," Maud scolded as she stood up, arms stretched out to take her granddaughter. "You shouldn't be doin' so much liftin' so close to your time."

Rose laughed. "What do you think I do the rest of the week when you're not here?" She set Christine in Maud's arms. "And I'd love for you to tell me that you weren't liftin' children every time you were expectin' another one."

Maud chuckled as she thought back to the years when her children were being born. Rose was right. A woman's work didn't go away just because she was pregnant.

"Why don't you let Christine come back to town with me tonight?" Maud suggested. "Your mother would like to see her, and she could meet the little Branigan boy. I imagine Robby'd like someone to play with. Mr. Branigan's gone to register his homestead claim, and Mrs. Branigan's scarcely come out of your old room." She shook her head sadly. "I think she must be feelin' terrible lonely and a bit frightened of what's ahead. I remember what it was like. I was terrible scared myself when we first come out here."

Maud turned her gaze over the tilled farmland, remembering once again the early years when she and Bert were starting out.

"What's her name, Mother Farland?"

"What?" She turned a blank look on Rose.

"Mrs. Branigan? What's her given name?"

180

"Angelica. She looks like an angel, too. A real sweet thing, from what I can tell, but unhappy. I'd like to see if I can't be of some help. Maybe havin' Christine with me will help break the ice." She shook her head again. "I sure would like to see that pretty lamb happy."

"Mother Farland"—Rose leaned forward and kissed her mother-in- law's cheek—"has anyone ever told you how wonderful you are?"

Devlin guided his gelding along the narrow track. The collar of his coat was pulled up around his neck, and he dipped his head forward against the cold wind that rustled the trees and brush surrounding him. He tried not to think about Angelica, but all this time alone made thinking about her all too easy.

He kept remembering the way she'd looked when she'd told him to stay away from her. He kept remembering the icy reserve she'd shown him when he'd left to file for the homestead. The memories had been cold company on his trip to the land office and back.

For eighteen years he'd only had to look out for himself. That wasn't something he'd aimed to change. All he'd wanted was to put aside his gun, to put the Devil Kid to rest. He hadn't been looking for anything else. He *liked* being alone.

Sure, he'd wanted to see his family. What man wouldn't after such a long time? But that didn't mean he was hankering to be part of one again.

Him? As a farmer?

It was crazy. It would never work. This was just a job. A means to an end. Nothing more.

He eased back on the reins as he lifted his head. There it was. Their quarter section of land, nestled in a fertile valley. A visit to the General Land Office had registered the homestead in their names. Five years of living on it and working the soil would make it theirs.

No. Not theirs. Hers. It would make it *hers*.

It was little more than a jungle now. The underbrush was so thick it was difficult to walk through it. A forest of trees covered much of the land, except for the meadow that made up the center of the long valley. Months of back-breaking work stretched before him, clearing the land, building the cabin, planting the crops.

Months of living with Angelica.

He wished it were years.

Devlin let the air out of his lungs in a long sigh. A cold band seemed to tighten around his heart.

He didn't have any right to be wishing for a life with Angelica. Hell, he wasn't the sort of man to think of settling down with a woman. Any woman. And he certainly wasn't the sort to make a woman like Angelica fall in love with him. Even if he did want it, he wouldn't know the first thing about ...

He swore suddenly and dismounted. Shoving his hands into the pockets of his mackinaw, his shoulders hunched and his head bent, he started off through the underbrush.

Once again, he saw her in his mind, this time leaning forward, smiling as she handed Robby a piece of bread at the dinner table. He saw her with her burgundy hair spilling over her shoulders as she brushed it in the morning. He saw her with her dark green eyes wide, her mouth pink and freshly kissed. He could almost hear her voice, warm, breathless, husky.

And then he heard her fear. *Just stay away from me.*

He was a gunslinger. He didn't have anything to offer the likes of Angelica Corrall.

Angelica Branigan.

That's how folks in Morgan Falls knew her.

God help him. He was beginning to wish it were true.

Angelica pulled the blankets up over Robby's shoulders, then leaned down to kiss his smooth brow. She smiled, thinking how sweet he looked. It was hard to believe she'd had to scold him so severely just an hour ago for throwing a toy at Mary Brighton's granddaughter.

Straightening, she turned and walked to the window. She brushed aside the ruffled pink curtains and stared out at the muddy thoroughfare below. It had stopped raining. In fact, there was even a break in the clouds. She could actually see a patch of blue sky.

All this rain would make anybody feel restless and unhappy, she told herself. Her spirits would lift with just a little sunshine. She'd been holed up in this house too long. She needed to get out, do something, see something.

But, of course, it wasn't just the rain or being cooped up at Mrs. Brighton's that troubled her. It was the frosty silence that separated her and Devlin. In the weeks since they'd arrived in Morgan Falls, they'd scarcely shared more than a dozen words between them. He rose every morning before dawn and straggled in after the sun had set. Mrs. Brighton kept his supper warm for him, and he ate alone in the woman's kitchen long after Angelica and Robby had turned in for the night.

When the two of them were together in their room, they both kept their eyes averted. If Devlin so much as brushed against her, she would jump as if she'd been burned. They slept with their backs to the other, each clinging to their own side of the bed. Their room had become like a prison cell, cold, silent, lonely.

It was driving her mad.

It was time, she decided, that Devlin show her the land he'd found. After all, it was really *her* land. She would insist that he take her out to the homestead he'd gone to register at the General Land Office. Once she'd seen it, once she knew it really existed, she would feel better. Maybe then she could find some way for them to live together in peace and harmony.

She sighed. Perhaps a separation would do them both some good. Perhaps if she didn't see him for a while she could make sense of her jumbled emotions.

She closed her eyes as she leaned her forehead against the cool windowpane. It was no wonder Robby was misbehaving. Most of the time, the tension in this room was thick enough to cut with a knife. Robby couldn't help but be upset by Angelica's and Devlin's icy behavior toward each other.

Unconsciously she laid her hand over her heart, as if to still the dull ache within the walls of her chest.

She didn't want it to be like this. She wanted them to get along, perhaps even to be friends. She'd never wanted them to be enemies. But how else could she control this ... this *feeling* that happened to her whenever he drew near, whenever he held her, touched her, kissed her?

Her heart began to race. She groaned helplessly as she turned from the window and sank into a chair.

Better that they should hate each other than to risk her heart again. Far, far better that they should hate.

Chapter Twenty-Four

"I'd use just a pinch more salt," Maud said as she passed the ladle to Angelica.

Angelica tasted the broth, then, with a nod of agreement, reached above the stove for the salt.

"It'll be mighty good to have the men home again." Maud sat down in a chair at the table. "I never did like travelin' the river, and I always find myself frettin' when Bert makes his pilgrimage to Seattle. It's not like he has to go there himself. He can pick up anything he needs right there in Snohomish." She sighed. "Guess the truth is, I'm just missin' him. I don't much care for havin' Bert gone more'n a day or two. Just don't seem right without him here. Guess that's what comes from bein' married so many years."

Angelica glanced in the woman's direction. "How long have you been married, Maud?"

"How long?" The woman frowned thoughtfully. "Land sakes. I guess next March it'll be forty years. Goodness me. I hadn't realized. It don't seem so very long ago."

"Forty years?"

"Mmm" A smile crinkled Maud's face. "I was just sixteen when Bert come to see my pa, askin' for my hand. Pa took me aside and asked me if that was what I wanted. I said yes right off, and there's never been a day I've regretted it. Not even in the bad times." She fixed shrewd gray eyes upon Angelica. "Lord knows, love can see a man and woman through the worst of times, if they'll let it."

Angelica nodded as she turned back to the simmering stew and began to stir. "You were ...you were lucky. You fell in love with the right man. It doesn't always happen like that. You're lucky to be so happy."

"Lucky?" Maud laughed. "I don't know that luck has much to do with it. I reckon God knows when a man and woman are right for each other and tries to help them get together. Sometimes we listen to Him. Sometimes we don't. But even when we do, it's not luck that keeps a couple happy. It's hard work and plenty of it." She paused.

Angelica thought she could feel the woman's gaze on her back.

"But I reckon love and happiness are something worth workin' for. Don't you, Angelica?"

"Of course." The two words caught in her throat.

She heard the scrape of the chair against the

wood floor, listened as Maud's footsteps brought her closer to the stove. She felt a hand alight on her shoulder.

"Whatever's been troublin' you and that man o' yours, it's time to put it to rest, lamb. Take it from an old woman who's weathered some mighty bad times and seen the same with a lot of other folks, too. You an' Devlin can work through your problems if you try. You're right together, you two. When the men get back from Seattle, you and he sit down and talk it out."

Angelica swallowed hot tears. She wanted to deny that there was anything wrong, but she couldn't, even if she'd been able to speak. The truth was, everything seemed wrong to her these days. And it only seemed to be getting worse.

The tiny bell above the shop door jingled, breaking the lengthy silence. Maud patted Angelica's shoulder several times before leaving the kitchen.

As soon as she was gone, Angelica set down the ladle. Sniffing, she wiped her eyes with her fingertips.

She was being foolish. What had she to be unhappy about? She and Robby had escaped Wood Bluff. Lamar didn't know where she was, and she was beginning to truly believe he wouldn't ever find them. Before long, she would have a house on a piece of land that would be her home for many years to come. Robby was healthy and happy. And Devlin had honored her demand not to try to kiss and hold her again. He'd stayed away, just like she'd asked.

No, she had no call to be unhappy.

Only, she was.

She remembered her resolve of a week ago. She'd been all set, the moment he returned from filing the homestead, to demand that he show her the land. She'd been determined that they find some way to live together in peace.

But when he'd returned, he hadn't stayed. He'd announced that he was going with Bert for supplies. The two men were going to Snohomish and then on down to Seattle. He hadn't bothered to tell her how long he'd be gone. He'd scarcely bothered to say hello or goodbye. He'd acted as if getting within speaking distance of her was the worst thing that could happen to him.

She'd tried to be angry with him but had failed. She'd tried to forget him but had failed in that, too. In fact, she'd thought about him much too often for her own comfort.

"Something smells mighty good in here."

Angelica gasped as she spun around. "Dev..." His name came out on a soft breath of air.

Framed by the doorway, he stood with hat in hand. His black hair was pushed back from his face, and she knew he'd raked his fingers through it only moments before, as she'd seen him do countless times. He had several days of dark stubble on his chin. His ebony eyes revealed a deep weariness.

She'd missed him.

The realization hurt in some hidden part of her heart, a part she wanted desperately to *keep* hidden.

"We didn't expect you back so soon," Angelica whispered, the thickness in her throat increasing.

Devlin shrugged. "We were lucky. We got all the things we needed our first day in Seattle. Would've been back sooner, but Bert wanted to visit some of the general stores in town, see what he might want to stock in his own store." He dropped his hat on a chair. "Bert and some of his boys are going to come out to the place tomorrow and help me finish puttin' up the house. We'll be out of Mrs. Brighton's by Saturday." He took a step forward.

Her heart was doing the crazy flippity-flop it did all too often when she was near him. It made it difficult for her to think straight.

Another step brought him within a few feet of her.

He looked even more tired than she'd thought at first. His eyes were bloodshot from lack of sleep, and the tiny lines around his eyes and across his forehead seemed deeper than usual. She wished she could ease his fatigue. She wished . . .

Unexpectedly, Devlin took hold of her hand, folding it within his much larger one. "How 'bout a truce, Angelica?" he asked softly.

There was a muted buzzing in her ears.

"We can't go on this way."

She tried desperately to control her careening emotions. "No." She swallowed. "No, we can't. I...I'd rather hoped we could be friends."

Devlin's smile revealed no joy. It seemed more resigned than anything else. "Friends it is, then." He squeezed her hand once, then released it. "I thought you might like to ride up to the homestead this afternoon. I know you've been dying to see it. Maud would be glad to keep Robby while we're gone."

"Yes," she answered in a small voice, hardly aware of what he'd said to her. All she could think about was that she wished he were still holding her hand.

The idea of a future with Angelica was a nebulous one. By choice, Devlin had tried to keep it that way. He had no right to want more from her than what she'd offered him.

Still, there were times, like now, when he knew that a year and a half with her would never be enough. Times when he knew that friendship wasn't enough either.

Devlin glanced behind him. She sat astride the rangy sorrel gelding, her skirts bunched around her legs. Her luxurious dark red hair was hidden beneath a plain bonnet, and her eyes were fastened on the narrow path before her. Light and shadows played across her face, revealing only glimpses of the beautiful face he had long since memorized.

But Angelica Corrall had more than come-liness. She had brains and spirit, too. Gumption. Angelica had plenty of gumption. He admired her for that. She was a fighter. She would never knuckle under to life, no matter how bad a hand she'd been dealt, and she showed her strengths in a dozen different ways every day.

Lord, he'd missed her while he was in Seattle with Bert. Even the weeks of icy silence had been better than not being near her at all.

He faced forward again, his mood darkening.

He'd better get over missing her. He'd be spending the rest of his life without her. One day, he would be moving on, and that day would come before he knew it. Angelica would have her house and her farm and her first crops, and she wouldn't need him anymore. Then he would mount his horse and tip his hat and ride away, and she'd be the Widow Branigan. All nice and neat and final.

Of course, a gunslinger was supposed to be a loner, a drifter. Gunslingers didn't think about settling down in any one place for long.

And like it or not, he *was* still a gunslinger. He could take off his gun belt, but he was still what he was. He'd tried to deny it time and again over the past weeks, always with the same results.

He knew what he was. And so did Angelica.

Sure. He might be able to make the Devil Kid disappear. He might live out the rest of his life without ever having to use his fast draw or worry about taking another bullet in the back. But that didn't change diddly squat.

How could it? He'd lived by the gun for too long. He'd seen too much of the ugly underbelly of society. He'd spent too many years living with the discards, the outcasts, the rejected of mankind.

Hell! Look at him. Truth was, he wasn't much of a man. He wasn't even much of a gunslinger, for all the reputation of the Devil Kid. He hadn't had more than two bits to call his own when Angelica found him in Jake's dilapidated cabin. He'd been living on *her* money since the day they'd met. What hope had he of ever having anything more than what he had now? What could a man like him offer anyone that was worth having?

Better he crush his undefined thoughts now before they took more concrete shape. Better they remain nebulous and unspoken. Better for him. Better for Angelica.

They had a truce. They would be friends. Fine. He could use a friend. A man in his profession had too few to ever turn one down.

Devlin stopped his horse, then glanced back at her, as if waiting for her to speak. Suddenly she realized that they'd reached their destination. The trail had broadened, and the trees weren't nearly as thick as before.

As her gelding drew up beside Devlin's buckskin, Angelica's gaze scanned the narrow valley before her. Trees had been felled, only their stumps remaining as evidence of their existence. Logs, trimmed and notched, waited beside the start of the cabin that would soon be her home. A crystal-clear brook cut a swath through the patch of land, gurgling and bubbling over the smooth rocks that lined its bottom. Here, on the western slopes of the majestic Cascades, the air smelled fresh and green and promising.

She was home.

"Oh, Dev . . ."

Angelica rode down the hillside, then dismounted and walked into the center of the clearing. In the past weeks, while she'd treated him with cold reserve, he'd searched for and found this place and then had slaved to build her a home and the farm she'd wanted. He'd been working so hard, and she'd been so heartless.

"It's wonderful," she whispered, turning around to find him standing behind her.

"Won't be much to the house. Couple of rooms and a loft. But it'll have a wood floor and a couple of windows."

"It doesn't matter. It will be perfect, no matter what it looks like. You've already accomplished so much, and I . . . I haven't . . ." She let the words die out.

Devlin stared down at her for the longest time, his midnight black eyes so intense. He had that "hunter" look about him now. She didn't know how else to describe the severity of the gaze that he turned upon her every now and again. She felt helpless beneath it. She wondered if he might try to take her in his arms.

And then the look was gone. He turned abruptly, pointing toward a stand of regal firs. "There's some volunteer blackberry and blueberry bushes over there, and the soil seems good and rich. 'Course, I don't know much about farming, but I think we ... *you* should be able to grow plenty of produce to sell to the logging camps. Bert suggested cabbage, peas, carrots, beets, onions, and beans. I thought I'd put in some apple trees, too."

I'm falling in love with him.

"I'll put up a shed for the horses before winter comes, and there ought to be enough money left to get a milk cow or two. Bert says whatever milk and butter you don't use you can sell to him for the store."

It stung each time he said "you" instead of "we." *I'm falling in love with him, and I'm going to lose him when our agreement is over.*

"Next week I'll work at getting rid of those stumps and getting that patch plowed up so we can begin planting. You won't get much of a crop this year—just enough to help feed us through the winter—but by next year ..."

In less than eighteen months, he'll be gone, and I'll be alone again.

Devlin turned his face toward the sky. "It's clouding over. We'd better get back before it starts to rain."

I didn't want to fall in love with you. Why did

you make me do it? Why?

His hand slipped beneath her elbow, and he guided her back toward the horses. She moved stiffly, blindly, torn between wanting to run away from his touch and wanting to throw herself into his arms where she could cling to him forever.

"Angelica?"

She heard the concern in his voice but didn't dare turn her head to meet his gaze.

"Is something wrong?"

"No." She was never more thankful than at that moment for her years of theater training. Her voice never wavered. "Everything is perfect."

Everything except for loving you. It wasn't part of my plan, Devlin. It wasn't part of my plan.

Chapter Twenty-Five

The cabin smelled of fresh-cut lumber. One of the small windows faced west, the other south. This time of the afternoon, a stream of golden light topped the cedars beyond the clearing to splash a window-shaped square upon the plank board floor.

Angelica turned slowly, her eyes taking in every minute detail of the cabin's main room.

A small oven was built into the left side of the stone fireplace. A cast-iron cooking pot hung from the chimney crane in the middle of the hearth. A black kettle and a dark blue coffee pot sat upon a trivet placed near the grate.

She'd had a range in her little house in Wood Bluff, and except for heating quick meals over the campfires on their way to Morgan Falls, she'd never cooked over an open flame. She hoped they wouldn't all starve to death before she got the hang of it.

To the left of the fireplace was the dry sink.

Above it, several shelves had been nailed into the logs. Blue and white plates, bowls, and cups were stacked on the lowest shelf, none of them new, a few with chips and cracks, but plenty of them. The dishes were a gift from Bert and Maud.

"Good gracious!" Maud had exclaimed, seeing Angelica's portmanteau. "Is *that* all you have? How do you suppose to set up housekeeping? What happened to all your things? Surely you had more back where you came from. Is it bein' sent out by rail?"

Angelica had only shaken her head mutely.

"You poor lamb. Whatever happened to you folks back east must've been a terrible ordeal. You let me see what I have that's just gatherin' dust in the attic. I reckon I can come up with a few things you'll need."

Angelica was grateful, not so much for the money Maud's generosity had saved them, although that was certainly appreciated, but because of the kindness of the gesture. It felt good to have such a friend.

To the right of the fireplace, her gaze lit upon the hip bath stuck in the corner. A picture flashed into her head, suddenly and uninvited. An image of Devlin sitting in the tub, steam rising around him, causing his black hair to curl, his long legs dangling over the sides as he soaked away the soreness from a day in the fields.

She felt heat rising in her cheeks and turned her back to the offending object.

A wood table and matching benches took up the center of the room. A worn, well-used high chair, another gift from the Farlands, stood at one end, and Devlin was just now putting Robby into it.

When he looked up, their eyes met and held. Neither moved, neither spoke for the longest while. Angelica wanted to say something to break the silence, but words failed to come to mind. Only the mental picture of Devlin in the hip bath remained.

He straightened. "The bedroom's through that door." His voice was low and warm. It caused a river of shivers to run up her spine.

She followed his gaze to the narrow door in the middle of the only inside wall. She felt the warmth in her cheeks increasing rather than fading.

Hesitantly, she rounded the table, coming to a halt before the closed door. She drew in a breath, then closed her hand over the latch and lifted it, pushing the door inward.

She'd known what she would see there. A bed, just big enough for two, covered with a patchwork quilt. She'd also been afraid that her rebellious mind would conjure up a new image.

And it came, just as she'd known it would.

She envisioned him, lying in bed, the quilt pulled down to his waist, his chest bare except for the light furring of black hair that narrowed as it approached the blanket. It made her want to see more of him.

Angelica quickly closed the door before her imagination could go any further.

"I should probably start supper," she mumbled, not allowing herself to glance in Devlin's direction.

Devlin slipped the rope latch over the gate post and turned away from the corral. Dusk was quickly settling over the land, lengthening shadows and turning the sky to gunmetal gray. A ribbon of smoke curled upward from the stone chimney of the cabin, an occasional orange spark contrasting sharply against a somber sky.

Supper was probably ready. Angelica would call for him soon. He felt a comforting peace descend upon him, a peace totally at odds with the turmoil that had surrounded him for days on end.

He was tired, bone weary after weeks of felling trees, wrenching stumps from the ground, hacking at creeping vines and stubborn underbrush. He ached in parts of his body where he'd never ached before.

And then it occurred to him that it felt good. He was filled with a delicious sense of accomplishment. That small patch of cleared ground, not much more than a few acres, if that, was clear because of him. It was *his* sweat, *his* sore muscles, *his* calluses that had rescued it from the wilderness.

It would take years to clear off the entire hundred and sixty acres, and forever to keep back the conifers and hardwood, vines and underbrush that would try to reclaim it. It would always be a battle, man against the elements. The soil was rich, the rain plentiful, but nothing would come easily here. Not for a man. Not for a woman.

He glanced again toward the cabin. He'd built it. With his own hands, he'd built that house. For far too many years, he'd used his hands in more destructive pursuits. But this time, he'd built something good with them.

He looked down at rough, callused hands that hadn't drawn a gun since arriving in Morgan Falls, and the sense of peace grew stronger.

He hadn't thought about his shoulder in days, maybe weeks. Perhaps it was because *all* of his muscles and joints hurt now, or maybe it was because the bullet wound was no longer a constant reminder of what and who he was. Maybe it was because it no longer seemed so important to remember it.

Perhaps...just perhaps, he *could* build a new life. Perhaps both he and Angelica had been able to leave their pasts behind. Perhaps...

The cabin door opened, spilling a stream of yellow across the boggy Washington soil. Angelica stepped through the opening, a dark silhouette against the lamplight.

"Supper's ready," she called softly.

It was a good, satisfying sound to a man who'd just caught a glimmer of hope.

* * *

Hot orange flames danced among the logs on the grate. As Angelica leaned forward over the simmering cook pot, her face bathed in the glow of the fire. She felt the flush of her heated skin. Damp tendrils of hair clung uncomfortably to her face and the back of her neck, and her plain brown dress was moist beneath her arms.

Devlin entered the cabin just as she pulled the chimney crane out from the fireplace. She hated to turn toward him. She felt wilted and knew she looked even worse.

"It's only stew," she said apologetically.

"I love stew."

She heard the splash of water as he washed up, then heard the scrape of the bench against the floor as he sat down at the table.

"Where's Robby?"

"He's already asleep. Too much excitement, I guess. He was worn out."

She reached for a bowl and ladled meat, onions, carrots, potatoes, and broth into it. Then, brushing her wayward hair away from her face with the back of her hand, she turned and carried his supper to him.

"Thanks."

Their eyes met.

"You're welcome."

"Looks good."

"It's only stew," she repeated.

"I love stew," he said again.

She turned away, frightened by the strange hammering of her heart, confused by the change in the way he looked at her, spoke to her, and perplexed by the change she felt within herself.

Angelica picked up the lamp. "I'm going to check on Robby," she whispered, then hurried toward the bedroom.

Closing the door behind her, she leaned against it, fighting a sudden onslaught of tears. Dashing them away with her free hand, she set the lamp on the small table beside the door, then crossed to her son's small cot and knelt beside it. She smoothed the blankets over his shoulders and felt another wave of tears thickening her throat.

"It wasn't supposed to be like this, Robby. I wasn't supposed to fall in love with him. And now ... when he goes ..."

I'm not about to marry you or anyone else. She closed her eyes as his emphatic protestation echoed in her ears.

He might live with her. He might even share something more intimate with her in that bed than mere sleep. But Devlin Branigan wasn't looking for anything beyond that.

Again, she recalled Devlin's words. *I'll get you to Washington, get you settled in on that farm you think you want, and after that, I'll be on my way. You've got my promise on it.*

"What do I do now?" She swallowed the lump in her throat.

It was too late to keep herself from loving him. She'd tried and failed. She already loved him.

She would get her heart broken, and this time it would be for good. She wasn't the foolish girl who'd thought herself in love with Lamar, a girl easily flattered by flowery phrases, dazzled by expensive gifts. The Lamar she'd thought she loved hadn't even existed.

But this was different. This time she was in love with Devlin Branigan. She was in love with a real person, a man with real faults and strengths. In six weeks, she'd seen Devlin's laughter and his anger. She'd seen him grumpy and amused. She'd seen the hurt he tried to keep hidden. She'd seen the man he wanted to be, if only honor and hope could be restored to him.

Angelica sat back on her heels, her eyes rounding in wonder.

Devlin Branigan *needed* her love. Was she going to give him up without a fight? Was she going to hide and do nothing, as she'd done when Lamar took her to Wood Bluff? Hadn't she learned *anything* from her past mistakes?

"I have more than a year to make him love me," she said to herself. "Somehow, I'll manage it. And once he knows he loves me, he won't ever leave."

You need me, Dev, and somehow I'm going to make you see that.

She tipped forward again, this time placing a feather-soft kiss on Robby's forehead.

"Your pa's going to stay with us, Robby. You'll see. He's going to stay."

* * *

She'd been in the bedroom a long time. So long that Devlin began to wonder if she'd gone to bed without saying good night. As if in answer to his thoughts, the door opened and Angelica returned to the main room. She glanced his way for only an instant before picking up the supper dishes and carrying them to the dry sink.

She was so damned beautiful, even in that drab brown dress and with her hair disheveled. Nothing could hide the creamy perfection of her skin or the sensuous curve of her mouth or the sultry charm of kelly-green eyes trimmed with sable lashes. Come to think of it, he'd seen her at her very worst and still couldn't think of a moment when he hadn't thought her beautiful.

Or a moment when he hadn't desired her.

The peace he'd found earlier this evening vanished. The urge to stand up and pull her into his arms slammed into him like a blow to the solar plexus. He knew better than to give into the impulse. He'd tried that method before, and all it had gained him was her anger. Angelica didn't welcome his kisses, and unless he wanted to spend more weeks in chilled silence, he'd better remember that.

He considered offering to help her with the dishes but didn't. If he stood beside her at the dry sink, where he could see the lush curve of her breasts and smell the warm scent of her cologne, it would be his undoing.

If he wanted a chance with Angelica, he

would have to proceed with care.

A chance? What did he mean by a chance? What was it he wanted from Angelica Corrall? Just what did he hope for the future?

He thought of the bed just beyond that door and imagined her in it. Imagined ...

"I was thinking," he began quickly, trying once again to stanch the flare of desire.

She turned toward him.

"I was thinking you might want the bed to yourself." He cleared his throat. "Now that we don't have to pretend we're living as man and wife, I mean. Nobody would know the difference. I could rig up a cot or something."

Her gaze was direct and unwavering. She seemed to be weighing his words, giving them plenty of consideration. Finally, she shook her head. "I see no reason for you to go to that trouble. We've managed well enough up to now." Her smile came slowly. "I trust you, Mr. Branigan."

But you don't know how hard it's been for me, he wanted to say, *and how much harder it's going to be now. Something's changed, and I'm not sure what to do about it.*

Instead, he shrugged and said, "Suits me." He rose from the bench. "I think I'll check on the horses one last time before I turn in, make sure that corral gate is secure."

He hoped the night air would cool his desire. If he lingered outside long enough, perhaps she would be asleep when he climbed into bed beside her. Perhaps, if she were already asleep, it would make it easier for him to find sleep himself.

"You listen to me, Bellows, and you listen good." Standing, Lamar rested his knuckles on the top of his cherrywood desk and leaned forward. He spoke in a low but telling voice. "You've already wasted several weeks of my time and money. I don't pay you to come in here and tell me you can't find her." He narrowed his gaze as he stared at the man in the chair opposite him. "She *will* be found."

"Yes, sir, Mr. Orwell. We're doing our best. But it is going to take some time to get it done."

Lamar straightened, hiding the fury that raged inside him behind a calm facade. "Tell me what you've learned."

"Well, sir . . ." Bellows, a squat, balding man in a neatly pressed suit, cleared his throat nervously. "I think she came to Denver, but I can't be sure at this time. A woman matching her description, a Mrs. Branigan by name, was met at the stage depot by her husband the day after Miss Corrall left Wood Bluff. She had a little boy with her, about the right age. I think there's a good possibility she was traveling under an assumed name." He dropped his gaze to the floor. "But, again, I can't be sure. Not yet. The driver remembered her and was able to give me a rather detailed description. Said she had the prettiest wine-colored hair he'd ever seen. And he said her husband kissed her like they'd been apart for a long, long time."

That bitch! How dare she do this to him? It was bad enough she'd taken the boy when Lamar wanted him, but now she was with another man. She should have known better. She should have known she was *his* woman until he told her otherwise. She belonged to him. He would make her pay for her actions. *No one* defied Lamar Orwell and got away with it.

"The Branigans got on the train the next day. I . . . ah . . . I've traced them to Idaho."

"You've traced them? Then why did you say you can't find her? Is it Angelica or not? Did you speak with her?"

"No, Mr. Orwell. I haven't been there myself, but my assistant has sent word that the Branigans visited family there. He's had to be careful in the questions he's asked. We can't even be sure if they're still staying with Mr. Branigan's relatives. We're trying to—"

Lamar's control on his temper broke. "Damn it, man! I don't want your excuses, and I don't want to know what you have to do to get the job done. I just want results. And I'm not paying you to let some idiot do the work for you. I want *you* to find her. Do you understand me?"

"I understand you." Bellows rose from his chair. This time his gaze didn't waver as he looked at Lamar, his voice steady and firm. "Mr. Branigan's brother is a judge, Mr. Orwell. A judge with plenty of power. Power that reaches to Colorado if he wants it to. I don't think he'd take kindly to us poking our noses into his brother's affairs, especially if his wife *isn't* your Miss Corrall. I believe it behooves us to be cautious."

Lamar wanted to break something, smash something into a thousand pieces. Even more, he wanted to smash Angelica. He wanted to put his hands around her throat and ...

"I'm catching the train for Idaho today. I hope to have something to report to you by early next week."

"You do that, Bellows." Lamar dropped into the smooth leather chair behind his desk. "And, Bellows ... Don't disappoint me. I don't care what you have to do to find her. Just *find* her."

Chapter Twenty-Six

Angelica placed her hand in the small of her back and arched as she squinted up at the faultless sky. Not a single cloud marred the wide blue expanse. The sun beat warm against her face. She smiled, feeling that the sunny day was a promise of better things to come.

She heard Robby giggle and glanced toward the child-sized corral that Devlin had constructed to keep the toddler safely contained while Angelica worked outside. At the moment, her son was running around the "yard" (as they jokingly called it), trying to escape the wildly lapping tongue of a black and white puppy, a gift from Mrs. Brighton.

"You'll be needing a dog to keep the critters out of your fields," the woman had said when she'd come by the previous day. "Besides, every boy ought to have a dog. This pup's father is one of the best hunters in these parts.

He'll be a good one, too, once he's past the puppy stage."

Domino—as Angelica had named him for his half-white, half-black face—caught Robby by the seat of his pants, causing the boy to tumble forward in the dirt. In a flash, the puppy was bathing Robby's face with his tongue.

Angelica dropped the hoe and started toward the yard, expecting to hear Robby's cries of protest. She stopped when, instead, she heard laughter again.

Her smile broadened as pleasure warmed her heart just as the sun warmed her skin. She had come to Washington to escape an undesirable past. She'd never expected to find happiness waiting for her.

She turned her head toward the trail that led out of their little valley, wondering how soon Devlin would return from town. He'd been gone a long time already. Of course, he would have to spend some time chatting with Bert.

With a chuckle, she picked up the hoe and began working the furrows of the vegetable garden. Bert could be long-winded at times. Devlin might be lucky to get back before nightfall.

It was a good feeling, being part of a community. Although she'd grown close to some of the actors in the theater company, it had never been quite the same as *really* belonging, perhaps because nothing had ever been permanent. There had always been a new town, a new theater, a new director, a new leading man.

Living in Wood Bluff had been even worse. There, she and Robby had been scorned and shunned by the good citizens of the town. Loneliness had filled her days and nights, and she had lived constantly with her shame, punished by guilt over the future she'd given her son.

But here, she and Robby—and Devlin, too—were accepted.

She thought of Bert and Maud Farland, of their two oldest sons, Morgan and Paul, who operated the mill, of Joshua and Rose Farland, living on the original Farland homestead, and their little girl, Christine. She thought of Mary Brighton, Rose's mother. All of these people had done so much to make the Branigans feel that they belonged in Morgan Falls.

And they did belong. Morgan Falls was their home.

They belonged here....And they belonged together.

She thought about the last few days since they'd moved into their home. Devlin was happy here. She could tell. She often caught him watching her, as if wishing he could say something more personal than how many stumps he'd cleared that day or how the plowing was coming along.

She knew he desired her, too. That was a good sign. He *should* want her. That was how it was for men. And when the time was right, when he realized he loved her, when he married her, then she would willingly give herself to him.

She didn't particularly care for the act of lovemaking. She'd learned quickly enough from Lamar that it wasn't a pleasurable experience for a woman. But she did long for Devlin to hold her, to kiss her, to start all those delicious butterflies flapping about in her belly. She would love to spend the night in his arms and wake up with her head on his shoulder.

She thought of the way he looked in the morning, ruggedly male, mature yet surprisingly youthful at the same. Perhaps it was because all facade was stripped away by sleep. In the morning, all traces of the hardened gunslinger were gone, and she could see only Devlin. A pleasurable longing spread through her, catching her by surprise.

"Jimmy told me the Devil Kid had himself a farm and a woman. I didn't believe it. The Kid a farmer. But here it is, and here's the woman."

A tiny shriek slipped past her lips as she whirled toward the stranger's voice.

He let out a low whistle. "I figured a man like the Kid don't settle down with just any woman. I was right. You're a beauty, ma'am. A real beauty."

The man stood with one thumb slipped under his gun belt, his stance relaxed. He was smoking a cigar, and when he spoke he exposed a row of yellowed teeth. A heavy beard hid most of his face, but she could see his eyes clearly enough. Blank, soulless eyes. She felt herself growing cold, despite the midday sun.

"Sorry for startlin' you, ma'am." He glanced toward the yard. "Fine-lookin' boy you've got there."

"Who are you? What do you want?"

He took a long drag on his cigar, then slowly let the smoke trickle out of his mouth and nose before answering. "T'tell you the truth, I come to see the Kid. Him an' me, we got some business t'finish between us. Then I thought to myself, Murph, why don't you have a look at this gal Jimmy said the Kid was livin' with? Go see if she's a real looker. And ma'am, I gotta say, you're prettier than any gal I ever seen."

Angelica tried desperately not to let her fear reveal itself in her voice. "Thank you. That's very kind." She took a small step backward. "I'm sure Devlin will be happy to ride into town to see you, Mr. . . . ." Her voice rose in question.

"Murphy. But you can call me Murph." He took another drag on his cigar before tossing it aside. He grinned. "And I'm content to wait for the Kid here with you t'keep me company."

She felt his gaze slip to her breasts, felt it like a brand through the fabric of her blouse. She felt stripped bare before him, exposed and vulnerable.

Angelica lifted her chin in a show of courage. "You're welcome to wait if you like, Mr. Murphy. I'm sure Devlin will be home soon." She turned around, forcing herself not to run toward the fenced yard. "If you'll excuse me, I need to feed my son."

She walked with measured steps, not realizing that she was holding her breath. She leaned over the fence and lifted Robby into her arms. She crushed him against her chest, making him squirm and protest.

"Dom'o!" he cried. "Dom'o!"

"No, honey. Domino has to stay there for just a little while."

Murphy's fingers closed around her arm. "Leave the boy outside. We don't need him underfoot, now do we, ma'am?"

His touch felt as deadly as a coiled rope around her neck. She could hear the threat in his voice. She knew what he intended to do to her. And she knew what he intended to do to Devlin.

Please, God, help me. Don't let him kill Devlin.

Devlin backed his buckskin into the shadows just in time to see Angelica's frantic glance over her shoulder at Robby before she was shoved into the cabin.

He drew the rifle from its scabbard, then dismounted, his sharp gaze scanning the forest around their house. He spied the lone horse tethered to a bush. There was no sign of anyone else. It appeared there was only one man with whom he had to deal.

It was surprising, even to him, how calmly

and rationally he was thinking. Surprising because he was not unaware of the cold fury that gripped him. He was not unaware of his fear for Angelica.

He kept to the trees, moving with long, easy strides, silently making his way toward the windowless back of the cabin. He wished he had his Colt .45. A rifle had never felt as right to him as a revolver.

If that bastard touched her ... if he laid one hand on her ... if he harmed her in any way ...

He blanked the unwelcome images from his mind, pausing briefly, then stealthily left the cover of trees and approached the cabin. He placed his back against the logs and listened. No sounds came from within.

He began sidling his way around toward the front.

Angelica closed her eyes as Murphy slid his thumb along her jaw.

"Yes, sir, I'm gonna enjoy this," he whispered in her ear.

He'd forced her to sit on the bench, facing the door. Then he'd tied her hands behind her back and secured the rope to the heavy wooden table. She'd felt a glimmer of hope when he hadn't taken her to the bedroom. Now that glimmer was gone.

"Oh, yes. You know what I'm gonna do. And you're wonderin' when, ain't ya? Well, I'll tell you, ma'am. Just as soon as I take care of the

Devil Kid, I'll see that you're taken care of, too."

Murphy's hands covered her breasts, squeezing them harshly as he leaned around and kissed her.

She nearly gagged at the foulness of his breath. She jerked her head sideways, trying to escape him. He roughly pulled her back, his fingers biting into the flesh of her arms. Then, with a terrible ripping sound, he tore her blouse and chemise down the front, exposing her breasts to his dreadful gaze.

"You fight me, I'll bring that brat o' yours in here," he growled. "You understand me, woman? You want him to live, you do what I tell you."

Angelica whimpered in terror.

"Now, I figure the Kid ought to be here just about any time. He was jawin' with some fella in front of the general store when I seen him. Looked like he was ready to head back home with his supplies. I figure it won't be long 'fore he opens that door. You an' me, we'll just be ready to welcome him, won't we?"

Angelica's thoughts became a dervish, whirling and darting about, making it impossible for her to grasp hold of one. Panic reigned in her head, in her heart.

Robby...
Devlin...
Robby...
Devlin...
Oh, God! Devlin...

* * *

Robby saw him and squealed in delight. Devlin placed a finger to his lips, hoping the boy would understand the gesture, praying he would obey it.

Carefully he inched his way toward the window. What he saw with a quick glimpse made his blood run cold, then hot. Angelica, her dress torn open at the front, her body exposed. But worse still, a pistol pointed at the back of her head.

"Pa!" Robby shouted, trying to draw Devlin's attention.

It was the first time the boy had called him that instead of Bran'gan, but Devlin wasn't pleased to hear it at the moment. Any sound was unwelcome now. He held his breath, waiting, hoping.

"Pa!"

"I reckon that's you he's callin' for, Kid. Put down your gun and come inside. Me an' your woman's been waitin' for ya."

If it were anyone but Angelica, he would have tried to cut down the gunman first. There was a chance he could open the door and fire before the other man pulled the trigger. But it was only a slight chance, and it wasn't anyone else. It *was* Angelica.

Besides, he knew that voice. Ryan Murphy would kill her as easily as he'd swat a fly.

"I thought you were dead, Murphy," he shouted through the glass, his back once again pressed against the wall.

"I thought the same 'bout you, Kid. You take some killin'. My aim must be a bit rusty. I would've sworn that shot was mortal."

"So . . . it was you."

Murphy laughed. "It was me, all right. How'd you survive?"

"I got lucky. An old friend happened by and managed to stop the bleeding in time." His shoulder began to throb just thinking about it. "I never would've guessed it was you, Murph, even if I'd known you were still alive. I never expected you to turn coward and shoot a man in the back."

"No point us keepin' on shoutin'." The laughter had disappeared from Murphy's voice. "Come inside, Kid."

Devlin had left his gun belt hanging on the peg beside the door, beneath his slicker. Murphy probably hadn't seen it. If Devlin stopped just inside the door . . . if he had the chance before . . .

There couldn't be any "ifs." He had to get his gun. Somehow, he had to get Murphy to turn his weapon away from Angelica just long enough. He only needed a few seconds.

"All right, Murph. I'm putting down my gun and coming in. Don't hurt the woman."

Again Murphy laughed. "I wouldn't think of hurtin' her. I've taken quite a likin' to her."

Devlin's belly twisted. His mouth tasted like he'd been chewing metal.

Then, years of practice took over. The calm

returned. His hands were steady. So were his nerves. He thought of only one thing.

Ryan Murphy must die before he could touch Angelica again.

Chapter Twenty-Seven

Angelica started to shake. It came from the innermost part of her and spread upward, outward. Icy tentacles of fear inched through her veins, chilling her blood. Tears blurred her vision. She wanted desperately to wipe them away. She wanted to see Devlin when he came through the door. She wanted to see his face, memorize it. She wanted to be able to look him in the eyes and tell him she loved him before he died. Before she died.

Devlin pushed the door wide. Sunlight splashed into the room, blinding her, making it difficult for her to see him. Slowly she made out his relaxed stance as he leaned his left shoulder against the doorjamb, and then she looked at his face.

The Devlin she knew wasn't there. This man was someone else.

There wasn't a shred of emotion written in his eyes. Not fear or anger or concern. Nothing. Only a bored smile in the corners of his mouth.

Look at me, Dev, her heart cried. *Please, look at me*.

But he didn't . . . wouldn't.

"How'd you find me, Murph?"

"Wasn't lookin' for you. Like I said, I thought you was dead. Jimmy Foster an' me were hired to do a job in Seattle. Jimmy overheard you talkin' about your place and your woman to someone and recognized your voice. He told me if he'd just seen your face, he never would've guessed it was you. I sure as hell wouldn't have." He grunted. "Guess I'd shave off my whiskers, too, for a nice little hideout like this. 'Specially if it came with a woman to warm my bed."

The cold steel of the gun barrel slid down the side of Angelica's face, from temple to jaw.

Devlin didn't look at her even then. Not so much as a glance. She watched him, hoping, praying for a miracle, but she was certain they would both be dead soon.

Devlin scratched his chin with the fingers of his right hand. "You don't have to kill me for that. I was planning to move on anyway. If you want her, you can have her."

Angelica couldn't stop the tiny gasp.

She heard Murphy's throaty chuckle, felt him draw closer to her. She turned her head, tilting it to look up at him. He was grinning broadly, showing his jagged yellow teeth, his gaze feasting first upon her face, then upon her naked breasts.

Did she see Devlin move out of the corner of her eye or did she only think she had later?

The small room seemed to explode. Her ears rang with the sound of gunfire. Moisture spattered her face and breasts and arms. Murphy's smile was replaced by a look of surprise as he fell backward, crashing against the stone fireplace. She twisted on the bench, watched him fall, stared at the hole in his forehead between his sightless eyes, saw the crimson pool staining his shirt around a second hole in his chest.

For a moment, everything was still. Nothing moved. It seemed to Angelica that even her heart had stopped beating.

Finally, she looked away from the dead man. It was then she saw the blood on her arms. Saw it on her breasts. Knew it was on her face. Murphy's blood.

She felt the bile rising in her throat, burning, choking. She struggled against the ropes that bound her wrists, held her prisoner.

"Sit still, Angelica."

She hadn't heard his approach, but Devlin was there beside her. She couldn't look at him. She didn't want to see or talk to him. She wanted to run and hide. She wanted to pretend that none of this had happened. She wanted to wash Murphy's blood from her skin. The smell of it filled her nostrils, and she felt another wave of nausea.

The moment Devlin's knife severed the hemp rope, she bolted from the bench. Pulling her blouse closed as best she could, she ran out of the cabin. She ran as if her life depended upon it. She was vaguely aware of Robby's crying, but she couldn't see to him yet. Not yet.

She stumbled, caught herself, kept on going until she reached the creek. Sobs came. Racking sobs that tore at her chest and throat. Sobs of terror and relief.

You don't have to kill me for that.... If you want her, you can have her.

She waded into the water, then sank to her knees and began scrubbing herself.

If you want her, you can have her.

He'd said it to save her life. He hadn't meant it. Where reason dwelled, she knew that was the truth. Only she couldn't find the place where reason dwelled right now. First, she needed to cleanse away the memory of Murphy's loathsome, violating touch. First, she had to rid herself of the sight of death, the sound of it, the smell of it.

He'd wanted to hold her, but she had run from him. She'd run as if he'd threatened to shoot her down as he had Murphy.

Devlin stared at the gunman's body. Ryan Murphy had been one of the worst of his breed. He'd been willing to kill a man—or a woman—for little more than a bottle of whiskey. Murphy had always enjoyed hurting and killing.

Devlin's hands closed into tight fists at his sides. Murphy had tried to hurt Angelica. He'd torn her dress. He'd put his filthy paws on her body. God help him, he'd like to kill Murphy again . . . and again . . . and again.

The dream was over. He'd known it couldn't go on for long. He'd known he couldn't ever really put the past behind him. If Murphy could find him, so could others. Jimmy Foster, for one. Devlin would have to go after Jimmy. And then who would be next?

He remembered the look of horror on Angelica's face. She had despised him. She'd seen him for what he really was, and she'd despised him.

Devlin grabbed Murphy's legs and dragged him out the door and around to the side of the cabin. A cold emptiness crept into his chest.

He would have to take Murphy's body to the authorities in Snohomish. Then he'd have to find Jimmy before Jimmy came looking for Murphy and found Angelica instead.

And after that? After that, he'd leave Washington.

There was likely a bounty on Murphy's head. Devlin would use the money to pay for a hired hand to work this place. With any luck, it would be enough to get Angelica through next summer's harvest. That had been all the longer he'd promised to stay anyway. If that wasn't long enough . . . well, that was her worry, not his.

His chest felt hollow.

He *had* to leave her. He didn't have a choice. Even if she didn't despise him, he couldn't stay. He couldn't expose Angelica and Robby to the danger his presence brought to them. And if she didn't despise him now, she would when the trouble kept coming. She would when she or Robby got hurt because of him.

He cursed himself. Cursed the hope. Cursed the dream. He was what he was, and he'd been a blamed fool for thinking—if only for a short while—that anything could ever change it.

"Devlin?"

Her husky voice caused a physical pain in his chest. He'd liked it better when he felt empty inside. Emptiness was better than this pain. Much better.

He dropped Murphy's legs and turned around. "Yeah?"

She was sopping wet. Her hair was plastered against her scalp. Her eyes looked bigger, more round than normal, and they seemed slightly dazed. She carried her tearful son in quivering arms.

"What will you do now?" she asked.

"Take him to the law. Tell them what happened here."

"You won't tell them . . . you won't tell them you were the Devil Kid?"

He didn't hear the past tense. He only heard the name. "Not unless I have to. No need bringing that down on your head. It'll go better for you and Robby if we can keep that our secret."

226

Her gaze was locked with his, never once glancing at the body. "How soon will you come back?"

He wanted to hold her and never let go. He wanted to hold her and kiss her and drive away the memory of this day. He wanted to go back to pretending that his life had changed. "After I find his partner. Not before."

She opened her mouth, then turned away without speaking.

Angelica stood in the doorway of the cabin, Robby in her arms. She watched as Devlin stepped up into the saddle and drew the muscular buckskin around to face her.

I know what you're thinking, Dev. I know what you're feeling. Why can't I tell you it makes no difference to me? Why can't I tell you that you're not the Devil Kid anymore, that things are different, that I love you just the way you are? Why can't I thank you for saving my life, for saving Robby, for saving yourself?

Devlin bumped up the brim of his hat with his knuckles, revealing dark, remote eyes. "I still think you should go into Morgan Falls and stay with Maud or Mrs. Brighton. It may be quite a while until I'm back."

She shook her head. "I'll wait for you here."

What's wrong with us? Why don't we say the things that need to be said?

"I'll have Bert or one of his boys come out and check on you while I'm away."

"Thanks."

Come back, Devlin. Come back to me. I love you.

Devlin turned the buckskin and led Murphy's horse, with Murphy's body lying over his saddle, out of the once peaceful valley.

Chapter Twenty-Eight

Angelica brushed stray hairs away from her face with the back of her flour-coated hand. A refreshing breeze blew through the open doorway, relieving the heat emanating from the oven.

With a sigh, she began kneading the bread dough again. She'd already baked several loaves the day before, and if Devlin didn't return soon, she and Robby certainly weren't going to need them. But for some reason, baking helped her get through the long days, and so she continued to knead and bake.

Devlin had been gone more than a week now, but it seemed much longer than that to her. Had Devlin found Murphy's partner, she wondered, or had Jimmy found him first? Was Devlin even still alive?

Angelica tried not to think like that, but it was difficult to banish such thoughts when she kept reliving that nightmarish afternoon, when she kept remembering the moment Murphy walked out of the forest and changed everything.

Nights were the worst. Murphy came at her in her dreams, came with his rough, groping hands and his foul kisses. Time and again, she heard the gunfire, felt his blood on her skin, saw him lying on the floor, looked into his open but sightless eyes.

She groaned and turned away from the table. She pressed her hands against her stomach, trying to stop the sickness that swelled and twisted her belly.

Striding across the room, she quietly opened the door to the bedroom and looked in upon her sleeping son. He lay in the middle of his cot, arms and legs splayed, a lock of brown hair curled on his forehead.

She wished she were a child like Robby. She wished she could forget everything as quickly as he had. Startled by the gunfire on that terrible afternoon, Robby had wailed as if shot himself. But he'd quieted as soon as she picked him up. An hour later, he'd been laughing as he played with the puppy again.

How simple it would be if she were like Robby.

She closed the bedroom door, then walked out of the cabin. Turning her face up to the warm, caressing rays of the sun, she let her thoughts return once again to Devlin.

Time and again, she'd mentally punished herself for allowing him to leave without telling him what he'd needed to hear. She didn't know why she'd been unable to speak the words that could have—*would* have—made a difference.

He'd read something in her eyes that hadn't truly been there. Not for him anyway. She should have told him then that she loved him. She should have told him that nothing mattered except her love for him.

What if he doesn't come back?

He'll come back. He said he would.

But what if he doesn't?

He must. I have to tell him I love him.

"Angelica!"

She opened her eyes to see Maud striding down the hill on short, sturdy legs. She waved an envelope over her head as she marched across the clearing.

"This came for you this morning. Bert was busy in the store, and I needed a visit, so I thought I'd deliver it to you personally. I reckon a postmistress should get out to see her neighbors occasionally, don't you?" Maud stopped in front of Angelica. With a handkerchief, she patted her forehead. "My, it's warm for May." She glanced around her. "Goodness, you've been busy. Look at your garden plot."

Angelica wasn't listening. She was staring at the envelope, forcing herself not to reach out and grab it from Maud's fingers.

"Where's Robby?"

"Asleep. Maud . . . the letter?"

"Oh my. Yes, of course. I thought it could be

from your husband. With that terrible business that happened here last week, I thought it might be important. Here it is, dear."

Angelica couldn't remember ever seeing anything he'd written before, yet she knew without question that the letter was from Devlin. Each broad stroke of the pen made her see him in her mind. It was so like him, strong, hard, quick.

Angelica Branigan, Morgan Falls, Washington Territory...

She drew her fingertips over the name *Branigan* and felt a tightness return to her belly.

"Excuse me," she mumbled, turning away from Maud.

She walked toward the creek, the envelope pressed against her chest, her heart thudding beneath her hand. Her feet felt weighted. Her vision seemed blurred.

He's not coming back.

But he'd said he would. She'd asked him when he would return and he'd said it would be a while. That meant he would return in time.

He's not coming back.

Angelica slowly lifted the seal and removed the slip of paper from the envelope. For a moment longer, she stared at the folded stationery as if it were some sort of poisonous viper. Finally, drawing a deep breath, she opened it.

Angelica (Not "dear" Angelica. Just Angelica.)

Devlin's Promise

There was a reward for Ryan Murphy's capture, dead or alive. I have instructed that it be paid to you. Bert Farland can help you obtain it from the authorities in Snohomish. I have advised them that you will contact them shortly. Use the money to hire a hand to continue clearing and planting. I don't know when I shall be able to return to Morgan Falls.

Devlin

She couldn't argue with the truth any longer. He didn't mean to return. He hadn't been able to tell her so in this note, but it was true all the same. He'd lost hope for that bright and better tomorrow they'd both wanted, and it was her fault. She'd done that to him. She hadn't let him see the man she saw every day.

"Oh, Dev, I'm so sorry," she whispered. "You weren't a gunslinger anymore. You were just a man protecting his family. I should have made you see that. I should have let you see how much I love you. I should never have let you go."

Angelica reread the letter one more time, then slipped it into her skirt pocket. She shoved the desire to mourn and wail into a remote corner of her heart. Perhaps later, but not now. She lifted her chin as she faced Maud and walked toward her friend.

"You were right," she said as she drew closer. "It was from Devlin. He's not certain how soon he'll be able to return. He wants me to hire someone to help me run the place until he gets back. Do you know anyone who might want the job?"

Maud's eyes narrowed. She seemed to see right through Angelica's brave facade but thankfully didn't say so. "Lars Johnson's boy might be interested. Bert will know. If not, I'm sure you could find a hand in Snohomish."

"I think I'll walk back to town with you. There's another matter I need to discuss with your husband." Angelica turned toward the cabin. "Come inside while I freshen up and get Robby. Then we can go."

She would throw out the dough, she decided. She wasn't going to need those extra loaves of bread.

Jimmy Foster hadn't ever been very bright, but even he should have known better than to try to cheat at cards. Especially without Murphy there to help him.

Devlin stared down at the fresh mound of dirt where Jimmy had been buried two days ago. For a brief moment, when Devlin had first heard of Jimmy's death, he'd dared to hope again. Both Jimmy and Murphy were gone. No one else knew he was in Washington. Maybe the Devil Kid was gone, too. Maybe he was gone for good. Maybe now Devlin could . . .

He'd squelched the thought like a bug beneath his heel. He had to move on. He couldn't go back. Angelica didn't want him there. He'd seen her fear. He'd seen what she thought of him. He remembered the cold aloofness before he left, the silence that had surrounded them. No, he couldn't go back.

He walked away from the gravesite. He could go back to Idaho, but there would be too many questions waiting for him there. His family wouldn't understand why he had left Angelica. They would want to know what had happened, and he couldn't lie to them again. Nor could he tell them the truth.

Perhaps he'd give California a try.

But what would he do when he got there?

He felt the weight of his guns against his thighs. They seemed heavier than any of the logs he'd hoisted into place while building the cabin.

Torin Johnson—whose white-blond hair and pale blue eyes proclaimed his Scandinavian heritage even more clearly than his name—was more man than boy at the age of sixteen, although his fair skin still had a tendency to turn hot pink whenever he was flustered or embarassed. He was built like a mountain with thick biceps and a broad, muscular chest beneath his dark green shirt. He was a half-a-head taller than his father, Lars, who wasn't a short man by any means. Both Torin and Lars had friendly, if somewhat reserved, faces and nice smiles.

Angelica liked the Johnsons immediately.

"I'm going to Snohomish tomorrow with Mr. Farland," she told Torin after he'd accepted her offer of a job. "You be at my place on Monday, and we'll get started."

Torin blushed. "I do not mind starting now, Mrs. Branigan." His words rolled out of his mouth in a thick Swedish accent. He glanced toward the floor of the general store. "I could get much done before Monday. I am a hard worker."

"That's very kind of you, Torin, but I believe we should wait. Three days won't make much difference."

She didn't want to tell him she had to find out just how much money was waiting for her in Snohomish. Until she knew, she didn't dare put Torin to work. There was almost nothing left from the savings that had brought them to Washington, not after buying a plow and a saw and an ax and horses and rope and harness and . . .

She sighed softly, then shook her head. "No. We'd better wait until I return."

"I will be there early on Monday." He glanced at her for just a moment, his face growing ever brighter, then hurried out of the store, joining his father and Bert Farland on the boardwalk.

"Good people, the Johnsons," Maud said from behind the counter after the door had closed. "Mr. Johnson doesn't speak much English, but Torin worked hard in school back in Iowa so he could help his father get his own farm in this country." As she talked, she swirled a cloth over the countertop, cleaning away fingerprint smudges. "Torin's ma and sister both died of smallpox several years back. Guess that's why the Johnsons come to Washington. To get away from the memories."

Angelica stared at the men standing outside the store and wondered if the same thing brought everyone west. Was it always a desire to escape some unpleasantness in their pasts that drew people to faraway places?

"I know you and Torin are going to get on just fine," Maud proclaimed as she tossed the cloth aside and came out from behind the counter. "He's a hard worker, that boy. He won't shirk. I know you're going to like him a lot."

"I like him already," Angelica replied, and knew it was true.

Maud stopped beside Angelica. "Perhaps you won't feel so lonely when the boy's there."

Angelica didn't even attempt a reply. She didn't care to admit, to herself or to Maud, that she was lonely. Nor did she want to acknowledge that she would always be lonely without Devlin, no matter who else might be with her.

"I'd better get home. Thanks for agreeing to keep Robby while I go into Snohomish." She turned and hurried into the living quarters, where she snatched her son from the high chair near the table. "I'll see you in the morning." She left through the back door, never giving Maud another chance to speak.

Angelica continued her brisk pace until she was out of sight of the settlement. Finally, feeling winded, she stopped and set Robby on his feet.

"Oh, Robby, your mother is such a fool. How did I let this happen to us?"

Taking hold of the boy's small hand, she began walking again, slowing her strides to match his shorter ones.

She wasn't aware of the sunlight filtering through the latticework of branches or the whispering breeze waving the stately Douglas firs or the harsh call of a magpie winging its way overhead. She didn't see the tawny-colored doe watching her with wide brown eyes, long ears twitching. She didn't hear the rustle of small animals as they scurried through the dense underbrush.

As usual, her thoughts had returned to Devlin.

Chapter Twenty-Nine

A nameless saloon in another nameless town.

Devlin sat at a table in a corner of the dimly lit room, a bottle of whiskey and a shot glass for company. It was all the company he wanted.

At the next table was an elderly man with a bushy white beard and long white hair that brushed his collar. Just as Devlin's gaze lit upon him, the old-timer looked up. He reminded Devlin of the drawings of St. Nicholas in the books his mother had read to him at Christmastime when he was a boy. The old man smiled at him as if they were friends.

Devlin nodded curtly and returned his attention to the whiskey. He filled the glass to the brim, then stared at the golden-brown liquid in silence, thinking of the oblivion it would bring him.

"Mind if I join you, sonny?"

Devlin looked up from the bottle and glass.

The old man was standing beside his table now, already pulling out a chair and preparing to sit down.

"You look like you could use a friend." He glanced at the bottle in Devlin's hand. "Ain't no help t'be found in that there whiskey."

"What are you?" Devlin groused. "A preacher?"

The man chuckled, causing his thick white beard to sway against his rotund belly. "Ain't never had no one mistake me fer no preacher before. Been called an old busybody a time or two. Can't say as I care fer that much, but I suppose they had a right t'say it."

Go away, old-timer, and let me get drunk.

The man nodded, as if he'd heard Devlin's thoughts. For a long time they sat in silence, Devlin nursing his drink, the old man watching him do it. Devlin would have liked to tell him to leave but didn't. Maybe it was the old man's resemblance to St. Nick that kept Devlin silent.

"You're new t'these here parts."

Devlin didn't look up or reply. He didn't want to encourage the fellow. He didn't want him to keep talking, although he was tempted to ask just exactly where "these here parts" were. Was he still in Oregon or had he moved into California by this time?

"M'name's Martin, but most folks just call me Two-Bits."

Devlin couldn't stop himself from asking, "Two-Bits?"

The man laughed again. "Somebody told me once I wouldn't amount to two bits. Name just sorta stuck." He crossed his forearms on the table and leaned forward. "How 'bout you, sonny? You got a name I can hang on ya?"

What should he tell Two-Bits? Was he the Devil Kid or was he Devlin Branigan? He hadn't thought about much else since leaving that quarter-section outside of Morgan Falls—except when he'd been thinking about Angelica and Robby, and that had been most of the time.

"I guess sonny will do," Two-Bits said to break the ensuing silence.

"As well as anything." Devlin splashed some more whiskey into the shot glass.

"You know the sort of folk that wind up in a place like this? The ones who're runnin', usually from themselves. You runnin', sonny?"

"Listen, mister. I'm not much in the mood for conversation. If you want a drink, I'll pour you one, but then I'd just as soon be left alone."

"No thanks. I gave it up years ago. I just come in here to socialize. But you go ahead if you've a mind to."

"Thanks," Devlin replied sarcastically. He tossed the drink down the back of his throat, then waited as the warmth spread outward.

"She must be somethin', that woman."

He slammed the glass down onto the table. The bottle of whiskey tilted precariously, then

241

righted itself. "*What* woman?"

"The one you're longin' fer. A man don't look like you 'cept over a woman. Fella my age learns a thing or two, and that's one o' them."

Devlin picked up the bottle and stared at its contents.

"Is she a good woman, sonny?"

"The best."

"Then what're you doin' here?"

"I don't belong with her. I'm bad news."

"She tell you that?"

"No, but it's the truth."

"You oughta give her a chance t'tell you fer herself, don't ya think? Could be she don't agree with your thinkin'."

The whiskey was dulling Devlin's brain. He couldn't seem to remember all the good reasons for leaving Washington, for leaving Angelica, for riding away from the life he'd come to want more than anything else.

"Sonny?" Two-Bits leaned forward. "I'm a right good listener."

Devlin stared at the old man for a long time. He was suddenly reminded of Jake and his shack and the whiskey Devlin had consumed while he waited for his shoulder to heal. He'd wanted out then. He'd wanted a new life. Jake had given him a chance to find it by sending Angelica to him with her harebrained idea of a farm in Washington.

Now here he was again. More whiskey. Another old man ready to listen, trying to help. He didn't know why, but suddenly he wanted someone to listen to him. He wanted to talk.

"My name's Branigan," he began softly, "but most folks know me as the Devil Kid."

Angelica sat at the table scribbling figures on a piece of paper. As hard as she tried, she couldn't seem to make the numbers work out like she wanted them to. She couldn't make her money stretch all the way through next summer. Torin wasn't being paid half what he was worth as it was.

She put down the pen and rubbed her eyes with her knuckles.

It wasn't the money that was causing her to feel such despair anyway. She knew they would make it somehow. If she had to, she could spend her evenings sewing. Bert made frequent trips into Snohomish. She could arrange to make dresses for one of the shops there, or maybe she could even sell them in Seattle.

No, it wasn't money worries. It was the emptiness of the house without Devlin. He'd been gone two weeks now. Was it ever going to get easier? Was the ache and loneliness ever going to go away?

Two-Bits leaned back in his chair, the fingers of one hand stroking the length of his white beard while he stared thoughtfully at Devlin. "So you just up an' left her, huh? Just didn't bother t'go back."

"She wasn't safe with me around." Devlin

dropped his gaze to the whiskey bottle. He thought about having another drink, then realized he didn't want it. Two-Bits had been right about that. There wasn't any help to be found in it. "It was better this way," he added.

"An' ya reckon she's safer now that you're gone? Did ya think that maybe some of those men's friends might know where you were? That Jimmy fella, he mighta told someone he knowed where the Devil Kid was an' they mighta told someone else. If they come lookin' fer you and find your woman there alone..." He shook his head slowly. "Don't reckon she'd stand much of a chance against the likes o' such men. And what if ya haven't outsmarted that fella from Denver? What if he knows where she is?"

A knot formed in Devlin's belly as he lifted his gaze to the old man once again. He almost changed his mind about the whiskey. He almost wished that he felt drunk rather than stone-cold sober.

Two-Bits got to his feet. " 'Pears to me you've got some thinkin' t'do. Hope you find what ya want, sonny. I sure do hope you find what ya want." With that, he turned and shuffled out of the saloon.

They came at him in his thoughts, the men he'd known through the years, the men he'd faced with a gun. He'd made his share of enemies, just like any other gunslinger. Hard men. Dangerous men. Men without morals or ethics. Men who took what they wanted and didn't care who they hurt to get it. He imagined them at their worst and knew what they would do to Angelica if they found her living there alone.

What if Two-Bits were right? What if someone besides Murphy and Jimmy knew of his whereabouts?

He'd left to try to protect her and, in leaving, had placed her in more danger than before. He would have to go back. He would have to stay until he was certain no one knew that the Devil Kid lived there, until he was certain no one else would come looking for him, until he knew she was safe from his enemies as well as her own.

He didn't care that she didn't want him there. He didn't care that she despised him, perhaps was even afraid of him. He was going to stay until he knew she was safe. Then he would leave, like she wanted him to. But only then.

He stood up so quickly that the chair toppled over behind him. He didn't bother to right it before striding out of the musty-smelling saloon.

Devlin didn't realize it, but he was a man headed for home.

Angelica stood in the open doorway of the cabin, staring out at the star-speckled black-velvet sky. The wind had come up after nightfall. It moaned amidst the swaying trees even as it whirled around her ankles, causing her nightgown to billow and swell. She shivered as she pulled her shawl more closely around her shoulders. It wasn't so much that the wind was cold but that the sound it made seemed to mirror the loneliness of her soul.

Where are you, Dev?

Was there a wind where he was, too?

She placed her fingers against her lips, then blew a kiss into the darkness.

"It's from me. Let it bring you home."

She thought back over the days and weeks that had passed since they'd arrived in Morgan Falls. She thought of the fields that had been cleared and the plants that had been sown— both before Devlin had left and after. She'd been right. She could make it out here on her own. She could make this a prosperous farm and she could raise her son and she could even find a measure of contentment.

But it wasn't all she wanted anymore. It wasn't enough. She wanted to share it with Devlin. She wanted to stand in this doorway with his arm around her waist and her head upon his shoulder. She wanted to awaken in the morning and find him there beside her. She wanted to meet his gaze and share the laughter over something Robby had done.

She waited another minute before closing the door. Then she looked around the small but cozy room. Everything her gaze touched made her think of Devlin. His hands had built this house, shaped the table and benches, placed stone upon stone in the fireplace, hammered the pegs and shelves into the walls. He had labored and sweated to build this place for her and Robby. He had risked his life to keep her safe. This was his home every bit as much as it was hers, perhaps even more so.

He'll come back.

For the first time since Angelica had watched Devlin riding away, leading Murphy's horse, she believed he would return to her.

He's got to.

It wasn't chance that had brought them together. It was destiny. He belonged here. Here with her and Robby.

This is his home, and we're his family.

Angelica felt a slight smile curve the corners of her mouth.

He feels it, too, she thought as she put out the light and made her way to the bedroom in the dark.

Jonathan Bellows let the pink curtains fall into place over the window as he turned toward the bed. He removed his suit coat and placed it carefully over the back of the chair, then removed his trousers with equal solicitude. As an adult, Jonathan Bellows had never gone to bed without making certain that his clothes—unwrinkled and impeccably clean— were ready for him in the morning. That was what he hated most about the travel his profession required. Rumpled suits and dirty hotel rooms.

There were some who might have called Jonathan Bellows fussy. He preferred to think of himself as tidy and well-groomed.

Heaven knew, it was difficult to stay that way when he was living out of a carpetbag. At last it appeared he had reached the end of his journey. He'd located Devlin Branigan and his family. Tomorrow morning, after dining on another of Mrs. Brighton's delicious meals, he would pay a visit to Angelica Branigan.

While in Boise, he'd learned enough about the Branigans to convince anyone that he was a close friend of the family, even Maureen Foster's own son. It wouldn't be hard, using his usual disguise of a slightly bumbling, often lost businessman, to find out what he needed to know.

Bellows slipped his nightshirt over his head and climbed into bed. He let out a long, weary sigh. With any luck, he would be back on the steamship tomorrow, headed for Denver to make his final report to Lamar Orwell.

Lord, how he detested that man. Bellows didn't know how he'd ever let himself become indebted to Lamar. He would give anything not to have to do the braggart's dirty work any longer. So help him, this would be the last job he did for Lamar. The very last job.

As he closed his eyes, he wondered if this

Mrs. Branigan really was Angelica Corrall. God pity her if it was true. Imagining what Lamar was capable of doing, Bellows almost hoped he would find that he'd been following the wrong trail.

Chapter Thirty

"Look, Robby. Here's one." Angelica leaned over and pointed at the light brown egg hidden in the straw. "Be careful," she cautioned as the boy reached for it.

Robby beamed as he gently placed the egg in the basket, then looked up for his mother's approval.

"Very good. That's six eggs this morning."

"Six eggs?"

"Right. Can we find any more?"

Robby frowned, looking as if he were considering a very weighty problem. His mouth puckered, and he squinted his eyes. Finally he shook his head. "No more," he pronounced solemnly.

"Oh, I think there must be a few still hiding from us. Let's look, shall we?"

He grinned, responding to his mother's smile and cheerful voice. "More eggs." He clapped his hands together, then bent forward so he could peer into the straw.

"Good morning, Mrs. Branigan."

Angelica turned toward the door of the hen house. "Well, good morning, Torin. I didn't expect you for another hour."

"I want to get an early start. There are many stumps still to be cleared. I have brought my team today. They are very strong and will be of great help to me."

"You're a good worker, Torin. I'm lucky you were willing to help me on the place. I couldn't have managed without you."

He blushed to the roots of his pale blond hair. His glance fell to the ground near his feet. "I am happy to do it, Mrs. Branigan. I like to work."

"Have you eaten? Robby and I were just gathering eggs for breakfast."

"I ate before coming."

"But not enough, am I right?" She suspected, from what Torin had told her in snatches of conversation over the past week, that neither he nor his father were competent cooks. "Come inside. You can't be expected to work on a half-empty stomach. A growing young man like you needs a good breakfast before he starts his day."

The pink in Torin's face deepened, but he nodded his agreement.

Angelica picked up the basket with one hand and took hold of Robby with the other. "Why don't you feed and water my horse while I heat up the skillet?"

Torin mumbled an acknowledgment before disappearing around the corner of the hen house.

Angelica smiled to herself. She wasn't unaware of Torin's attraction to her. She'd seen the same look before when she was with the theater company. They'd hovered around the back entrance—boys becoming young men and eager to prove themselves but not sure quite how to go about it. Only, most of them hadn't been as shy and well-mannered as Torin Johnson, nor nearly as nice. She didn't want Torin's first crush to be a bad experience. She hoped she wouldn't inadvertently hurt him.

Less than an hour later, only crumbs were left of the fried bacon, scrambled eggs, and thick slices of bread which Angelica had prepared. Torin had't spoken a single word throughout the meal and had looked surprised and uncomfortable whenever Angelica had made an attempt to start a conversation. When he was finished eating, he thanked her politely and hurried out to begin his work.

As she stacked the dishes for washing, she wondered if there might be some girls close to Torin's age living near Morgan Falls. Surely there were. Hadn't Maud mentioned another family of homesteaders, one with several daughters? Angelica was certain she had. The Newmans? The Newtons? That was it. The Newtons.

Now, she thought, all she had to do was manage to get Torin and the Newton girls in the same place at the same time. Nature would take its course from there.

Suddenly her face lit with excitement.

"We could have a barn dance," she said aloud as she turned toward Robby's high chair. "Wouldn't that be fun, Robby? A barn dance with music and food and folks from miles around. Maud could help us. She knows everyone from here to Snohomish." She grinned as excitement began to well up in her chest.

Why hadn't she thought of something like this before? It wouldn't just be good for Torin. It would be good for her, as well. She'd spent far too many hours thinking about Devlin and wondering if he would come back to her. And although the feeling that had come to her last night—the certainty that Devlin *was* coming back—still lingered, she knew she had to keep her mind on other things or she would become obsessed with watching the trail leading into the valley.

It could still be several weeks before Devlin returned. What better way for her to spend her time than becoming friends with her neighbors?

Holding on to the kettle with a towel, she carried it to the dry sink and poured hot water into the round washtub. All the while she scrubbed the dishes and skillet, her mind was whirring with ideas. She could hardly wait to complete her chores so she could walk to Morgan Falls and have a talk with Maud.

She wasn't sure just what made her turn toward the open doorway. Perhaps it was the soft nickering of her gelding out in the corral or perhaps it was Domino's whimpers for attention from the fenced yard. Whatever it was, she turned—and then stopped dead still.

The hair rose on the back of her neck as she watched the lone horseman—a stranger—ride out of the trees and descend the trail on his way toward her cabin.

Angelica broke free of the fear-induced inertia. Drying her hands on her apron, she crossed quickly toward the door. She reached up above the coat hooks and removed the rifle from its rack. Then she stepped out into the morning light, her gaze locked on the stranger as he approached.

He was watching her, too, and she saw his eyes flick nervously toward the rifle, then back to her face again. He slowed his horse, finally drawing it to a stop while still some distance away.

"Good morning, ma'am," he called as he removed his hat. "Are you, by chance, Mrs. Branigan?"

Angelica nodded once.

"Thank goodness. I was afraid I'd taken another wrong turn. I'm frightfully bad at directions. Mrs. Brighton told me how to find your place, but..." He grinned sheepishly and shrugged his shoulders. "I'm afraid I've taken several wrong turns getting here." He placed the black bowler back over his bald pate, then stepped awkwardly down from the saddle. "Is your husband at home?"

Short, paunchy, and slightly rumpled, the stranger looked harmless enough, but Angelica couldn't shake the sense of foreboding he'd brought with him.

"Not at the moment," she replied, then added, "but he should return soon."

He took a step forward. His hand motioned nervously toward the rifle. "You won't need that thing, Mrs. Branigan, I assure you. I'm a friend of Mr. Branigan's family in Idaho. I've been conducting business in Seattle and had to come up to Snohomish regarding some of my lumber concerns. Mr. Branigan's mother asked me to pay a visit while I was up this way."

Angelica lowered the rifle slightly, although she still wasn't convinced. This could still be a trick. For all she knew, he was Murphy's friend Jimmy.

She glanced to the right and was encouraged to see Torin striding quickly toward the cabin.

"Mrs. Foster wanted me to bring back news of you and Mr. Branigan and . . . and . . ." He frowned. "Is it Bobby? No, Robby." He smiled, as if quite pleased with himself for remembering. "She wants to know how her grandson Robby is doing."

Angelica relaxed. No one like Jimmy would know Maureen Foster's or Robby's names. "Robby is fine." She set the rifle butt on the ground, leaning the muzzle against the cabin wall. She looked again to the right and raised her hand to wave at Torin, letting him know everything was all right. She saw him stop and wait, as if considering whether or not to believe her. She waved again, and this time he turned and started back toward the far end of the clearing.

"Your husband?" the man asked.

"No. He's our hired hand." She faced him again. "I'm sorry to have greeted you this way, sir, but we had some trouble recently. Won't you come in and have some coffee? You can see Robby for yourself and tell Maureen just how much he's grown since we left Boise."

"Thank you. I'd like that." He removed his hat again. "Allow me to introduce myself. I'm Johathan Bellows."

The morning passed quite pleasantly. Jonathan Bellows was an enjoyable conversationalist, and it wasn't long before she felt as if they were old friends. He told her that Tucker was working hard to see that Idaho became a state. Maggie and the children were all doing well, as were Neal and Patricia. Fiona was expecting another child in late winter. Maureen's husband, David, had been ill for a while but was doing much better when Bellows left for Washington.

As he talked, Angelica imagined each member of Devlin's family. It made her feel good, hearing about them. In the short time she'd been in Idaho, she'd come to care about the Branigans and the Fosters and the Whittiers, come to think of them as her own family. It wasn't true, of course. She was only pretending to be a Branigan, but still ...

"I understand you're an accomplished actress, Mrs. Branigan. Do you ever miss the theater?"

She blinked, brought back to the present by his question. "Miss the theater?" She thought about it for a moment, trying to remember the excitement of opening night, the thrill of applause, but it seemed almost a dream now. That girl, the actress Angelica Corrall, had been someone else, someone far different from the woman she was now. Angelica had found something on this little homestead in Washington far better than fame.

"No," she answered softly but assuredly. "I much prefer my life with Devlin and Robby."

"Well ... you're a very lucky woman." Bellows rose from the bench. "Now, I have taken up enough of your time, and I have a boat to catch in Snohomish. I really must be on my way. I'm eager to get home to Boise." He leaned forward to pat Robby's head. "He's a fine boy, Mrs. Branigan. You must be very proud of him."

"He and ... and his father are the most important things in my life," she whispered.

Bellows's eyebrows drew together, then relaxed. "Yes. Of course. Well, you tell Mr. Branigan that I'm sorry I missed him. Next time you visit your family in Boise, be sure to look me up. And thank you for the hospitality."

"You're welcome, Mr. Bellows. I've enjoyed meeting you."

She followed him outside, carrying Robby to the yard and lowering him over the fence, then turned and watched as Mr. Bellows untied his horse and climbed into the saddle. He glanced around the valley, then returned his gaze to Angelica.

"I'm afraid you'll have to point me in the right direction," he said with a self-deprecating laugh. "I can't remember which way I came in."

Angelica pointed. "Just follow that trail to the main road. Turn right, and it will take you straight into Morgan Falls."

He tipped his bowler. "It's been a pleasure."

"For me, too, Mr. Bellows. Give our love to Mrs. Foster and the others."

"I'll do so. Good day." He glanced at Robby as he played with the puppy. "Take care of yourself, son." Bellows turned his horse and rode across the clearing and up the trail.

When he'd disappeared into the forest, Angelica went back inside, buoyed by the unexpected visit. It felt good to hear from the family, good to know they were thinking about them, too.

Smiling, she tackled the rest of her chores. She still wanted to get into town to talk with Maud, but first she had to finish washing the dishes and make Torin some lunch. Then she would go to Morgan Falls, and she and Maud would make plans for a barn dance.

First she'd found a family. Now she'd found friends. Angelica had never expected her life to be so full.

She was going to have a lot to tell Devlin when he returned.

Chapter Thirty-One

Maud Farland had never been the sort of woman to let grass grow under her feet.

From the first moment Angelica brought up the idea of a barn dance, Maud embraced it with enthusiasm. She immediately called a meeting of the townswomen—Rose Farland, Mary Brighton, Rebecca Newton, and Angelica. They all met in Mary's kitchen and made plans while they stuffed themselves on Mary's delicious peach cobbler smothered in thick cream.

Lars Johnson's barn was chosen for the site. It was by far the largest barn in the area, and the Johnson farm was on the road to Snohomish, making it easily accessible to everyone. Bert Farland volunteered to organize the musicians—most of them being his own sons. Mrs. Brighton, whose culinary skills were indisputable, was put in charge of the food. Those dreary souls who had no interest in kicking up their heels to a lively fiddle would still come to the barn dance if only for a taste of her cooking.

The days seemed to fly by after that. Using the list Maud gave her, Angelica wrote and addressed the invitations while sitting at Maud's kitchen table. At home, she began baking again, but instead of bread, she made cookies. Some of them she frosted, and Robby got to help, although he wound up with more frosting on his face than on the cookies.

The day before the dance, Angelica left Robby with Mrs. Brighton and rode over to the Johnson farm in the back of Bert's wagon with Maud, Rose, Rebecca, and Rose's friend Esther Plum from Snohomish.

"This was a wonderful idea, Mrs. Branigan," Esther said, her freckled face wreathed in a smile.

Rebecca nodded. "I wondered how we'd ever get to meet people. Our place is so far back in the woods. My girls think we've fallen off the edge of the world. Now they'll know we've got neighbors."

All of the women chimed in, agreeing that Angelica's suggestion had been inspired. Angelica couldn't help but feel pleased.

Everyone's spirits were high as they strode into the barn, brooms and pitchforks in hand. Their hair hidden beneath kerchiefs and their faces soon smudged with dust, they swept and shoveled and pitched until the barn was nearly as clean as any house. Later that night, the men would come in and put up tables for the array of food Mrs. Brighton and the other women had prepared.

By the time Angelica returned home and tucked Robby into bed, she was too tired to think about anything but falling into bed herself. Not even thoughts of Devlin could keep her awake tonight.

"What's the matter, Maudie?"

Maud looked up from the flickering orange and yellow flames on the hearth. "What?"

Bert grinned tolerantly. "I said, what's the matter?"

She shrugged. "I don't know. Tired, I guess."

"Imagine you would be, the way you've been keepin' up with those young gals. Runnin' all over creation. Workin' from sunup to sundown." He sat beside her, draping his arm around her back. "But what's brought that frown to your forehead? You only look like that when somethin's troublin' you mighty fierce."

Maud felt an old and very familiar tightening in her chest. She touched his cheek, then laid her head against his shoulder. "You know me too well, Bert. Sometimes I swear you know what I'm thinkin' before I do myself."

"I should. We've been together a mighty long time."

Yes, a mighty long time, and she'd loved him every last minute of it, even when she'd been mad enough to scalp him for some of the fool stunts he'd pulled.

"Not one of the children, is it? Rose okay?"

She shook her head. "Rose is fine. I was just thinkin' about the Branigans."

"Oh." The concern had disappeared from his voice. A chuckle rumbled deep in his chest. "So you're tryin' to fix things for them, too. Is that it, Maudie?" He patted her arm. "Just can't stand not to see folks happy and in love, can you?"

She poked him in the ribs with her knuckles but didn't lift her head from his shoulder.

He cleared his throat, trying to hide the lingering traces of amusement. "Well, I don't see that there's much you can do when the fella's not around."

"I know . . . I know." Maud sighed. "But Angelica's so unhappy. She hides it most of the time, but every so often I catch that look in them green eyes o' hers. She'll be lookin' off down the road as if she's hopin' t'see him ridin' up at any moment." She lifted her head and met Bert's gaze. "But t'tell you the truth, I get the feelin' sometimes that she don't think he ever will. An' sometimes I'm afraid she's right."

"Well, Maudie, that's where you're both wrong. That boy's got more character than t'ride off and leave his wife and son. I can't say as I know what's keepin' him, but I'm tellin' ya, he'll be back. You can bet on it." Bert rose to his feet, drawing Maud with him. "Now, I think it's time we got you t'bed. I don't like seein' you so tuckered out, an' you're gonna need plenty o' rest before the big shindig tomorrow night."

Devlin had ridden hard for more than a week, but tomorrow he would reach Morgan Falls. Tomorrow he would be home.

He hadn't allowed himself to think about the possibility that Angelica could have been in danger while he was away. He simply concentrated on getting back to Morgan Falls as quickly as possible. He rested the horse only when he had to and bedded down for the night only when it was too dark to ride on.

And day by day he'd drawn closer to his destination, closer to Angelica.

The simple cotton dress was a soft yellow with short sleeves, rounded neckline, narrow waist, and full skirt. It had always been a favorite of Angelica's, perhaps because the color made her feel bright and gay. It was a perfect choice for the barn dance.

Angelica worked for a long time on her hair. Tonight she wasn't going to settle for a demure bun. Instead, she swept her hair high on her crown and arranged it in a mass of curls. She even added a spray of yellow wildflowers behind one ear.

Stepping back from the small mirror, she smiled. The woman who smiled back at her was young and pretty and carefree. She looked ready for a party. Angelica hadn't felt like that girl in a long, long time.

"What do you think?" she asked her son as she turned around.

Sitting on the bed, Robby clapped his hands together, as if applauding the results.

Angelica curtsied. "Thank you, kind sir."

When she heard a knock on the door, she grabbed her shawl off a peg even as Robby slid from the bed, then she followed her son to the door.

"Torin?" she exclaimed in surprise when she opened the door. "Whatever are you doing here?"

His pale hair was slicked back, and he was wearing a white shirt with a stiff collar. A pair of suspenders held up his dress trousers. He was also wearing a bright flush of embarrassment. "I did not think it right that you should have to walk to the dance alone."

"Why, Torin," she replied softly, touched by his thoughtfulness, "how kind of you."

"Tory! Tory!" Robby held up his arms and waited for his large friend to lift him up from the floor. Torin immediately obliged.

Angelica picked up the basket filled with cookies, then glanced behind her. "I guess I haven't forgotten anything. Let's go."

The walk to the Johnson farm didn't seem as far with Torin along for company. Angelica no longer felt the need to make conversation when she was with him. She simply enjoyed the companionable silence, content to be with a good friend.

Torin's presence did, however, remind her

why she'd thought of the barn dance in the first place, and she mulled it over in her head as they followed the path toward Morgan Falls. Over the past few days, she'd met Rebecca's daughters, and she was certain that every one of them would take a liking to Torin Johnson. The Newton girls were certainly pretty enough to capture his interest. And if not one of them, there were others coming up from Snohomish.

As they stepped off the forest trail and onto the main road, the sound of laughter caused their heads to turn. Coming toward them in their flatbed wagon was the Newton family—Ted and Rebecca and their daughters.

I couldn't have planned it better if I'd tried, Angelica thought, feeling just a bit smug as she raised her hand and waved.

They were invited to join the girls in the back of the wagon. Angelica was quick to agree, happy to be able to set down the basket of cookies and even happier to put Torin in the midst of the Newton girls. She hopped up onto the rear of the wagon, letting her legs hang down behind. Torin sat beside her, still holding Robby.

Silence was soon replaced by the babble of excited voices and laughter. Angelica sensed that all five of the girls were watching Torin, and a glance in his direction told her he thought so, too. His complexion had turned from pink to scarlet.

The closer they came to the Johnson farm, the more people joined them on the road.

Voices called back and forth from wagon to wagon. Newcomers were introduced to those who had lived in the area for many years. Children jumped down from one wagon and ran over to another. Others rode on horseback. Still others walked.

Angelica began to wonder if the entire town of Snohomish had decided to come to the Morgan Falls barn dance. She hoped Mary Brighton had prepared enough food.

Devlin watched the parade of people and horses and wagons as it turned off the main road and made its way toward the house and barn set back about a quarter mile. He wondered what had brought so many people there. He could tell the occasion was festive, merely by how dressed up everyone was.

Then he heard her laughter, a sound that made his heart quicken in relief. Angelica was safe. Nothing had gone amiss while he was away.

His eyes found her. She was dressed in yellow and wore yellow flowers in her hair. She looked like a girl, and yet she was unmistakably a woman. She was smiling and talking with those around her, glancing often at the young man beside her.

Another wagon turned off the main road, blocking his view, and he couldn't see her any longer. The sense of relief and joy dissipated, replaced by irritation. He'd been riding hard for days to reach her. He'd needed to make certain she and Robby were all right. And here she was, on her way to a party. She hadn't even cared that he was gone. She'd probably been glad of it.

Hell! What had he expected? Had he thought she would miss him? He was just a hired gun. Same thing he'd been most of his life. Angelica had offered him a job. That was all. She was his boss, not his woman. He'd quit, ridden away, left her. She'd probably hired someone else to take his place.

Devlin backed his buckskin deeper into the shadows of the trees and waited until the road was deserted once again. Then he turned his horse up the road toward home, trying not to think about how lovely Angelica looked in yellow—or about the blond man he'd seen beside her.

Angelica's face ached from smiling so much. She'd danced until her feet hurt. She'd eaten until she thought the seams of her dress would burst. She'd met so many people her head was swimming with names and faces.

Maud's arm circled her shoulders. "It's a grand success, Angelica. You should be right proud of yourself for what you've done here. You've made folks feel like neighbors."

Angelica was warmed by her friend's praise.

"It looks like our young ladies have discovered Torin," Maud added in a whisper.

Angelica followed Maud's gaze to a group of girls standing near the food table. The two oldest Newton girls, Carolina and Eunice, were among them, as were Virginia Ross and Laura Jane Smith from Snohomish. They were whispering and giggling, all the while casting covert glances toward Torin who was leaning against the side of the barn, his hands shoved into his pockets, his gaze locked onto the floor.

"Why isn't he dancing?" Angelica wondered aloud.

"Probably don't know how. Torin and his pa aren't much for socializin'. Friendly folk, just reserved, I guess. Torin's always been one to stay pretty much to himself." She shrugged. "Besides, without a ma, who was there to teach him to dance? Sure not his pa."

"I didn't think of that."

"Well, don't fret yourself about it. He'll do all right." Maud moved away toward another group of women, leaving Angelica to her thoughts.

This whole idea of a barn dance had been conceived so Torin could meet some young ladies his own age. If he spent all his time alone just because he couldn't dance—even if the girls noticed him—it wasn't going to do him any good. At least, not the way Angelica had planned for it to do.

Well, maybe she could just do something about it, she thought as she lifted her chin, straightened her shoulders, and took off in his direction.

* * *

Devlin hadn't planned to bathe and shave and put on clean clothes. He hadn't planned to step into the saddle again tonight and ride Angelica's sorrel back in this direction.

But then, neither had he planned to feel the emptiness of the cabin nor to continue thinking about the way Angelica had looked, dressed in yellow, her face wreathed in smiles. But that was exactly what Devlin had done.

He had just dismounted and was tethering his horse to a hitching post beside the other horses when he saw her. A nearly full moon bathed her and the young man with her in a soft white light.

He watched as she took the fellow's right hand and placed it on the small of her back. Then she gripped his left hand with her right and put her other hand on his shoulder. Their heads bent forward in unison, almost touching as they stared down at the ground and began to move awkwardly over the hard-packed earth beneath their feet.

"No, Torin."

Her voice wafted to him on the cool night air, light, happy, amused. A voice so familiar to him he'd heard it in his dreams.

"It's really quite simple. Remember to count in your head."

Devlin didn't consciously move forward, but suddenly he was there, standing behind her back. He reached out, laying his hand on her shoulder. "Perhaps if he watched us, he would understand."

Angelica gasped as she spun around. Her face turned up to him in the moonlight, revealing wide green eyes. He watched emotions flit across her beautiful face and was frustrated by his inability to read and understand what he saw there.

It didn't matter anyway. Not at the moment. Right now all he wanted to do was hold her.

"You do it like this," he said, his gaze never moving from Angelica.

He drew her into his arms, holding her as if she were a fragile vase. He was acutely aware of the warmth of her hand in his, the rise and fall of her breasts, even the tiny pulse of the vein in her throat. They turned around the barnyard in time to the music, but Devlin didn't really hear it. He didn't notice anything except Angelica—the feel of her in his arms, the way her eyes sloped up at the corners, the warm scent of her cologne, the sheen of moonlight on her hair.

Tomorrow he would have to admit to himself that this was all pretend, that his stay here was temporary.

But for tonight, if only for tonight, he wanted to believe it was real.

He was back. He'd come back to her. And there was something about the look in his eyes, the way his gaze seemed to caress her face, that made Angelica's heart swell with joy. She hoped the music would never stop. She hoped he would never let her go.

But, of course, it did stop and he did let go.

For a moment he stood before her, staring down into her eyes. She wanted to move back into his embrace, ached for it, longed for it, but she didn't know how to tell him so. She felt as shy and uncertain as a schoolgirl suffering from her first crush.

Devlin turned away from her. "Did that help?"

Angelica had forgotten that they weren't alone.

"I'm Devlin Branigan." He held out his hand toward Torin.

"Torin Johnson, sir," the boy mumbled in return as he accepted Devlin's handshake.

"Thanks for lettin' me dance with my wife."

Angelica glanced quickly, surprised by the harsh inflection she'd heard. Could it possibly be or did she only imagine it? Had Devlin been jealous of her dancing with Torin? But Torin was only a boy. Surely, she was wrong.

Still, she couldn't help feeling another surge of hope. If Devlin cared enough to feel jealous, maybe ... just maybe ...

"Well, I'll be. That you, Devlin?" Bert ambled out of the barn, following the path of yellow light that spilled through the open door. "Good t'see you back, son. We were gettin' a might concerned about you." He took hold of Devlin's arm with one hand and Angelica's with the other. "Come inside and let's get you acquainted 'fore this here shindig runs out o' steam."

Chapter Thirty-Two

"Bert?" Angelica touched the man's arm. "Have you seen Robby? He's not with the other children. I can't find him anywhere."

The older man must have read the near-panic in her eyes. He put his arm around her shoulders and squeezed. "Don't worry, Angelica. The little tyke was pure tuckered out, an' Maud took him t'our place and put him t'bed. Said she was a bit tired herself. You an' Devlin were dancin' and she told me t'tell you what she'd done, but I plumb forgot."

Angelica let the air rush out of her lungs. "Thank God," she whispered. "I thought . . ."

"I'm sure sorry for worryin' you."

"It's okay—" she smiled her relief "—now that I know he's all right. We'll just get him on our way home."

"Why don't you let the boy stay where he is for the night? I'll bring him home in the mornin'. T'tell you the truth, Maud does love havin' Robby stay with us. Guess he sorta fills that empty spot that livin' so far from our own grandsons has left her."

"Oh, Bert, I don't—"

"I'd consider it a favor. Sides, we go traipsin' in there t'get the boy and we'll wake up Maud. Tired as she is, I don't want t'do that. Now, you wouldn't either, would you?"

She shook her head at his wheedling expression. "All right." How could she argue with him? From the first day Angelica and Devlin had arrived in Morgan Falls, Bert and Maud had been helpful, so friendly and accepting. It would be nearly impossible to deny Bert such a simple request as this.

"Angelica?" Devlin crossed the barn with long strides. He was scowling. "I checked with the Newton girls. They haven't seen Robby. We'd better—"

"It's all right. Robby's with Maud."

She watched the worry erase from his face and knew just how he felt. She loved him all the more for caring so much about her son.

"Tell you what," Bert said, grabbing each of them by an arm as he'd done earlier in the evening, this time propelling them toward the darkness outside, "you two git yourselves on home. It's late an' you got a ways t'go."

"But, Bert," Angelica began, "I've got to help clean up and—"

"You done enough, puttin' this blame thing together. The rest of us can sure as heck manage to clean up after ourselves. Now git." He gave them both a tiny shove out the door.

Bemused, Devlin and Angelica looked at each other.

"Well," Devlin said, "I guess we don't have much say about it."

"No. I guess we don't."

"This was all your doing, huh? The barn dance, I mean."

"Not really. Everyone helped."

His voice seemed to lower. "I had a good time."

Her stomach reacted as if he'd just spun her around. Remembering the way it had felt dancing in his arms, she whispered, "So did I."

"Guess we'd best start home. It's late."

She nodded.

"Tired?"

She nodded again. "A little."

"Come on." His hand cupped her elbow, and he guided her toward the hitching post.

They paused beside the sorrel gelding. Devlin's hands circled her waist. She felt a tiny skip in her pulse as he lifted her up and placed her on the saddle. His hands lingered for a moment, and her eyes were drawn to his.

There were so many things she needed to tell him. So many things she wanted to say. But she was unable to speak. She could scarcely breathe.

The moment passed. His hands released her waist, and he turned away, taking up the sorrel's reins. Without a word, he led the horse toward home, their way lit by the glow of the moon.

Devlin didn't much care for the way he was feeling. For years now, he'd been able to sit back and coolly assess his thoughts and emotions. He'd left behind that hot-headed youth long before he'd left Georgia back in '69. He'd become a man who was able to disengage himself from his own sentiments. The skill had kept him alive more than once through the years.

But that sort of remoteness was impossible when he was around Angelica. He felt too much when he was with her, and it was difficult to keep his thoughts in order. Sometimes it was difficult to think at all.

He had come back to do a job, he reminded himself. He had come back to protect Angelica from men like Murphy who might be looking for him and harm her in the bargain. He had come back to protect her from Lamar, who might yet find her. Those were the only reasons he had come back. When he was sure she would be safe, when he'd finished his job, he would be on his way again.

He'd nearly convinced himself, during the long journey back, that he could do it with the same cool reserve he'd exhibited with every other job he'd ever been hired to do.

But it had only taken the sight of her to dispel that notion. It had only taken an instant of holding her in his his arms to remind him of the torture that was ahead of him.

Watching Devlin's back as he led the sorrel down the trail into their valley, Angelica could almost feel him erecting a barrier between them, distancing himself from her.

Not again, she thought. *You'll not leave me again, Devlin Branigan.*

When he stopped the horse in front of the cabin and turned toward her, she tried to see his face, but it was hidden in shadows. He hesitated a moment, then placed his hands on her waist. As he lifted her from the saddle, she leaned into him, holding on to his shoulders. She didn't pull away when her feet touched the ground but kept staring up at him.

"Why did you come back, Dev?" she asked, her voice more husky than usual.

As the silence lengthened, she damned the night that hid his ebony eyes from view.

"Dev?"

"I had a job to do. Don't worry, Angelica. I don't mean to stay any longer than necessary. I'll make sure you and Robby are safe and that you won't have any trouble making a go of your farm. After that, I'll be on my way, just as I promised." He pulled away from her. "I'd best put the horse up. May take me a while. Don't bother to wait up."

Angelica felt the cool night air swirl around her, causing gooseflesh to rise on her arms.

No, you don't, Devlin Branigan. You can't es-

cape me so easily. Not again. Not this time.

She went into the house, more determined than ever.

Devlin took the time to groom both the horses. He tossed them some extra hay, checked the corral fence, even reorganized the tack in the lean-to. He didn't try to analyze why he was avoiding Angelica now after spending the evening with her, after holding her in his arms as they danced around the Johnsons' barn, after standing beside her as he was introduced to their few neighbors and the others who'd come up from Snohomish. He just knew he had to keep some distance between them until his equilibrium returned.

Finally, there didn't seem to be any excuses left that would keep him away from the house. He figured she was asleep by this time anyway.

Exhaustion washed over him. Relief came with it. As tired as he was, he would be able to fall asleep without thinking about Angelica. As tired as he was, he wouldn't even notice that she was in bed beside him.

At least, he *hoped* he was that tired.

He saw the soft flicker of firelight through the window as he approached the front door. The rest of the house was cloaked in darkness. All was silent except for the chirping of frogs somewhere in the distance.

Unsuspecting, he opened the door.

And then he stopped in mid-step.

She stood before the fireplace, the light turning her nightgown into little more than a gossamer mist, a mist that highlighted the shapeliness of her form. She was clearly naked beneath the flimsy material. Her silhouette was outlined in gold by the firelight at her back. Cascading hair fell in waves over her shoulders and down her back, the dark red tresses glowing with warmth.

Never had he known a woman so lovely. Never had he wanted a woman as much as he wanted her. The desire began as a slow heat, devouring him by inches until he was consumed with it.

"Angelica," he whispered thickly.

Put something on, his mind protested as he struggled to remember all the reasons he couldn't allow this to happen. *Put something on before I do something we'll both regret later.*

She moved toward him. She was barefoot, and it occurred to him that even her feet were lovely, delicate, inviting. She stopped, her eyes locked with his. For a moment neither of them moved, neither of them seemed to breathe. Then her arms encircled his neck as she raised up on tiptoe.

"Angelica, you don't know what you're doing."

Her breath was warm against his skin. "Yes, Devlin, I do." Her mouth brushed against his as she spoke.

His will to resist was shattered by the sound of her husky voice. He reached for her, crushed her against him. He claimed her lips with a fury, tasting, sampling, devouring. His tongue prodded her mouth until she opened to him. His hands ran over her back, down to her buttocks, and back up again.

You're wrong, Angelica. You don't know what you're doing, and neither do I. But there's no going back.

He cradled her face, slowed their kisses. There was no stopping their lovemaking, and now that he'd acknowledged it, he knew he wanted to savor every moment. He wanted each touch to bring pleasure, not just to him but to her.

They were alone. They had this night before them. He would make this one night a night of magic.

Tomorrow would have to take care of itself.

Angelica felt the change in him, and for a moment she feared he was going to turn away, reject her.

But he didn't pull away. His kisses became gentler, softer, slower. In response, her body weakened. The need to draw closer to him, to become a part of him, was almost painful in its intensity. It was something she'd never felt before. It both frightened and excited her.

His hands began to move again, to explore her body with agonizing thoroughness. When he cupped her breasts, she heard a low groan, then was surprised to realize it was she who had made the sound. She felt her nipples harden beneath his gentle teasing, and again she groaned.

His hands slid up from her breasts, pausing to free each tiny button along the front of her nightgown. Finally she felt the coolness of the night air brush against her skin as he pushed the gown from her shoulders. It slid down her arms, over her back and hips and legs, until it rested in a cottony puddle around her feet.

Devlin stepped back from her. She could see his face clearly in the firelight. She could see the desire in his ebony eyes. His black gaze burned a slow path over her body, all the way to her feet and then back up again. She felt branded by the look but deliciously so.

"You're like an angel," he whispered. "Angel ..."

She wasn't ashamed of her nudity. Beneath his gaze it felt right. She felt beautiful. She almost felt like an angel.

Suddenly she wanted to see him in the same way. She wanted to see him naked and know that there was no shame in it. She wanted to feast her eyes on him. She wanted to know every inch of him, even better than she knew her own body.

She fumbled with the buttons of his shirt. Her fingers seemed unable to achieve even this simplest of tasks. The mounting tension in her belly tempted her to rip the buttons off rather than be delayed further.

"Here." Devlin's voice held an odd mixture of amusement and frustration. "Let me help."

Together they removed his shirt, then his trousers, and finally his underdrawers. She thought for certain he would be able to hear the thudding of her heart as she stared at him.

He's beautiful, she thought as she took in the breadth of his chest, his tapered waist, his slim hips. *He's beautiful*, she thought again as she stared at his male arousal.

She was amazed by her discovery. She hadn't known it would be so. These feelings were all new to her. She'd thought herself experienced, but she realized now that she'd been an innocent still.

She touched him, winding her fingers through the dark mat of hair that covered his chest. She caressed the taut muscles beneath his skin. Unable to stop herself, even if she'd wanted to, she began to explore his body with her hands.

When she heard his groan, she felt something burst inside her, a need so strong it was almost painful, a need that only Devlin could quench. She moved toward him until their bodies met.

Their mouths sought each other, gloriously, frustratingly restrained, controlled. A flame ignited inside Angelica, a flame that any moment would burst into a firestorm, raging out of control.

"Devlin." She moaned his name against his lips.

He swept her feet off the floor, cradling her in his arms, his mouth never leaving hers as he carried her to the bedroom.

He placed her carefully on the bed, then lay

beside her. Once again his hands explored her body, stroking, petting, caressing. Her desire rose to a fevered pitch. She cried out his name, needing release from the fury that scorched her.

It was then he rose above her. The moment she felt him brush against her burning, aching flesh, she arched, pulling him to her, joining them together with a suddenness that took her breath away—and his, too.

There was a pregnant pause, as if the very earth itself suddenly stood still, and then he began to move.

She moved with him, to a silent rhythm as old as time, yet as fresh and new as the first blossom of spring. Angelica marveled in each sensation, wondered at the feel of him, the sound of him, even the smell of him. She marveled until the rhythm had quickened and she could think no more. She could only feel.

As passions raged, they climbed together toward a moment of shattering bliss.

Exhausted, replete, Devlin pulled her against the contours of his body, her head nestled against his shoulder. He nuzzled her ear. Her hair tickled his nose, its fresh scent making him think of mountain streams and wildflowers.

He shouldn't have allowed this to happen. No matter what they had shared this night, he didn't belong in her life. Angelica was merely lonely. Perhaps she was frightened that he would leave again and another Murphy would come and threaten her. Maybe this was her way of making him stay.

Or perhaps she truly cared for him.

But it didn't matter. He couldn't stay. Not for long. He would only bring her heartache.

The Devil Kid didn't belong with an angel.

Chapter Thirty-Three

Angelica awakened to the rat-a-tat-tat of a woodpecker and Domino's eager yapping. A songbird trilled in the distance. She smiled to herself, feeling pleased, as if she were somehow responsible for the sounds of nature.

A heartbeat later, her smile faded and her pulse quickened. A sixth sense told her that he was watching her, and she felt her body responding to him. She opened her eyes to meet his gaze.

He was propped up on one elbow. His black hair swept roguishly across his forehead. His cheeks and jaw were covered with dark stubble. His mouth was set in a grim line, and his eyes were as cool and remote as she had ever seen them.

She was suddenly quite afraid.

Devlin turned his back to her as he sat up and put his feet on the floor. "I shouldn't have let it happen. I never meant to make love to you. That wasn't why I came back."

Angelica sat up, too. She clutched the blankets to her bare breasts. She reached toward him with one hand, longing to touch him, to feel him, then drew her fingers back unrewarded.

"Why *did* you come back, Devlin?" She'd asked him the same question last night. She hoped his reply would be different this time.

It wasn't.

"Because it was pointed out to me that I was putting you in more danger by leaving than I was by staying. We don't know that Jimmy and Murphy were the only ones who saw and recognized me. There could be others. Besides, Orwell might still be looking for you and Robby. We haven't been in Washington all that long, and he isn't the type to give up easy." He raked his fingers through his hair. "You hired me to do a job, and I'm going to do it."

"You came back to finish a job." Her voice sounded small and distant in her ears. "Is that the only reason?"

A long silence followed her question before he replied, "I've never cheated an employer yet. I took your money. I'll stay till the job's done."

There was a pain in her stomach. "I see. How very admirable of you, Mr. Branigan."

"Look." He turned his head, glancing at her quickly, then turned away again. "It's my fault what happened last night. I can promise you that I won't forget myself twice."

This time she didn't draw back. This time her hand touched his shoulder and remained there. "It wasn't your fault, Devlin. I wanted you to make love to me. I wanted you to stay. I still do. Don't you see that I—"

He shrugged off her hand and stood up. He dressed quickly, wordlessly. Angelica watched him and felt her fears increase.

When he was fully dressed, he turned around, his ebony eyes impaling her on the bed. "Get this straight, Angelica. I'm a gunslinger, and that's not ever going to change. You know it as well as I do. Besides, I'm a loner. I'm not used to staying in one place for long, and I'm sure not cut out to be a farmer. I never even meant to stay here as long as we'd agreed."

Angelica shook her head, trying to deny what he was saying.

"I lied to you, Angelica. I never meant to keep my promise to stay till next year's harvest. I was going to find someone else to fill in for me once I'd healed up. Well, my arm's healed."

"But you've never cheated an employer yet," she whispered. "You came back to finish the job you were hired to do. You said so yourself."

He acted like he didn't hear her. "My draw is as quick as it ever was. You saw that for yourself when I shot Murphy. Have you forgotten what it was like, seeing a man shot down in front of you? How many times do you want to see something like that, Angelica?"

She quailed before him, not wanting to confront the mental picture his angry words summoned.

He sounded disgusted as he continued. "I'm going to stay to see this through because I don't want to be responsible for anything happening to you. But then I'm leaving. Is that clear?" He stepped toward her. His voice rose. "Do you understand me, Angelica? I'm not going to stay!"

"But you don't understand," she protested softly, unaware of the tears that streaked her cheeks. "I don't care about your past. I care about you. It's you I—"

"Don't say anything more," he said sharply. "I won't say I didn't enjoy myself last night. I've wanted you since the first moment I saw you. There isn't a red-blooded man that wouldn't. But even *your* body isn't enough to make me stay here for long. You think I want to rot in this rain bucket for the rest of my life? There are other places to see and other women to warm my bed."

Devlin saw her mouth open, although she made no sound, saw her flinch as if he'd struck her. Unable to bear his own cruelty, he spun and strode out of the bedroom, slamming the door behind him. He kept on going, out the front door and across the fields until he was standing at the far end of the clearing. It wasn't until he stopped that he realized he was shaking. He sank onto a stump and rested his head in his hands.

He'd had to say it. He'd had to stop her. She'd been going to tell him she loved him. He'd felt it in his gut. He didn't know what he would have done if she'd spoken the words aloud. He didn't know what he would have said.

Or perhaps he did know.

Even your *body isn't enough to make me stay here for long.*

Angelica flinched again as the angry words resounded in her head.

Even your *body isn't enough to make me stay here for long.*

She curled into a tight ball and covered her head with the blankets. She wanted to go to sleep and never wake up again.

Even your *body isn't enough to make me stay here for long.*

She saw them in her memory, the people of Wood Bluff, the way they'd looked down their noses at her, the way they'd shunned her as if she had leprosy. Whore, they had called her, because she had a son but no husband.

Then their faces changed. Suddenly they were the faces of her friends in Morgan Falls. But they weren't her friends any longer. They knew what she'd done. They knew what she was.

Whore...soiled dove...an actress...so common...never a lady...

How could she have been so wrong again? How could she have given her heart, given herself to Devlin? Had she no pride? No shame?

But I love him, and I thought . . . I thought he loved me.

She'd thought she loved Lamar at one time, too.

But this was different. This time it was different.

Was it?

This time it was Devlin.

But he'd rejected her, just like Lamar had rejected her.

He isn't like Lamar. He's nothing like Lamar. He's Devlin. He's Devlin.

Her chest ached with an unimaginable pain.

He doesn't want me. He doesn't love me.

She wanted to die. God help her, she wanted to die.

Devlin attacked the tree with all the pent-up frustration and anger that roiled inside him. Again and again he swung the ax, hacking away at the bark and the meat of the tree, tiny wood chips flying all around him. Sweat trickled down his spine. It beaded on his forehead. His muscles burned and his back ached, and still he kept at it. If he stopped, he would start thinking again.

And Devlin didn't want to think. He didn't want to remember.

If he thought about last night, about the look of wonder in Angelica's green eyes or the tiny cries of ecstasy that had slipped through her sensuous lips or the creamy softness of her skin or the beauty of her wine-colored hair . . .

If he thought about the way she had come to him and given herself to him . . .

If he thought about the way she made him feel, not just last night as they'd made love, but day in and day out, whenever he was with her or whenever he was apart from her . . .

If he thought about the cruel words he'd used to stop her declaration of love . . .

If he thought about any of it, he'd go mad.

And so he kept on working, kept on chopping down trees, mindless of the wide arc of the sun, mindless of the ticking away of the hours, mindless of the emptiness that encircled his heart.

Angelica had to force herself to get out of bed. She had no idea how long she had lain there trying to hide from reality. Her head was pounding and her body ached, but it was nothing compared to the pain she felt in her heart.

She splashed water into the washbowl and quickly sponged herself before putting on a clean blouse and skirt. It seemed a major effort to lift her arms to brush the snarls from her hair. Finally she settled for twisting the tresses into a knot at the nape.

Stepping outside, she was surprised to see that the sun was already positioning itself above the western skyline. Had she really stayed in bed all day?

She heard an ax striking against wood and followed the sound with her eyes until she found Devlin. She saw him raise the ax, then watched it fall. Rise and fall ... rise and fall ... rise and fall.

The pounding in her head increased, as if echoing the sound of the ax. She closed her eyes and drew a steadying breath.

She could survive this. She had been through hard times before. She'd survived them, and she could survive this, too.

Straightening her shoulders and holding her head high, she started across the field. The scent of newly turned dirt, pungent and warm, mingled with the fragrance of the tall cedars. Her footsteps were muffled by the rich earth.

She'd almost reached Devlin before he saw her. He hesitated a moment, his eyes locked with hers, then he looked at the tree once again and finished the swing of the ax. With slow, deliberate moves, he rested the ax on the ground, drew a kerchief from the pocket of his denims, and wiped his forehead. His bare chest glistened with sweat, defining the muscles that rippled beneath dark skin.

The silence was tense with unspoken feelings. She watched him, saw the way he avoided her eyes, and for a moment she almost hated him. Almost ...

"Bert should have brought Robby home by now," she said at last. "I'm going after him."

Devlin nodded without turning toward her.

She waited, hoping for some other form of reply, of acknowledgment. Hoping for something more.

He raised the ax above his shoulder and renewed his attack on the tree.

Defeated, Angelica turned away.

"Maud isn't here," Bert told Angelica. "Mary Brighton's took sick. Plumb wore out from all the bakin' she did for last night's shindig, I reckon. She's not a young thing like you."

Angelica didn't feel young. She felt old. Intolerably old.

"Anyway, Rose come over this mornin' an' told Maud she needed her help. I shoulda sent Robby home to you, but t'tell you the truth, the boy an' I've been havin' a right good time together."

Angelica started to lift Robby in her arms, then decided against it. He was getting so big. He was too heavy to carry anymore. She definitely didn't have the strength for it today.

She smiled weakly, knowing it wasn't a very good effort, but she hadn't the energy—or the heart—for anything more. "Tell Maud thanks for letting Robby stay with her last night."

"Angelica?" Bert laid a hand on her shoulder. "You all right?"

"I'm fine. Just a bit tired." Briefly she considered asking Bert how she could make Devlin love her. But, of course, she couldn't do that. She could never reveal the truth to Bert or anyone else. It would be bad enough when Devlin left her for good.

"Imagine you are. The ladies of Morgan Falls did themselves up proud last night. You gotta right t'be tired. I know Maudie is. I think she'd still be in bed if'n it weren't for Mary takin' sick." He patted Angelica's shoulder. "You get on home now and get some rest, too."

She nodded as she took hold of Robby's hand. "Let's go, honey."

"Bye! Bye!" Robby shouted gaily to Bert as his mother led him toward the door.

"Bye, Robby. You come see me agin real soon."

Somewhere beyond the hammering that grew ever louder in her head, she was aware of the tinkling sound of the bells above the shop door. She glanced up the road that would lead her home. It seemed to stretch endlessly before her.

With conscious effort, she took the first step in that direction.

Jonathan Bellows lived in an attractive two-story house on a quiet Denver street. While not wealthy, he was "pleasantly comfortable," as he liked to put it. He was a man of simple needs. He enjoyed his work, and through the years he'd built a solid reputation as a top-notch investigator, a reputation of which he was unashamedly proud. He had a cook and a housekeeper to take care of his home life. He had his club when he wanted companionship and entertainment.

He was also a man who took great pride in never being ill. Illnesses were the product of a weak spirit and a weaker mind, he'd told his housekeeper on more than one occasion. Sickness was a mere excuse for sluggards and sloths.

And so it was with some alarm that his housekeeper summoned the doctor to the Bellows residence early in the morning the day after his return from Washington Territory.

"I'm sorry to have bothered you on a Sunday, Dr. Horton, but I didn't know what else to do." Mrs. Hodgekiss wrung her hands as she led the way up the stairs. "Mr. Bellows has never seen a doctor in all the years I've worked for him, but I heard him mention that you attended his club."

"It's quite all right. I'm more than happy to look in on Bellows. Knowing how he feels about my patients and their ailments, I confess to being curious to see what has laid the man low." The doctor patted the woman's shoulder as they paused outside the bedroom door. "You wait right here while I examine him. If I need you, I'll call."

"Yes, sir."

While she waited, Mrs. Hodgekiss busied herself with dusting the hallway outside the master bedroom. She could hear the clicking of the grandfather clock that stood at the base of the stairs and wondered how long it would be. Time seemed to drag by, and with each passing minute her anxiety grew.

Her fears seemed to be confirmed when the door opened and the doctor stepped out into the hall, his face pinched with worry.

"What is it, Dr. Horton?" she asked.

He removed his eyeglasses before meeting her gaze. "I believe it's typhoid fever, Mrs. Hodgekiss."

The housekeeper drew in a sharp breath.

"I'm going to send a nurse over to care for him. Get rid of any milk you have in the house. It might be contaminated. And I want to know where you bought it so that I can stop the spread of the typhoid, if that's the source."

"But he's not had any milk. He's not eaten a thing. When he arrived yesterday, he said he wasn't hungry and went straight to bed. I couldn't even get him to drink his evening tea."

"Arrived? From where?"

"I don't really know, sir. Washington Territory, I think he said. But he never tells me much. His work is confidential, you know. He's been gone for some time. He may have been several places besides Washington."

The doctor rubbed his forehead. "Did he travel by train?"

"I believe so, sir."

"Lord," Dr. Horton said with a sigh. "He could have contracted it anywhere. In Washington. From a food vendor at any of the stops. Anywhere." He sighed again, then turned a piercing gaze upon the housekeeper. "Bellows speaks well of you, Mrs. Hodgekiss. He says you're a superb housekeeper. I want you to prove it. I want this house to be cleansed from top to bottom. Wash your hands before you touch any food. That goes for any of the other

staff as well. Throw out the food in the icebox.
Boil your water before drinking it. And don't
let anyone into this house except me and the
nurse."

"Yes, doctor."

"I'll be back with the nurse soon."

"Is there . . . is there anything I can do for Mr.
Bellows, sir?" Mrs. Hodgekiss asked as she
watched the doctor descend the stairs.

He glanced back at her. "If you're a religious
woman, Mrs. Hodgekiss, I suggest you pray."

Chapter Thirty-Four

Devlin looked at the freshly plowed furrows and waited for his now familiar feelings of satisfaction. They didn't come. Nothing he did had brought him any pleasure since he'd tossed his cruel words in Angelica's direction yesterday morning and marched out of the bedroom.

He han't seen or spoken to her today. When she'd returned from the Farlands' with Robby yesterday afternoon, she'd left the boy in his child-sized corral and retreated to the bedroom. When Devlin had opened the door later in the evening, intending to put Robby to bed, Angelica had mumbled for him to go away and leave her alone. So he and Robby had slept on bedrolls under the stars.

Remembering how it had felt having the child snuggled against his back during the night, he turned and glanced toward the fenced yard where Robby was playing with his puppy. Devlin grinned at the sight.

Robby caught him watching. "Pa!"

Possessive pride welled in his chest. Pa. Robby Branigan's father. It sounded so good.

If only it were true.

"Pa!" Robby ran over to the fence and peeked through at him, giggling as Domino nipped at his pant legs.

Devlin left the sorrel standing in the field, the reins wrapped around the plow, and walked toward the fence that kept the boy out of trouble. Once there, he leaned over and scooped Robby up into his arms, causing squeals of delight to fill the air.

"Your mother must be plenty angry, boy. I'm afraid I hurt her."

No, he wasn't just *afraid* that he'd hurt her. He *knew* he had. He'd wounded her just about as badly as he'd known how, just to protect himself.

"I didn't have any choice, you know. She's got to understand that I can't stay. I can't be her husband. I can't be your pa. It'll be better in the long run, doing it this way." He shook his head as his gaze moved to the house. "I can understand her ignoring me after what I did and said, but it's not like her to take it out on you. I suppose I'd better do some fast talking before the two of us die from my cooking."

Robby nodded solemnly as if he'd understood everything Devlin had said.

Devlin heard the sounds of a horse's hooves

striking the earth and turned around just as Torin Johnson's enormous workhorse lumbered into view. Torin didn't slow the animal's speed as it descended the hillside into the Branigans' valley. For an instant, Devlin feared the horse and rider would end up rolling down the incline.

But despite the horse's clumsy size, it was sure-footed, and it carried its rider down the hill and across the clearing without mishap, then plowed to a stop not far from Devlin, tossing up dirt clods several feet into the air.

Trouble rides a fast horse, Devlin thought as he looked at the young man's face. "Torin? What's wrong?"

"We have trouble in Morgan Falls, Mr. Branigan," Torin answered breathlessly. "Mrs. Brighton . . . Mrs. Farland . . ."

"What about them?"

"They are sick. Mr. Farland learned that there is typhoid fever in Snohomish, and he thinks—"

Devlin set Robby back into his pen and whirled toward the house. He didn't walk. He ran. He shoved open the cabin door, letting it crash against the wall as he crossed the small main room and let the bedroom door fly.

"Angelica?"

Anemic light filtered into the bedroom and onto the bed.

"Angelica?"

He slowed his steps now, even as he tried to still the panic that filled his chest. Somehow, he knew what he would find, even before he reached her side and pulled the blanket back from her face. He touched her forehead, then pulled his hand back as if it had been singed. She was burning up.

Angelica stirred. Glazed and feverish, her eyes lifted to meet his. "Robby?" she whispered hoarsely.

"He's fine. He's okay."

"My head . . . it hurts."

"I know."

She closed her eyes again.

Devlin stared down at her. She looked so pale, so small and helpless. And he felt every bit as helpless as she looked.

"Mr. Branigan?"

He turned to find Torin standing in the cabin doorway, holding Robby in his arms. "Stay there. Don't come in." He headed toward them. "Take Robby outside."

Torin backed away from the door. As soon as Devlin had stepped into the sunlight, Torin asked, "Mrs. Branigan, too?"

"Yes."

"Typhoid?"

"Yes." Devlin didn't have to wonder. He'd seen it before. He'd watched several die from it. He'd nearly died from it himself. "Torin, will you take Robby to your place? If we're lucky, he wasn't exposed to it and won't take sick."

"I will help, Mr. Branigan. I can—"

"No, you can't help. I've had typhoid. I'll be

safe. You might not be. You and your father and Robby just stay at your place. Don't let anyone come around. When the danger's over, I'll come for the boy." His gaze moved to Robby. "Take good care of him, Torin."

"I will, sir."

"If the doctor gets up to Morgan Falls, send him out here."

"I will, sir."

Clutching Robby to his burly chest, Torin returned to his steed and mounted up. He glanced back at Devlin, telling him with his eyes what he couldn't say with his voice. *And you take care of Angelica.*

Devlin nodded. "I will."

"What do you mean he can't see me?" Lamar exclaimed. "He sent me a note, advising me that he had important information." He waved the slip of paper that had arrived at his office two days ago.

"I'm sorry, sir," the housekeeper replied. "Mr. Bellows has taken to his bed. He's not to be disturbed."

Lamar pushed his way past the woman. He wasn't about to be put off any longer. The note had said Bellows had information about the boy Lamar wanted to adopt. That could only mean that the investigator had found Angelica and her son. "I won't keep him but a moment."

"Sir!" Mrs. Hodgekiss stepped into his path again. She placed her hands on her ample hips and thrust out her ponderous breasts as if they were battering rams. Her expression said quite clearly what she thought of Lamar Orwell. "You don't understand. Mr. Bellows might not live. He's got the typhoid fever."

Cold fingers of fear clamped about Lamar's throat. Long-forgotten memories from his childhood intruded. Memories of the epidemics that swept through the city tenements, wiping out entire families. He'd watched his mother die an agonizing and slow death. He'd lost two sisters to disease as well.

Cholera, yellow fever, smallpox, typhoid. Just the words made him break out in a cold sweat.

"I'll tell Mr. Bellows you were here, sir, when he's well enough to hear it." The housekeeper closed the door in Lamar's face.

Lamar stared at the door. Slowly the memories receded. Despising himself for allowing the recollections of his youth to return, he unconsciously summoned anger to replace his fear.

Damn Bellows anyway! Why couldn't he have waited another day before he took sick? This was going to make things inconvenient. He wanted the information about Angelica. Typhoid could take weeks to run its course, and death could as easily be the outcome as recovery. If Bellows died, Lamar would have to start searching all over again.

He swore as he turned around to face the street. Bellows had better recover. Lamar wanted to know about Angelica and her brat. He wanted to find them and take the boy away from her. That would teach her that she couldn't cross Lamar Orwell. And it would keep Penelope and her father off his back.

He grunted as he settled his hat onto his head, thinking of his horse-faced wife. He never should have hinted that he'd found a child for them to adopt. She would be after him constantly, wondering when she could see the boy. He'd have hell to pay if Bellows didn't pull through this, and soon.

He marched down the walk to his carriage, cursing the fates that continually seemed to be working against him.

Devlin laid another blanket over Angelica's shivering form. Only moments before, he had been sponging her forehead as she complained of the heat. He knew that the pattern of alternating chills and fever had only just begun. He knew that it would grow worse as the week progressed, that her fever would rise to frightening levels, that her head would ache until she thought it would explode.

He sat in the chair that he'd pulled close to the bed. He took her hand in his, holding it gently, as if any pressure might bruise it. He stroked the back of her hand, then turned it over and repeated the gesture across her palm. He felt the roughness of her hands and remembered how hard she'd worked to make a go of this farm.

"You're too beautiful for this sort of life," he said, his gaze moving to her pale face. "You should have a wealthy husband. Someone honorable and upstanding that you can be proud of. You should have a fine home with plenty of servants. You shouldn't have to settle for life with a gunslinger, scraping to survive on a measly little homestead and a two-room shack, wondering if men like Murphy will try to hurt you. You deserve better, Angel. You deserve the best."

He thought of her as she'd been the night of the barn dance, alive, vibrant. Her voice, crying out his name as they made love, seemed to echo in his head. How could two days make such a difference?

Her eyes opened, but he didn't think she saw him sitting there. Her gaze was unfocused. He leaned forward, gently calling her name, but she didn't look at him, didn't acknowledge that she'd heard him in any way.

Her eyes closed again, and he thought she'd fallen back to sleep. He released her hand, then pulled the blankets up over her arm, tucking the wool fabric snugly beneath her chin. Finally he stood and turned toward the bedroom door.

"I love you."

He froze, then whirled about. His gaze darted to her face, hoping ... But her eyes remained closed.

Had he only imagined that he'd heard her whispered words? Was it only because he wanted to hear them, now when it might be too late for her to ever say them again?

"Angel?" He leaned over her. "Angel?"

She didn't move, gave no sign that she'd heard him.

I love you, too, Angel.

The realization shook him to the core.

Or perhaps it wasn't the realization. Perhaps he'd known it all along.

Yes, he *had* known that he loved her. It was only admitting it that unnerved him. He'd tried hard enough not to face it. He'd run from it. He'd sought to leave her rather than acknowledge it. He'd struck out at her with cruel, hurtful words just to keep from facing the truth.

I love you, too, Angel.

It was easier to think the words the second time, but he knew he couldn't ever say them to her. He could never speak them aloud. To do so would only bring her more unhappiness. She deserved that wealthy, upstanding husband and a fine home. She would have them one day if he weren't around.

Devlin would stay by her now. He would fight to make her well again. But he wasn't going to stick around long enough for her to hate him because of what and who he was.

Angelica groaned again and began to toss restlessly. She shoved at the blankets, knocking them onto the floor.

Devlin didn't have to touch her forehead to

know that her temperature was rising. Knowing what had to be done, he picked up the bucket and went to fetch cool water from the stream.

Chapter Thirty-Five

By the end of the first week, Angelica's fever had risen to an alarming height, with no sign of abating. Her lips were dry and cracked, and her nose frequently bled. Her skin was covered with bright red spots, marking the places where the typhoid had eroded the blood vessels. She was tortured by an unappeasable thirst. Her normally husky voice became little more than a croak.

Devlin left her side only when it couldn't be avoided. He fed the horses, tossed scraps to Domino, and fetched more water to bathe Angelica's fevered body. He often forgot to feed himself and only remembered when his stomach growled relentlessly.

Everything within Devlin was focused on defeating the typhoid bacteria that was spreading through Angelica's system, attacking her and trying to steal her life. He talked to her constantly, whether or not she appeared awake. He reminded her of her stubborn spirit. He told her she had to keep on fighting. He spoke of Robby and what it was going to be like watching him grow into a man. He talked until he was hoarse, and still he talked on.

"Hang on, Angel. You've beaten everything else that ever tried to knock you down. You've beaten Lamar. He'll never find you and Robby now. You've beaten me, too. Now you've got to beat this. Just hang on a little longer."

A blanket of yellow sunshine spread over the quiet valley. It left glittering tracks upon the surface of the stream. It warmed the rich, dark brown soil. It cast shadows of tall trees across the green ferns and colorful wildflowers that bordered the cleared ground of the Branigan homestead.

But Devlin wasn't aware of any of it as he tossed a forkful of hay into the corral. His thoughts were still inside the cabin with Angelica.

How much longer could her body endure such a high fever? She seemed so weak already, yet he knew that she still had a long ways to go to recovery.

He closed his eyes and leaned against the fence rail. Twice before, he'd known the ravages of typhoid. The first time, he'd been sick with it himself. He didn't remember much about his illness except that there were times he'd wished he would die. The second time, he'd been in Chicago, arranging the sale of some cattle for his trail boss. The buyer had been one of the first to sicken. A doctor, soliciting help with the victims of the epidemic, had told Devlin he was immune to the disease since he'd had it before.

Devlin had never forgotten what it was like. He'd watched men and women, young and old, sweat and shiver their way through the disease. He'd watched many of them die. When the fevers went too high or lasted too long, they always died. Always.

"Mr. Branigan!"

He turned toward the shout and watched as Torin rode down the trail.

Torin reined in his horse while still some distance away. He glanced toward the cabin, then back at Devlin. "Mrs. Branigan, is she . . ."

"She's holding on."

"We heard from the doctor. He will not be able to come to Morgan Falls. The typhoid is very bad in Snohomish."

Devlin stepped away from the corral, squinting as he looked into the afternoon sunlight. "How are Mrs. Farland and Mrs. Brighton? Is anyone else sick?"

"No, no one else is sick." Torin's gaze dropped to the horse's neck. "Mrs. Brighton died last night."

Devlin felt a stab of pain in his chest. Trouble still rode a fast horse.

He pictured the stout, rosy-cheeked woman who had welcomed them so cordially into her home, treating them not as boarders but as a part of her family. Mary Brighton had been a woman of easy smiles and joyous laughter. She probably hadn't been more than fifty years old, if that. Now she was gone forever.

"Robby is fine," Torin added. "Papa is watching him. I thought I would come and work in your fields. You will fall too far behind." He dismounted. "I will take care of your livestock so you can take care of your wife."

Take care of your wife... take care of your wife...

Typhoid had killed Mrs. Brighton.

Take care of your wife... take care of your wife...

He wasn't going to let it take Angelica.

With a nod, he spun toward the cabin. He'd been away from her too long already.

It was so terribly hot in the theater. It was nearly impossible to remember her lines. Her leading man was speaking, but his voice was muffled. She strained to understand him.

Suddenly the theater was empty and she was alone on the stage. Her footsteps echoed against the balcony, returning to her like the ghosts of actors who had gone before. Fear crept into her heart, grating against her spine.

"I told you you couldn't leave me."

She tried to scream, but no sound came from her throat. She tried to run, but her shoes seemed nailed to the boards. Heart pounding, she watched as Lamar walked across the stage. Where his face should have been she saw only blackness, yet she knew it was him. She could feel him. She could feel the evil in his soul.

"I keep what's mine, Angelica. I told you that. Why didn't you listen? Why?"

Robby!

"You'll never see him again. You're not worthy to be a mother. You haven't a husband. Look at you. No one could love you. No one." He began to laugh.

No...no...it's not true. Devlin loves me. Robby loves me. It's not true...It's not true.

The laughter continued, filling her head, pounding against her temples. Laughing... laughing...laughing.

Stop! Please stop!

"Stop...please stop..."

Her words were so soft he could barely understand her. Devlin leaned forward and saw the tears streaming from the outer corners of her eyes.

"Stop...please stop..."

"Angelica." He brushed dark strands of hair away from her pale face. "It's all right, Angel. I'm here. I'm right here with you. Nothing's going to hurt you. It's all right."

"Please..." The sound was more whimper than anything.

Helplessly he continued to croon comforting words, hoping against hope that she could hear him.

* * *

Murphy's fingers bit into the flesh of her arms. Then he tore her dress and feasted his gaze on her body. She tried to scream, but once again she was mute. She wanted to run, but her hands and feet were bound and she couldn't move.

And then she heard the explosion. Devlin had saved her. Devlin had come in time and saved her.

Suddenly she realized there was blood everywhere. It was on her skin, her clothes, around her feet. It ran down her face, blinding her, turning her vision red.

Angelica looked at him. Her green eyes were alight with panic.

"The blood," she cried. "The blood. Get it off me. Please . . . get it off me."

"Angelica, there isn't any—"

"You shot Murphy. You shot him."

As suddenly as she'd awakened, her eyes closed and her body stilled. Devlin was left only with the memory of the terror that had filled her eyes, the horror his killing ways had brought to her dreams.

One day bled into another. Devlin stayed relentlessly by Angelica's side, leaving her only when forced to by the needs of her illness. He changed the bedding frequently, boiling the soiled sheets to sterilize them, hanging them in the sun to dry. He prepared broth and tried to tempt her to eat but met with little success.

He bathed her hot, rose-spotted body, always conscious of how alive and vibrant it had been such a short time before.

As the fever worsened, there were times when she was delirious, others when she was gripped by a stuporous calm. Occasionally she knew him. Usually she didn't. She had terrible nightmares. He could tell by the fear on her face as she thrashed weakly in the bed.

Sometimes he wanted to grip her by the shoulders and shout at her to wake up, to get well, to stop torturing him this way.

Sometimes he felt as if he himself might die as he saw her slipping further and further away from him.

And always he remembered that he loved her.

When Angelica opened her feverish eyes, she saw it waiting for her. It stood in the far corner, a black wraith cloaked in shadows. Perhaps it thought to hide from her, to take her by surprise, but her illness had not dulled her senses. Even should her eyesight have failed her, she still would have felt the presence of Death and known it waited for her.

Although it hurt to do so, she rolled her head to the side, her gaze finding Devlin. She'd known that he, too, would be waiting for her. Whenever she opened her eyes, he was there. His chin rested against his chest. His eyes were closed, and she knew he slept the sleep of exhaustion.

God in heaven, how she loved him.

"Dev?" she whispered through cracked lips.

He straightened instantly.

"Robby?"

He leaned forward, his ebony gaze caressing her face. "He's okay. He's with the Johnsons."

"You'll take care of him ... for me?"

"Sure. You know I will. And you'll be up and around in no time."

From the corner of her eye, she saw movement. A rustle of blackness. Death had stepped from the corner.

Angelica stared up at Devlin's beloved face. "It's come for me." She tried to lift her hand, wanted to touch him, but she hadn't the strength. "I'm not ready for it."

"For what, Angelica? What aren't you ready for?" He pressed a cool, damp cloth to her forehead.

She looked toward the corner again. The wraith had drawn closer still. "For Death," she answered hoarsely. "Do you see it there? In the corner ... It's been waiting ... for me. So dark ..."

"No. No, Angel, I don't see it. Listen to me. You're going to get well. You're not going to die."

Death took another step forward.

She was so tired. Her body ached. She hadn't even enough strength to keep her burning eyes open. "I ... love you. I wanted ... to be your ... wife ... so very much ..." She drew in a deep breath. "Would you ... have ... married me ... Dev? Would ... you ..."

"Angelica? Angelica?" Devlin gripped her by her shoulders. "Look at me, Angel."

Nothing. Not so much as a fluttering eyelash.

He glanced toward the corner of the room, almost expecting to see something dark and deadly waiting there, just as she'd said. But there was nothing but ordinary shadows.

His gaze returned to Angelica, and his heart nearly stopped. She seemed so utterly still. He couldn't detect a rise and fall of her chest.

"God, no!" he whispered. "Dear God, no. Don't let her die. I'll do anything. *Anything.* Please, God, don't let her die."

He pulled her to him, pressing her ear close to his lips, crushing her chest against his.

"I'll marry you, Angel, if that's what you want. Just don't die. Don't die ..."

He squeezed his eyes shut as he drew her head to his shoulder.

"God," he prayed, "if You'll pull her through this, I'll do whatever she wants. I'll be a farmer. I'll be a husband. I'll take care of her. I won't ever leave her again. I promise. I'll do anything. Just, please, don't let her die." He swallowed the thickness in his throat. "I know I've got no right to ask. I know what I am. But, God, I'll do my best to change, if that's what You want of me. Just don't take Angelica."

It was crazy, he knew, but he would have sworn he heard the whisper of the wind moving through the room. When he opened his eyes, it seemed that the corner wasn't quite as dark as before.

And then he heard her sigh.

He laid her back upon the bed, pressed his forehead against the blankets over her chest, and for the first time since he was a boy, Devlin Branigan wept.

Chapter Thirty-Six

Angelica was ravenous when she awoke. Through the bedroom doorway she could hear Devlin moving about the kitchen, and she could see sunlight on the floor. Bright sunlight, not the weak light of early dawn.

Why had he let her sleep so late? Why hadn't he wakened her so she could prepare his breakfast before he went out to work?

She tossed aside the blankets, rose from the bed, and immediately crumpled to the floor, a surprised cry slipping from her lips.

Devlin's tall figure filled the doorway. "What the . . ." He hurried toward her. "What on earth were you trying to do?" He lifted her off the floor, cradling her against his chest. "Why didn't you call me if you needed something?"

She met his scowling gaze. "I was hungry and thought I'd fix something to . . ." Her words trailed off into nothing, choked off by his stern expression.

"Do you have any idea how sick you've been?" He laid her on the bed.

"Sick?"

One dark eyebrow lifted.

She frowned, concentrating, and little by little, the images came to her. Images of Devlin sitting by her bed. Images of him trying to coax her to eat. Images of him holding a cup of hot broth to her lips or a cool compress to her forehead. Images of Devlin.

And then she remembered something else. Death had come for her, and Devlin had sent it away. That part was hazy, the images unclear. Yet she knew in her heart that it was true.

She looked up at him. Her gaze traced the shadows beneath his eyes, the shaggy length of his hair, the deep lines etched in his forehead. Did he look older or was he simply tired? No, it was something more than either of those. There was something different about him, she thought, but what was it?

His eyes, she thought at last. It was his eyes.

What was it about his eyes? They looked weary, red-rimmed, as if he'd gone days without sleep. But that wasn't what was different. It was something more. Something . . .

They were watching her with love.

Her heart skipped, almost faltered, then began to race from the sheer joy of discovery.

Devlin had learned to love her.

He straightened. "You stay put, and I'll bring you something to eat."

She smiled and nodded.

"Don't try to get up again."

She shook her head, and her smile grew.

He stared at her a moment longer, obviously confused by her strange response. "Stay put," he said firmly, as if to make sure she meant to obey. Then he turned on his heel and strode out of the bedroom.

Angelica closed her eyes, weariness stealing over her. But she didn't want to give into sleep again so soon. She wanted to savor her discovery a little longer.

Devlin loved her.

How long? How long had he loved her? Had he only just begun to feel that way, or had he loved her for a long time? Had he even realized his feelings for her yet, or was he still trying to deny them?

Again, thoughts of her illness flitted through her mind. Had she been ill as long as it seemed to her now? Had Devlin truly stayed by her side for days on end, caring for her so tenderly, so personally, or was it all an illusion, a residual of the illness itself? The harder she tried to analyze it, the harder it became for her to concentrate on the puzzle.

By the time Devlin returned to the bedroom carrying a tray, Angelica was fast asleep.

Devlin whistled as he tended to his evening chores, his thoughts never far from Angelica. He couldn't believe the change in her. Only three days ago, he'd thought he'd lost her. Today, she'd actually sat up for almost an hour. She'd eaten four bowls of soup, drank two glasses of milk, and complained that she would rather have had fried chicken and potatoes. She'd even asked him if he could help her wash her hair. He'd promised her he would do it in the morning.

Domino raced around the corner of the lean-to at just that moment. Long ears flapping and mouth open, the pup flew past him, then spun about and attacked Devlin's trousers, growling with as much ferocity as he could muster.

Devlin chuckled as he bent over and picked up the squirming canine. "You miss having Robby around, don't you, fella?" He ruffled Domino's ears. "Me, too. Maybe it's time Torin brought the boy home."

He realized then how often Angelica had asked about her son in the past couple of days. He supposed he'd ignored her hints because he'd wanted to have her to himself just a little longer. He'd come so close to losing her and now . . .

He glanced up, watching as sunset painted the clouds in varying shades of orange and pink and purple. The evening air cooled, and shadows lenghtened across the tilled earth of the Branigan homestead.

Devlin turned and looked at the house, wondering if Angelica remembered anything she'd said while the typhoid had tortured her with fever and chills. Did she remember that she'd said she loved him? Did she remember that she'd said she wanted to be his wife? Had she meant it, or had it only been part of the delirium?

He wished he knew.

Angelica was discouraged by her lingering weakness. She wanted to be able to get out of bed, to do things for herself. She wanted to be able to bathe and dress herself and brush her hair and look nice for Devlin.

If truth be told, above all else she wanted him back in her bed. She wanted him to lie beside her and hold her in his arms. She wanted to share the warmth of his body as they snuggled beneath the thick quilt. She wanted to feel his breath in her hair and hear his whispered endearments in her ear.

She wanted him. She wanted Devlin. Ah, yes, how very much she wanted Devlin. She wanted to touch him, to be a part of him, to feel . . .

She felt the heat rise in her cheeks. More clearly than any other moment in the weeks since, she remembered their night of lovemaking. Often, when she caught him watching her, when she saw the love in his eyes, she was filled with a yearning so strong, so poignant, it was almost painful. Even while she knew she hadn't yet the strength to make love to him, the desire was still there.

Even your *body isn't enough to make me stay . . .*

His words echoed once again in her head,

but they no longer carried the sting she'd felt when he first uttered them. The words had lost their ability to hurt her, for she knew now that he hadn't meant them, that he'd spoken out of fear or regret or uncertainty. Yet, she wondered if those same words weren't the cause of Devlin's silence regarding his love. She wondered if they weren't what kept him from professing his true feelings for her.

She wished she knew what to say to him now. She wished she knew how to thank him for what he'd done for her, how to tell him she loved him and wanted him to stay with her forever. She wished she knew how to draw his own confession of love from him.

Angelica sighed as she closed her eyes. She was too tired to work it out in her mind just yet. For now, it was enough to know he loved her. She would find a way later to help him say the words.

After all, they had an entire lifetime ahead of them. That was something she believed with all her heart.

Three days later, Devlin carried Angelica outside and set her on a blanket spread by the gurgling stream. Then, without a word, he left her there, returning to the house with purposeful strides.

Angelica turned her face up to the sun, loving the glorious vitality she felt in its warming rays. It seemed like forever since she'd seen the sun, since she'd been outside the dim, closed bedroom. She felt new strength seeping into her blood, into her bones, and reveled in it. She breathed deeply of the fresh mountain air.

Glancing down at her dress, she silently lamented the way the fabric hung on her emaciated frame. She'd almost wasted away. She was hardly anything more than a rack of bones. She'd seen herself in the mirror for the first time yesterday—sunken hollows beneath her eyes and in her cheeks, her hair dull and limp—and the image had frightened her. More than any time since she'd awakened from the fever-induced stupor, she'd realized how truly close to death she'd been.

But today wasn't a day for such grim thoughts. She hadn't died. She was alive, and Devlin was with her. He loved her. Nothing else could possibly matter beyond that.

She glanced toward the cabin, wondering where Devlin had gone and what he was up to. She'd known he was keeping a secret about something when he entered the bedroom this morning and asked if she'd like to go outside later in the day.

It pleased her to know him so well that she could read the excitement in his eyes. It pleased her very much indeed.

He stepped through the cabin doorway, one hand carrying a black skillet covered with a checkered cloth and the other hand carrying a basket. She knew, of course, what was in the skillet. She'd smelled the delicious odors coming from the kitchen while she lay in bed. Her stomach growled just thinking about it.

Angelica grinned as Devlin drew closer to her. "Fried chicken?" she asked.

"Fried chicken." He set the skillet on the ground beside the blanket. "I'm afraid it didn't turn out too good."

"I'm sure it's delicious."

Devlin knelt beside her and pulled back the checkered cloth, revealing the unevenly cooked pieces of meat. Most of them looked suspiciously close to raw, although a few held some promise of achieving a nice, golden brown if only they'd been allowed to cook a while longer.

Angelica raised her eyes from the unappetizing chicken in the skillet to Devlin. For a moment they merely stared at each other, and then she giggled. She tried to stop, but it escaped her anyway. She covered her mouth, as if that would hide the sound.

He looked wounded.

"Oh, Dev, I'm so sorry," she managed to say, her laughter continuing, growing. "You tried so hard to give me what I wanted. I know you did, but ... but ..." She tried again to swallow her mirth.

Stiffly he replied, "I can see you don't think much of the chicken. Perhaps you'll like these better." He pulled the cloth from the basket as he spoke, this time revealing biscuits, charred to a crisp.

Angelica tried. Lord knows, she tried. But the gale of laughter couldn't be stopped. She picked up one of the rock-hard, solid black biscuits and held it in the palm of her hand.

"I guess this means I'm about to lose my job as cook on the Branigan farm?" he asked, a suspicious lift curving the corners of his mouth as he looked at her.

Still not certain if he'd been hurt by her laughter, she sobered enough to reply, "Except when we want soup. You make a delicious soup. Honestly."

"But you don't care for my chicken and biscuits, huh?" There was no mistaking his smile as he shook his head. "And I was so sure you would."

In unison their gazes dropped to the unsavory food he'd brought out to her, and in unison they began to laugh. They laughed until tears ran down Angelica's cheeks and Devlin's ebony eyes sparkled with amusement.

"It's that damned fireplace," Devlin managed to say as the laughter waned. "How have you managed to cook anything edible since we moved in here?"

She shook her head helplessly, mentally picturing him pulling the burnt biscuits from the oven.

"Well, I'm telling you now. First bit of profit we turn, we're buying a stove. I figure we should get some lumberjacks in here. A couple of Bert's boys work for a logging outfit down river. Maybe they'd be willing to do it. They could clear the ground for farming a lot faster than I can do it alone, and we would make some money from the sale of the trees. Maybe we still couldn't get the stove until next summer, but it wouldn't hurt to try."

Angelica's laughter had disappeared. She stared at Devlin, a strange feeling of detachment overtaking her as she realized what he was saying. He was talking about "we," about what they should do on the farm, about buying a stove by next summer. He was talking about staying.

Devlin stretched out on the blanket, lying on his back, one arm beneath his head as he stared up at the sky. "We're going to need to add onto the house by next year, too. Robby's growing fast, and he'll need a room of his own before long."

"Ah-huh."

"I thought we could put a door in the south wall and add the room there. What do you think?"

"Yes." That seemed to be all she could say. At the moment, she felt too dizzy and light-headed to think of anything more profound.

She lay down on the blanket beside Devlin.

"Feels good, doesn't it? Warm without bein' hot."

"Yes," she whispered again.

"Look up there." He pointed. "Do you see it?"

Angelica followed the direction of his finger until she spied the outstretched wings of an eagle. The majestic bird circled above the treetops, swooping low, then climbing higher once again.

It was a little like the reaction of her heart as Devlin drew her close against his side and slipped his arm beneath her head.

Jonathan Bellows entered his office accompanied by the vocal protests of his housekeeper. "You shouldn't be workin' so hard, Mr. Bellows. The doctor told you to stay in bed, and here you are, workin' two days in a row. If it weren't for that Mr. Orwell..."

He closed the door firmly.

The woman waiting in the chair in front of his desk did not turn her head toward the doorway nor did she indicate in any other manner that she had either heard him enter or heard Mrs. Hodgekiss's objections.

As he crossed the room and stepped behind his large oak desk, he tugged at the front of his wool jacket, even though he knew it was impossible to make it look right. He'd lost far too much weight during his illness, and now his expensive custom-made suit hung on him like a tent.

He hadn't liked looking like this when Lamar Orwell had come to see him the day before. He liked it even less when he was meeting a new client.

Bellows studied the woman a moment before sitting on the chair behind his desk. Her identity was hidden behind a heavy blue veil that swathed her face as well as her fashionably large hat. She wore a striped wool gown in golden brown shades. The bodice was trimmed with a blue velvet vest and high collar. Her hands were clothed in fine kid gloves.

"Thank you for seeing me, Mr. Bellows." She sat forward on the chair, allowing room for the ample bustle of her gown. "Your housekeeper told me you've just recovered from an illness. I wouldn't have insisted on seeing you if the matter wasn't of some importance."

"That's quite all right, Mrs. . . ." His voice rose in question.

"Miss Pen," she provided.

He scribbled the name on a piece of paper. "And what is it I can do for you, Miss Pen?"

She reached into her blue velvet reticule and pulled out a thick envelope. Leaning forward, she pushed it across the desk. Bellows picked it up and opened it. It was filled with money.

"There's two thousand dollars in there, Mr. Bellows, as a retainer for your services. I will pay you two thousand more if you are able to supply me with the information I want. I will pay you a bonus if I feel you have told me everything you can possibly learn."

He swallowed hard. "What information do you need, Miss Pen?"

"I want to know everything you can tell me about an actress named Angelica Corrall."

Bellows dropped his gaze to the money in the envelope and felt his mouth go dry. "Just what do you mean by everything?"

"I want to know about her past, her family,

her childhood. I want to know about her activities when she was in Denver a few years ago. I want to know where she went when she left our fair city and what she's done since then." The woman tightened the drawstrings on her reticule. "I want to know about the people in her life. Her friends. Any family." There was a pause. "The men."

"Well...I..."

The woman rose gracefully to her feet. "I have every confidence that you are the *one* man who can provide me with the information I want, Mr. Bellows. I'm also certain that you won't reveal anything about my visit to anyone else."

"Of course not, but Miss Pen, I'm not sure that I should—"

"I promise you, sir, that I mean Miss Corrall no harm. The information is for my eyes only."

"Well, I—"

"If I'm pleased with your work, Mr. Bellows, the bonus will be *most* rewarding. I will let you know how to contact me. Good day, sir." She swept from the office without a backward glance.

Bellow's gaze fell from the empty doorway to the envelope in his hand. Two thousand dollars and he had yet to say a word. What information about Angelica Corrall could be so important to this Miss Pen that she would offer so great a reward?

He frowned.

It couldn't be a coincidence that she'd chosen him. This woman had to know something about his investigation for Lamar. But what did she know? And how had she found out?

He pulled the green bills from the envelope and fanned them between his fingers. There had to be a logical explanation. If he just gave it enough thought, he would discover the truth. He was sure of it.

And then, suddenly, he knew why this woman had come to him. He knew as certainly as if she'd never bothered with that heavy blue veil. He knew it as well as he knew his own name.

He thought of the less than reputable tasks he'd performed for Lamar over the years. He thought of how very much he'd wanted to tell the man that he couldn't work for him any longer. He thought of what this money meant to him now and why this woman wanted the information.

He grinned.

"Well, *Miss Pen*, it looks like you've hired yourself a detective. And I think I can tell you just what you want to know." He stuffed the money back into the envelope and placed it into his suit coat pocket, then rose from his chair. "Almost makes a man feel sorry, even for a crook like Lamar."

Chapter Thirty-Seven

Robby tore away from Torin the minute his feet touched the ground.

"Mama! Mama!"

With choppy, short-legged strides he ran across the grassy stretch of earth and tossed himself into his mother's waiting arms.

"Oh, Robby," Angelica cried as she crushed him to her, "I've missed you."

"Missed you," he proclaimed in return.

"Let me look at you." She held him away from her, her gaze moving slowly over his face, looking for any small change that only a mother would notice after not seeing her child for nearly four weeks. "Oh, you're such a big boy."

Devlin stepped out of the cabin, stopping behind Angelica's chair placed off to one side of the doorway.

Robby's attention shifted to the tall man.

"Pa!" He immediately strained toward Devlin.

Reluctantly Angelica let go of her son and watched as Devlin lifted him high above her.

"Tory's house," Robby said as he pointed toward Torin. "I stayed Tory's house."

"I know," Devlin answered, squeezing him tightly.

Angelica turned her head to see Torin walking toward the cabin. His face was flushed. His gaze was fastened on the ground. He paused while still a few yards away.

"You are well, Mrs. Branigan?" he asked.

"Yes, Torin, I am well."

"My father and I, we have prayed for you." His complexion reddened further. "I am glad you are all right."

"Torin?" Angelica leaned forward, held out a hand toward him. She waited patiently until he garnered the courage to step forward and take it. "There's no way I can ever thank you enough for taking care of Robby for me. If anything had happened to him..." She squeezed his fingers. "You're my *very* dear friend, and I'll never forget what you've done for me." She glanced up at Devlin and Robby. "For what you've done for us," she added softly.

Devlin's gentle smile was almost a caress.

Torin pulled his hand from her grasp and stepped backward, his gaze once more locked on the ground near his feet.

"Have you heard how Mrs. Farland's doing?" As Devlin spoke, he returned Robby to Angelica's arms.

"Mr. Farland told me she is much better. Rose Farland has stayed in town to help care for her, but Mrs. Farland says there is no need for it. She says Rose should be resting before the baby comes."

Angelica shook her head. Poor Rose. Losing her mother to typhoid and almost losing her mother-in-law as well. And Rose so close to delivering her baby. She wished she'd been able to help.

"I should go visit Maud. To see if there's something I can do," she said thoughtfully.

Devlin's hand closed over her shoulder. "Not yet. Not till you're stronger."

The tenderness in his voice made her heart constrict. If Torin hadn't been standing there, watching and listening, she would have asked Devlin if he loved her. She was tired of waiting to hear him say the words she knew were true.

She would also have asked him if he meant to marry her.

I'll marry you, Angel, if that's what you want. Just don't die.

Sometimes she could hear those words echoing in her head. Sometimes she would have sworn that he'd spoken them to her while she was ill, and then she would wonder if it were only part of a dream, if she were merely wishing she'd heard them. Everything was such a blur from those days and weeks she'd lain in bed, caught in the fever's grip. It was hard to separate the dreams and nightmares from reality now.

She should be content just knowing he loved her, she told herself, but she wasn't. She wanted more. She wanted forever.

Devlin stood behind Angelica as she tucked Robby into bed for the night. She leaned over and kissed the boy's forehead, smoothing back his hair with her fingertips.

"Good night, sweetheart," she whispered. "Mama loves you."

"Ni', Mama." Robby's umber eyes moved to Devlin, almost expectantly.

"Good night, son."

"Ni', Pa," Robby mumbled, then rolled onto his side and closed his eyes. Within a heartbeat, he appeared to be asleep.

Devlin felt a surge of emotion. He couldn't have loved the boy more if Robby had been his own blood kin. "Good night, son," he whispered again.

Devlin glanced at Angelica, marveling at her beauty even after so long an illness. Her dark red hair fell in thick waves over her shoulders and down her back. Her complexion was flawless, if a bit too pale, and there was new sparkle in her green eyes now that her son was home with her. Still, he could see that she was weary.

"It's time you were back in bed, too," he told

her. "It's been a long day."

She turned her head and looked up at him. "Are you turning in?"

"After I've seen to the horses." He stepped away from her. "I'll try not to wake you when I come in." With that, he turned and strode from the bedroom.

The evening air was pleasant, the heavens clear and star-studded. A sliver of moon hung suspended above the treetops.

Devlin jammed his hands into the pockets of his trousers as he made his way swiftly toward the lean-to. He couldn't explain the sudden sense of panic he'd felt back inside the house. He just knew he was afraid.

No, that wasn't true, he thought as he leaned his forearms on the top rail of the corral and stared at the buckskin and sorrel geldings. He *could* explain it.

He was afraid because he'd begun thinking in terms of a future with Angelica, yet she had never again said that she loved him, never indicated that she wanted him to stay beyond the terms of their bargain. He'd promised God he'd do whatever she wanted him to do. What if it turned out she wanted him to leave?

He remembered her terror the night she'd dreamed about Murphy. He remembered the way she'd pleaded with him to get rid of the blood. She'd looked at him with horror. *You shot him.*

He'd thought then that she must hate him.

He'd thought then that she would never want to look at him again. It was just as he'd said. He was a gunslinger. He belonged with others like him, not with a woman like Angelica.

Devlin laid his forehead against his arm, feeling another wave of confusion.

Yes, he'd expected her to hate him, but instead, days later, she'd looked at him and told him she loved him. She'd asked him if he might have married her.

Heaven help him, she'd made him believe, if only for a little while, in a better future. She'd made him believe he could really forget his past. He'd even sworn to God that he would change, that he would become the man she wanted, if only He would let her live.

But what if he couldn't change? What if Angelica had realized it and no longer wanted him? Or worse, what if she'd been delirious, perhaps even thought she was speaking to someone else? What if she hadn't meant what she'd said or hadn't meant to say it to him?

Coward, his mind taunted.

He turned and stared at the cleared land. He wanted this. He wanted Angelica for his wife. He wanted Robby for his son.

He looked toward the cabin, pale yellow light spreading out from the open doorway. Angelica was inside.

He wasn't a coward. He'd never turned away from a fight in his life, and he wasn't about to start with this one. This one wouldn't be fought with guns and he was plenty unsure of himself, but he wasn't going to give up without at least giving it a good try.

"I love you, Angelica, and I mean to stay, if you'll let me."

With purposeful strides, he headed back toward the cabin.

After Devlin left the bedroom so abruptly, Angelica sat down on the side of the bed. She stared across the room at her sleeping son in his cot.

That's where Devlin had been sleeping ever since she first become ill. Now he had made himself a bed on the floor. It seemed he was doing all he could to avoid her.

Could she be wrong about his feelings for her?

No, she silently answered her own thought. *No, I'm not wrong.*

She rose and crossed to his makeshift bed, quickly bending down to pick up the blankets and pillow. She carried them back across the room and dropped the blankets on the floor. Then she kicked them underneath the bed. The pillow she placed next to her own.

They were going to talk about this tonight, she decided. She wasn't going to continue wondering what he meant each time he opened his mouth to speak or worrying whether or not he intended to stay.

Angelica heard his footsteps as he entered the cabin, then listened as the door closed behind him. She sank onto the side of the mattress, feeling suddenly weak and apprehensive. She tilted her chin in a show of courage, designed more for herself than for Devlin.

He paused in the doorway, his ebony gaze darting across the room to meet hers. "I thought you might be asleep."

"I was waiting for you. We need to talk."

"Yes, we do."

Angelica's fingers tightened around the footboard. "Devlin, I..."

"Angelica, I..."

They both broke off at once.

"Let me go first," Devlin said softly, "or I might never get it said."

Angelica's mouth was dry. "All right," she whispered.

He took a step into the bedroom. Light and shadows played across his handsome face. His mouth was set in a grim, determined line. His feet were braced apart, as if he were prepared for a physical blow from some unseen foe.

"You know what I am, Angelica. You've seen it for yourself. I've used my gun as a way of life for a lot of years. Oh, I can say I've stayed inside the law, but that doesn't change what I've done. You hired me to protect you and Robby, to get you here and to help you start over, but just by being with me, I've put you both at risk."

"Devlin, it doesn't..."

He held up a hand. "Let me finish."

She nodded, afraid of what he was about to say.

"I never will know when someone else with an old grudge or a determination to gain a reputation as a gunfighter might turn up. It makes my future uncertain." He took another step forward. His voice lowered. "I've lived hard, Angel. I've done a lot of things I'm not proud of. I don't know that I have anything good left to offer anyone."

Her heart started to pound in her chest.

"I tried to leave you once, but the truth is, I'd like to stay. God knows, you wouldn't be getting much if you allowed it. You'll probably regret it because I don't know if I can change, if I can be the type of man you'd want. I might just end up hurting you."

Angelica rose from the bed. "What is it you're trying to say, Devlin?"

"I'm trying to say I'd like you to be my wife, if you'll have me."

"Why?" The single word came out a strangled whisper.

"Why?" he echoed.

For what seemed an eternity, he stared at her, their gazes locked. Neither seemed to breathe. Neither moved. It seemed to Angelica that her heart had stopped beating as she waited for his reply.

She didn't know how it happened, wasn't aware that he'd stepped closer. Just, suddenly, he was holding her. Suddenly, he was pressing his lips against her hair and whispering the words she'd longed to hear.

"Because I love you, Angel. Because I love you."

Chapter Thirty-Eight

Angelica had never been so frustrated in all her life.

Since their friends in Morgan Falls already thought they were married, Devlin and Angelica couldn't just go to the preacher in Snohomish to tie the knot. Devlin thought it better that they go to Seattle where both of them were strangers, but he wasn't certain how long it would be until they could leave the farm for a few days.

In the meantime, he had laid out his makeshift bed on the floor once again.

"I may have forgotten it before," he'd told her when she'd objected, "but my mother brought me up to act like a gentleman and to treat a lady like a lady. We're going to do things right from now on, Angelica. I'm not getting into your bed again until we're properly and legally wed." He'd grinned wickedly as he'd drawn her into his embrace. His voice had been husky as he'd added, "I couldn't share your bed without doing a lot more than sleeping."

Tingles of desire tortured Angelica as she remembered the way he'd kissed her then.

She uttered an unladylike curse beneath her breath as she walked along the track from the Branigan homestead to the main road. If they couldn't leave for Seattle soon, she was going to have to seduce him again—and to heck with how his mother had raised him, to heck with what was right and proper. Either Devlin was going to make love to her or she was going to go stark raving mad.

Why, she wondered, with so many other things clouded in her memory by the typhoid's raging fever, did she have to remember their night of lovemaking so clearly? She wished she'd forgotten it completely. Knowing what was being withheld from her made the waiting all the more agonizing.

With sheer will and determination, Angelica forced her thoughts elsewhere.

First she thought about how wonderful it felt to be out walking. She felt stronger with each passing day. Her appetite was certainly healthy. She ate enough for three women her size and was still always hungry. Very soon her figure would properly fill out her dresses again. In fact, if she didn't control her eating, she would be too large for her own clothes before long.

She grinned, wondering if Devlin would love a plump wife.

She shook her head, pulling her thoughts away from Devlin once more.

This time her musings moved ahead to Morgan Falls. She was anxious to see Maud after so long a time. Torin had brought news of her friend's improvement, but Angelica was impatient to see for herself. She still couldn't bear the thought of Mary Brighton being gone. Perhaps it was harder to face because she hadn't been able to attend the funeral and say her own proper farewells.

"Mrs. Branigan! Angelica!"

She stopped where the trail met the road and looked to her right. Rebecca Newton and her oldest daughter, Carolina, walked toward her, baskets in hand.

As soon as they reached her, Rebecca took hold of Angelica's hand. "Oh, my dear, we were terribly worried when we learned you'd been stricken with the typhoid. We're delighted to see you looking well."

"Thank you, Mrs. Newton."

"Thank God your husband returned when he did. I shudder to think if you'd been out there alone with no one to care for you." Rebecca released her hand. "And thank God the epidemic didn't spread. I've heard there are many dead in Snohomish. We were lucky hereabouts. We've just been to see Mrs. Farland. We took her some of Carolina's preserves. That must be where you're headed now. To see Mrs. Farland."

"Yes. How is she?"

"I couldn't believe it. She hardly looks as if she's been sick, except for being thinner. I think Mr. Farland's going to have a difficult time convincing her to rest and stay out of the store." Rebecca patted Angelica's shoulder. "You've lost weight, too, my dear. Remember, it isn't healthy to be so thin. Do take care of yourself."

"I will."

"Mrs. Branigan?" Carolina said softly.

Angelica's gaze moved to the strawberry blonde.

"Is Torin Johnson still working for you?" The girl glanced at her through lowered lashes, obviously uncomfortable about asking after the boy.

"Yes. A few days a week."

"When you ... when you see him, will you tell him I ... I said hello. I haven't seen him since the barn dance."

Angelica smiled. "I'll tell him."

Rebecca's eyes twinkled as she looked at her daughter, then at Angelica. "Well, we must be getting home. Do take care of yourself. And you and that husband of yours come callin' when you can."

"We will."

The two women moved on. A moment later they disappeared beyond a curve in the road.

So, Angelica thought as she turned once

more toward Morgan Falls, her idea for the barn dance hadn't been for naught. Torin *had* caught the eye of at least one young lady of the district. Perhaps she could find an errand for Torin to run that would just *happen* to take him up to the Newton farm.

She grinned to herself. She wondered if all women in love automatically became match-makers.

"Seattle?" Maud repeated. "When?"

"I'm not sure. Just as soon as we can get away." Angelica poured some more tea into her cup. "Devlin has some business to take care of and he doesn't want to leave me at home alone. At least, not yet."

Maud harrumphed. "I should say not. He was gone for far too long the last time."

"We fell so far behind while I was ill. We've a lot of ground yet to clear. Devlin says we must get it done before winter or next year's crops will never be enough." Angelica sighed. "Maybe we'll have to wait until fall to go to Seattle."

Maud seemed to be contemplating some-thing of great seriousness as she stared at the dregs in the bottom of her teacup. When she glanced up, she leaned forward in her chair. "Angelica, I've got no doubt that Bert would scoff at what I'm about t'say, but I swear it's the truth. I've always tried my best to keep my nose out of other people's business, and I've tried to do the same with you and Devlin. But

I'd be lyin' if I said I hadn't noticed that things ain't been right between you and that man o' yours for some time."

Angelica said nothing in response.

"I think this trip you got planned to Seattle is just the thing you two young folk need to put things right again. And I think you need to go real soon, too. The farmin' will get done, one way or another, and you need to think 'bout the two o' you for the present."

You don't know how right you are, Maud, Angelica thought. The trip would make her Mrs. Branigan, and she could stop living this lie with her friend, for one thing.

"But what you don't need is a young'n taggin' along," Maud continued. "Why don't you just leave Robby here with me when you go? That way, you an' Devlin can have some time for sparkin'. Make a real holiday of it."

"Oh, Maud, I couldn't do that."

The older woman reared back in her chair. " 'Course, you could."

"But you've been sick—"

"And you haven't? You think, just because I'm older, that I'm not goin' t'be myself again? I took care of Robby before, and I can jolly well take care of him now."

"But there's more to think of than that. Rose will be having her baby soon, and she'll need your help. I just couldn't impose—"

Maud twisted in her chair and shouted, "Bert!"

Her husband appeared instantly in the doorway to the store.

"You tell Angelica that we want to keep Robby here with us while she and that husband o' hers run down to Seattle for a spell. She seems to think I couldn't take care of that youngster anymore."

Angelica was having a hard time arguing with the woman. Not simply because Maud was so determined, but because Angelica couldn't have wanted anything more than a few days alone with Devlin for a honeymoon. She loved her son, and she'd missed him while he was staying with the Johnsons during her recuperation, but it would be heaven to have Devlin all to herself for the first few days of their marriage. She couldn't believe her secret wish was being handed to her so easily, almost as if it were fate.

"No point in arguing with her, Angelica," Bert said with a wry smile. "I never would've thought it possible, but since she's got her strength back, Maudie's twice as stubborn as ever before. You might as well just bring the boy on over and be off with you 'cause she'll have it her way, no matter what you or I say."

Angelica ignored the twinge of guilt she felt for deceiving her friends. She wasn't hurting them by her silence. In fact, she was making things right. As soon as she could get to Seattle, she would be Mrs. Devlin Branigan.

"Well," she said softly, "since there's no point in arguing..."

Maud sat back, a look of satisfaction lighting her face. "I knew you'd see the wisdom of it. You just get that boy over here to me and be on your way. We'll see that everything's taken care of for you."

Lamar pushed the sheer curtains away from the window and looked down on the busy Denver street. He ground his teeth in silent frustration as he spun back toward his desk.

Why was he saddled with so many idiots and incompetents? Didn't anyone take their responsibilities seriously?

Jonathan Bellows, for instance. Where was the man when he needed him? First, he had nearly died from typhoid fever, which could have made Lamar start from scratch with another investigator. Then, after making a brief report to Lamar that Angelica, her son, and her husband were living in some godforsaken place called Morgan Falls, Bellows had left town. When Lamar had returned to tell him how to proceed, he'd learned from Bellow's housekeeper that the fool had gone off on business for another client.

Another *client*! The cretin had no business taking on other clients. Lamar paid him far more than he was worth, and Bellows should damn well be available when Lamar wanted him.

He ground his teeth again.

Damn Angelica! Damn her for every last problem that he'd faced since she ran off to

Washington. She'd been his woman, and Lamar Orwell didn't let anyone else have something that was his, even if he didn't want it—or *her*—any longer. Angelica should have remembered that. Hadn't he taken her to Wood Bluff himself? Hadn't she understood that *that* was where he'd wanted her to stay?

Fool woman!

Lamar swept his arm across the top of his desk, sending blotter and paper and pen flying.

Idiots, all of them!

He sat in his leather-upholstered chair, his thoughts turning to his wife. As if he hadn't enough problems, he also had to deal with Penelope. She had been driving him crazy about the little boy they were going to adopt, wondering when Lamar would be bringing him home.

Lamar leaned back, closed his eyes, and drew a deep breath as he massaged his temples. There was only one thing for it. He would have to see to things himself. He couldn't count on anyone besides Bellows to handle such a delicate matter. This had to be handled with extreme caution, and the fewer people who knew about it, the better. Lamar couldn't take any chances that Alexander would find out about Angelica and that brat of hers. The old man was a most unforgiving sort and would never tolerate his son-in-law's transgressions.

How much simpler things would be once Alexander was dead. Lamar would be in charge of the vast Venizelos fortunes then. His father-in-law's will would, of course, leave everything to Lamar. And once he was in control, he wouldn't have to worry if Penelope knew about Angelica or any of his other women. Hell, he wouldn't even have to ever see her again. She could rot in that house of hers for all he cared.

If Alexander weren't surrounded by so many loyal to him, Lamar would have been tempted to try to speed along his demise, but he'd realized long ago that it was smarter for him to bide his time and play the devoted husband to the old man's homely daughter.

In the meantime, he thought, there was a little matter he needed to see to in Washington Territory.

Chapter Thirty-Nine

In the pale light of early morning, Angelica gave Robby another tight hug before passing him into Maud's waiting arms.

"Be a good boy," she called as she walked up the ramp onto the steamship *Sarah Jane.* "Mama will be home soon. I love you."

Devlin's voice was gentle, tolerant. "We won't be gone all that long, Angelica. Robby'll hardly have a chance to miss us. Not with Maud stuffing him full of cookies and spoiling him with presents the way she always does."

"I know." She glanced up at him. "It just seems we've been apart so much lately. I feel so guilty, leaving him behind again."

"We could still take him with us."

She loved Devlin enough already, of course, but she loved him even more for suggesting it. She shook her head. "No. I think it best if this time be ours alone."

His arm tightened around her shoulders as

his eyes darkened. It was almost as if she were being siphoned into their swirling black depths. She felt her body weakening in response. Her stomach twirled and spun. Her knees wobbled, and it was only his arm that held her upright.

"Yes." His voice was husky. "I believe it is better if we have this time to ourselves."

His unspoken promise of what was awaiting her after the wedding left her body quivering with anticipation. Impatiently, she wondered how long it would take them to reach that preacher in Seattle. No matter how quickly, it wouldn't be fast enough.

With a loud scrape and a bang, the boarding ramp was pulled clear of the landing. The steamer blew its horn as it left the Snohomish pier. Angelica jumped and her gaze darted back to the trio waiting on the dock.

"Have a wonderful time," Maud shouted, waving her free hand madly. "And don't you worry about a thing. We're gonna be just fine."

Standing behind his wife, Bert also raised his arm in farewell.

Angelica brought her careening desires under control long enough to return their good-byes. "We'll be back in a week," she called. "Thank you for keeping Robby."

Maud's reply was muffled by the sounds of the steamship and the churning river. "Don't hurry on our account. Just have yourself a nice holiday."

Angelica waved one last time as the steamship rounded the bend in the river, removing the landing from view. She felt foolish for the tightness in her throat and the glitter of tears in her eyes.

Devlin didn't know what to say to her. She looked so unhappy.

Old insecurities raised their nasty heads and whispered to him that she was probably having second thoughts about marrying him, that he would never be able to make her happy, that she would regret this decision for the rest of her life.

He tightened his grip on her shoulder, as if afraid she would suddenly bolt away from him, as if at any moment he could lose her.

Angelica tilted her head to look up at him. Wisps of burnished auburn hair fluttered against her milky skin and kissed the back of her neck. Tip-tilted green eyes were wide and clear. The smile curving her full mouth was tempered with sadness.

"I've never been separated from Robby until this summer when I was too ill to care for him. It feels strange, leaving him on purpose, that's all." She turned her whole body toward him, slipping easily into his embrace. "I love you, Devlin," she whispered. "I hope the *Sarah Jane* is a fast steamer."

His own words of love seemed to catch in his throat, held there by his self-doubts, but his arms drew her closer as he kissed her forehead. "I hope so, too."

* * *

Angelica lost count of the number of logging camps they passed on their trip down river. Time and again, mingled with the chug of the steamship and the lapping sounds of the river, she heard the song of the saws, the bite of the axes, and the sobering crash as another mighty red fir or cedar fell to earth.

Standing at the rail, she stared across the infinite green sea of towering trees. "Will they cut them all down before they're through?" she wondered aloud.

"Not in our lifetime." Devlin leaned his forearms on the railing. "Nor in our children's or our grandchildren's."

"It seems endless, the forest."

"Nothing is endless."

Her heart skipped. *Except my love for you.*

As if he'd heard her thoughts, he drew closer and took hold of her hand. Although she didn't turn toward him, she knew he was watching her, felt his love in the very nearness of his body.

"We mustn't cut all the trees down on our homestead, Devlin. We must keep some trees, just to enjoy."

"When we get back, you can mark all the trees you want to save. That way our children can look at them and say, 'Our mother kept these, just so we could enjoy having them to look at.'"

She glanced in his direction. "You're making fun of me."

"No." His teasing grin faded. He caressed her cheek with his fingertips. "I want whatever you want. But it's you I enjoy looking at, not the trees. You're prettier than a thousand acres of red cedar, and worth far more besides."

She flushed with pleasure and found it difficult to think about the forest any longer.

Hours later, Angelica had a glimpse of what she thought was the Pacific Ocean.

"It's not the ocean, Mrs. Branigan," the captain informed her. "This is Puget Sound. To reach the open sea, we'd have to sail through that passage—" he pointed "—and out through the strait. You wouldn't see the ocean until tomorrow."

That might all be well and true, Angelica pondered as the steamship pitched about on the choppy waters, but it looked like an ocean to her, and it certainly wasn't as smooth as the river had been.

It was very quickly apparent that Angelica was a much better horsewoman—poor though she was—than she was a sailor, and she was more than merely thankful when the lights of Seattle appeared through the settling dusk.

The dining room of the hotel was aglow with sparkling chandeliers and stark white tablecloths. Crystal goblets and fine china edged with gold glistened at each place setting.

Standing on the threshold of the beautiful room, Angelica tightened her hand on Devlin's arm. He'd told her to put on something special for the evening, but she'd never expected *this*.

"Devlin," she whispered urgently, masking her concern from the head waiter with a smile, "we can't afford this place."

"Tonight is a special occasion. I think we can afford to be a little extravagant."

"I don't belong in a place like this."

"Why not?" Tenderness softened his ebony gaze.

"I just don't..."

"This way, Angelica."

His arm at her back was firm, and there was no fighting against it as he guided her through the elegant room.

Angelica had worn her finest dress, but she knew with only a glance around the room that it was terribly outdated. She'd forgotten how very long ago it had been since she'd worn the yellow and golden brown damassé silk and satin evening gown. The bustle was much too small to be fashionable, the train too long. It had been all the thing when she'd bought it upon arriving in Denver back in '81. Now, she felt...

"You are the most beautiful woman in this room," Devlin said softly as he pulled out a brocade-upholstered chair for her. "I thought I might have to knock a few heads together, the way the men were staring and wishing you were with them instead of me."

Angelica looked quickly about her, but it wasn't the men she noticed. It was the women.

They were all watching Devlin with barely disguised relish. She had a very unpleasant desire to scratch their eyes out.

Turning her own gaze onto the man taking the seat across the table from her, she couldn't deny that it would be difficult for a woman not to want to feast her eyes on him. His suit displayed the breadth of his shoulders and chest to perfection. Half a head taller than most of the men in the room and without an ounce of fat, he radiated good health and vitality, not to mention a strong measure of masculinity. And she hadn't even considered yet his dark good looks.

She had a sudden vision of the way she'd seen him in that old shack of Jake's. He'd been so unkempt, so...so raw. His face had been pale and sallow beneath a scraggly black beard. Each movement he'd made had been stiff. His shoulders had been bent like an old man's. His eyes had been dulled by pain and alcohol. She hadn't thought him a man she would have glanced at twice on the street and had seriously doubted the wisdom of hiring him for the job ahead.

She must have been blind.

Devlin leaned forward. "What are you thinking?"

She started in her chair. "What? Oh...nothing really." She knew she was blushing.

"Nothing?" He was grinning at her.

"All right. If you must know, I was thinking that you are scandalously handsome and that if some of these women don't quit looking at you as if they'd like to take a bite of you, I'm going to pull someone's hair out by the roots."

He appeared to choke on his laughter. "That would be interesting to see. I doubt a lady has ever started a riot in this restaurant before."

Angelica frowned as she shook her head, thoughts from the past trying to intrude on the beauty of the evening. "I don't know where you ever got the notion that I was a lady, Devlin Branigan."

Devlin straightened as the waiter approached their table. He ordered a sumptuous meal of roast beef and sweet potatoes and baby peas and carrots. He finished by ordering a bottle of champagne.

As soon as the waiter had retreated, Devlin took up the conversation where he'd left it. "I knew you were a lady the moment I set eyes on you, Angelica Corrall. A finer one I've never known. It's in your soul."

"Real ladies don't become actresses, Mr. Branigan, and travel around the country, living out of a trunk. Real ladies haven't seen the things I've seen or done the things I've done. Real ladies don't become enamored with married men, even by accident, and give up everything to stay with them. And real ladies don't *ever* find themselves pregnant with an illegitimate child."

"So, *real* ladies never error. Is that what you're telling me?" He stretched his arm across the table and took hold of her hand.

"You couldn't be more mistaken, Angel." Intense black eyes captured her gaze, refusing to let go. "There isn't a man or woman in this room who hasn't done something they regret, something they wish they could do over again, differently this time. That doesn't make them less than what they are, does it?"

Angelica shook her head.

"Tell me. Would you really change things if you could? Would you change your life so that Robby had never been born?"

Her answer was immediate and emphatic. "No!"

"Me neither." His fingers tightened around hers. "Tell me about when our son was born. That's something a father should know."

Angelica had a hard time fighting the tears his words brought to her eyes. In fact, it was impossible to fight them, so she just let them stream silently down her cheeks, loving him more all the time.

Devlin listened as she talked of the months of loneliness and fear before Robby was born. He'd expected to feel jealous, knowing that Lamar had been Angelica's lover, but it seemed too distant, too removed from the reality of now. When she looked at him, her love was as clear as anything he'd ever seen.

His only real fear was if he would be able to keep her love.

"I don't know what I would have done without Marilla. Everyone else treated me like a leper, but she was always good to me, right from the beginning. She was with me the night Robby was born."

She sipped the champagne in her goblet. "I'll never forget the first time I saw him. I thought he was the most beautiful thing in the world, even though he was so red and wrinkled and he had the most ear-splitting cry you've ever heard. It was like music. I wish you could have heard him."

"Me, too," he said, enjoying the special look that had come over her face.

"I held him in my arms, and I knew nothing else mattered. I named him for my grandfather, Robert Trent. There are miniature portraits of both my grandparents in my mother's locket." Her expression grew wistful. "When Robby is older, I want him to know that he comes from a loving family and that he's got every right to hold his head up and be proud."

Devlin wished he hadn't brought her here. He wished he'd found a Justice of the Peace, dragged the man out of bed if necessary, and had him marry them tonight instead of waiting until tomorrow. He wished he had Angelica alone with him in a hotel room this very moment. He wanted to hold her and kiss her and make her forget all of the sad times. He wanted to make her think only of love and happiness.

He had to settle for trying to let his heart shine through his eyes. "He'll be proud just to be your son."

God forgive me, he added silently, *if I ever bring you anything but happiness.*

Angelica had forgotten the din of civilization. She had grown used to the simple song of birds and the wind whistling through trees tall enough to pierce the heavens.

Awakened just before dawn by the sound of a wagon clattering down the street, Angelica lay staring up at the ceiling, pondering the day before her.

Her wedding day.

It still didn't feel real to her. None of it. Not Devlin's proposal nor his avowal of love nor the trip down river nor the supper last night. She was afraid that if she pinched herself she would awaken and discover it was all part of a dream. How could a person tolerate such happiness?

As if to save her from such a fate, the memory of Lamar intruded on her thoughts. She remembered her despair, her humiliation, when he had taken her to the saloon of his former mistress and dumped her there. She remembered the dark days of depression that had followed.

She had been so young, so foolish, and she had thought for certain that her life was over. She had been convinced she would never trust a man again, let alone allow herself to fall in love.

The unpleasant memories were replaced with a sense of triumph.

She'd beaten Lamar. He had taken her innocence and then had left her to face the harsh realities alone. But in the end, she had beaten him. She had her son and she had her home and she had Devlin.

Devlin...

He hadn't slept all night.

Every time he'd closed his eyes, Devlin had remembered another reason why he shouldn't marry Angelica, why it was wrong. He'd remembered the faces of the men he'd ridden with through the years, most of them hard, dangerous, desperate men. He'd remembered the times he'd used his guns, wounding and killing. He'd even remembered the whores who had warmed his bed when no decent woman would have looked at him twice.

But the worst memory, the one that tortured him again and again, was the look of horror on Angelica's own blood-spattered face as she stared at Murphy's lifeless body.

He'd sworn to God that, if He let her live, he would change. But how did a man change his past? How was Devlin to keep Angelica from discovering the man he really was?

Chapter Forty

Angelica opened the door to her hotel room before Devlin had a chance to knock. Her eyes widened momentarily, and then her face lit up with a radiant smile.

"I...I was about to come to your room," she said as she backed away from the door. "You were late."

She looked so incredibly lovely he nearly forgot the speech he'd been practicing all morning. She was wearing dark green this morning, the same color as her eyes. Her lustrous hair was twisted up on her head and hidden beneath a perky little bonnet trimmed with a dyed ostrich feather.

Angelica reached for her matching reticule. "I'm ready."

"Wait. Angelica, before we go—"

"If you think for one moment that you are going to back out now, Mr. Branigan, you've got another think coming." She flashed him a second brilliant smile. "This is our wedding day, and I intend to enjoy every minute of it." She hooked her arm through his and pulled him toward the door.

He knew she was teasing with him. She couldn't have known he was about to give her one last chance to change her mind. He'd thought long and hard about it and had known it was the right thing to do. He had to help her see who and what he really was.

He wasn't the man who'd pretended to be her husband. He wasn't the man who'd built their little cabin and then masqueraded as a farmer. He wasn't the man she'd created in her mind just because he'd tended her when she was ill.

He was a hired gun, a quick draw, and one day, if she married him, she would realize she couldn't love the man he really was. If she married him, he would constantly live in dread of that day.

But looking down into her upturned face, seeing the light dancing in her eyes and the smile curving a mouth ripe for kissing, he forgot everything except that he loved her. Despite himself, he loved her, and he would have the love she offered him now.

To the devil with tomorrow.

There wasn't even a wisp of clouds to mar the canopy of blue sky. A refreshing breeze blew in off the sound and tugged at Angelica's skirts as she and Devlin traversed the board-walks.

Once again, Angelica noted how foreign the busyness of the town seemed to her, and she marveled at what a difference only a few months in the wilderness had made in her. One would have thought she'd never lived in a city, yet she'd spent almost her entire life in bustling seaports and thriving cattle towns, state capitals, and Washington D.C.

She'd loved the excitement of it once, but no more. Now she longed for the serenity of Morgan Falls and the quiet life she'd found with Devlin and Robby.

She glanced sideways at Devlin and felt her heart skip nervously. She'd tried to ignore it, tried to pretend she hadn't noticed, but she knew with a sixth sense that Devlin had come to her room to tell her he couldn't marry her. Not because he didn't love her. She knew in her heart that he did. Was he regretting the notion of settling down? Was he feeling the pull of wanderlust?

"Well, I'll be damned. Is that you, Kid? Hell-fire, if it ain't. What you doin' so far west?"

She felt Devlin stiffen before he stopped and turned toward the saloon doorway. She turned with him.

"Whooeee." The red-bearded man let out a long, appreciative breath as his gaze slid over Angelica. "Guess that answers my question. Your taste in women is better than ever, Kid."

The air seemed to crackle as Devlin drew

Angelica closer to and slightly behind him.

"Mind steerin' me to the place where you found her? Maybe there's another looker like her. I wouldn't mind havin' a go with..."

Devlin's hand darted toward his thigh. The reflex action found no holster strapped there and his hand was forced to come away empty. Angelica sensed his frustration. She saw the man pale, as if he'd just looked into the face of death.

A moment later, Devlin had his fingers wound in the fabric of the man's shirt, lifting his feet up off the ground. "I didn't like you when we drove cattle together, Perkins, and I like you even less when you talk like that about my wife."

"You...your...wi...wife?" he croaked, his frightened gaze darting past Devlin's shoulder toward Angelica.

Devlin's grasp tightened, choking off Perkin's air. He slammed the man up against the wall of the saloon.

"That's right. My *wife*."

Angelica watched the man's face begin to turn red as he struggled to draw a breath. When it appeared that Devlin had no intention of putting Perkins back on his feet, she stepped forward and laid a hand on Devlin's arm.

"Put him down," she said softly.

He turned his head to look at her, his gaze hard, his expression twisted with fury. "This is what's ahead of you. Men like this thinking you...you're..." He floundered, unable to speak what they both knew was true. "Just because you're my wife, they'll think it."

"Put him down, Devlin," she repeated. "It's not important."

"Not important!" Devlin shoved Perkins through the doors of the saloon. His fingers closed around her upper arm, and he began pulling her along the sidewalk. Even the low tone of his voice couldn't soften the full blast of his fury. "Not important that he thinks you're some soiled dove from one of these saloons?"

"It's been thought of me before," she reminded him with gentle stubbornness, all the while holding her head high, her gaze not wavering from his. "What that man thinks of me isn't important. You taught me that, Devlin. You told me I'm a *real* lady. Did you mean it?"

He stopped his mad dash along the boardwalk abruptly. His black gaze narrowed as he scowled down at her. "Don't you understand what happened back there? What if Perkins wasn't just a two-bit saddle bum full of lust and an itch to scratch it? What if he'd been someone with a gun and a score to settle?"

Both of her arms were now captured in his viselike grip, and he jerked her toward him.

"You might have been hurt. Just because you're walking with me in the street, you could be hurt. And I didn't even have my gun with me to protect you. Next time we might not be so lucky."

She stared at him in silence for what seemed

a very long time, understanding finally dawning. This was what had been bothering him last night and this morning. It's what he'd tried to tell her the night he proposed. It's what he'd been telling her in little ways all along.

"It's Murphy, isn't it?"

He made no reply.

"It's Murphy and all the men you've known since you left Georgia and learned to fire a gun."

Devlin released his grip on her arms as he backed away from her. The look on his face was wary, lingering anger mixed with apprehension, as if he expected her to bolt.

Her own anger caught her by surprise as much as it did him. Hands on her hips, she thrust her upper body toward him, her chin set in a stubborn line. "How did you get your reputation with the ladies without learning anything about women, Devlin Branigan? Do you think I'd turn tail and run so easy? I was the one who came looking for you, remember? I hired you to bring me to Washington. We both wanted new lives, new identities. Well, we found them. And we found each other. I don't care one lick what a man like *that*—" she jerked her head back toward the saloon "—thinks of me. I care what *you* think of me."

Her temper increased with each word she spoke. A quick step brought her almost up against him. She bent her head back to look up at him.

"The Devil Kid wasn't so famous that folks

won't forget him with time, and Devlin Branigan sure as heck doesn't need a gun to work his farm. And if problems come, then we'll face them together. Now, let's get married and go home where we belong."

In sight of any and all who happened to be on the street that morning, Devlin pulled her into his embrace and kissed her, full and hard. Street noises receded. Sunshine seemed to encircle them in a private cocoon of gold. Angelica felt herself go soft, then ignite with the pleasure of his lips against hers.

When he raised his head, he grinned the same devilish grin that had caused her heart to pound, her pulse to race, the very first time they'd met. "It's the only way I could shut you up," he said by way of explanation.

"Do it once more," she responded huskily, "before I start babbling again."

He obeyed without hesitation.

The minister was a tall, bean-pole-thin fellow with a receding hairline and muttonchop sideburns. His wife was short and stout. Both of them observed the couple with stern glares that would have frightened off less determined lovers.

Devlin and Angelica were made of sterner stuff.

"Marriage is an honorable estate, not to be entered into lightly . . ."

Devlin stared into eyes of kelly green and prayed Angelica would never think he had entered into this marriage lightly.

"If anyone knows any reason why these two should not be wed ..."

He knew plenty of reasons. He'd tried to explain them to her, but she refused to listen.

"Do you take this woman to have and to hold ..."

God help him, he wanted nothing more than to have and to hold, to love and to cherish.

"... until death do you part?"

It would be death to be parted from Devlin, Angelica thought as she smiled softly, then said, "I do."

The words came out on a breath, but even so, she knew Devlin heard her reply.

"... I pronounce you man and wife."

They stood stock-still, the enormity of the moment holding them both captive.

Finally he drew her to him. "Mrs. Branigan," he whispered, his lips hovering above hers.

She wondered, as he kissed her, if two more beautiful words existed.

He undressed her in daylight.

Not so very long ago she might have been scandalized to think of two people coupling in the daytime. But then, she'd never felt this sort of impatience for a day to end, for the sun to set.

Neither had she ever felt such a torrent of passion.

Angelica drank in the sight of him, wondering anew at the beauty of his body. The corded muscles in his shoulders, arms, stomach, and thighs were rock hard. He was strong enough to break her in two, if he chose. Yet she feared nothing about him.

Their first joining was fierce and quick, two hungry people starved for the feel of the other. They feasted in haste and found the satisfaction they sought.

Afterwards, they lay in each other's arms, gently stroking, constantly touching, until the fires of desire were stoked again. This taking was done at leisure and with a different—but just as great—pleasure.

Time had no meaning. The rest of the world had ceased to exist. There were only Angelica and Devlin. That was all that mattered for now.

Chapter Forty-One

Afternoon sunlight streamed through the window at the back of the house. From the doorway to the store, Maud watched Robby and Christine playing with blocks on the rag rug in the center of the room. For the moment—their small bellies full of a hearty lunch—peace and quiet reigned between them.

Maud let out a sigh of satisfaction as she crossed the room and sank into a chair.

"Tired, Mother Farland?" Rose asked. She was seated in a rocking chair which Bert had placed near the back door in hopes of catching an afternoon breeze.

"A bit." She saw her daughter-in-law grimace as she leaned forward to pick up Christine's doll from the floor. "You should be lyin' down. You do too much, Rose."

"Mmmm." Rose closed her eyes as she leaned back in the chair again.

"There's a new family settling in north of

the Branigan place. Name of Orson. The mister's in the store right now, gettin' supplies. Nice-lookin' fella. Hair like gold and the bluest eyes I've ever seen. Even bluer than Torin's. My guess is Mr. Orson's never walked behind a plow before. Bit of a dandy. Hands as smooth as silk. We didn't even know he an' his kin was up there." She nodded to herself, remembering. "Not like when the Branigans come through. Soppin' wet, they were. Ridin' in on horseback all the way from Oregon instead of comin' up the river. Never could understand such foolishness when there's a perfectly good riverboat that could've brought 'em to Snohomish."

"Mmmm."

"Guess Mr. Orson's met the Branigans, bein' neighbors and all, 'cause he was askin' about 'em, wonderin' when they'd be back and askin' about the boy there." Maud's gaze turned out the back door. Sunshine had cast a cloak of yellow-gold over the warm earth, and the room seemed to fill with the fresh scents of summer. "I hope Angelica's holiday is everything she wanted. Never seen two people more right for each other . . . nor more in love neither, than her and Devlin." She grinned as her eyes slipped back to Rose. "Maybe Robby'll have himself a baby brother or sister come next spring. Be nice for yours to have a little friend to play with. 'Sides, can't never be too many young'ns about."

Rose chuckled. She opened her eyes to stare

at Maud while one hand came up to stroke her rounded abdomen. "I think you've forgotten what it's really like," she suggested in a wry voice.

"No, I haven't forgot. I remember when each one of my own was born. Morgan, he was the easiest, bein' the first. Jacob, his birthin' was the hardest. Like as not he was mule-headed long 'fore he was born. Ruth and Naomi, they were so small, like little porcelain dolls. After all my boys, so full of juice and mischief, my girls were a pleasure." She smiled, lost in her musings. "Your Joshua . . . Lord, I thought I'd never draw a full breath again when I was carryin' him."

"Mother Farland?"

Their gazes met and held.

"Have I told you how glad I am I didn't lose you to the typhoid, too?" Rose's eyes misted as she tried to hide the sadness and loss she felt. "I love you so much."

Maud swallowed the hot tears that rose quickly in the back of her throat. She felt afresh the pain of losing her dear friend Mary and knew that what Mary's daughter was feeling was far worse. "Why, daughter, I love you, too." She cleared her throat and fussed with the mending in the basket beside her. "Lord knows, I wasn't ready for the other side, and I'm right sure the Almighty wasn't hankerin' to have me there yet, causin' Him trouble. And I don't plan on askin' Him why He didn't take me till I see a few more of my grandchildren."

The two women exchanged sorrowful, understanding smiles. Then they settled into a lengthy but companionable silence, Rose watching the children at play, Maud taking up her darning.

"Mother Farland?"

Maud glanced across the room again, surprised by the suddenness of Rose's voice.

"I think you're mighty close to seein' another one of them."

"What?"

Rose's eyes rounded and a tiny moan escaped her lips. "Another one of your grandchildren," she replied with a gasp.

"Oh my!" Maud hopped up from her chair. "Bert! Get in here quick."

Her husband stepped into view, Mr. Orson standing behind him in the doorway.

"Don't stand there gapin', old man," she snapped at Bert. "Help me get Rose into the bedroom. Her time's come."

"She'll know," Angelica whispered as she snuggled against Devlin's warm body, the bedroom cloaked in the shadows of dawn. "Maud will take one look at me and know the truth."

Devlin's fingers played through her hair. "What truth?"

"That we've been on our honeymoon."

He chuckled, soft and low in his chest.

"I wish we could stay longer. The days have gone by so quickly. I don't feel like I've even seen Seattle."

Again he chuckled. "You haven't seen much outside of this hotel room," he conceded. "You'll just have to see the city some other time."

"I feel a little guilty."

"Why?" His breath was warm upon her forehead as he whispered the word.

"Because I haven't missed Robby more."

Devlin rolled her onto her back, then covered her with his body, holding himself above her with an arm on each side of her head. "Robby will be with us the rest of our lives. These days were ours."

Angelica smiled, feeling a delicious warmth spreading through her veins. She was constantly amazed by her husband—the feel of him, the sound of him, the smell of him, the taste of him. She'd discovered how much she loved to hear him laugh, and she'd heard it often in the past few days. She loved the way their bodies fit together so perfectly. She loved the way she could read his thoughts upon his face, long before he ever voiced them. She'd wondered once, in the middle of the night when she could hear him breathing softly beside her, how she could ever have found his face hard or closed or dangerous. She loved the way he made her feel about her own body, about making love, about giving and sharing and taking from the other.

She also loved the way his eyes darkened whenever he wanted her.

He wanted her now, for instance, but it was

more than just his eyes that told her so. She felt him growing hard against her even as he lowered his mouth to hers.

She sighed—a pleased sound of acquiescence—as her body responded to his. They didn't have to catch the steamship for nearly two hours. There was no point in rushing to the docks just yet.

Devlin couldn't wipe the grin from his face. If he lived to be a hundred, he thought, he would never know what he'd done that was good enough for him to deserve Angelica's love.

As the steamer made its way upriver, Devlin leaned against the ship's railing and pondered his good fortune. After four days and nights in her arms, it was difficult for him to remember any other way of life than as her husband.

He thought of the Devil Kid, the way he'd reached so automatically for his gun, the way he'd watched for danger at every turn. He remembered the wounded man with a hangover who had opened the door of Jake's shack to Angelica's persistent knocking. It seemed he was thinking about another man, a total stranger.

He'd done it. He'd left the old life behind. He'd found a new and better identity. He *was* Devlin Branigan.

He took a deep breath, enjoying the freedom he felt.

"We're almost home," Angelica said softly

as she slipped up beside him, her hand gliding through the crook in his arm, her head touching his shoulder.

Bound to another, yet freer than he'd ever been in his life.

He grinned. "Yeah, we're almost home."

"I wish I could tell someone how happy I am. I wish I could tell someone about that dour-faced minister and his wife. I wish I could tell someone what it's like to love you so much that sometimes I think I'll burst."

He kissed the crown of her head. "You can tell me."

She shot him a vexed grin, but her irritation was mere pretense. "You know good and well what I mean."

"Yup." He put an arm around her shoulders. "Tell me anyway."

"Not a chance, Mr. Branigan. Not even if you try to force it out of me."

"Just what sort of force did you have in mind, Mrs. Branigan?"

She blushed a particularly lovely shade of pink, and he laughed aloud, loving her all the more because, even as she blushed, he knew what she was thinking.

His laughter echoed off the banks of the tree-lined river, coming back to him and multiplied tenfold by the wind. To Devlin, it seemed that the whole world laughed with him.

Later, Angelica would wonder why she hadn't known. She would wonder why, even before they arrived in Morgan Falls, she hadn't felt something to warn her. A mother should sense these things. A mother should know when her child is in danger.

She did know that something was amiss the minute they walked into the Farlands' general store and she caught a glimpse of Bert's face. "What's wrong, Bert?"

The older man glanced from her to Devlin, then back again.

Dread shivered up her back. "What's happened?"

"Angelica, I . . ." Despair lifted his shoulders in a helpless shrug.

She grasped Devlin's hand in a death grip. "It's Robby. What's wrong with Robby?"

Was he sick? Did he get the typhoid after all? Had he fallen and hurt himself?

A dozen possibilities flashed through her mind in the moment between her question and Bert's halting response.

"He's gone. We can't find him." Again Bert looked at Devlin. "We've looked everywhere."

Angelica wasn't aware that she screamed her son's name. She had no warning of the black sea that rose to envelop her, pulling her down into blissful oblivion.

When she came to, she was lying on Maud's bed, concerned faces swimming above her.

"Robby?" she whispered as she tried to focus on one of them.

"It's my fault," Maud responded, wringing her hands near her waist. "It's all my fault.

The children were playin' and then Rose's time come and Bert and I got her back to our room here. Then I sent Bert to get Joshua. I heard the young'ns laughin' and hoped they weren't gettin' into mischief, but Rose was havin' a hard time and I couldn't leave her. I thought ...I thought ..."

"The boy wandered off," Bert continued when his wife couldn't. "We been out all night an' agin today lookin' for him."

This couldn't be happening. It couldn't be.

Angelica sat up. Her vision spun, and she closed her eyes against it, clinging desperately to consciousness. "Robby was out there all night?" She reached out, and Devlin's hand was there to take hers. "Dev," she whispered, utter helplessness lacing the single word.

"Don't worry, Angel. We'll find him." Still holding her hand, he turned toward the older couple standing on the opposite side of the bed. "Tell me everything. Every little detail. Was Torin in the store? Maybe Robby tried to follow him home. He always likes to be with his friend Tory. If Robby saw him, he might have—"

Bert shook his head. "Neither o' the Johnsons have been in for days. Store's been quiet since yesterday mornin'. 'Cept for that new fella. You know, the one livin' above the ridge north of your place. Mr. Orson, I think his name was."

"North of us? I didn't know there was anyone up there."

381

"No? Well, he acted like he knew you. Anyway, he was in the store when Maud called for me to help Rose into the bedroom. Guess he left 'cause of the commotion. Didn't even take his supplies with him. I reckon he'll be back later."

"Orson..." Devlin spoke the name slowly, as if trying to see the man it belonged to. "Are you sure that's the name he gave? What'd he look like?"

As Bert described the newcomer, Angelica kept her eyes on Devlin, not really listening at first. Then she sensed the tension increase in the air around them. She felt herself grow cold, reading Devlin's thoughts as if they were her own.

"Lamar?" she asked hesitantly.

He immediately tried to reassure her, as if he hadn't been thinking the same thing. "Bert and I will ride up to the ridge. I'm sure we'll find that Mr. Orson doesn't know a thing."

But Angelica knew better. Lamar had told her that he always kept what was his, whether he wanted it or not, and he always got what he did want. He'd wanted Robby and had come after him.

Falling in love had made her complacent. She'd allowed herself to believe they were safe because he hadn't found them sooner. She'd allowed herself to believe that Lamar had quit looking weeks ago, if he'd ever looked at all. She'd fooled herself and Devlin into believing that the past was forgotten.

His past, perhaps, but not hers.

She never should have left Robby in Morgan Falls. She never should have let him out of her sight for a moment. This was her fault. Her own fault. She'd been so eager to marry Devlin, to have him all to herself, to lie in his arms and make love with him for hours. She'd wanted that so much that she'd forgotten to protect her own child.

Meeting Devlin's gaze again, she saw her own doubts and recriminations reflected in his eyes. She saw his agony and fear and guilt, and she knew that his suffering was the same as hers.

"He's taken our son," she whispered, her hand tightening around his, seeking to draw strength from him and, perhaps, share a little of her own. "Devlin, he's taken our son."

Devlin stood beside the open doorway of their cabin as he fastened the gun belt around his hips and strapped one holster to his right thigh with deliberate, controlled motions. The look on his face was like granite—hard, unmovable, cold.

Looking at him, feeling his icy rage, Angelica shivered. "I'm going with you."

He didn't look at her. "No, you're not."

"I've got to be with you. I've got to be there when you find Robby. He's going to need me. He'll be frightened."

"You'll stay here where you're safe."

Her chin tilted upward. Her back stiffened.

"If you leave me here, I'll just follow on my own. Lamar's got no right to Robby. He's never claimed he's Robby's father. The law won't let him just come in and take my son away. He can't just take him from me."

Devlin straightened and turned his head toward her. Unmistakably, there was murder written in his eyes. "Do you think the law has anything to do with this, Angelica? Lamar Orwell *owns* the law. When you've got the kind of money that Orwell does, you decide what's right and wrong, and the law turns its eyes away until you tell it to look. He'll do what he damn well pleases unless I stop him. And I *mean* to stop him. It's what you hired me to do. Remember?"

"He's already taken my son," she shot back, anger raising her voice. "I won't let him take my husband, too."

Without a word, he bent to his task, lacing the other holster to his left thigh.

Angelica drew in a deep breath. When she spoke, it was in a low voice, none of her inner panic revealing itself in her words. "You're right. Lamar does own the law, and if you go after him with a gun, he'll see that you hang. You won't get a trial, let alone a fair trial. You won't stand a chance." She stepped toward him. "You're not the Devil Kid anymore. You're *my* husband and *Robby's* father. I don't know how we'll do it, but we'll get Robby back without the use of your guns. And we'll do it together."

Once again, Devlin straightened and met her gaze. "Lamar won't have a chance to see me hang. I plan to find him before he even knows I exist, before he suspects that someone might try to take Robby back."

"Then you'd better teach me to shoot, too," she retorted, anger finding its way back into her voice, "because I plan to be right beside you. If this is the only way to get Robby back, then I mean to help, and there's nothing you can do to stop me."

"Angelica—"

"We're wasting time. Either let me go with you or I'll go after you've gone."

They stared at each other, stubborn wills doing silent battle in the space that separated them.

Finally, Devlin sighed in defeat. "All right, Angel. Let's go."

Chapter Forty-Two

It had been incredibly easy to snatch the brat.

Lamar leaned back in the plush seat of his private car. He drew heavily on the fine cigar, then blew the smoke upward where it formed a bluish cloud above his head.

He smiled, remembering his good fortune. He'd just stood there in the general store, talking to the idiot that owned the place, trying to find out information about where Angelica and her husband had gone and when they would return. He hadn't known that the boy was playing in the other room. At least, not at first.

And then that woman had gone into labor. Lamar had stood in the doorway, watching the commotion, not believing his luck. It had been simple enough to slip outside and wait by the back door until he was certain no one would see him enter and then leave with Robby in his arms. A little chloroform had kept the kid quiet until they'd reached Portland and boarded the train for Colorado.

"Mr. Orwell?"

He turned his gaze upon the slender blonde standing in the doorway to the sleeping compartment.

"The boy's asleep. Is there anything else you'll be wanting of me?"

He'd hired Suzanne Wagner in Portland. He'd needed someone to care for Robby during the journey back to Denver. Suzanne was perfect for the job. She was young and poor, desperate for the money he'd offered, and wasn't the type to ask questions. She only wanted to earn enough to get her to her sister's in Connecticut.

Looking at her now, Lamar realized there might have been one other reason he'd chosen her. It was a long, tiresome trip from Portland to Denver. Suzanne wasn't beautiful, but she was attractive enough to help the miles go by a bit faster, with just the right sort of persuasion. Wide-eyed and innocent, she didn't look like she'd cause him too much trouble.

"Yes. Come sit with me. I'd like some company before I turn in for the night." He smiled and pointed to the seat opposite him.

Angelica stared blankly out the window. She could see nothing of the passing landscape. The night was as black as ink, like a mirror image of her heart. Black and empty.

Around her, other passengers shifted in their seats as they tried to find comfortable positions. A few luckier souls actually snored. She couldn't sleep, no matter how hard she tried.

She knew Devlin wasn't asleep either. He sat next to her, his arms crossed over his chest, his head dipped forward. He rested and waited, like a coiled snake waiting to strike, but he wasn't asleep. She could feel it.

They'd spoken little since leaving Morgan Falls. It was difficult for her to think of anything except Robby. Was Robby crying for her? Would he make Lamar angry? She remembered well Lamar's violent and sudden bursts of temper. Would he hurt her son if Robby displeased him?

Please don't cry, Robby. Mama's coming. Mama's coming.

The wait for the next steamer out of Snohomish had been almost unbearable. The wait for the eastbound train from Portland had seemed to last an eternity. And the train itself seemed to be traveling so very slowly. She wanted to go up to the front of the train and tell the engineer to stoke the engines, to make the train go faster. They had to hurry.

Still, Angelica knew she should be grateful to be on the train at all. If it weren't for the money the Farlands had given them, she and Devlin never could have afforded to travel by steamboat and rail. They would have been forced to go overland by horseback. It would have taken them weeks to reach Denver, weeks to find Robby.

She closed her eyes, a sick feeling tightening

her stomach. For the hundredth time since they'd returned from their honeymoon, she silently flayed herself for leaving Robby alone. She should have known better. She should have remembered the type of man Lamar was. How could she have forgotten what had sent her running from Wood Bluff? How could she have forgotten why she'd taken her son into hiding?

A tiny moan escaped her chest.

Lamar has Robby...

Lamar has Robby...

"It'll be all right," Devlin said softly. His arm went around her shoulders and he pulled her toward him. His fingers stroked her hair as he tried to calm her shivers of fear. "I promise, it'll be all right."

Long after Angelica's quivering stopped, Devlin continued to caress her head, thinking about the promises he'd made since first meeting this woman.

He'd promised to take her safely to Washington and stay with her for eighteen months. He'd broken that promise when he'd headed for California after shooting Murphy.

He'd promised God he would marry her, if only she would live. He'd promised he would be whatever she wanted, that he would make her happy, that he would never leave her. He'd tried to break those promises, too. Only Angelica's stubbornness had made him go through with it, so certain was he that she would one day regret it.

And now he'd promised that everything would be all right. He'd promised that he would find Robby and bring the boy home and that everything would be all right.

What if he couldn't keep this promise, either? What if he couldn't return Robby safely to his mother? What if . . .

His mouth brushed the top of her head. "I'll keep that promise, Angel, no matter what it takes. No matter what I have to do. I won't fail you, Angel."

Penelope saw her visitor to the door and watched as the man sauntered down the walk toward the street. At the wrought-iron gate, he turned and tipped his hat to her, revealing his balding pate.

"Good day, Miss Pen," he called to her, a wry smile curving his lips as he spoke the name.

Then he stepped through the gate and disappeared behind the tall green hedges that closed the Orwell mansion off from the dusty Denver street.

She wasn't surprised at the news Jonathan Bellows had brought to her, although she thought he'd been surprised by how calmly she'd received the information. Of course, Bellows didn't know how many other lovers her husband had entertained through the years. Penelope did. Penelope had always known about Lamar.

She could leave her husband. She had more than enough money to do anything or go anywhere she wanted. The trouble was, what she wanted was Lamar. She'd always wanted Lamar, even knowing the truth about him.

Penelope closed the door and returned to the drawing room, her silk skirts swishing around her ankles. She paused before the large, gilt-framed mirror and assessed her image.

She was homely.

When she was a child, her mother had often told her that she would grow into her oversized features, but it had never happened. Her protruding nose, her wide mouth, her flat forehead had just grown along with her. She'd never had a beau as a young woman; no man had ever sparked her on the porch; never had anyone tried to steal a kiss at a cotillion.

Lamar, on the other hand, was devastatingly handsome. Women fell under his spell so easily, and he knew how to use his charm to get whatever he wanted. The first time her father had brought home the ambitious Mr. Orwell, Penelope had decided she wanted him for her husband. She'd recognized in his eyes that he wanted what she had, too. Wealth.

She'd decided it was a fair exchange.

Penelope turned away from the mirror, her gaze moving about the high-ceilinged room. It was filled with furniture and rugs and figurines from all over the world. She had spent months, years, decorating this room, this house, turning it into the showplace it was.

But that didn't make it a home. She needed a child to make it that.

Perhaps if she'd been able to conceive her own baby, she never would have learned about Miss Corrall and her son—or cared. Of course, she'd known about the beautiful actress her husband had kept for his mistress while she and her father were traveling abroad, but she hadn't learned about the child until a few months ago.

She traced her fingers lovingly along the marble fireplace mantel before walking across the spacious room to stand before the window. She moved aside the sheer blue curtains to stare out at the yard.

Overconfidence was probably Lamar's biggest weakness. He never believed that anyone was smarter than he. He mistakenly thought, because she was homely, that she was also stupid. He thought he was the one with all the power.

Shaking her head, Penelope smiled. Perhaps, she thought, his audaciousness was one of the things that had attracted her to him. At times she wondered why she wanted to keep him so much. Was it merely because she—plain Penelope—liked to be squired about Denver on the arm of its most handsome citizen?

Perhaps. Or perhaps it was simply that she loved him just as he was, despite his faults. Whatever the reason, keep him she would.

"Poor Lamar," she said aloud to the empty

room. "He thinks he can leave me once Papa dies."

Foolish, foolish man, to have underestimated Penelope Venizelos Orwell.

Lamar clenched his jaw as the carriage passed beneath the arched entrance to the driveway. He was home at last, and it was about time. He was sick to death of the brat sniveling for his mama. Suzanne had bounced the boy on her lap and sung softly to him and fed him sweets, but nothing seemed to quiet him. Finally he could turn him over to Penelope and be rid of looking at him.

Hell and damnation! Penelope had better be pleased with the boy. She'd wanted a child, and he was giving her one. And his choice was the only logical one. At least Robby had some right to wear the Orwell name, bastard though he might be. Taking Robby in and adopting him was at least better than raising someone else's by-blow for them.

The boy whimpered again, and Lamar clenched his fists in his lap. Like the brat or not, Penelope better get him out of Lamar's sight before he made sure the boy stopped his infernal sniveling.

Glancing out the carriage window as it drew up to the house, Lamar let out a groan. Alexander was there. He cursed again. He wasn't in the mood for playing up to the old man today. It was bad enough he had to pretend to be a doting husband for his horse-faced wife.

Besides, he still had work to be done. First thing he needed to do was tell his men to watch for a green-eyed beauty with burgundy-colored hair getting off the train. He knew she would follow him. In fact, he'd counted on it. That was why he hadn't tried to disguise himself when he'd taken the boy. He wanted her to figure it out and then come after him.

A malicious grin curved Lamar's lips. He had a matter or two to take up with the rebellious Angelica Branigan, but he wanted it to take place on his own turf. He wanted to make certain she understood just how much trouble she'd caused him. He wanted to make sure she learned a lesson about defying him.

Oh yes, Angelica would follow him, and he didn't want her—or her husband—to miss out on a proper reception. He had plans for the both of them. Very definite plans.

Chapter Forty-Three

"Devlin Branigan? Angelica's husband?" Lamar grinned at the man standing just inside the door of his office. "You're sure he's the Devil Kid?"

Duncan smoothed his soft leather gloves over each finger, his face a mask of indifference. "I'm sure, Mr. Orwell."

"I can't believe it. How did you find out?"

"It wasn't easy, but I convinced Marilla to tell me a few things she hadn't told you." The henchman's grin revealed the pleasure he received from his work. "Like, the old miner who called on Miss Corrall when he came to town and who his friends were." Duncan shrugged. "Folks see and hear things in a small town like Wood Bluff. A bit more nosin' around, and I put two and two together."

Lamar picked up a decanter and removed the crystal stopper. "Join me in a drink, Duncan? I think this calls for a celebration."

"No, thanks, Mr. Orwell."

Lamar stared at the brandy he'd poured into his glass, toying with the possibilities, enjoying each scenario as it played in his head. "A gunfighter . . . Well, well, well," he muttered, a plan taking shape before his eyes. "A man like Alexander would never stand a chance against a gunfighter, would he?"

"No, sir, he wouldn't."

"No. No, I doubt Alexander has even ever held a gun. He wouldn't know how to shoot one." Lamar took a drink and savored the taste of the expensive liquor.

Duncan watched him in silence for a long time. Finally he asked, "What do you want the men to do?"

"I want them to watch every train that comes through. Angelica and her gunman will be on one of them. You can bet on it. When they arrive, I want them met at the station by the law. Make sure the men look and act the part, just in case there are any witnesses." He tapped his fingernails against the glass in his hand. "Take Miss Corrall up to the old Chamberlain place and keep her under lock and key. Have one of Kelly's girls stay there, too, to watch over her and make sure she has everything she needs. Take Branigan out to the jail at the Token Mine. No one's been up there for years so there's no chance he'll be discovered until we need him."

"And then?"

Euphoria spread through Lamar, that and

the brandy making him feel warm and satisfied. He grinned in triumph. "Then my father-in-law is going to get into an argument with a stranger in town. A known gunslinger. Later that night, Alexander will be shot down in the street. His killer will be seen, however, and captured." His gaze met Duncan's. "The Devil Kid will hang, of course, for his crime. My wife will be distraught. I will encourage her to take a long trip, away from the terrible memories of what happened to her father. Perhaps I'll suggest she go stay with her relatives in Greece."

Duncan picked up his hat. "I like the way you think, Mr. Orwell." With a nod, he turned and left the office.

"So do I." Lamar chuckled. "So do I."

The July sun blasted down on Denver at midday. In the wake of passing carriages and wagons, clouds of dust rose from the parched earth.

Angelica squinted against the bright sunlight as she stepped down from the train. Sweat trickled along her spine and between her breasts. Tendrils of damp hair clung to the back of her neck.

Devlin took hold of her elbow. "We'll get a room at the hotel first. Then I'll check around."

"But I want to go to Lamar's. I want to get Robby."

"Angel, be reasonable," he replied with tenderness. "Orwell didn't go all the way to Washington to take Robby just to give him back to you when you demand it. We'd better know that Robby's there at his house before we go barging in. Otherwise, we might not find him."

She knew what he said made sense, but she didn't want to be reasonable. She just wanted her son. Everything inside her insisted that she rush out to the Orwell mansion and rescue her child from Lamar.

"Come on. We could both use something to eat, and I'd like to clean up a bit."

She nodded in agreement, too weary and disheartened to argue at length. She had put her trust in Devlin months ago, before she hardly knew him. Now that she loved him, how could she not trust him to do what was right?

"What will you do first?" she asked as they rounded the corner of the depot.

Their way was suddenly and completely blocked by several men bearing guns and wearing badges. Angelica gasped as she gripped Devlin's arm.

"What a surprise, fellas. I do believe it's Mr. Branigan," the man closest to Angelica said. He spit a wad of chaw onto the sidewalk. "Not very smart for a wanted man."

Devlin's eyes narrowed but he didn't move or speak.

"Don't try 'n' do nothin' stupid, *Kid*, or the lady might get hurt. Just come along, nice and quiet like."

"Devlin?" Angelica looked up at his remote expression.

"You'd best be on your way, ma'am. It ain't smart t'be seen consortin' with a killer."

She felt shock jolt through her body, followed by cold terror. Devlin had warned her that Lamar owned the law.

She turned to look at the man before her, hoping against hope that this was all a mistake. "You have the wrong man, sheriff. My husband is not wanted for anything."

"I got a warrant that says he is. Devlin Branigan, alias the Devil Kid—thought you'd fooled everyone, didn't ya, Kid?—wanted for murder. Seems he killed a very important man here in Denver. Whole town is outraged. Venizelos didn't even have a gun on him. The Kid just stepped out of a dark alley and shot him cold. Never gave him a chance."

Angelica's gaze darted quickly to each of the men. She was nearly paralyzed by their hard, relentless faces. These were not men looking for the truth.

Still, she had to try to convince them they were mistaken. "That's a lie. Devlin would *never* shoot an unarmed man."

"Rod—" the sheriff turned to one of his deputies "—see the lady to her hotel."

Rod reached for Angelica's arm.

Devlin moved to intercept him. "Don't you touch her or I'll—" The rest of his sentence died abruptly as he was struck on the head with the butt of a revolver.

Angelica cried out as Devlin pitched forward.

"Get her out o' here," the sheriff snapped at Rod. To the others he said, "Pick him up and let's go."

She hadn't even time to scream before she was being dragged toward a waiting carriage and shoved inside. She tried to scramble out the other side but was jerked back. A second later, a cloth was clamped over her mouth and nose. She struggled against the sickening sweet smell before slipping into darkness.

Not knowing what they'd done to Angelica or where they'd taken her made his captivity a thousand times worse than he'd ever imagined.

Devlin paced the small cell from end to end, stopping each time he turned to grip the iron bars and stare at the sliver of light beneath the jail door, then resuming his pacing. Occasionally he touched the back of his head, fingering the lump and congealed blood, trying to ignore the pain that knotted the muscles in his neck and shoulders.

He cursed himself for being so careless. He cursed himself for losing the edge, now when it had mattered so much. He cursed himself for a thousand and one things, but none of it changed his circumstances.

Stopping again, he glared at the door. He hadn't heard a sound from the room beyond for hours. He didn't know where he was, although he was certain it wasn't the Denver jail. There was only one cell, and the room smelled musty and unused. There were no sounds of the city filtering through the walls. No, he wasn't in Denver.

He crossed the cell, glancing toward the door again as he turned at the far end. Was it daylight he saw or lantern light? He didn't even know what time of day or night it was. Nor did it really matter to him. He was concerned with only one thing now. Where had they taken Angelica, and was she all right?

He stopped his pacing. "Hey, out there!" he shouted.

There was no response.

Perhaps they'd left him alone. Perhaps they hadn't left a guard. If he could find some way to open the cell door . . .

His eyes had grown used to the darkness of the room, at least well enough to know that his jailers had made certain they hadn't left him anything he could use as a weapon against them. There was no cot with iron legs or wire springs. There was only a thin tick mattress lying on the wood floor. They hadn't even left him a bucket of water.

He shook the bars, in futile hope of jerking it free. Rage roiled in his chest.

If Orwell dared touch Angelica—if any of his men harmed one hair on her head—he'd kill them all. With his bare hands, if he had to, but he would kill them all.

Lamar was dining with Penelope when the butler brought him a message from Duncan.

He read it quickly, then again more slowly, savoring the information. He tried unsuccessfully to hide the satisfaction he felt. Finally he refolded the note paper and slipped it into his vest pocket.

"Good news, dear?" Penelope asked.

"What? Oh, yes. I've just learned a shipment I've been awaiting has arrived in Denver even sooner than I expected."

"How nice." She smiled at him.

Lord, how he loathed looking at her at the end of his table. He couldn't abide the sound of her voice, either. He hated it when she called him dear or darling. Worst of all, she was stupid. She was so easily fooled. She believed whatever he told her. She even believed he loved her.

"Did I tell you Papa is coming over this evening?"

Hell! He finally had Angelica in his grasp. He wanted to see her. He wanted to make her squirm and regret leaving Wood Bluff, and now he had to play host to his father-in-law.

"He's very excited about being a grandfather."

Lamar inclined his head.

"And I couldn't be more pleased with Robby. I do wish you would spend a little more time with him, Lamar. He should get to know you. I don't believe you've even looked in on him since you came home." She tapped her chin with her forefinger, frowning thoughtfully.

"Do you know, darling, I think he looks just a little like you."

Lamar's fork stopped midway to his mouth. His gaze darted down the length of the long mahogany table.

"His chin, I think, and perhaps his nose," Penelope continued, her eyes on her plate as she speared some asparagus. "And he's so well mannered." She shook her head sadly. "But he never stops asking for his mama and papa. So tragic, their dying so suddenly."

"Yes." He resumed eating, although his stomach was beginning to knot up. "Tragic."

"I do believe, if I could do so, that I would bring his parents back so he wouldn't miss them so very much. As much as I love him, I would do it if I could. I know how I would feel if my father were taken from me so suddenly."

He wished she'd shut up.

"Lamar?"

He ignored her.

"Lamar?"

Repressing a groan, he looked up.

"You do know how much I love you and that I wouldn't want anything to ever separate us, don't you? I want nothing more than for us to have a very long life together."

"Of course, Penelope. I want the same."

The butler stepped into the doorway again. "Excuse me, madam, but your father has arrived. He's gone up to the nursery."

"Thank you, Harrison. Tell Papa that Mr. Orwell and I will join him soon."

"Very good, madam."

There was no avoiding it. He would be spending the evening at home. He would have to wait until tomorrow to see Angelica.

The room Angelica had awakened in that morning was large and airy. Thick Persian rugs covered the highly polished wood floors. Upholstered chairs were grouped near the fireplace. A ceiling-to-floor bookcase was built into one wall, its shelves filled with leather-bound books. The wall coverings were ornate. The four-poster bed with its canopy and sheer curtains was placed against the wall opposite an enormous gabled window. The only thing that marred the second-story view of the manicured lawn and colorful gardens were the iron bars outside the window.

It was an attractive jail, but a jail nonetheless.

Angelica stared down at the gardeners who were working among the flowers. She'd tried calling for their help earlier, but they either couldn't hear or were ignoring her.

She tried to remember how she'd arrived here, but nothing was clear after the moment she was pushed into the carriage outside the train depot. She vaguely recalled awakening once or twice, only to have a cloth placed over her face again, sending her back into a drugged sleep. She felt slightly nauseated by the smell that seemed to linger in her nostrils.

One memory, however, was all too clear in

her mind. She could still see the gun striking the back of Devlin's head. She could see him crumpling to the ground. Time and again, she'd replayed the scene in her mind and wondered if he were alive or dead.

She heard a key turn in the lock and spun to face the door as it opened. She wasn't surprised to find Lamar standing there.

"Angelica, it's good to see you." He stepped into the room and closed the door behind him. His blue eyes assessed her critically. "You do look a bit worse for wear. I hope my men didn't use more force than necessary. You're unharmed, I trust."

"What have you done with Devlin?"

"You mean that gunfighter you married? I believe he's to be tried for murder." He grinned as he crossed the room. "It's bad enough that you ran off to Washington, my dear Angelica. Did you have to compound your error by marrying a wanted criminal?" His fingertips brushed her cheek.

She jerked away from him. "You know he's not a criminal. You know he didn't shoot anyone. He wasn't even in Denver. We'd just gotten off the train."

It was like he didn't even hear her. "I hope you like this room," he said as he turned away. "It's yours now."

"You can't keep me here if I don't want to stay." She clenched her hands in front of her dress, trying to sound calm and reasonable. "Just give me back my son and release Devlin.

We'll go away and forget that any of this happened."

He laughed. "You always were delightfully naïve, Angelica. Perhaps that was one of the things I liked best about you. I never should have left you in Wood Bluff for so long." He crossed to a dark blue chair near the fireplace and sat down. He brushed at some imaginary lint on his trousers before looking up at her again. "I think you'll come to like this house. I'll see that you won't be lonely. Of course, I won't be able to visit you again until my wife's father passes on—I can't take any chances right now—but that won't be much longer. Then I can do what I please and see who I want."

"You can't mean to make me your mistress again," she whispered, horrified. "I'm a married woman."

"A mere technicality, my dear, and soon enough you'll be a widow. You see, your husband is to be tried for the murder of Alexander Venizelos, my revered father-in-law. He will be found guilty and hanged. Then you and I shall both be free. Before long, we can be together like in the old days."

She flew at him in a fury so sudden it caught them both by surprise. She struck at him several times before he was able to respond with a violent backswing, catching her beneath the jaw and knocking her to the floor. She braced herself on her elbows as he rose from the chair and came to stand over her.

He touched his cheek where she'd scratched him. His blue eyes were as cold as ice. "You'll be sorry you did that, Angelica. Very sorry."

"Never." Her voice shook with hatred. "I'll never be sorry. But you will. I swear it."

"I believe you used to be more civilized, my dear. You may have been just an actress, but you did know how to pretend to be a lady." He headed for the door. "It must be living with that gunman in the wilderness that's done it to you. I'll help you remember your manners some other time." He didn't look behind him as he left the room.

Angelica heard the key turn in the lock, then rolled onto her stomach and gave into the hot sting of tears.

"You'll be sorry, Lamar Orwell," she whispered. "So help me God, you will."

Chapter Forty-Four

For two days, perhaps three, Devlin didn't see or hear anyone. He was beginning to believe his captors didn't mean to hang him or shoot him. They simply planned to starve him to death.

He thought it was evening, although he couldn't be certain, when he heard sounds from the other room. He scrambled to his feet as the door opened, letting in a flood of blinding light. He squinted and shielded his eyes.

A man stood in the doorway. "Brought you somethin' to eat."

Footsteps sounded on the wood floor, then the tray slid under the cell door.

Before Devlin's vision could clear or he had a chance to speak, the man was gone, the door slammed closed behind him, leaving Devlin once again imprisoned by darkness.

The smell of the food filled his cell and made his stomach growl. He groped his way toward the iron bars, then felt along the floor until he found the tray of food. He sat down beside it and started to eat. He scarcely tasted it, didn't know if it was good or not. He simply shoved it into his mouth and swallowed, washing it down with the strong coffee they'd brought with it.

When he was finished, he leaned his back against the bars and forced himself to think clearly. Several days without food or drink, surrounded day and night by darkness, constantly wondering about Angelica and Robby, had left him feeling disoriented. He knew he couldn't afford the luxury of madness. He had to be ready the next time the door opened. He had to find some way to escape.

He drew a deep breath. *Concentrate, Branigan.*

If this wasn't the city jail, it was a pretty safe bet that the men who'd taken him weren't deputies. But if they were Lamar's men and his "arrest" had merely been orchestrated to fool any witnesses, why hadn't they just killed him? They were keeping him alive for some reason. Why? Obviously, Lamar needed Devlin for some reason of his own, but what?

Whatever the reason, Devlin was thankful for it. It meant he still had some time. It meant there was still a chance for him to escape.

Lamar slammed his fist down onto the desk in frustration, spilling the ink pot. He cursed loudly and shoved his chair away before the ink could drip onto his suit.

His office door opened, revealing a thin, nervous-looking fellow. "Mr. Orwell, what—"

"Clean that mess up," he shouted at his secretary.

Culver nodded. "Right away, sir."

"I'll be at the Cattlemen's Club."

"Yes, sir."

Lamar stormed out of the office, glowering at anyone who dared get in his way.

It should have been so easy. It had been such a simple plan. His father-in-law, out at night, accosted by a known gunman. Shot, his killer captured before he could get away. A quick trial. A hanging.

So if it was so simple, why wasn't anything going according to plan?

He had the Devil Kid rotting in that cell out at the old deserted mine. Now, he only needed to get Alexander's cooperation. He only needed one night, just one chance. But he'd been thwarted at every opportunity. Alexander hadn't gone to his club once in the past week. Nor, did it seem, was he ever alone.

Lamar thought of Angelica and swore again. She was waiting for him in the old Chamberlain house, and he couldn't get away to see her.

All week, Penelope had had a list of obligations which she insisted they keep. Alexander had usually been in attendance as well, giving Lamar little choice but to go. As long as the old goat lived, Lamar couldn't take a chance of offending him or his daughter.

Well, damn it, somehow he'd make his plan
work, and once Alexander Venizelos was dead
and Lamar had inherited his vast fortune, he
would pay many a visit to the beautiful Miss
Corrall—or rather, the Widow Branigan. He
planned to teach her the things he'd neglected
to teach her three years ago. She'd been so
naïve, so easily pleased with a few vaguely
worded promises back then.

He frowned, remembering the way she'd
struck him. She wasn't quite so pliable anymore.

Yes, he would have many things to teach her.
And her first lesson would be that no one *ever*
defied Lamar Orwell.

No one.

Devlin's head pounded and his stomach
hurt. It felt like his belly button was shaking
hands with his backbone. He figured it must
be close to feeding time.

For the past few days, his jailer had brought
him one meal daily. There was only just
enough food to keep him alive, never enough
to stop the persistent hunger and thirst.

Were they doing the same to Angelica? Was
she going hungry? Had she been harmed?

Devlin squeezed his eyes shut, forcing himself to think about something else, trying to
concentrate on some way to trick his jailer into
lowering his guard, some way to trick him into
opening the cell door. If he thought about Angelica anymore, if he pictured her in his head

as hurt or hungry, he would go stark raving mad.

Instead, he imagined Lamar and what he was going to do to the man when he managed to escape. There wouldn't be a safe hiding place for the worthless cur after this. Lamar had kidnapped Robby, then he'd stolen Angelica, and Devlin wouldn't rest until he'd evened the score.

Devlin opened his eyes when he heard voices from beyond the door. A few low words were exchanged, followed by a cry of surprise. Something crashed to the floor. Suddenly the door banged open. Devlin sat up, covering his eyes from the light.

"Mr. Branigan?" The voice belonged to a woman.

He scrambled to his feet. "Who is it?"

"There isn't time for that now, Mr. Branigan. Come. We must hurry in case others return."

He heard the key turn in the lock, then the iron-barred door opened before him. He stepped forward, swaying unsteadily on his feet.

"Are you injured, Mr. Branigan? Can you ride?"

"I can ride," he answered through clenched teeth.

The woman's hand took hold of his arm. "Come along, then. I've got horses waiting outside."

She pulled him forward. In the front office, he saw his jailer lying in the middle of the floor.

Outside, two men sat astride horses, intently watching the hills around them.

"Mount up," the woman said as she dropped his arm and picked up the reins of a sleek palomino. "I'll explain everything to you once we've reached safety."

It could be a trap, he thought as he glanced at the woman and her accomplices. This could be why Lamar had been holding him. He drew a deep breath of fresh air, trying to clear his head.

He hadn't the strength to overpower the two men with her. However, one of them was holding his rifle across the pommel of his saddle, the business end pointed in the opposite direction. The man's eyes were moving over the surrounding hills instead of watching Devlin. If he could reach him first, knock him off his horse, he might be able to get the rifle before the other fellow . . .

"Mr. Branigan, please. We need to get out of here. Mr. Schultz usually goes to the Redbird Saloon around seven each night. When he doesn't show up, his friends will come looking for him. We want our trail to be completely cold before they do. If they discover who helped you escape, we might never find your wife."

His instincts told him to trust her. He supposed he had no real choice, anyway. This was his chance to escape. Besides, the woman knew about Angelica. He had to find out what she knew. She might be his only clue to help him find Angelica. He could find out who she was and why she was helping him later.

He moved toward the remaining horse, ignoring the pounding in his temples. He stepped into the saddle. "Let's go, then."

The thunder of galloping hooves glanced off the mountainsides as the small party rode away from the deserted mining camp.

Devlin had no idea how long they traveled at breakneck speed, but when they finally slowed their tired mounts, the sun was resting atop the ragged peaks of the Rockies. They left the road and guided the horses into the middle of a fast-running creek. They proceeded downstream in silence for close to another hour. Finally, as darkness began to fall around them, Devlin followed the others out of the water and down a narrow pathway that led to another old mining shack.

The woman looked over her shoulder. "There is food inside, Mr. Branigan. While you eat, I will explain everything."

"First, tell me who you are."

She shook her head. "I am merely a friend."

Devlin didn't move. She was a stranger to him. Why was she helping him this way? Why had she risked her life to rescue him from his prison? How had she known he was there?

"Mr. Branigan, we both love someone whom Lamar would hurt in order to get what he wants. I cannot let that happen, and neither can you. We must work together." She dismounted. "Come inside, and I will tell you my plan to find your Angelica."

Still, he didn't move. "Who are you?"

"You may call me Miss Pen."

The Orwell mansion was filled with people that night, eating and drinking, talking and laughing. Wall sconces and chandeliers glittered with light. Musicians played from the balcony in the hall while couples waltzed in the ballroom.

Lamar stood near the open window, hoping for a gust of cool air to drift through. He let his gaze slide disdainfully over the guests while pretending to be the caring host.

They were, for the most part, friends of Alexander's, but many of them were there because of Lamar, because they feared him and the power he wielded. He liked to see them bowing and scraping. He remembered all too well the days when it was he who had to obey the whims of others. Only Alexander was left, and soon he would be gone, too.

He saw a flash of yellow out of the corner of his eye and turned his head as Penelope entered the room. She paused, her gaze sweeping the room until she found him. She smiled.

Lord, she was ugly. She was skinny and shapeless, and the color of her gown made her resemble a stalk of ripe corn. Her face was flushed, as if she'd been running and was still winded. To think he'd been saddled to her all these years. He couldn't wait to be rid of her. There was a city full of beautiful women waiting for him once he was free of Penelope—and he would start with Angelica.

Penelope swept across the room, nodding to her guests but not stopping until she'd reached her husband's side. "I'm sorry I am late, Lamar. I've been in the nursery with Robby. He is the most remarkable child. I just couldn't pull myself away. I lost all track of time, and then I had to hurry to dress."

Lamar didn't want to hear about the brat again.

"Do you know what Papa has suggested?" She turned and waved at her father across the room. "He thinks we should take a trip back to Greece, to show the family his grandson. Don't you think it's a wonderful idea?"

"How long would you all be gone?"

"Oh, Papa meant for you to come, too. It's time for you to meet the family in the old country. Especially Papa's brother, George. You will like Uncle George. He is a lot like Papa."

Lamar sipped his brandy. "That wouldn't be possible, Penelope. Someone has to stay here and manage business. Between your father's companies and my own investments . . ."

"Papa has many capable men, Lamar. The Venizelos enterprises would succeed, even without you here. Papa is no fool. He has made certain that his daughter should always be provided for, even after he is gone."

He glanced at her, angered by her superior tone and bothered by her words. He quickly subdued the fury before anyone could see it.

After all, what had he to worry about? Soon Alexander would be dead. Then he could send Penelope to Greece or Europe or wherever. He didn't care as long as he was rid of her.

Penelope patted his arm. "Think about it, Lamar. I believe you'll decide it's the best thing for us." She smiled again, flashing her buckteeth at him. Then she turned and began to make her way about the drawing room, greeting her many guests.

Lamar tossed the rest of his brandy toward the back of his throat and let it burn its way down to his stomach, unconsciously gripping the glass as if he wished to crush it.

He had to find a way to get Alexander alone so Duncan could take care of him. The rest would be easy. A few carefully selected witnesses. A judge who owed Lamar a favor. No one would look beyond the surface, no matter how much the gunslinger professed his innocence.

But Lamar was damned tired of waiting. He had to do something and do it soon.

Chapter Forty-Five

Dawn's paintbrush splashed a pink blush over the smattering of clouds dotting the blue-gray sky. From the window of her room, Angelica watched as the brilliant colors faded with the rising of the sun. She watched until the sky was pure cerulean and the clouds were stark white. She watched but didn't see the beauty of it. She merely noted that it marked the beginning of another day of captivity, another day of wondering what had happened to Devlin, another day of worrying about her son.

She didn't turn when she heard the bedroom door open. She knew it would be Emma with her breakfast tray.

Emma Kelly—young, friendly, and not overly bright—was a creature of habit. She came to Angelica's room six times each day, three times to bring the food, three times to take away the dishes. Angelica could tell the time by her coming and going.

Once, Angelica had actually managed to push past Emma, only to find the front door guarded by one of Lamar's lackeys. One look in his eyes, and she'd known what her fate would be if she tried to escape again.

"Mornin', Miss Corrall," Emma greeted her brightly.

"Good morning, Emma." Her hands clenched at her sides. "And please, remember that my name is Mrs. Branigan." Angelica knew the girl had been told not to call her that. She knew it was just part of Lamar's little game of torture.

As expected, Emma acted as if she hadn't heard. "I brung you somethin' special this mornin', Miss Corrall."

"Just leave it. I'll eat later."

"I don't mean your food."

Angelica glanced over her shoulder, watching as Emma set down the breakfast tray with its gleaming silver coffeepot and fine china. She knew the plates were filled with tempting breads and meats and eggs, but she had no appetite.

"I brung you this." Emma drew a small box from the pocket of her dress and held it toward Angelica.

"What is it?"

"I think you should open it an' see for yourself." The girl grinned, her brown eyes sparkling with excitement.

Unless it was news of her husband or son,

Angelica really didn't care what was in the box. "Who sent it?"

"Who do you think?" Emma giggled.

Angelica turned her gaze back to the window. "You may have it, Emma."

The girl gasped. "You don't know what it is, Miss Corrall. It's from Mr. Orwell."

"My guess is it's something glittering with lots of diamonds. From the shape of the box, I'd say it was a bracelet. Lamar was always partial to diamond bracelets." She leaned her forehead against the cool windowpane. "Whatever it is, you may have it. I won't tell him I gave it to you. I'll tell him I threw it out in the chamber pot with the other sewage. That way you won't get into trouble."

"Miss Corrall . . ."

"It's Mrs. Branigan, Emma. Mrs. Devlin Branigan."

Morning was Lamar's favorite time of day in the Orwell household. His horse-faced wife never joined him for breakfast. Penelope always took her first meal in her room, and Lamar preferred it that way. He could enjoy his breakfast without looking at her, without hearing her chatter, without thinking about what he had to put up with just to get where he wanted to be.

"Excuse me, sir."

Lamar glanced at the butler.

"Mr. Duncan is here, sir. He's waiting for

you in your study. He says it's a matter of some urgency."

Lamar didn't like the sound of that. He wiped his mouth on his napkin, then laid it neatly beside his plate and rose from the table. He hid his sudden tension behind measured, unhurried steps as he left the dining room and walked to his private study.

Duncan turned toward him as Lamar entered the room. One look at his henchman's face, and Lamar knew that trouble was afoot. He closed the door before speaking.

"What is it, Duncan?"

"It's Branigan. He's escaped. Schultz said a man he'd never seen before came up to the mine. While he was talking to him, someone hit him from behind. Branigan was gone when Schultz came to."

Lamar reacted with fury, knocking over a table covered with priceless figurines, scattering shattered glass and porcelain across the floor. "What kind of damn fool are you? Why weren't there more men at the mine watching him?"

Duncan's eyes narrowed, but he didn't reply.

"Am I the only one who can think in this outfit?" He swept a pile of papers from his desk, then shoved his chair back against the wall. He whirled to face Duncan. "Find him, damn it. I don't care what it takes. Find him!"

"Yes, sir, Mr. Orwell."

Duncan placed his hat on his head and turned to leave. Before he reached the door, it was flung wide, revealing a distraught Penelope, still in her dressing gown, her dark hair hanging loose about her shoulders.

Lamar's gut tightened, wondering if she might have overheard his tirade.

"Lamar," she screamed as she entered his study, "something terrible has happened. It's Papa."

"What about him?"

"He's been shot. Someone was waiting for him when he arrived home last night. He ... he's dead." Tears spilled down her cheeks as she drew near to him. "Oh, Lamar, Papa's dead. Whatever am I to do without him?" She laid her head upon his shoulder. "I don't understand. Why would anyone want to kill Papa?"

Lamar was taken aback only for a moment by Penelope's startling news. Who could have beaten him to the punch in killing Alexander? Well—Lamar's cunning mind swiftly saw— whoever it was, it would be Devlin Branigan who would pay for it.

Lamar suppressed his smile and began to stroke his wife's hair. "Don't worry, my dear. I'll be here to help you." Lamar's gaze met Duncan's across the room. "See to that matter we were discussing."

"At once, Mr. Orwell." Duncan left, closing the door behind him.

"Don't worry, Penelope. If it's the last thing I do, I'll see Alexander's murderer brought to justice. Your father will be avenged."

He couldn't contain his smile any longer. After all, he was free at last. Alexander was dead, and Lamar hadn't even had to arrange it.

What a perfect turn of events.

Devlin's hand tightened on the reins when he recognized Lamar riding through the gates. It was tempting to follow hot on Lamar's heels, but caution held him back. Finally assured that he wasn't being watched, Devlin pulled the sombrero low over his forehead, hunched his shoulders, and urged his mount forward at an unhurried but steady pace. Despite his lazy appearance, his sharp eyes never once lost sight of his quarry.

On the outskirts of town, Lamar turned his horse up the drive of a small but elegant house. Devlin kept his head lowered as he rode idly past, not stopping until the road was obscured from view by a number of tall trees. Then he left the road and dismounted.

Carefully, keeping to cover, he made his way back toward the house. He didn't know how she'd known, but Miss Pen had assured Devlin that Lamar would go to see Angelica this morning. If she was right, then Angelica was inside that house. Devlin's stomach knotted. If Miss Pen was right, then Lamar was with her now.

Go slowly, he reminded himself. He had to move slowly. He couldn't risk being stopped, not when he was so close to finding her.

You must promise me one thing, Mr. Branigan. Miss Pen's voice echoed in his head. *You will not harm Mr. Orwell. You will leave his punishment to me.*

He fingered the butt of the revolver riding his thigh. It had been easy enough to give his word to her last night. It would be harder to keep the promise now, especially if Lamar had harmed Angelica.

Angelica had seen Lamar riding up the drive, and she was ready for him. Her back was to the window, and behind her she held the fork from her breakfast tray. She was wearing the same dress she'd worn all week, the one she'd had on when she got off the train in Denver. She'd refused to wear any of the fancy gowns he'd sent to her. He could not fool her with expensive gifts this time. He couldn't buy her affections or her favors. She wasn't the same naïve girl he'd met three and a half years ago.

She waited, her heart pounding, not sure what his visit meant. Had his plan to frame Devlin for murder succeeded? Was Devlin, perhaps, already dead? She quelled the sickness that rose in her throat. She wouldn't give in to weakness. Not now. Not ever.

The lock clicked.

The knob turned.

The door opened.

Lamar stood smiling at her from the doorway. "Angelica." His cool gaze flicked over her. His smile dulled. A frown drew his brows close together. "Why are you wearing that filthy dress?"

She didn't answer him.

"Where are all the gowns I sent to you?" He stepped in and closed the door.

"I didn't want them."

One corner of Lamar's mouth turned up in a twisted grin. "But you don't understand, my dear. *I* want you to wear them."

"No."

"Dear, dear, dear," he muttered, then sighed as he sat down in the chair near the door. "I can see we need to clear up a few things. I realize that I spoiled you when you lived at the Windsor. However, it cannot continue as it was before. I am normally a quite reasonable man. You know that's true. I treated you well before, didn't I?" He waited for an answer but didn't get one. "I don't expect a lot from you, Angelica. I only want a pleasant smile now and then. I want you to look attractive and dress well. I want you to come willingly to my bed when I ask it. Is that so much to ask?"

She swallowed the outraged tears that burned her throat and eyes. "I will *never* come to your bed, willingly or otherwise."

Lamar clucked his tongue and shook his head. Without another word, he rose from the chair, locked the door, then dropped the key into his suit coat pocket. As he faced her, he removed his coat, hanging it neatly over the back of the chair.

Angelica sidled to the opposite side of the

bed. Her right hand ached from clenching the fork so tightly.

"Angelica ..." His voice was low and coaxing. "Remember how beautiful it used to be for us."

She lifted her head proudly, showing her scorn for him both by her actions and her tone of voice. "It was never beautiful for me. I just didn't know it because I'd never been with a *real* man. You know nothing about making love to a woman, Lamar Orwell. I know that now. I would rather service the town drunk than you. I'm sure I'd find it more pleasurable."

She'd expected her insult to incur his anger. She'd suspected he would try to hit her. But she hadn't anticipated the crazed gleam she saw in his cold, unforgiving eyes. She feared his calm far more than a violent outburst.

"You forget where your son is, Angelica," he said softly. "He is in my house, under my care, and no one knows you even exist. You forget that I could go home now and smother him in his bed if I chose to. And I just might choose to if you don't cooperate with me."

"You wouldn't," she whispered in horror.

"Wouldn't I? Don't try me. Now, take off that dress." He slipped his suspenders off his shoulders.

"Lamar—"

"Take it off, Angelica, or you'll never see your son alive again. I'm tired of sparring with you. Do as I say."

"I can't. Please."

"Is it that husband of yours you're thinking of?" He laughed as he unbuttoned his shirt. "Don't waste your time. He's probably dangling at the end of a rope right now."

She pressed her back against the wall. The prongs of the fork dug into her flesh through her bodice, but she ignored the pain. It was nothing compared to the pain in her heart. "Lamar, please."

He tossed his shirt on the chair and moved toward her. "Perhaps you'd prefer it if I undressed you. It'll be my pleasure."

Chapter Forty-Six

Devlin tied the gag snugly at the back of the girl's head.

"Sorry, miss," he whispered as he looked into her frightened brown eyes. "I'll see that you're freed just as soon as I can."

He checked the ropes binding her wrists and ankles, then leaned over to do the same with the unconscious man lying on the floor. Satisfied that neither would be able to free themselves, he stepped out of the closet and closed the door.

Devlin drew the gun from its holster and stealthily made his way through the house. Finding nothing on the ground floor, he climbed the stairs, pausing each time a floor-board creaked, but no one appeared to try to stop him. He was beginning to doubt that Lamar had even come inside, let alone that Angelica was here.

Had it been a ruse? Had Lamar known he

was being followed and led him here, then escaped out a back way?

He heard a sharp protest from behind the next door.

"Damn you!" It was a man's voice. "Damn you to hell!"

Devlin heard a sharp noise—a slap—followed by Angelica's cry of pain.

Fury exploded in his head. He didn't bother to try the door to see if it was locked. He simply kicked out with his right leg, his rage adding strength beyond anything he'd known before. Amidst the sound of splintering wood, the door crashed open before him, and he burst into the room, his .45 cocked and ready.

He heard Angelica whisper his name in disbelief. His glance in her direction was brief, his gaze returning almost instantly to Lamar, but every detail was seared into his brain.

Her cheek bore the red mark of Lamar's hand. Her complexion was pale and wan, and tears streaked her cheeks. She held a fork before her chest in one hand; the other was braced against the wall for support. One sleeve of her soiled dress was torn at the shoulder. Her hair tumbled loose down her back. He'd even noticed her feet; they were bare.

In the next instant, he saw the blood dripping from Lamar's cheek, several small holes puncturing his skin beneath his left eye. Devlin observed Lamar's naked chest, saw the suspenders hanging against his thighs, noticed the bulge of Lamar's arousal even as it shriveled.

"You yellow dog," Devlin said in a low, deadly voice. He raised his gun, aiming it at a precise spot between Lamar's eyes. He watched as sweat beaded on the man's forehead.

"Devlin..." Angelica choked on a sob. "Devlin, don't do it."

He didn't want to listen to her. He wanted his revenge. He'd thought of little else for days. He wanted to kill the man who'd hurt Angelica. This was what the Devil Kid knew how to do. This was what he did best.

"Dev, he isn't armed. If you kill him, he'll have won. He'll have made you what he's told others you are. A cold-blooded killer. They'll hang you for murder."

"He doesn't deserve to live. Look at what he's done to you."

From the corner of his eye, he saw her move away from the wall. The fork slipped from her fingers and clattered to the floor as she crossed the room.

"He hasn't hurt me, Dev. Believe me. He didn't have a chance. You came in time. You took care of me, just like you promised."

Devlin met her beseeching gaze for an instant, torn by his need for vengeance and an even greater need to be what she wanted him to be.

"Either way, you'll hang, Kid," Lamar sneered, seeing Devlin wavering. "I've got witnesses that say you killed my father-in-law. You won't get out of this town alive. The law's looking for you right now."

Lord, he wanted to pull the trigger. He wanted to rid the earth of that pile of horse dung, rid the stench from his nostrils. He wanted to make sure that Lamar Orwell could never hurt Angelica or Robby or anyone else again.

Angelica's hand touched lightly upon his left arm. "You're not the Devil Kid anymore. The Kid disappeared back in Washington. You're Devlin Branigan, and he doesn't live by the gun. We'll find an honest lawman. We'll let him handle this. Please, Dev. For me. For Robby." She paused. "For all of us."

He looked into her eyes and saw a love so great it shook him to the depths of his soul.

She *really* didn't see the Devil Kid. Not even when he stood right in front of her, filled with hate, his gun drawn and ready to fire, ready to kill. She only saw Devlin Branigan. She only saw a homesteader, a man who'd built a cabin in a small valley beyond the Cascades, a man who'd cleared the land and tilled it and planted crops. She only saw a man who loved his wife and his son.

Somehow, miraculously, he saw himself through her eyes, and in that instant he knew it was true. He wasn't the Kid anymore. The Devil Kid was dead at last.

Devlin lowered the gun to his side.

"Thank you, Mr. Branigan. I was afraid you'd forgotten our bargain."

He turned toward the voice. "Miss Pen."

"Penelope!" Lamar exclaimed at the same time.

Angelica's hand tightened on Devlin's arm as the woman entered the room, walking slowly toward Lamar.

Penelope shook her head as she looked into his surprised gaze. "You have made many mistakes, my dear husband, but this...I didn't expect this. I am afraid we will have much to discuss when we get home."

Husband? Devlin was stunned by the word. He'd never suspected it. Why had she done it? Why had she rescued Devlin when she must have known he meant to kill Lamar?

Lamar's face twisted into a grotesque mask of hate and disgust. His mouth opened as if he would speak, and then he seemed to choke as a sudden movement drew his eyes to the doorway.

"Isn't it wonderful, Lamar?" Penelope said, looking behind her at the men standing there.

Devlin recognized the two taller men from last night's rescue. Both of them were holding guns. The third—a much older man—was a masculine version of Penelope. Devlin assumed he was her father.

"Papa wasn't killed," Penelope told Lamar. "There wasn't even a shooting. I know you must be very relieved, since he has left full control of everything to me in his will, and when I die, if I have no children, it all goes to Uncle George in Greece."

The look of shock on Lamar's face would

have been comical at another time. It almost made Devlin feel sorry for him. Almost, but not quite.

Penelope's gaze returned to her husband. "I do have a piece of unhappy news which I don't think can wait until we get home. We have had word from the bank. I have no head for business, as you have so often told me, and I don't claim to have understood what it was all about, but it seems that we are broke. Your investments have all failed. Our money is gone. If it weren't for Papa, we would be destitute. We are penniless, completely ruined."

"No! It's not true!" Lamar looked from his wife to Alexander. "It can't be true. Someone is lying. We've been cheated. It couldn't happen. Alexander, you know . . ." The protest died in his throat as realization began to sink in.

"Don't worry, dear." Penelope kissed his cheek. "By the time we return in a year or two from our trip to Greece, we can start over again. Papa will guide you very carefully. Won't you, Papa?"

"You can be sure of it, daughter." Alexander's gray eyes were like steel as he stared at his son-in-law.

"Now," Penelope continued, "you put on your shirt and coat. It isn't like you to be so careless with your appearance."

She turned away from her husband. The look on her face softened as she approached Angelica and Devlin. She lifted her fingers toward the red mark on Angelica's cheek, then thought better of her action and let her hand fall once again to her side.

"I'm so sorry, Mrs. Branigan," she whispered. "I should have done something sooner. I should have known. It is my fault."

Angelica didn't know what to say to the woman. She thought of the pain Penelope must have felt when she'd learned of Lamar's unfaithfulness. She hated herself for her part in it, just as she'd hated Lamar for deceiving and hurting her.

As if Penelope had read her thoughts, she said, "You were not the first nor the last of his lovers, Angelica, but I believe you were the most innocent. I knew what my husband was before I married him. You didn't know. Perhaps if I'd not gone to Greece with Papa, if I'd been here . . ." She shrugged her shoulders.

"I didn't know about you. I—"

"I know. You aren't to blame." Penelope glanced toward the door. "Colleen, are you there?"

A white-capped woman stepped into the room. She carried Robby in her arms.

Angelica began to shake so hard she almost couldn't stand. She leaned against Devlin for support. "Robby . . ." Her voice quivered. "Robby . . ."

"Mama!" Robby squirmed out of the nanny's arms and ran across the room.

Angelica fell to her knees and embraced her child, tears flowing unchecked. She felt Devlin's arm encircling her back, holding her, lending her his strength as he knelt beside her. It was a long time before she looked up again.

Penelope's smile was a sad one. "I wish he were my son, Mrs. Branigan, but he belongs to you. You are a lucky lady, to have a husband who loves you and a beautiful child, too." Her gaze shifted to Devlin. "Take them back to Washington, Mr. Branigan. There is nothing left for you to do here. My husband shall never trouble any of you again."

Devlin cupped Angelica's chin with his hand, drawing her gaze to his. "She's right, Angel. A homestead doesn't take care of itself." He kissed her forehead. "Let's take our son and go home."

Suddenly the anguish of the past two weeks seemed unimportant. Little more than a bad dream. Nothing mattered but that they were together, the three of them, the past forgotten. Robby had a father and a name. Angelica was no longer a scorned woman, shamed by the mistakes of yesterday. The Devil Kid had passed into the place of myths and legends. A new future stretched before the Branigan family, clean and full of promise.

"Yes," Angelica whispered, "let's go home."

Epilogue

A gust of wind twirled a funnel of gold and red leaves across the field. Overhead a flock of geese flew south, a perfect V against a fair blue sky.

Angelica leaned against the doorjamb, drawing a deep breath of crisp fall air, then letting it out with a sigh of satisfaction. Memories of the past eighteen months flitted through her mind, stirred like the autumn leaves before the wind.

Glimpses of Devlin—Devlin in Jake's cabin ...Devlin as he kissed her beside the Denver stage ...Devlin as he nursed her through the fever ...Devlin on their wedding day ...Devlin as he made love to her....A glimpse and then they were gone, settling back into the private corner of her heart where the joys of life are stored.

Eighteen months had seemed like a long

time when she'd struck her bargain with a wounded gunslinger on that fateful day. It had seemed long, but it had flown by so fast.

She heard laughter—Robby's and Devlin's—and turned toward the sound. A smile played across her lips at the sight that met her eyes. Robby was riding the big plow horse they'd bought from the Johnsons last spring, his short legs sticking almost straight out over the animal's broad back and sides. Devlin was right behind him, carefully not touching the boy, letting Robby do it alone, and yet ready to grab him in an instant if the need arose. Domino trotted alongside the horse, his tongue hanging from the corner of his mouth, looking as if he were smiling, too.

Robby looked up and caught sight of Angelica. "Look at me, Mama. Look at me."

"I'm looking, Robby."

Devlin leaned forward. "Okay. Stop him, son. Just pull back on the reins real slow. That's it."

Brown eyes glittering with excitement, Robby drew the horse to a stop. Once again he looked at his mother.

Angelica clapped her hands. "You're going to be as fine a horseman as your father," she said as she left the house and walked toward them. "You already ride better than me."

"That's what Pa says."

She shot a look of mock anger in Devlin's direction. He had the decency to look ashamed.

"Some things should just be between us

men, son," he whispered into Robby's ear. "You'd better learn that now."

Angelica's laughter bubbled over. "Maybe *you* should learn to be careful what you say."

"I think you're right about that." Devlin swung his leg over the animal's back and hopped down, then turned and caught Robby as he mimicked the motion. He set the boy safely on the ground at his mother's feet.

Angelica ran her fingers through Robby's wind-tousled hair. "You'd better take care of Lady and her puppies before it gets dark. I left the scraps on the table for you. Make sure you fill the water dish, too."

In an instant, Robby was scurrying off to obey, Domino chasing after him just like he'd done ever since he was a pup.

Robby's growing up so fast. Where has the time gone?

She felt Devlin's arm go around her waist, felt his lips nibbling on her neck just beneath her ear. She tipped her head to the side, giving him better access to the tender spot even as chills raced up her side.

"Got any scraps for me?" he whispered in her ear. "I'm kind of hungry myself."

"I might have something for you," she replied, followed by a husky laugh. "Later."

Devlin straightened. "Think I'll take care of the horse and then wash up." He started to turn away.

"Dev?"

"Hmmm?" He glanced back at her.

"Oh . . . nothing. I'll go see that your supper is ready."

Angelica hurried back to the house, feeling foolish. She didn't know why her tongue seemed tied in knots. There was so much in her heart that she wanted to share with him, and yet the words just wouldn't seem to come.

She wanted to tell him how glad she was that she'd found him in Jake's cabin eighteen months ago. She wanted to tell him that he'd given her what she'd wanted so badly—a home. She wanted to share the very special discovery she'd made since falling in love with him. She'd learned that home wasn't a cabin made of logs on a farm in Washington.

Home was the place she'd found in Devlin's heart.

After tucking Robby into bed in the boy's own room—the room Devlin had added to the cabin last spring—Devlin walked across the main room and paused in the doorway to their bedroom. His gaze settled on his wife, and he felt a loving warmth spread through him.

Angelica sat on a chair near the bed. She was dressed in a pure white nightgown that covered her from throat to ankle.

How, he wondered, could a woman wear something so decorous and yet appear so seductive?

Her expression was pensive as she braided her hair, her head tipped to one side. Devlin marveled at how well he knew and understood her. He sensed what she wanted to tell him, felt it in his soul. Perhaps it was because he'd been thinking the same things, remembering, wondering at the changes this woman had made in his life.

She was so beautiful. It wasn't just her expressive green eyes or her abundant burgundy hair or the feminine curves of her body. It was a beauty that came from deep inside her, something uniquely Angelica, something good and honest and true. Like an angel.

His Angel.

He crossed the room and knelt beside her chair. He placed his hands over hers, slowly pushing them away from her hair. Then, gently, he loosened the braid and spread the heavy tresses over her shoulders. When he was done, he raised his eyes to meet hers.

"The harvest is in, Mrs. Branigan."

She nodded.

"Better than I ever thought it would be when we first came here."

"I know," she whispered.

He eased her from the chair, bringing her down to her knees before him, fitting her against his body as he nuzzled his face in her hair, breathing in the warm scent of her cologne. "I don't like to break promises to you, Mrs. Branigan, but there's one I made some time back that I just can't keep."

"What's that?" she asked in a small voice.

"I'm not leaving just 'cause the harvest is in. Eighteen months isn't long enough. I plan to stay for good." He cupped her face in his hands and looked into the swirling green eyes that spoke so eloquently. "I'll make you a new promise. One I *can* keep."

She smiled up at him, trust and happiness lighting her face.

"I promise to love you forever, Angel. Forever."

Angelica's heart swelled with a joy almost too great to hold. She knew he could see her love for him in her eyes. She knew he could see all the treasured memories that he'd given her, and she knew that he treasured them, too.

She raised her lips and kissed him, feeling passion warming her blood, like molten ore over a blazing fire. It was the way she always felt when she kissed him. It was the way she would always feel.

Tomorrow, she would tell him there was another crop they'd planted which had yet to be harvested. Tomorrow, she would tell him there would be another Branigan come spring.

For tonight, she wanted nothing more than to bask in Devlin's promise of love.

Author's Note

Dear Reader:

Almost immediately after the release of the first Women West book, PROMISED SUN-RISE, I heard one recurring question: What happened to Devlin? When can we read his story?

The readers were right. I couldn't leave Devlin's fate untold. So, while I was writing my second book in the series, PROMISE ME SPRING, it was I who kept wondering: But what happened to Devlin?

Devlin and Angelica—two hurting, imperfect people who had lost faith in themselves—became very special to me during the course of this book. Their story represented my belief in the redemptive power of love.

Thanks to so many of you who took the time to write to me regarding the Women West series. I hope you will watch for my next book, MIDNIGHT ROSE, coming from Leisure Books in the fall of 1992.

All my best,

Robin Lee Hatcher

WOMEN OF COURAGE...
WOMEN OF PASSION...
WOMEN WEST

This sweeping saga of the American frontier, and the indomitable men and women who pushed ever westward in search of their dreams, follows the lives and destinies of the fiery Branigan family from 1865 to 1875.

PROMISED SUNRISE by Robin Lee Hatcher. Together, Maggie Harris and Tucker Branigan faced the hardships of the Westward journey with a raw courage and passion for living that makes their unforgettable story a tribute to the human will and the power of love.

_3015-2 $4.50 US/$5.50 CAN

BEYOND THE HORIZON by Connie Mason. The bronzed arms and searing kisses of half-breed scout Swift Blade were forbidden to her, yet Shannon Branigan sensed that this untamed land that awaited her would give her the freedom to love the one man who could fulfill her wild desire.

_3029-2 $4.50 US/$5.50 CAN

NORAH HESS

"Overwhelms you with characters who seem to be breathing right next to you!"

—*Romantic Times*

HAWKE'S PRIDE. Forced into an arranged marriage, young Rue thought Hawke Masters was the most arrogant man she had ever met. But on their bridal night, she found an unexpected fulfillment in his strong arms.

_3051-9 $4.50 US/$5.50 CAN

DEVIL IN SPURS. Lovely Jonty Rand had posed as a boy to escape the notice of rowdy cowboys, especially Cord McBain. So when Cord suddenly became Jonty's guardian, she despaired of ever revealing her true identity. Determined to change her into the toughest rawhider, Cord made her life a torment — until one night he discovered that she would never be a man, but the one woman who could claim his heart.

_2934-0 $4.50